The Reunion

The Reunion

Geoff Pridmore

The Book Guild Ltd

First published in Great Britain in 2020 by
The Book Guild Ltd
9 Priory Business Park
Wistow Road, Kibworth
Leicestershire, LE8 0RX
Freephone: 0800 999 2982
www.bookguild.co.uk
Email: info@bookguild.co.uk
Twitter: @bookguild

Copyright © 2020 Geoff Pridmore

The right of Geoff Pridmore to be identified as the author of this
work has been asserted by him in accordance with the
Copyright, Design and Patents Act 1988.

All rights reserved. No part of this publication may be
reproduced, transmitted, or stored in a retrieval system, in any form or by any means,
without permission in writing from the publisher, nor be otherwise circulated in
any form of binding or cover other than that in which it is published and without
a similar condition being imposed on the subsequent purchaser.

This work is entirely fictitious and bears no resemblance to any persons living or dead.

Typeset in 12pt Adobe Jenson Pro
Printed and bound in the UK by TJ International, Padstow, Cornwall

ISBN 978 1913208 714

British Library Cataloguing in Publication Data.
A catalogue record for this book is available from the British Library.

Gnossienne

n. a moment of awareness that someone you've known for years still has a private and mysterious inner life, and somewhere in the hallways of their personality is a door locked from the inside, a stairway leading to a wing of the house that you've never fully explored – an unfinished attic that will remain maddeningly unknowable to you, because ultimately neither of you has a map, or a master key, or any way of knowing exactly where you stand.

The Dictionary of Obscure Sorrows

Prologue

I am a spy.
Correction: I was a spy.
Well, not so much a "James Bond" spy,
I was a surveillance officer.
It was a job I did.
It had its limitations.
No "friends" with which to share.
A spy – sorry! – surveillance officer doesn't get to choose his friends or the story.
No choice.
Only this time, I have a choice.
My subject(s)? One family occupying two very different worlds.
What follows is the transcript of a former surveillance officer; it begins quite a while ago…

Chapter 1

Hanne's Story, 1963

17th June 1963	School Report: Hanne Constance Mauer
Summary of academic year September 1962 – June 1963	Hanne has had the most amazing year! As she nears the end of her primary school years here at St Caradoc's she is busy preparing herself for a place at Helston Grammar School. However, there is still a way to go yet. Patience is a virtue, as we on the staff often remind her. In all, she has excelled in her work, especially in this last term. Her strongest subjects are: Geography, English and History, whilst dragging her feet somewhat in Arithmetic, but to her credit she is an able all-rounder. Outdoors, she lacks co-ordination and I suspect this may be an eyesight problem? There are still tensions in the playground as I'm sure you're well aware, but I have no doubt these will ease as the years pass. Overall, she is a friendly and bright child who exudes confidence. Her imagination knows no bounds and never ceases to amaze those who like a good story. I was sorry to note recently that her "Andalusian Gypsy" phase has passed, as I always found her stories so colourful and amusing. Eleven Plus notwithstanding, providing she continues to put the work in, Helston Grammar will have a chair and desk awaiting her for 1965.

Departure

Hugo Mauer pulled tight on the cord with one hand, looped it and tied a knot that nine-year-old Hanne Mauer didn't recognise but admired tremendously for its obvious steadfastness. That knot wasn't going anywhere and would keep their luggage safe for the long journey ahead.

Oma must have taught dad how to tie a good knot. Oma must have taught him everything he knew. Dad could do anything. Hanne believed he was "dexterous", having learnt the word "dexterity" only six weeks before and through her own unprompted inquiry.

Sitting patiently, she admired her father through the distance of his reflection in the van's wing mirror. Once he was in the driving seat, having satisfied himself that all was secure and complete, they could be underway.

'You have the list I made?' From the back of the van, Hugo's inquiry sounded more like a command than a question.

'I have it in my top pocket.'

"Uncle" Wally seemed a tad frustrated with the question, as if it had been asked a hundred times in the past week. She heard the sound of his hammer dropping onto the concrete as if he might be making some sort of gesture or protest, but she knew in her heart of hearts that that would be most unlike him. He'd never lost his temper – never ever.

In the wing mirror, if she angled her head down enough, she could see his top half; see him pull a note out of his top pocket – very briefly – then immediately push it back down again.

'Here,' said Wally.

'Let me see it again.'

Typical dad! Can't let things rest. She almost protests but thinks better of it. The tiny, rectangular mirror makes everything look far away. Wally pulls out the list again, with thumb and forefinger, unfolds it, checks to make sure that it really *is* the only piece of paper that's ever occupied the outer top pocket of his tattered old tweed jacket in at least twenty years, before handing it to his old friend to study one last time.

'Come on, Dad! We'll be late for the ferry!' Hanne was losing patience.

'Hush now!'

'Hanne! Dad's got to make sure…' Rene, patient as always, finishes her sentence with a gesture to the lips. Like all good mothers she leads by example: mum can sit quietly; baby Marco is sitting quietly and he's only two; therefore, Hanne must sit quietly. Hanne, however, is quite unaware of such etiquette.

'Make sure what?'

'That everything's going to be all right while we're away.'

'Uncle Wally will look after everything. He's very good at looking after things.'

'Yes, he's very good.'

'And it's not like we've got real animals on our farm – not like a proper farm.' Rene has to agree, Hanne is quite right; it's not a farm in the traditional sense of comprising animals in stone-wall barns, hens pecking, fat geese waddling about their business, pigs and goats awaiting their needs, a sturdy old cob ready to ride scratching his hind quarters against the gate. What had been a romantic vision of growing flowers for a living had become an industry in its own right; this new property was nothing more than industrial premises in all its concrete block ugliness, and nothing was ever going to make it pretty. *Maybe Germany will be pretty. It has to be!*

By the time she checks the mirror again, Wally has picked up his hammer and turned away to carry on banging silly nails into silly fences. *Isn't the world full enough of silly nails and fences and walls? Does it need any more dividing lines and divisions?*

Hugo drops his long frame into the driver's seat, slamming the driver's door because that's what it needs, but in doing so rocks the van on its springs like a boat rocking on water.

'Dad's too big for this little van.'

'What are you bellyaching about now, young lady?'

'I'm not bellyaching, but it's warm in here and Marco will be sick if we don't go soon and he'll probably be sick all over me!'

'I do not think the ferryboat captain will want you on board if you are going to complain.'

Rene also thinks her husband is far too tall for such a little van; his long legs and big feet overwhelm the driving space and floor pedals so that he looks like a large child squeezing into a toddler's pedal car.

Behind, Hanne shifts awkwardly in her makeshift forward-facing seat because she can't see enough over his broad shoulders. She wants to see the road ahead, and to do this she will have to sit either very upright or tilt to the side. Tall for her age: 5' 4" at nine years, eight months, eight days, dad tells her that good height is a family norm – good height coming in this instance from both parents. Everyone remarks on her height, which is normally a wonderful compliment, but in this instance she has nowhere to put her lanky legs other than outstretched in front of her because this is the van variant of the Morris Minor – a working vehicle never meant to have seats in the back or overly tall children.

Two weeks ago, in an effort to introduce herself, she had written to Oma using special airmail paper, telling her – in best primary English – that dad had to have a van because he is a flower grower and men like him need vans for their produce, which has to be taken to the railway station or a lorry depot, depending on cost and "availability" – another word she'd only recently learned, and one of her favourites. Come this morning's post and time of departure, Oma had still not replied; but had she done so she might have asked: *Can't he have a proper car for holidays?*

Hugo's shovel-like hands cover the wheel like a giant's hands. Never mind Hanne's comfort; dad doesn't look at all comfortable and he's in the driver's seat!

In preparation for her own driving lessons that she will book in 1970 she takes note of all starting procedures: he opens the choke, turns the key, pulls the starter, engages first gear, releases the handbrake and away! Pulls out of the yard just like any old day of the week, but this time everyone is on board. How is the old dump going to manage without them?

She glances back out of the tiny rear windows to wave to Wally, but he is already busy again wiring a fence that dad needs in order to partition something that needs partitioning if it is to function properly and make money. There seems to her to be an utter lack of sentimentality. Nobody says goodbye, nobody waves farewell and there are no animals. What's more, she won't miss the house one jot. It is the creepiest, coldest farmhouse in the world and if she weren't to see it again, so what!

She makes a mental note of the milometer: 33030. Her estimate is that it will read 34030 by the time they reach Oma's in Bavaria, and this will be her private obsession for the journey. Nobody else need know as she is testing herself on her keen ability with figures, which is much better than Mrs Williams thinks it is.

Sitting beside her, wrapped up in his own little world of wonder, two-year-old Marco is so young he doesn't even know what "three" is – he hasn't even reached the age of three, so she can't share anything with him. At least he's quiet, and that's a mercy for all concerned.

Through town the needle on the speedometer mesmerises her as it flickers between 20 and 30 mph then quickly down to zero as dad stops to let someone cross at a zebra crossing; it's Saturday morning and the townsfolk are busy shopping. Hannah carefully observes each and every single one of them. There just might be someone they know, and she desperately wants to wave to them with a view to letting them know – if they don't already – that the Mauers are off on their holidays – abroad, not Torquay – and it's well deserved.

Out of town, once the A30 straightens out a bit, their average speed should increase to around 40 to 50 mph, and perhaps even over that when crossing Bodmin Moor and Dartmoor (Hanne's estimate). She's planned the route on the map and memorised it. Mrs Williams didn't give her any great marks for memory, probably because Mrs Williams' own memory is suspect.

In France and Germany – apparently – people drive extremely fast, and there will be no saying just how fast dad can take the Minor once he puts his foot down. In Cornwall, and in England too, the police are always hot on speeding motorists and won't allow for any recklessness – especially as dad is a German. They'd really throw the book at him given half the chance and he'd be a prisoner of the British authorities yet again.

Hanne would tell anyone that the Cornish were good with dad because the war hadn't affected them as much as those poor folk living in the cities in the southeast. In this far western peninsula, people hadn't been bombed in the way that mum's family had been bombed in London, and that's why so many of the German prisoners had been taken to Cornwall because the Cornish were not seething for revenge in the way that Londoners were. Cornwall was as it had always been.

That's not to say that the children of the Cornish were so good with Hanne, because they weren't. Well, not all were so rotten, but those who were made the most impact.

'Small village, small school, small minds!' Rene would say by way of some comfort, but even this wasn't enough. To the bullies, Hanne was the daughter of a Nazi, meaning that *she* was a Nazi. Nazis were not to be tolerated. Stones were thrown, along with mud, or snow, lumps of ice, punches, too. Mostly, it was the words that cut deepest of all, as words always do.

Ironically, similar methods to those used by real Nazis.

ONE HOUR, 48 MILES LATER...

'There's Jamaica Inn!' exclaimed Rene in a bid to excite her bored daughter.

'Jamaica Inn?'

'Daphne du Maurier was a famous writer who lived in Cornwall, and she wrote a story about that inn.'

'When?'

'Ooh, years ago! Long before you were born.'

'Perhaps I could read it when we get to Oma's?'

'Oma cannot read English, and if so we must not think she would be reading about Cornish public houses.' Hugo was beginning to relax a little in the driving seat, his mission to reach Dover in good time for the ferry. Idle banter regarding pubs and novels was never likely to interest him.

'Why can't Oma read English?'

Hanne waited all of two seconds for a reply at the very time the van was struggling with a steep gradient, its engine screaming for a more suitable gear. Rene was expecting dad to reply.

'Can't Oma speak English, then?!' shouted Hanne.

'Oma speaks only German!' Rene shouted back.

'How are we going to know what she's saying, then?'

Rene, seeing her anxious husband preoccupied with leaning forward over the wheel trying to coax the van up the hill, had her own misgivings about possible communication with a mother-in-law she'd never met.

'People can say more with a gesture than they ever can with words. It won't matter if we can't say a lot. Dad will do a lot of the talking, and he can tell us what Oma is saying, can't you, Dad?'

Hugo, in the middle of changing down a gear, could not be interrupted, his powerful fist grappling with the skinny gear lever. Rene's task was to navigate and keep the children amused.

'But I sent her a letter two weeks ago telling her all about us because I thought she wouldn't know and she'd want to know!'

Unable to stop the blush, Rene turned her profile away from Hanne's accusing glare as if she'd spotted something scenic. Children – especially girls – could spot embarrassment at a hundred yards. The shame of it: the letter was actually secreted upstairs in a wardrobe too high for even lanky Hanne to reach when exploring. *Damn expensive airmail!* It was one thing to fib to a child, but she wouldn't destroy the letter either; it remained secreted in a box all her life.

'I'm sure you'll pick up a few words of German when you're playing with your cousins.'

'Who are my cousins?'

'Heike and Heidemarie. Heike is slightly younger than you – she's your father's sister's girl. And Heidemarie is probably a little older than you, though not by much, and she's your father's brother's daughter. They've also got brothers and sisters, but the three of you are very close in age, so I'm sure you'll all be good playmates for one another.'

Rene noticed Hanne glance anxiously at her baby brother, who seemed happy and content thus far into the journey.

'Don't you worry about Marco. He's not going to hold you back. We'll take care of Marco, won't we, boy, eh?'

Marco responded to his mother's touch with a beaming smile and chuckle – probably the only member of his family to be sitting comfortably in the claustrophobic van and with no anticipation of just what lay ahead.

'Marco might as well start by speaking German as he doesn't speak any English yet!'

'I'm sure Oma will teach him a few words, as she will you! You'll both be bilingual by the time we come home again.'

'What does "bilingual" mean?'

'It means someone who asks too many questions!' Hugo's irritation with his chatterbox daughter was likely to get worse as the journey progressed and this worried Rene. Ever since the arrival of Hanne, and most latterly Marco, their father had worked harder and harder. He saw little of either child and barely knew them. She didn't doubt that he loved them, but for some reason he was having difficulty relating to them. Marco was easy enough as he wasn't saying anything other than a few garbled words and was happiest amusing himself, but Hanne had a unique ability to get under her father's skin. She was in every way her father's daughter; nothing of Rene's family was to be seen in her and it was as if Rene had played no part in her daughter's genetic make-up.

What would Oma make of her English granddaughter? Hanne had been named after her German grandmother. For that matter what would Oma make of her English daughter-in-law? The situation reminded Rene of an article she'd read in a women's magazine about the arranged marriages of Europe's royalty in days gone by; how princesses would be shipped off to a foreign land where they couldn't speak the language, trapped in a loveless marriage, never to see their dear homeland again.

Rene's marriage was by no means loveless: she adored Hugo; and at least married life was on British soil, but six weeks in Bavaria was going to be quite a trial with only Hugo and Hanne for conversation.

In his many recollections of his homeland and family, Hugo had never claimed a fond relationship with his widowed mother. She had come across as something of a tartar who took perverse pleasure in taking back whatever she had given to her children. These stories always left Rene with the impression that her mother-in-law would be a difficult woman to bond with.

And what if "the war" came into conversation? Rene wasn't the type to hold her tongue if someone wanted to have a go. It might not come from Oma; it might come from somebody else. How would she deal with it? It shouldn't arise. There were times when she got quite defensive with Hugo if he mentioned Dresden. So she'd come back with London, Birmingham, Coventry, Manchester and all those non-strategic cities that were bombed and "rocketed" (her word).

'Rene? Get the map ready. We are closing to Lown-ceston, nah?'

'*Nearing* Launceston, Hugo. Nearing Launceston.'

Devon and onward...

Hugo drove as he worked – hard. There were plenty of places to see along the way, but Rene and Hanne could only marvel as such places flashed by.

Rene had experience of two places – her native East End of London and the far west of Cornwall where she'd worked as a Land Army girl. Of the 300 miles in between she knew little other than what she'd read or seen on the television. She knew Devon bordered Cornwall, but all the other counties were something of a mystery: Somerset, Wiltshire, Hampshire, Surrey. She would make a mental note on this journey, just as Hanne was making her own personal note of the mileage. She would try and make a note of Germany, too. What came where? Was Bavaria in the south and, if so, what surrounded it?

Hanne kept up a barrage of questions about whatever she saw and caught her fancy, but Rene had no answers that could be drawn from experience.

Hugo, too, had not travelled since arriving at St-Erme station on a train in 1944 – a confused POW detained by Churchill until such time as it was considered he would no longer be a threat to national security. He had often recalled it in this way to Hanne, as if Churchill himself no less had ordered the particularly dangerous Hugo Mauer be kept under guard until such time as "Mum" Rene insisted he be released into her care. As a Londoner, her credentials in this respect satisfied Churchill and the War Office. Had mum been a simple Cornish maid then dad would probably still be incarcerated just like the equally dangerous Rudolf Hess – whose story fascinated him.

The little van, working hard climbing hill after hill, was rarely in one gear for too long. Hanne sympathised with it because she knew what it was like on a bike with only three gears. She hated hills, unless they were downhills.

Holland would be different, with its flat roads. Hugo would be able to rest the gearbox in Holland; rest his cramped left foot and left leg. Hopefully, they could speed through Holland and make good time, especially if they didn't stop.

Hanne felt that, if Saturday morning cinema was anything to go by, there would be so much to see in Holland. There would be windmills and charming folk in national dress wearing clogs. Dad would have to drive carefully as so many of the Dutch people rode bicycles (like her) and they wouldn't be expecting a Morris Minor van from Cornwall with a German at the wheel to come racing along and blow them off the road and into a dyke.

She had seen a film once where the narrator had said that the fishermen of Yorkshire could understand the Dutch fishermen without translating, and vice versa. Many words and phrases were the same or very similar, so she should be able to talk to some of the people and not need a translator. If she said, 'I want a cup of coffee', she would be understood perfectly because the phrase was very similar in Dutch. It would be enough to get by; she wouldn't need mum or dad to translate for her.

Rene thought Hugo would be bound to stop in Holland to look at the flowers and compare notes with the growers. Surely he wouldn't miss such an opportunity to compare notes?

A day later: The end of the beginning – at last

Dover was not what Hanne had expected – not at all. She'd expected a quayside like the one at Penzance, where they would drive down the quayside and be lifted onto the ferry by means of a crane and ropes. Hopefully, they would remain in the van while it was being lifted. Dover didn't disappoint: it was just very different to what she had thought it would be; and, horror upon horror, the sea was brown! She'd never seen the sea so brown as this and suspected that rusty sewer pipes running into the sea were the cause.

The ferry was much, much bigger than she'd expected. There was room on board for a thousand Morris Minor vans parked bumper to bumper.

The speed limit for boarding the ferry – in the approach – was ten miles an hour. This caused the speedometer needle to jump like mad; it couldn't cope with such a snail's pace, especially having worked so hard from Cornwall. It wouldn't matter if it broke completely in Holland because the continentals have a different system of measuring speed, so the van's speedometer would be useless anyway. Hanne could take her eye off it then, though hopefully it wouldn't affect the milometer, which she needed for checking the total mileage to Oma's.

Chapter 2

Hugo's Story

Prisoner Release form 8975	POW Hugo Heinrich Mauer
Release date: 28th September 1947 Rank: Private Delete as appropriate: Wehrmacht / Kriegsmarine / Luftwaffe / Other Nazi Party member: YES/NO	*POW No. 375734 Mauer* *General overall discipline, works hard, does as ordered. Not known to have been a party member. No reason to hold further. Suggest repat or agri job here. Some English but not fluent.* *Signed: Major P.H. Redmond, Commandant*

Hugo had tied a steadfast knot that wasn't likely to give at any point on the journey ahead, but every time they stopped he'd pay it some attention. All the luggage was waterproofed in clear plastic sheeting covered by a tarpaulin, so a downpour shouldn't dampen proceedings.

What would his platoon commander have said? "Check, check and check again. Only move out when you're happy with your check."

'You have the list I made?'

Wally was not a happy man this morning, which was most unlike him. Hugo was not insensitive to people's moods; he just made a point of never showing concern. A mood was destructive for all concerned as it was selfish and should not be indulged with some pathetic enquiry.

Maybe Wally was "under the weather", as the British say, but it was totally out of character. He'd been fine last night, joking and talking too much as he always did. Meg, his wife, was fine and would be into work soon after making sure their boys were in school, so nothing wrong there. Perhaps it was something he ate? Whatever, no time to muck about; best to go now or never.

The list is in order – straightforward.

'Anything you do not understand? Nah? Good! Better go or the ferry will leave without us.'

It bothered him all day the fact that Wally seemed so down – didn't even say goodbye. There must have been a reason. Maybe he was jealous that he wasn't coming along, too. How could they have taken everybody? But that's all Hugo could think of by way of explanation. Wally had been paid in advance to look after the operation. He wasn't alone, there were plenty of staff on hand and, although things were never quiet, this was the best time for what he had in mind.

Wally had always had time for Hugo. He'd never been discriminatory in any respect. He could have shouted: 'Hey, you Jerry! Move your arse!' as others had done. Wally was never like that. He'd made a point of catching the eye of the sullen, beaten POW with a smile and a thumbs up: 'You'll be all right, mate. You're with us now. We'll look after you.' And he had – good as his word.

Thinking about it, yes! He should have come with us. How thoughtless not to invite him! He's always had an interest in the language, learning whatever words and phrases he could pick up. He was always asking about Bavaria.

'We should have brought Wally!' said Hugo, quite out of the blue, as they crossed the Devon county boundary.

'Too late now. I don't think we'd have had room.'

'Not in the van! He could take his car – the Hillman. We should have offered. He loves Germany… He loves Germany, you know,' he repeated, fearing that Rene couldn't hear him properly. 'Remember, he helped me learn English and I would teach him German words, nah?'

'He taught you how to play chess.'

'No, I knew to play chess. He took me to the St Ives Chess Club. We would make chess pieces on the lathe. Without chess I would not be here. We would not be on this journey.'

'He'll get over it,' Rene reassured him. 'You needed him to run the farm while we're away. Maybe next time when the children are older he and Meg could come with us.'

'The children must come with us – always. This is for *them*.' His forefinger tapping the rim of the steering wheel, Hugo was adamant, and that surprised Rene.

The van was too noisy for conversation, though it did help Hanne in learning to project her voice over the noise. She wasn't about to wait for quieter opportunities and chatted away regardless about all manner of sights that she was seeing from the back.

'Ford Zodiac.'

'Pardon?'

'Ford Zodiac. I think he wants to get by. We're too slow. He looks very impatient.'

'He would do with you staring at him.'

Rene responded dutifully to the vast majority of these observations, but not Hugo. This lack of response, on the surface, might have seemed un-fatherly, but the truth was that

Hugo was really quite deaf in his left ear, with diminished hearing in his right. He kept this to himself and mostly no one noticed, though some folk did think he was either ignorant or just typically German, or both.

"Typically German" is a rather silly phrase though, despite the fact that English or British people used it quite often, as if they, somehow, could not be categorised as being "typical".

Looking in the rear-view mirror, Hugo glimpsed Hanne studying him. Embarrassed, she glanced away to the road ahead. This had been a good way of looking at dad up until then because he didn't use the mirror nearly enough; he tended to use the wing mirrors, and generally he was not a backward looking person.

Hanne had learnt from various sources that Germans were typically blue-eyed and blond-haired. This contradicted what she could see with her own eyes: Dad was not blue-eyed. Hugo had black hair combed back and thinning, and his eyes were brown – definitely brown. She pressed him on the subject. At first, he didn't hear, then Rene nudged him. 'Dad! Hanne is asking you something.'

'Yes! What?'
'Are you really German, Dad?'
'Of course. Why would I be not?'
'Because you have brown eyes.'
'Yes. I have brown eyes. That is Bavarian, nah.'
'And you have black hair.'
'That is Bavarian.'
'Mum has blue eyes.'
'Too many questions, I think.'
'Hitler said that all Germans had blue eyes and blond hair.'
'No, I think the English said all Germans have blue eyes and blond hair.'

'And you've got a big nose. Hitler didn't like big noses. That's why he killed the Jewish people.'

Rene couldn't believe her ears. 'What do you know about that, young lady? What have they been teaching you at school?'

'Nothing. I saw it on television about how he killed Jewish people because they had big noses. I've got a big nose, everyone says I have.'

'I don't think you should be watching programmes like that, do you?'

'It was a schools' broadcast programme I was watching when I had flu and I was off school last year. It was for schoolchildren – like me.'

Hugo glanced across at Rene, as if it were her fault for inventing TV, or at least leaving it in a place where Hanne could switch it on unaided. 'We can't be there all the time,' she snapped.

'It's the price we pay for running our own business.'

'Would they have killed you, Dad? Because of your nose? And me too?'

Hugo didn't answer. He was good at keeping his thoughts to himself and diverting thoughts that disturbed him. Since his arrival in Cornwall in 1945, in order to help his English he'd read books and any articles he could find on the war. He'd read how Germany had originally prepared to invade in the southeast and along the south coast in Operation Sea Lion in 1940 – the summer he was apprenticed to a sales clerk. Barely audible, he started to talk to no one in particular: 'Looking at the countryside today, an invading army would have found it hard with the hedges and large oaks, beeches, elms, ditches, valleys... If the British had dug in, this would have been hard country to take. Panzers need flat, open ground because the infantry follow. If the British had not given up, and they would not have done, each kilometre would have been hard fought, just as Normandy had been hard fought in 1944.'

'Go on, Dad! Tell us some more.'

'Like Arnhem – the big mistake of Montgomery – paratroops would have dropped into fields to open fronts in the west and the north. The infantry would have been beaten. Troops would have landed along England's south coast from Kent to Land's End, up the Bristol Channel and Welsh coasts. I learned more about the war since, than Hitler's government ever told me.'

End of big nose question.

Saved!

Hugo had known nothing about the war at all – only what he'd experienced. His news had come direct from Joseph Goebbels and his propaganda ministry. Goebbels had reassured everyone. The Allies were falling back on all fronts, and they'd soon be suing for peace. 'Today, everyone has the news – ITN, BBC – all they ever broadcast is news, news and more news. Where does it get anyone?'

'Nowhere, I suppose?' said Rene.

In respect of his dark hair and large nose, he kept this thought to himself: *There had been others – at school and on the parade ground.* 'I'm a Bavarian and proud of it!' seemed to come from nowhere.

'I know, dear. Don't worry.'

Yes, there were those who questioned his appearance. His facial structure would not have stood up to rigorous measurements from the professors of Aryan ideology. Not so much in respect of his brother or sisters: they were quintessentially Northern European; but Hugo was different. The difference was enough to concern him that there might have come a day when someone would have called to the house in Oberwinkel to demand proof of the bloodline, because something was clearly amiss.

'Did you adopt him, Frau Mauer?' they might have asked.
'What did you know of his father?'
'Does he have a different father to his siblings?'

It was ridiculous of course! Hugo was quintessentially German. *Look at Rudolf Hess; look at Goebbels; look at Speer; look at Himmler – who looked Japanese, for goodness sake! And look at raven-haired Adolf Hitler – no small nose on him either!*

There were plenty of examples, but protesting that from behind the wire of a Nazi internment camp would have carried little weight.

If the war had gone the other way, and Germany had successfully landed in Britain, Hugo would by now be someone quite senior in the Luftwaffe. Not as a commissioned officer, but an NCO at least. He might very well have been posted to Cornwall where his work might have been in airfield construction. He liked construction; he was no flyer and had not even considered that he might have been pilot material, but on the ground he might have excelled in building runways. It did not occur to him at the time that the British would have fought tooth and nail for every centimetre of their sacred ground. He might have had a handle on the English language, but he had no idea who the British were.

By nightfall they'd reached Ringwood, which was good progress considering traffic and the little van. 'The Germans would have built *autobahns* here,' Hugo exclaimed, pushing forward his national pride. 'No silly little roads and bends, but proper straight roads to take you from A to B. Our journey would be quicker today.'

'Would we be at Oma's by now if we had proper roads?' asked Hanne.

'Maybe not, but nearly. Also, I would have a better car – a Mercedes Benz. We would break the speed of sound.'

Hugo dreamt of owning a Mercedes Benz. The little Moggy Minor was a beginning, but the dream would finalise with a Mercedes. He was prepared to be patient.

As the overly warm little engine cooled, emitting little burbles like a hungry tummy, Hugo and Rene set about putting up a tent on the open parkland that was to be their resting place for the night. 'I think this is the New Forest.' Hugo wasn't absolutely sure, but there were no fences to be seen and the grass and shrub were as neat as any heathland he'd ever seen.

'I'm not sure we can park here,' said Rene, anxious that some authority – suspecting them to be vagrants with no purpose in life – would arrive and move them on.

'We'll be gone by daybreak,' Hugo assured her. Hanne would sleep in the van while Marco slept between his parents in the tent.

The oddness begins at sea

For Hugo, if there were any problems behind them at home, Wally would phone the port or ferry company and get the message through. Now was the time to receive any such messages as, once they landed on the Continent, there would be no such opportunity.

He searched the faces of the crew busy marshalling the boarding motorists. Nobody had said anything when the van was checked prior to boarding. Surely somebody would spot his Cornish registration and approach him with the news that they would have to turn back as there had been a disaster at home.

Nobody did.

Even at sea he expected an officer to dash down the steps leading from the bridge with the awful news that they would have to go about and return to port because Mr Mauer would have to get back to his business as the farm could not cope without him.

Initially, that was what was in the head of Hugo Mauer. He even rehearsed an apology in his head. He knew Hanne would be particularly disappointed and even quite bitter in her response. He would say something along the lines of: 'I am very sorry, but we are needed at home and we have had a holiday in the van. You enjoyed your stay on the New Forest, nah?'

Hanne would protest, of course; so his reply would be like this: 'We will try again later. I want you to meet your cousins. For me it is very important that you begin a friendship with them that will last always. When you are friends, you will be friends forever. Blood ties you to them more than you can know. Now we have to return.'

The rehearsal was not needed. The call to return to Cornwall never came. Something else happened though and it's worth mentioning.

As the ferry steamed out of Dover, Hugo made his excuses and separated himself from the family. 'I need to take some air,' was all he said.

'Can we come with you?'

'No. It's cold out there. You stay here in the café where it's warm.'

He left Rene with some change for tea and cakes and was gone in a second, swiftly stepping out of sight as if he'd forgotten something most vital.

Seasickness and he doesn't want to admit it!

Rene knew her husband well enough to know that the sea was not in his blood and he'd avoid boat rides like the ones at St Ives where boatmen sped you around the bay, performing tight circles for a shilling. She was sure now that this was the reason behind his disappearance; it made sense.

Hanne, occupied with staring at lorry drivers eating pies and chips, not content with the café, pestered to explore. 'We'll all go,' said Rene.

'What if Dad comes back looking for us?'

'We won't go far. I need a walk. How about you, Marco? Stretch our legs?'

Marco was unsure as to whether to burst into tears or go with the family, but if Hanne was going, then of course everyone must go.

For the next half hour they searched the ship inside and out. Fruitless. They even asked the AA man sitting at his desk handing out leaflets and warning people that they must remember to drive on the right-hand side when leaving the ferry.

'Sorry, madam? Tall, dark gentleman with a heavy accent and a tweed jacket? No, no one fitting that description has come my way. Do tell him though when you find him to make sure that he—'

'Drives on the right – yes, he's… he was born on the Continent, so I think that will come naturally to him – thank you. And, if for any reason you do see him, please tell him his family are looking for him, would you?'

'Yes of course, madam. We'll be docking soon, don't forget. Short trip this one!'

Rene immediately regretted not having referred to her husband as "German", but she feared that an AA officer just might scowl at the mention of the word. All civilian men who wore uniforms were ex-military because they liked the order and the discipline. Stands to reason.

Grocers might not wear uniforms, but they were particularly bad. She had been ordered out of a veg shop once when she innocently enquired about a particular type of apple that her "German" husband liked and from which a fracas ensued. She told the indignant grocer what to do with his fruit using a very East End London manner of vocabulary, which made her feel considerably better, but in pre-supermarket days her rebellion simply left her with a longer walk to the other side of town for fruit and veg.

The AA man was right in respect of the fact that they would be docking soon. They needed to find Hugo and find him quickly.

The majority of passengers were on deck, loving the occasional burst of sun and the race of the ship through the waves, all watching intently as the horizon dipped and rose again with the Continent looming closer and closer. D-Day all over again.

'Look! I can see Calais,' exclaimed one cockney voice.

'I can see the French tricolour flying from the town hall,' said another.

'I can see Dad!' shouted Hanne. 'Look, down there.'

Sure enough, there was Hugo, sitting not on a bench but on the bare steel-plated deck with a ventilation shaft almost completely obscuring him. He looked tired and dejected, not sick. What was strangest was the fact that he appeared to be talking to himself – mouthing and gesticulating as if someone else were there, listening and exchanging words with him; but clearly there was no one else.

Hanne didn't notice this oddness – dad was dad as always – and she called out to him. It was Rene who noticed – and wondered.

Behind them the waves

The ferry crossing had enforced a period of rest for a couple of hours. Now, on the other side of the water, the marathon was on again. Sandwiches were made with salami and rolls bought on the ferry and eaten while on the move. Only when it got dark did Hugo find a place to pull over and erect the tent for the first time on the Continental mainland. Camping: putting up a tent in the dark – a skill that the Luftwaffe had taught him and one that he could put to good use. He and Rene would share the tent with Marco while Hanne slept in the van.

What the Luftwaffe had not taught him was to erect a tent on a municipal tipping site during the hours of darkness: an easy mistake after nightfall, but a shock upon awakening for their first morning on the Continent.

Holland did not disappoint the family, particularly Hanne – her expectations were precisely as she'd hoped. There were windmills in the very places she had expected them to be, people were riding bicycles and some were even dressed in traditional costume.

The books in school were spot on! The canals went on forever and ever and ran in parallel to the road. Even the trees were actually in neat lines and not higgledy-piggledy as they were at home. Uniform height, uniform distance apart, as if each tree commemorated the life of a soldier who might have marched along these roads in Napoleonic times and later in WW2. Holland in the flesh was like a premonition that had been proved correct. Providing dad didn't knock a cyclist into a dyke then this would be the most marvellous part of the journey so far. What's more, the milometer was on course for her predicted mileage of 34030.

The road less travelled

Rene was a very capable navigator who could balance the needs of a two-year-old whilst reading a map; but they reached a point where Hugo was confident he knew the neighbourhood so the map wasn't needed. He clearly had a plan but he wasn't about to explain what that plan was. They needed a cuppa and a break for a while where they could picnic and let the little engine cool. Hugo knew just the place – if it was still there.

Left here, follow the lane, then right and left again. No signs of a café; no café signs. They were leaving the beaten track now, leaving tarmac and civilisation behind and nosing further down a track that posed more questions than it could possibly answer. Dad was clearly confident, and the whole thing was thoroughly exciting if you were aged nearly ten or thereabouts.

Hugo was not a sentimental man; at least, not that anyone could tell. The idea of setting off down "memory lane" to revisit old haunts did not interest him at all – he would tell you. Yet here he was back at a place that he knew only too well – like a burglar revisiting the scene of a crime.

After what was probably a good five minutes of bumping down a track, fearing he'd break a spring or shock absorber, he stopped the van within walking distance of a pleasant but unremarkable farm, quite isolated and obscure in its situation.

The engine cooled for a while, but the van's occupants had grown lazily used to its space capsule-like interior. It was cosy; no one wanted to get out. Besides, Oma's must surely be just around the corner from Holland.

'Where is this?' asked Hanne, looking out at a wide expanse of flat, cropped meadow.

'It's just a farm,' Hugo replied calmly. 'I will get some fresh milk for our tea. They have very green grass so I am sure they will have some fresh milk, nah?'

'I'm sure they will,' agreed Rene, only too happy for the rest from map-reading.

Hugo stretched out of the van and stood for a few moments, propping himself against the roof of the cab, patiently waiting for the spasm in his lower back to subside. Unbeknown to him, he was being watched from a nearby hedge. He had come under the scrutiny of two boys armed with toy rifles, dressed in denim jeans and wearing, as headgear, olive-green plastic helmets US Army style. From this secret observation post they were watching his every move and preparing to fire off their caps.

Hugo couldn't see the boys who lay as quiet as church mice observing a cat, but he could see something far more disturbing as he made his approach to the farmhouse door. He could see the past, and he could see it vividly.

Stepping back to... 1944

Karl and Thomaz urge their friend and comrade to make his move.

'Go on, Hugo! This is a recce, after all. You go and knock on the door.'

'And what if the Americans are in there?'

'If the Americans are in there, you surrender. They'll have you on board a ship for New York before you know it and you'll be in the lap of luxury, you lucky devil! Better than dying of hunger, Hugo.'

'And if they shoot me?'

'They won't shoot an unarmed man! Give me your rifle; we'll cover your back. If the coast is clear, signal with your raised hand. Remember, we need what's in that farm. Now, go on!'

Reluctant, ever cautious, Hugo makes his way across the yard to the farmhouse and knocks at the door. He fears what may be on the other side of the door – Dutch resistance, Americans, British, or just an angry farmer armed with a shotgun.

For what seems an eternity, he waits for an answer. The farm appears to be deserted, the barn door banging on its latch in the breeze as if some furious poltergeist were wrestling to open it from inside. Hugo is about to signal an all clear when the door opens, cautiously.

As if resigned to her fate, the farmer's wife holds the door open for him to enter. She neither invites nor beckons nor makes him welcome in any respect. He turns and waves for his hidden comrades to join him – the drawbridge is down; the castle is open without a shot being fired.

There in the kitchen, as if expecting their arrival, is the farmer sitting at the table, lean, muscular arms folded tightly as if annoyed that his tea has been interrupted. The table laid with Delft china plates and bone-handled cutlery; a loaf fresh out of the oven, sliced and steaming; cheese and hard-boiled eggs ready for consumption.

Jan Rensburg had been working in a field when he caught sight of the indiscreet little recce party long before they'd happened upon the farm. He'd returned to the house in the hope that they might wander past and leave it all alone – leave it for the Allies to arrive.

Had the three youngsters not been so starved, they would most definitely have left it alone. It wasn't just them, it was their entire platoon. Everyone was out on the lookout for food; little groups all split up that day and with one task in hand – to survive.

The Führer wasn't supporting them anymore; they had to find their own way. That's what Oberfeldwebel Gondorf had told them.

In four long years of occupation, Rensburg had succeeded in keeping a low profile with his German occupiers. They'd bought bits and pieces from him, vegetables and milk mostly. Faces had come and gone, but largely they'd been mature faces; war-weary, middle-aged conscripts. The Nazis and the Gestapo were principally occupied with the towns and cities, which they controlled with iron pragmatism. There had been incidents though: Rensburg's farm had been searched twice – once by soldiers looking for Allied aircrews – a bomber had crashed nearby. The local gossip was that it was an RAF Wellington, but that had been contradicted by someone else claiming it was an American Liberator that had been carrying a VIP. Whatever, the soldiers came and went with no damage done and that was all that mattered – the farm left alone for a while.

The second visit was rather more sinister and nasty and involved the combined forces of the local constabulary led by officers of the SS. They were looking for Jews in hiding. Rensburg had never met a Jew in his life, didn't know what one was or even what they looked like, but that didn't stop the intrusion or prevent the house and farm being turned over without apology. Floorboards were pulled up, doors busted with axes and hammers, pictures pulled off walls, windows broken.

It wasn't the raid that disturbed them so much, despite its violent impact; it was the thought that someone in the community just might have pointed a finger at the Rensburgs. Long after the Nazis had fled – in fact as long as the Rensburgs lived – they suspected that someone, somewhere close by, had suggested to the Nazis that they be paid a visit.

Jan Rensburg had never considered his own part in the war. A simple man for whom farming was all he'd ever wanted, he was forty-nine at the outbreak when Holland had been quickly overrun. This was his childhood home and he loved the isolation. It was only when the war finally came to *him* that he decided to take a more positive role. Only in those past few months, now that the Allies were so near, had he started to open his door at night at the sound of approaching Allied bombers coming in low and fast across Holland. Like a lighthouse or beacon, the Rensburgs, along with hundreds, maybe thousands, of other householders were using their doors and drapes in open defiance of the Nazis to flash a message of goodwill and support to the bomber crews who briefly glimpsed their welcome as they thundered overhead.

The three young men who now occupied their kitchen were as frightening as any Gestapo officer on the lookout for escaping airmen or Jews. To Jan Rensburg, the boys were thin, dishevelled, clearly starving and quite likely unbalanced. Without a senior officer in their midst, there was no saying what they might do. He'd heard of the most appalling horror stories from all across Europe of how soldiers when retreating and without leadership turned to the most inhumane savagery.

He stood up and appealed to them in the only language he knew – his native Dutch: 'You can eat what we have, but then you must go. The Americans will be here soon.'

'What's he saying?' demanded Karl, who was a bundle of nerves and probably more on edge than the Rensburgs.

'I don't know!' replied Thomaz.

Only Hugo seemed to grasp the farmer's request. 'He wants us to leave.'

'Oh! You speak Dutch?' spat Karl with incredulity.

'No, but that's what he wants.' Hugo was determined to remain calm – keep a cool head.

'We'll go when we've had our fill,' said Thomaz, eyeing up the meagre feast before them.

'Eat up, my friends, and enjoy! We've come a long way.'

The Rensburgs stood aside as the young Luftwaffe soldiers took their chairs and grabbed at the food with such desperation that Hilda Rensburg considered them savages.

The recce party had been trained well enough to make sure that their rifles remained strapped on their shoulders, even when sitting. Jan Rensburg considered the possibility that if he could get hold of just one rifle he could use it like a club to break at least two heads before turning the barrel on the third; but there was no way of knowing just who was out there. To murder a German soldier now at this late hour would be to sign their death warrants. At the very least they'd be hanged from the nearest branch, and their only daughter – working away in Nijmegen – would be sent to a concentration camp.

Besides, Rensburg couldn't even kill an animal let alone the boys gorging at his table. He was known far and wide as the dairy farmer with a heart – a man who loved his animals.

'Do you think the farmer has a daughter?' asked Karl of his comrades, his mouth full of bread spitting crumbs onto the table. Rensburg understood enough of his German and glanced nervously at Hilda. *Thank God Sonje left for the city a year ago.*

'Why?' asked Hugo.

'So that we could take her hostage for when we leave. She would be ours for bargaining should we run into Americans or British. We don't want these people raising the alarm when we leave.'

'It is better to shoot them!' said Thomaz with all the assurance of a boy who'd never killed anyone in his life.

'No! We are not murderers!' snapped Hugo.

'Thomaz is right. We don't want them to raise the alarm. The Americans could be very close.'

It looked as if Hugo might be outvoted. 'We don't have to shoot them!'

'You have a better idea?'

'We tie them up or put them in the cellar.'

'Yes,' said Karl, his panic beginning to dissipate. 'Put them in the cellar. All farms have cellars.'

Thomaz reached behind his shoulder and pulled his rifle onto the table. The farmer, having understood much of their conversation, raised the palms of his hands in surrender. 'Merciful God, don't shoot us!'

Now, Hilda Rensburg, who so far had been stoic, who so bravely in the past had calmly dealt with the intrusions of soldiers, police and Gestapo, who had stood and watched her home being broken up in front of her, feared the worst. They were to be murdered in their own house and their remains left for the rats to devour. Poor Sonje! What would she find? What would they tell her?

She began to cry, collapsing to her knees, shoulders heaving, tears spilling to the stone floor from a cloudburst of terror. Jan grabbed her awkwardly in a desperate attempt to hold her up while comforting her, but he couldn't manage it. He too dropped to his knees in an effort to cradle and comfort his one and only love. Convulsing, she lifted her eyes to the bewildered trio now gathered around them, completely at their mercy.

Thomaz lifted his rifle and pointed it at Hilda's bowed, shaking head.

'Where's the cellar, farmer?' he demanded. Ashen-faced, Jan could do no more than look up at the barrel now pointed at the bridge of his wife's nose.

'WHERE'S THE CELLAR?!' screamed Thomaz.

Karl reached for the rifle barrel, gently pulling it away from the woman's face.

'He doesn't understand! Hugo?'

'Yes, Karl?'

'Look for a cellar.'

He turned to engage Thomaz, looking him straight in the eye. 'Don't shoot them, Thomaz!'

'I might do if the old lady doesn't shut up!'

Thomaz Binder was surprising everyone, including himself. He had never shouted at anyone in his nineteen years. No one who knew him would describe him as ever being a shouter or a bully and certainly not someone to lose control; a pragmatist – yes.

'Certain things have to be done.' That's what he'd said to both Hugo and Karl during training when they were discussing a massacre that had occurred in rural France some years earlier. When asked why such things had to be done, he didn't, or couldn't, answer.

They made sure that the door to the cellar was secure, but it was not locked in such a way as to be beyond the ability of the Rensburgs to break out, by which time their jailers would be long gone.

The Allies couldn't shoot them for imprisoning a farmer and his wife. No one was dead, no one would starve in the cellar as there was some food and wine and also some natural light. There was no alarm to be raised so there was nothing to fear, but, of the three, Hugo had been the most concerned for the plight of the Rensburgs.

His widowed mother farmed and had done since he'd been small, since the father he could barely remember had died of smoke inhalation having fought a neighbour's house fire; his chest already weak having suffered a gas attack in the Kaiser's war.

Hugo's feelings toward the farmer's wife were ambiguous at that moment in time. He didn't want to hurt her, it was nothing personal, but there was a part of him that couldn't empathise with her plight. He wanted to punish her because he was sure that she too lacked the emotion he had sought for so long from his own mother. He was sure that all farmers were like this; they all lacked the capacity to love truly because the land and property were the most important things to them.

The land consumed all their natural and spiritual energies. The purpose of children was to continue the running of the farm and to care for their parents when they became infirm; it was clear and simple – a rule of life; of that, nineteen-year-old Hugo was convinced.

He didn't want the farmer and his wife to suffer, to starve or be short of food, and he made that plain to both Karl and Thomaz. He told them that he wouldn't wish starvation on his worst enemy because he was always hungry and there was nothing worse in life than to be without food and water. As a Catholic boy he'd had to go hungry when he was made to fast for a day each week. He'd hated it! What good did fasting do anyone? The smokers were better off because they just didn't seem to have an appetite at all, but not even a world war was about to start him smoking.

Thomaz reassured him with a hand on his shoulder: 'They won't starve. There's some food in there – some cheese. Dutch cheese. They even have a tap. Does that satisfy you?'

Hugo nodded solemnly.

Karl urged them on. 'Let's get this food back or all this foraging will have been in vain.'

There was a handcart in the yard; they could use that.

*

A brief history of the Morris Minor:
Designed by Alec Issigonis, over one million were manufactured between 1948 and 1972. Variants included saloons, convertibles, wood-framed estates, pick-ups, and panel vans like the one in this story. They were small but very gutsy.

*

In the van, Rene buttered the sandwiches, buttered the rolls and spread beef spread, passing the first to Hugo and then Hanne before preparing a special treat of banana for Marco.

She might not have noticed had Hanne not prodded her on the arm, so preoccupied was she with feeding Marco, but Hanne *had* noticed. Dad was staring straight ahead at the farm as if suddenly he had become frozen and unable to speak or move. Strange.

Like on the ferry, he was oddly inanimate, as if in another world.

'Are you still hungry, Hugo? ... Hugo?'

'Yes, I'm hungry.'

'Was it something they said to you at the farm?' asked Rene, confused as to why her husband seemed so quiet and withdrawn.

'No, she was a good lady – the daughter of the farmer, nah.'

'Do they have cows? Proper farm animals like a proper farm that we can go and see?' asked Hanne excitedly.

'I do not think so,' replied Hugo.

'Do they grow flowers? Perhaps you could compare notes?' asked Rene.

'No, they do not have flowers. I think they are produce growers – vegetables – nah.'

A fib, of course, rather similar to Rene's fib about the letter to Oma that she didn't post. There were a brace of Friesians grazing nearby and milked daily, hence the fresh milk.

There was to be no explanation of the last twenty minutes; there was nothing to tell really. Hugo had not asked what kind of farm it was when a woman of similar age to him opened the door. He had begun by asking her whether she spoke English and she affirmed that she did, so he told her that he was English and that his family were English and that they were hoping they might be able to buy some milk. He didn't recognise her and she didn't recognise him, or at least she appeared not to.

When she returned with the milk, he asked how much and put his hand into his deep trouser pocket, but she refused, telling him how good the English had been to them during the war. He asked whether she'd been farming there at that time but she replied, 'No'; her parents had been farming whilst she had trained and worked briefly as a secretary in Nijmegen before returning to the farm after the war. 'I hope your parents survived the war?' he enquired.

'They did,' she replied. 'Do you need anything else?'

He thanked her and said it was 'Just the milk' they required. Of course, what he really needed to know was the fate of her parents. He wondered, as he walked back to the van, whether she'd realised who he might have been – one of those guilty young German soldiers who had robbed them of food and locked them away in their own cellar. She might not have been able to recognise him, but she would have been told the story many times. His German accent – heavy accent – would have been so easily picked up on by her. He didn't even look English yet here he was claiming to be English, claiming to be passing by and in need of milk. Where would an Englishman be going in this district in 1963? No real Englishman who had known the war would want to return for the sake of sightseeing! What would he be after seeing? The ruins? The graves? There was a generation of men who had no wish to return to the "bloody Continent", least not in their lifetimes – a curious youngster maybe, but a thirty-eight-year-old?!

Just as he had come under the scrutiny of the boys on his approach to the farm, now on his return he was watched by the woman's father, who momentarily stopped his repair work on a wire fence, anxious for the uninvited stranger to leave.

Jan Rensburg preferred his daughter to answer the door; he preferred to be somewhere else when people arrived unexpectedly. Still hard at work, with good eyes and a clear memory, there was, he feared, something horribly familiar about this visitor, so he gripped the hammer tightly and recited a silent prayer.

So, that would have been the explanation, but why bother anybody with the details?

Inside the van, Rene had boiled a kettle on the primus. 'Tea? Here!'

'Thank you.'

'Can I have some tea? Can I see their cows?' asked Hanne, not at all convinced that it was only an arable farm.

'Not just now,' Hugo replied as he stared out of the windscreen at the events of 1944.

The last thing the picnickers were expecting happened suddenly with no warning whatsoever: Hugo turned the ignition on and pulled the starter. He hadn't finished his rolls or tea, nor had Rene or Hanne, who complained: 'I haven't had my tea!'

'Oh, we'll stop again soon. Oma will be waiting.'

'Are we nearly there?' Hanne asked excitedly, quickly forgetting her tea.

'We've a long way to go. There's a border to cross.'

'Is the border a river?'

But Hugo wasn't talking to his daughter; he was talking to Karl and Thomaz.

*

Thursday (Donderdag) 14th September 1944, Holland.
Where the Allies had not been able to penetrate in the north, a national railway strike was called by the Dutch government in exile and a German embargo on all food transports to Western Holland. The "Honger Winter" (Hunger Winter) was just around the corner.

*

They departed the farm along the very same lane that he, Karl and Thomaz had pushed the loaded cart away in search of their platoon. In 1944, they didn't want the main road for fear of running into an American or British patrol, so they pushed further into the Dutch countryside certain that they could use their only compass and map to work their way around to the last known position of the platoon.

They also didn't want to run into a Waffen-SS patrol for fear that they might be seconded into its ranks and forced to murder, rape and pillage as part of an initiation ritual. Thomaz and Karl had both heard various rumours that it had happened recently to a band of hapless infantrymen who lacked a senior officer and the courage to defend themselves. They were, apparently, a band of admin clerks in search of food and a unit. Such were the rumours.

'Stop taking food off the cart! Think of your comrades!' Karl snapped at Hugo. 'Didn't you eat enough at the farm?'

'My meal was interrupted by our good friend Thomaz wanting to kill the farmer and his wife.'

'Well, I didn't kill anyone,' replied Thomaz, now feeling quite ashamed, 'but I can tell you now, comrades, my boots are surely killing *me* with every step.'

Karl and Hugo empathised with their friend. An army marches on its feet primarily and, although they were a little more comfortable than they had been, the constant walking was causing foot problems. Socks, if an individual was lucky enough to have them, were wearing thin, causing the skin of the heel to chafe against the inner lining of the boot, so all three limped to some degree. Athlete's foot plagued each and every one in the platoon.

'The Americans have better boots than we do. Even the British have better boots because they lace up. My feet sweat so.'

'Thomaz? When the war is over I will buy some Italian boots. I will buy my entire family Italian boots.'

'Your entire family, Hugo?'

'Yes, my mother, my brother and my two sisters.'

'Dreamer! Where will you get the money? Eh?'

Yes, Hugo the dreamer. He dreamt of making money once the war was done. He could clearly see what was to come; no fortune teller required. In his mind it was already written as a promissory note to self: Hugo the businessman driving a big car, living in a big house, taking advantage of all those post-war opportunities for ambitious young men like him.

Dreams kept him going that day, helping with every laboured step.

Property development was his plan. The bombing and shelling would mean rebuilding on a vast scale. It would require hard work and commitment, but should the Good Lord see fit to spare him there would be plenty of scope for an entrepreneur of his ambition. And he wouldn't squander his money on booze, tobacco and women. He'd be a wise investor in foreign markets. Not so wise perhaps to mention it now while pushing a cart over uneven ground.

Pragmatist Thomaz was scathing. 'The Americans will take all our money, and if they don't the British will. They still have all their Jews in place.'

Karl the historian wasn't quite so sure. 'There are no Jews in England.' Of that he was certain: 'One of their kings killed them all in the Middle Ages. I read it – King Henry or King Edward, someone like that. He put them all in a tower and set it alight. But first he made them sew yellow felt badges onto their clothes. Where do you think Himmler got the idea from?'

Thomaz guffawed. 'Are you saying Himmler isn't an original thinker?'

'I'm just saying there isn't a new idea under the sun.'

Hugo reminded him that he wouldn't dare say that if Himmler were actually stood in front of him, to which Karl begrudgingly agreed. 'True, but I would ask him to take his turn in pushing the cart!'

*

Hanne had read somewhere that the Dutch didn't use umbrellas in the rain, so she made another mental note to spot an umbrella user in a downpour. Infuriatingly for her, it didn't rain during her brief time in the country, so this was never put to the test.

*

It seemed no time at all since leaving the farm that the border post hove into view – in fact, it was an hour's drive at a steady 45 mph. Hugo prompted Rene to find the passports *schnell* as this was the German border and the guards would not be amused if they were kept waiting.

He had no experience of German borders in 1963, so this was his assumption based on experience from the immediate post-war period and American border guards. (There were no borders when Holland, Belgium and France were occupied, so what did he know.)

'Passports!' was the one-word request from the guard, who seemed anxious to be relieved of his tedious duty. His job: to stop and check any vehicle with a foreign registration. He was not at all impressed by the blue/grey farmer's van that had so valiantly got the Mauer family to the border from West Cornwall without mechanical incident.

Rene had expected a more British reaction from the guard. 'My! You've done well! Come all the way from Cornwall have we in this little Morris? I remember seeing the boffins from Oxfordshire test this particular type of car some years ago. A number of them came right through this very checkpoint. Would it be possible to see your passports, please?'

A little more like the AA officer on the ferry.

But in the here and now she thought that he looked very much like a guard of World War 2, with his black, calf-length boots, peaked hat and tunic with its piping and those baggy trousers. He looked smart but depressingly grey in a severe sort of non-democratic way, as if all the Nazis were still in place and no one was prepared to soften their image.

'He could look like a guard without all that!' she remarked. 'And a beret would help, with a white shirt and blue tie and a nice pair of creased flannel trousers with tan shoes. The French looked very smart and very handsome, and so unthreatening. Not so here – shame.'

She was confident in the belief that he did not speak English.

'Rene? You have the passports?' Hugo urged her to search her handbag without delay. He was only the driver; Rene was the holder of the keys to the kingdom.

She reassured him that she would find them in just a moment, but both husband and guard were intimidating her by the very nature of the whole ridiculous exchange.

As she fumbled, seconds turned to minutes. She began to exhale knowing that all eyes were upon her – Hugo, the guard and, from behind, Hanne and Marco. Where was Oma's house from here? Where's the plate of bratwurst and sauerkraut and would it be cold? Would this silly man stop them in their tracks?

She felt as if she wanted to make it quite clear that she was in fact a British citizen. She had a God-given right therefore not to be impeded from entering a country that was correctly hers through victory. Montgomery had not been forced to wait at the border or had his passport scrutinised by some self-important, heel-clicking jobsworth.

It was not the time for remembering the debacle that had been Arnhem.

A queue was forming behind, and the guard was determined to clear it by ordering Hugo to park in the adjacent layby in order to allow a much more important German-registered Mercedes Benz to come through without further hindrance. How embarrassing! What sort of return to the Fatherland was this? A German gives orders and he does as he is told.

Switching off, Hugo decided it would be prudent to talk German with the guard now towering over the roof of the van.

'This is the first time I have crossed the border in… many years. I was captured on this border and I've wanted to see it again. So, I'm doing it now with my family.'

Even with Hugo speaking in German, the guard seemed unwilling to partake in any small talk, but Hugo persisted, feeling it was better and more honest to be friendly rather than demonstrate a possible guilt or animosity through silence. During the war, he'd seen people shot at roadsides for not explaining who they were and what they were doing, for not having the right papers, and he found it difficult now to convince himself that the war was in fact over and that this wouldn't happen.

He'd known men who'd talked of women and children being shot without a second thought – their bodies thrown into ditches. At this moment, he felt like a traitor – he'd capitulated and stayed away in a foreign land for far too long. Why should this young guard talk to him? He'd allowed himself to fall into the hands of the enemy! Now he was trying to return, slip in unnoticed, and he didn't even have the courtesy to have the passports ready for inspection. What sort of soldier had he been?

Clearly inept.

Hugo looked at the guard and immediately saw parallels with his younger self – so often detailed for guard duty rather than the flying training he'd been promised. He cast his eyes down at the guard's boots, enquired: 'Do you find your boots get very hot in this weather?'

'Yes, very hot.'

From the back of the van a young English voice piped up: 'Are we at Oma's?'

'Ah, you think Oma has her own private policemen?' For once on the long journey, Hugo was pleased that his ever-inquisitive daughter should interject at this point. His relationship with the border guard needed fresh impetus whilst poor Rene searched high and low for their passports.

'Maybe?' came the little voice, its owner unseen by the guard.

'I have a daughter,' he told Hugo.

'I have a son also,' said Hugo. 'He is asleep. It's a long way from England. It's a long way from Cornwall. This is very important for them – for their education.'

'Here! I've found them!' An exultant Rene proffered the passports to the guard, who took them without acknowledgement to her or her efforts and proceeded to examine them in detail. Hugo's passport was German and this made the difference.

'They're in order. *Willkommen*, Herr Mauer!'

Hugo thanked him, started the engine and pulled away into traffic, so very pleased to have heard what he'd been hoping to hear ever since his capture nineteen years before; so pleased was he that tears welled, causing him to sniff and glance out of the side window for fear that his emotion might be picked up on by the family, the guard's words echoing in his mind: 'Welcome home, Herr Mauer!'

'Marco's going to be sick, I know he is!' came the little voice from the back and, closing his eyes tightly as if pressing the shutter of a camera, Hugo Mauer found himself back in the past.

*

The only reason that the Rensburgs were saved from their cellar prison was the arrival at the farm of a hungry man seeking to trade an antique clock for any food they might have. Unable to get an answer at their door, he was about to break in when he heard faint shouts from a ground-level vent.

*

'What's in this coffee? I feel sick!' choked Karl as if he had just swallowed poison. 'Rum. They've put rum in the coffee. Liquid courage,' said Thomaz, smiling serenely, liking the very idea of the normally forbidden rum in an enamel pot of normally mundane coffee. This occasion, he felt, was like the Last Supper and hopefully what it was leading to would not be so tragic.

'I thought it was to celebrate the commander's birthday?' quipped Hugo.

'Dutch courage is what it is. This is what they mean by "Dutch courage".' Thomaz was happy – very happy. And he hadn't killed anyone, at least not yet and not in cold blood.

The combination of rum and coffee seemed to cause something of a very profound effect on Hugo's interpretation of that evening in the Dutch schoolhouse. Looking across the table at his friends, he felt that he could also see himself from their viewpoint, as if *he* was also *them* – Karl and Thomaz – and that they were all one and the same. He wanted to take a picture of the scene and would have given everything he owned for a camera at that moment. Not that he normally had any interest in cameras.

Despite their travails, their hard labour, their walking with aching feet and legs for kilometre after bloody kilometre, despite their fear that a battle was looming that might not go their way, they had survived this far, and their commitment to one another was stronger than ever.

Hugo was impressed at how disciplined his friends were. They should all have turned savages by this point, tearing at meat and bread with their bare hands, gulping down alcohol by the metre. They should have captured women in the local towns and villages and brought them here for their depraved desires, yet here they were in an abandoned school, sitting upright with their uniform tunics tightly done up, their unwashed hair greased back over their scalps and tidy. It was as if they were still schoolchildren and the teachers expected them to be good, especially in someone else's town.

Above the heads of Karl and Thomaz a Spanish guitar hung on the wall: a teacher's guitar maybe? Perhaps a teacher who used to accompany the children's voices as they sang some merry ditty about the old Netherlands, its kings, queens and folk heroes. How they must have loved seeing their teacher remove that guitar from its hook on the wall so that they could play and sing.

It might have been like that in Oberwinkel had the Nazis not replaced the school's resident teacher. He was a good man. He'd have played guitar for them and sang of Germany and its heroes.

The Nazis stopped that from happening.

That night in the old school, had it not been for Oberfeldwebel Gondorf, the whole thing just might have descended into chaos, for he was the "teacher" who kept them in order. Teacher/chieftain of the tribe, older brother/veteran warrior, Gondorf stood no nonsense: a tough but likeable NCO whose natural charisma was proving him to be a great leader of men.

Karl particularly admired him, though he tried to play this down, and it was he who would say that if Gondorf were captured, the Allies would soon fall under his spell and follow *him* rather than their own NCOs, staff officers, generals and the like.

Gondorf was one of life's natural movie stars in looks and voice; standing at 6' 2" he was solidly built, with golden hair and green eyes. He was as much Polish as German through his mother's line, and if he had divided loyalties he did not share them, but, of course, that was not surprising in Hitler's Germany. A professional soldier, he was a signals instructor by trade and a paratrooper by training. He even wore a para's smock; no one objected to such individualism in this woebegone Luftwaffe unit of mothers' boys.

He was there to whip them into shape, and he did his duty in this respect but without filling their souls with fascism, fear and dread. He taught them quietly and confidently, bringing all his experience to bear, yet showing none of the damage either mentally or physically that they would have otherwise expected. Not so much as a finger was missing, and the troop suspected that in Russia and later Italy he'd been parachuted in and then quickly brought home again for ceremonial duties – an Aryan idol to be paraded rather than sacrificed along with all the miserable ugly wretches, their bodies stinking up the never-ending graveyards of conquered territory.

Karl was convinced of this thesis: Gondorf must have been saved by a homosexual Nazi because that's what most Nazis were in his opinion and certainly sexual deviants. Thomaz, however, thought it more likely that Gondorf had married well and that it was his wife who'd brought him back from the Winter Line by insisting her handsome husband have a safe training job. Thomaz did not believe that most Nazis were deviant in any way.

'Hugo? Thomaz?' whispered Karl, nudging his friends. 'Look at Oberfeldwebel Gondorf.'

'Yes?' They looked across the room at folk hero Gondorf – the defiant individual, an impotent cigarette dangling from his lips, his dress tunic stained and casually opened at the collar, a neckerchief tied around his throat and several days of beard growth that irritated him.

'How old do you think he is?' asked Karl.

'Forty-five?' replied Hugo, not really sure.

'He looks it, doesn't he? Truth is, he's not much older than us.'

'I hear he was at Monte Cassino with the First Paratroop Army before coming to us. He would use the Enigma machine for sending codes,' said Thomaz.

'The First Paratroop Army? They were all but annihilated,' said Hugo confidently repeating the gossip he'd heard from someone better informed than he.

'Then we needn't worry because Gondorf is a lucky omen for us. He always survives conflict. He is always pulled out because he is a favourite of someone – someone who loves him enough to keep him safe. And if he's safe, we're safe!' Thomaz was not called "naive Thomaz" for nothing.

For his part, Karl was not so confident that "safe" was coming their way.

'Tonight we say goodbye to our youthful good looks, my comrades, because tomorrow morning our job will be to reconnoitre again, and I've a feeling that this time it will not go so well, as the Americans are in this district. If Gondorf *is* a lucky omen then we'd better stick close to him. Our futures depend on it.'

*

In the weeks before setting off for the reunion, Hanne compiled a list of famous Bavarians, headed by Hugo Mauer, Oma Hanna Mauer, Beethoven, Mad King Ludwig II, Robert Wagner (she meant Richard), Levi Strauss and his brother Richard, Rudolph Diesel, Hermann Goering and Thomas Mann. This was not a definitive list.

*

It had been a long day's driving and, although now in Germany, Oma's house seemed as far off as ever when Hugo decided that it would be prudent to pull off the main road and camp on the edge of a wood for the night.

'Tonight we sleep here.'

'How far now to Oma's?' asked Hanne.

'Not far. Tomorrow we will be there. Come on, Mum, pitch the tent with me. You children make yourself comfortable in the van.'

*

Rene would often tell Hugo about the work of Sigmund Freud and how his theory was changing the way people thought about themselves. She'd read about Freud in the Reader's Digest while waiting at the dentist's, but Hugo was having none of it, refuting Freud's theories as a load of bunkum!

*

Hugo had woken that morning from a fitful sleep to see Karl and Thomaz still slumbering in a sitting position under the guitar and in the very same place they'd eaten. Someone had taken away the table. Maybe they'd removed the table to sleep on? He couldn't recall for certain. Thomaz's head was resting on Karl's shoulder, their field caps pulled down across their faces in a vain effort to afford themselves some privacy at least. He thought their faces looked like shopfronts with the shutters pulled across. No business today.

Of course, there would be business that day. The British and Canadians had suffered heavy losses at Arnhem, so now was the time to take advantage of the situation. Germany could negotiate with the Allies who were on the back foot. The propagandists were forecasting the Allies withdrawing to the sea and suing for peace. Hugo's platoon may well have been hungry and tired, lacking in men and munitions, but it was still operational.

There was a sense of hope and optimism that morning among the "filthy fifty" as they called themselves. They could at least give the Americans a hard time and, if there was support from a Panzer unit or artillery, there would be no stopping them. The Führer himself would give out the citations when news reached Berlin. *This* would be the platoon to save the Fatherland.

The sun's rays beaming in through – as yet – unbroken, cobwebby windows seemed a good omen.

*

Hugo's favourite English language book was The Time Machine by H.G. Wells, given to him by Wally Johns, Christmas 1950, as a device to help him learn English. Once Hugo had mastered the language, he was convinced that time travel would one day be possible.

*

By the time Hugo and Rene had finished putting the tent up in the dark wood it was ten o'clock exactly. Hugo would not have considered himself a watcher of time, but he was. His watch was his reference in life; its luminescent dials had seen him through the war and had come into his possession the day he left school to start work at the local agricultural merchants, an urgent gift from his elder brother who feared his younger sibling might be late without it and therefore let the family name down in the process.

The watch – a Heuer – was travelling through time, ticking as happily as ever in 1963 as it had done in 1943. Treated with care as his brother had advised, it would require only occasional winding and in return would last him his lifetime and those of his children and even grandchildren. It was Swiss and efficient, and it was the same make as those favoured by the Luftwaffe air aces. Shining the torchlight on it now at precisely ten o'clock reminded him.

It had one little flaw: a hairline fracture of the glass caused by the manic throws of a dying man.

In 1916, Germany becomes the first country to adopt Daylight Saving Time (DST). In 1944, Oberfeldwebel Gondorf uses DST for one, last advantage.

*

October 1st was the day the clocks went back. There would be an extra hour. Gondorf, leading his young recruits from the front, kept glancing at his watch, causing Hugo to wonder just what he expected to happen in the next few minutes. It was no good asking as the troop was now under silent orders, all following in line, not too close should the man in front tread on a mine. The only unnatural noise was the sound of leather boots trudging heavily on wet grass, the chink of gun metal catching metal uniform fastenings, the laboured breaths of tired, apprehensive men – the clumsy sounds of an army on the move. Not at all what Hitler had envisioned, but then again, he'd been a soldier of the trenches; and they'd only marched twice.

It wasn't a mine that shattered the silence; it was a smell – the smell of rotting flesh. The farm they were approaching was in ruins; the decaying carcasses of its "live" stock lying bloated in what remained of the yard – the farmer missing, perhaps dead, perhaps taken for forced labour. That had been Jan Rensburg's fate that day, though unknown to Hugo, Thomaz and Karl. Saved from confinement in the cellar, only to be taken by a Wehrmacht unit with direct orders from Berlin to take him and others that morning for removal to Germany for forced labour.

Hugo wondered to himself just who had killed the cows? People were starving all over Holland – starving in the true sense of the word. Famine is the best description. Had the

SS been here first? Were the Americans denying the Germans food by slaughtering the livestock?

He didn't even know whether this was a German farm or a Dutch farm. He'd been told that morning that their objective was to take over a German village close to enemy lines, close to where the Americans had placed their artillery. They were expecting trouble and the extra hour would give them an advantage was what they were told.

He heard a faint voice behind him.

'What's that disgusting smell?' It was Thomaz addressing no one in particular.

'You most likely,' replied Karl.

'Dead cows in that farm over there.' Hugo gestured with his head.

'Trust farmer's boy Hugo to notice that.'

Hugo rounded on his friend: 'How could anyone not notice the smell of rotting animals?!'

A furious Oberfeldwebel Gondorf turned to urge quiet by drawing his forefinger across his neckerchiefed throat. He'd lost his sense of smell at Monte Cassino.

*

Hugo rarely boasted in company, but he was only too happy to show off his Heuer watch to anyone who showed an interest.

*

Hugo reckoned his Heuer watch had not stopped since that day on October 1st 1944. Nineteen years seemed like yesterday. He thought for a second or two about abandoning the visit to Oma and driving on to Switzerland to congratulate the TAG Heuer factory on manufacturing such a perfect timepiece. It might even make the papers in Switzerland and Britain. "Cornish-based, German-born flower grower and former Luftwaffe POW takes his watch home to the factory that produced it." They could use it in their advertising. They might even want it in their museum. He wanted to tell Rene but she was already asleep, or appeared to be.

He studied the back of his hand in the half-light. A bigger hand and wrist than that of the young Luftwaffe soldier attached to the Second Paratroop Army. He'd replaced the watchstrap in 1949 at a jeweller's in Penzance. The strap – Italian leather – was expensive in its day but came highly recommended by the jeweller who said it was a perfect match for such a fine watch and that it would last for many years.

Before sleep overcame him, in the quiet dark of the wood, he thought he heard the children in the van – devoid of parental discipline – being silly. Or maybe, he speculated with dread, he could hear the ghosts of 1944 calling for his return.

*

Hugo's favourite English language film was the first one he ever saw: A Matter of Life and Death. He took Rene to see it as a first date. Though he understood little of the dialogue, he made a point of watching it whenever it was on at a cinema. He identified with David Niven's character, Sqn Ldr Peter Carter, believing that he, too, had "borrowed" extra time on Earth – time that, it could be argued, he was not entitled to.

*

The houses in the village were alight – flames and rising smoke from smashed roofs, walls and windows, craters making the ground appear like the devil's own golf course, automatic gunfire and tracers engaging the advancing party causing them to drop to the ground.

'Everybody, get down! Now!'

Gondorf gesticulated for a crawling advance toward the carnage ahead. Incoming rounds made sure that his men remained as they had been trained to do under such circumstances – on their bellies.

Craters enabled some cover but rifle fire from a house was becoming evermore intense and succeeding in the objective of stopping the advance and keeping heads in the dirt. Gondorf suspected they were encountering the Americans – a presumption based on the distinctive sound of American small arms fire, which he knew only too well from Monte Cassino. Maybe Canadians? They were known to be in this district; but possibly British, though following the debacle at Arnhem he doubted it. If it was the free Polish then each man in the recce party had better fight to the last because the Polish would not take German prisoners alive. There was even a slim chance of it being the Prinses Irene Brigade. They, too, would fight to the death.

Gondorf, noticeably calm and collected under fire, ordered Hugo to take out the house where someone was pinning them down with rifle fire.

'Take it out with the Panzerfaust.'

Hugo, keen to impress his leader and keen also to put his training into action, lifted the weapon and took aim. His first shot fired in anger. On pressing the firing lever, the rocket blasted into the house with such force that it took out both the front and rear walls. The incoming rifle fire stopped immediately. Job done – for a moment at least.

It was an expression of doubt that Hugo noticed next on Gondorf's face. The destruction of the house and its lethal occupant had surprisingly not brought satisfaction to the veteran's weathered features; rather a very slight dribble of blood from the temple mixed with perspiration.

With bullets whipping past their ears, completely out of character, Gondorf rose to his feet as if to rally his men with a cheer.

What are you doing, teacher?

Felled by an unseen axe from behind! Knees buckled, his helmet falling forward hitting the ground, whereupon his face fell into its upturned rim, his solid body crashing like an oak into the churned earth.

Hugo, keeping flat, turned every which way looking for the assailant.

Who wielded the axe?! Where is the slayer? I can't see him!

There followed a grotesque display of convulsions as Gondorf – brain dead – lifted himself from the dirt before kicking and thrashing his limbs in a spastic, grabbing effort to regain his feet and life itself, with blood and plasma pumping from his nostrils and mouth, eyes rolling with wild accusation at those near enough to witness his dying throes.

For what seemed an eternity, Gondorf's wretched, animated corpse writhed, whilst his blood drained into the crater.

By the time darkness began to fall over the burning village, the remains of the recce party had assembled in the basement of a house, the most able survivors bringing with them wounded comrades in varying states of distress. One young soldier cried of ferocious pain emanating from a wound to his wrist, while others mortally wounded screamed incessantly for morphine, their mothers and Christ.

There was little anyone could do to comfort the poor wretches: no morphine, few bullets. Their only hope was to wait for reinforcements, and the only kindness they could realistically offer was to talk-up the arrival of reinforcements.

'There's a division on its way. General Guderian and his panzers. You'll see! He'll blow the enemy away. Hang in there, comrade. Not much longer now.'

Truth was, they had only ever been a recce party in the hands of an experienced soldier. They were little more than boy scouts who had spent the last eighteen months since conscription guarding railway sheds and sightseeing across Europe.

The hope for relief from some approaching friendly unit was a slim hope indeed. The flare pistol used to signal lay with Oberfeldwebel Gondorf's body on the other side of the road. It would need retrieval if they were to stand a chance, but even then no one knew just what colour flare should be fired for help. The wrong colour would bring artillery fire onto their heads. Therefore, a codebook was needed too.

*

Rene was determined to learn some German for reasons of getting to know her husband's family and in case an emergency should occur. Mark Twain's experience in learning the language, however, troubled her: "One might better go without friends in Germany than take all this trouble about them."

*

'It's not like him to cry like this. I don't think he's very well. Can we stop the van?' Hanne pleaded with her parents.

'Ooh, are you not feeling well, my love?' Rene reached back to feel Marco's forehead. 'He's got a temperature all right!'

'We can't stop now. We're almost there. He can rest at Oma's.' In Hugo's mind, he was only saying what Oberfeldwebel Gondorf would have said and what Oma would have said.

*

"Do generals and politicians know of the expertise of sergeants? Probably not." (Hugo Mauer speaking to a noted professor of Twentieth Century History).

*

'There was nothing I could do for Oberfeldwebel Gondorf – nothing! He just stood up. I don't know why.'

Hugo felt guilty. The recce party's lucky omen was gone. Slain by his own misadventure. The much loved professional who'd trained them so well had done the inexplicable by ignoring his own advice; the very thing he'd always warned them never to do. Now *they* – his pupils – were alone in the world.

*

Working as a nanny for a prominent Cornish family in 1946, Rene had read Dr Spock's Baby and Child Care, a book recommended by her employers. She could recite passages from the book verbatim. Coincidentally, their journey to Bavaria that day took them past Spock's ancestral Dutch home.

*

Sobbing, Marco's condition appeared to be worsening with every kilometre. 'I think we ought to stop. He's not very well, are you, Marco my love?' As Hugo pulled the van into the side of the road, Rene reached back, lifting the tired little boy into her loving arms. Switching the engine off, Hugo, exhausted, covered his face with his hands, pressing his fingers tightly against his ears to cut out the noise of incessant crying.

*

The screams of the dying would not subside and the walls of the cellar merely trapped and amplified the cacophony. Prayers went unanswered. Thomaz considered it would be better to leave the confines of the "hellhole" and take his chances elsewhere because he couldn't stand it anymore. This, despite the death he'd already seen.

Karl reminded him: 'Did you see Gondorf? Did you? Did you? Is that the fate you want? Eh? Eh?'

'Gondorf knew better than to stand up in the middle of a fight!'

'And you know better than to walk out there now!'

But Thomaz would have walked out despite Karl's protestations. It was only the bombardment of incoming shells that caused him to stay, as they impacted all around them, shaking the foundations and threatening the fragile ceiling with imminent collapse. The devil was playing golf and the cellar was smack in the middle of the fairway. Maybe the devil was German, maybe American. It didn't matter because the devil was non-partisan. Whoever "golfballs" they were, no one was going anywhere – least of all Thomaz.

'No reinforcements are going to come. We're going to be blown to hell if we can't get that pistol from Gondorf and the codebook. No one's going to know we're here,' exclaimed Karl.

Just as it seemed as if the occupants of the cellar could take no more, the continual shock of bombardment and gut-wrenching screaming came to an abrupt stop.

'Merciful heaven! Either we are dead or they are!' said Thomaz.

Hugo checked the condition of the last of the seriously wounded. 'They're at peace.'

'They're fortunate, because that's more than we are!'

'Now is the time to retrieve that flare gun and see what is out there.' Karl was the nominal leader now and fully prepared to step up to the mark.

'Without a weapon? We're out of ammunition,' snarled Thomaz. 'Any volunteers?'

Metz was the youngest. 'Where's Metz?' someone asked.

'Metz is dead,' Hugo told them with certainty. He was looking at what remained of Metz – the nervy boy with a gaping hole in his stomach who had been brought in to die. Hugo wondered what the Führer would think if he were here now looking at Metz – or what had been Metz, the promising academic and musician. His facial muscles strained by the slow passage of agonising hours spent pleading for death; his mouth gaping wide now like a landed fish, glass eyes staring into blackness.

Hugo searched for a sign that might have been Metz's spirit rising from the body but could see nothing. He reprimanded himself for not having the faith to be a priest as his mother wanted him to be, or to be able to see beyond death – whether it be the death of a bloated cow in a burning farmyard or a German youth no older than he.

Karl reminded him that if Metz was dead, then he was now the youngest.

*

By the time of the family reunion in 1963, the population of Germany had risen to just over 73 million, with the preservation of large areas of forest considered vital for the nation's well-being.

*

'Where's Dad going?' asked Hanne.

Hugo got out of the van without saying a word, before stumbling as if drunk to the edge of the forest where he fell to his knees.

Unable to see his face, Hanne and Rene watched in silence as he leant forward and started to sweep the forest floor with the palms of his hands as if trying to uncover a hidden, precious object from the debris of twigs and leaves. Something personal and utterly special that was lost in this very spot nineteen years previously. Hanne turned to her mother for an answer to his bizarre behaviour.

Rene was not slow to respond: 'Dad knows a special German medicine for sick children. You find it in the woods here. Oma taught him all about it.'

'Can I go with him?'

'No, he'll be back in a minute once he's found it. Won't he, Marco? Eh?'

*

Of all Hugo's recurring nightmares, this was the worst.

*

Out in the fresh air, crawling as he had been taught to do, like some earthworm, Hugo silently prayed that he be spared the sniper's bullet because he was certain there had to be a sniper – somewhere.

Ahead, he could see through the smoking rubble the figures of two men, both recognisably German in their green uniforms. For a moment, it appeared that all was okay after all. Problem solved. Their presence suggested that they'd held the road and that there was no need to hide because clearly these two fellows were alive and animated. Hugo's first instinct was to call out or make some sort of noise to attract them; but maybe it was illusionary – a mirage – and so caution prevailed. He continued to worm his horizontal approach until he could see with clearer, starker clarity that these men were indeed an illusion of sorts. One poor wretch was suspended on a wire fence – caught like a fly in a giant web. Why was he trying to climb a fence? His bizarre entrapment made no sense.

The other figure was sitting back against the fence as if taking a breather. Then it dawned on Hugo that an explosion must have blown them against the wire.

From his right side a voice approaching his position, drunk – grotesquely drunk – singing in strangled tones some desolate song that he can make no sense of. It's a woman, quite young and eminently pretty, empty wine glass in hand, dressed for an evening ball in heels and long black gown over which she has draped, like a jacket, a man's white collarless shirt; the ashen skin of her face and exposed arms bruised and mottled with white dust, her fine fair hair cascading loose to her bare shoulders, her voluminous breasts swinging seductively as she trips and topples on broken heels, her awkward path to a destination that Hugo cannot begin to imagine.

Now the worm becomes a timid cat crouching ever deeper to the ground, he watches her pathetic, limping steps, but without pity, for in his base desire he so badly wants her.

Stopping within metres of his position, she pauses as if suddenly able to sense his presence, glancing around her as if responding to some unheard call for her attention. Hugo holds his breath. Trembling, unable to focus, she steps forward, momentarily easing his tension, her bizarre song begins again and this time she accompanies it with a dance: step – close – step, step – close – step. She discards her empty glass on the broken ground where it shatters into tiny shards, which impact Hugo's face just as she reaches out for an unseen partner.

Eyes shut tight instinctively; the shards do not penetrate – thank God! The woman stumbles on out of sight, out of resonance.

However, in the years to come she will return to his nightmares many, many times.

*

Rene made a note in her diary of the date and time they entered Bavaria:
Donnerstag (Thursday) 20th Juni 1963, 11.37 am

*

At last, dad's country! Wind down the windows, the air is warm and still. The bunting will have been strung out in Oberwinkel; they'll be boiling water for that welcome home brew. Biscuits will have been bought or baked especially for this day. The miles and kilometres have flown by; the years have flown by; 1944 is a long way behind us now. Cornwall is a long way behind us. The parish priest will mention the reunion at Mass and give thanks for a loved one returned to the flock.

*

'Why are there no barbed wire fences surrounding the fields?' asked Hanne. 'No fences at all!'

'That is because in Germany we have no need of wire fences as they do in England.'

Hugo's answer could not placate his ever-inquisitive daughter. 'Why?'

'You will see when we get to Oma's.'

*

Montag 2nd Oktober 1944, 1.45 pm
Another cellar

His eventual return to the dark cellar, his return to the living who complained of the dead because they were beginning to smell; but the living smelt almost as bad.

'Is there any hope, Hugo?'

He felt giddy and as tall as a giant as he brushed the dirt from his uniform with his hands, having forgotten the sensation of what it was like to stand again. Two hours' crawling does that to a man; makes him feel 10 feet tall.

He had this to tell them:

'The Americans have withdrawn behind the safety of the barbed wire. There's no way back over the open ground in daylight – not without weapons. And there's no way through that barbed wire – it's at least 2 metres high.'

'Then we stay put,' affirmed Karl. 'Thomaz? You man the first lookout.'

Uncomplaining for once, Thomaz dutifully went to his post – the only aperture open to them.

*

20th Juni 1963, 3.03 pm
Oberwinkel

Their arrival in the village of Oberwinkel coincided with the 413th utterance of the question that trip comprising the sentence: 'Are we there yet?' the sentence that Hanne had been asking on a regular basis ever since the van left Cornwall. The only word missing this time was: "nearly".

Hugo had shut his mind off to the frequency of the question in much the same way as he had learned to do in the cellar with the screams and moans of the dying, whereas Rene had kept a secret tally for her own amusement.

There was no bunting that they could see; no band waiting to beat the drum; no welcome committee headed by the parish priest. No fanfare. Perhaps they were ahead of time and it would all be performed tomorrow. After all, how could the villagers know they were to arrive at this particular minute in the afternoon?

'Hooray! We've arrived at last in Rip van Winkle!' squealed a jubilant Hanne, forgetting in her excitement to check the mileage.

*

Montag 2nd Oktober 1944, 2.07 pm
The end in sight

Thomaz had not been at his station long before calling for quiet. The survivors had been consoling one another with whispered stories of home and family and just what the future might hold for them once this mess was over.

He could see just far enough through the smoke and wreckage to get the impression of an armoured unit approaching.

'I can see Americans – 200 metres to our right.'

Each of the twenty surviving men in the cellar reached for their weapons; weapons with near empty magazines. They might fire off a few rounds between them by way of a gesture, but an empty gesture was all it would be and more likely suicidal.

'They're approaching and they've got prisoners.'

Karl joined him to peer out of the tiny aperture. 'It cannot be so?'

Always the optimist, he wanted to see a German contingent bringing American prisoners captured with food and boundless other supplies; but no, clearly it was indeed a large American contingent approaching their position with prisoners – a good number of men whose ranks seemed to outnumber their captors. Gone were the steel helmets of battle, for these men wore their field caps, and far from being the saviours of the so-called "glorious Third Reich" they were nothing more now than the defeated remnants of a once all-conquering army.

'We're tired, hungry and thirsty,' commented Karl quietly and philosophically. 'We should join them.'

*

20TH JUNI 1963, 8.09 PM
GUEST BEDROOM, OBERWINKEL

Hugo not only loved his English wife, he admired her. She'd just put the children to bed having received a courteous welcome from his mother with little more than a handshake. Rene loved to talk but there would be few opportunities to share her thoughts with anyone else in the coming weeks of their holiday. Hugo would be busy on the farm and she deserved better, he thought.

Over the past few days since leaving Cornwall, she'd navigated them across southern England, Belgium, Holland and Germany all the way to Oberwinkel with only occasional errors that were not her fault. She'd organised the maps, planned the route, pitched camp at night, and got them underway the following day all the while keeping the children amused.

In that very bed where he'd last laid his head in 1942 he recalled those pre-war days of school and farm work. Then, he'd never given the English, or Cornish, a second thought. Why should he? Travel had not concerned his young mind, nor had language. Now, he was "British" of sorts; he spoke English; his children were English; his wife and her family were English; he drove an English car. Hitler and his cronies with all their so-called meticulous planning had only succeeded in turning a Bavarian boy into an Englishman – of sorts.

'The children are not at all well. All that travelling!' said Rene as she laid out her nightwear in preparation for her first night's rest in Germany – their first night in a proper bed in nearly a week of travelling. What luxury!

She turned to Hugo for a response.

'Hanne too, nah?' he asked.

'Yes, Hanne too.'

Finally able to relax, Rene slipped off her shoes and immediately massaged her poor, swollen feet; it was like she had walked all the way from Cornwall.

Hugo reassured her, 'They will be all right; this is important for them. They are here to meet their cousins.'

'Your mother gave them a good welcome.'
'Which is more than she did me!'
'Oh, come on now! She just hasn't seen you in a long while.'

Pushing open the bedroom window, Rene stared out at the lights of the little village set against the blackness of the Bavarian night, which to her seemed so much more black than a Cornish or English sky.

'This is such a peaceful little place. Doesn't look like the war ever came anywhere near here.'

'Ah! So it might seem, but an American tank blew a hole in this wall.'

He pointed to the entire gable end.

'New wall. A hole in this very bedroom. Thank God I wasn't in residence! I was a POW. Maybe it was the same Americans who captured us?'

*

Montag 2nd Oktober 1944, 3.11 pm
Border village

Outside, squinting in the daylight, assembled on the road as if awaiting a bus, the shabby remains of the recce platoon stood resigned and trembling while a chatty GI snapped their photo for posterity. *Better to shoot us with a camera than a gun*, thought Hugo.

Their helmets replaced with peaked field caps, their useless weapons collected, the troop took stock of their surroundings; the only thing left to them in which they could take stock.

How ironic – they'd achieved their objective of securing the road; they'd secured it for over twenty-four hours and at great cost. They'd arrived guns blazing "saving" what they believed to be a German village.

Hugo congratulated himself on having done a magnificent job with the Panzerfaust. He'd held his nerve. He'd watched over the dying and braved being shot when venturing outside to get information. The Führer would have personally pinned a medal to his chest were he to be informed – most certainly.

Now that the battle was over, they could see the environment for what it was. They'd come running into the smoke and flames, they'd seen buildings alight, and those that weren't they set ablaze as if it were the buildings that were the enemy and not other men. This morning they were redundant, standing outside what had been a shopfront window, its glass under their feet, its produce buried under dust and rubble.

Today, they would limp out. Yesterday, they'd forgotten hunger and thirst; forgotten sex and love; forgotten for a moment just who they were; forgotten that there might just be a tomorrow.

For a brief moment yesterday they had been strong and fit; they had been at least capable. Today they would be children again – barked at, sworn at, pushed, shoved and cajoled toward a destination over which they had no choice; slaves in a new order.

No sooner had the photographer taken their collective image, than he turned his lens on a GI tending to a wounded German combatant with a flesh wound in his right forearm. The wounded lad looked to be in tears, or close to. A corporal called to the photographer to take another picture, this time of three GIs tending to another wounded German who was in need of water. Hugo assumed the injured men were of the first group to be captured, as he didn't recognise them from his platoon of what had once been 150 men.

He looked across to where Gondorf had fallen, to see if he could see the body. It was there all right, he hadn't imagined it; he hadn't risen miraculously.

That grisly image. Don't care! Stop caring now! Look away, dummkopf! He meant nothing to you. You didn't know him!

In the cellar Karl had reassured him that Gondorf would have been brain dead instantly the bullet entered his skull; that his heart must have been strong and so it continued to pump. That's why he convulsed. That's why he bled so. That's what he witnessed.

They were to be searched again. Hugo quickly understood the gesture from the fierce GI glaring at them. His undisguised loathing would have had them line up for execution right there and then. There was no time for prisoners, no resources such was the whole bloody essence of capture. Thank God this morning something spared them from such a fate. Maybe they were so obviously kids – amateurs, cadets, raw recruits. Waffen-SS men would not have fared so well.

The words uttered by the GI were not understood, but his gestures most certainly were – open coats, jackets, take off your caps. Something nasty is bound to be concealed.

Again, the photographer was on hand, snapping away with his German camera loaded with American rolls of film.

'Do the Americans make cameras?' Hugo whispered across to Thomaz.

'I don't think so,' returned the whisper.

'Hey! He's taken my wallet!' growled Karl. 'Thieving crook!'

Such indignation simply earned him a smack round the head like a naughty schoolboy. Lucky that's all it amounted to.

Hugo thought it was probably just as well that the photographer was there as his presence was probably preventing a bigger crime. He feared for his watch and kept it concealed by holding his jacket open, his sleeve obscuring the beloved Heuer. He had nothing else worth taking.

Once the search was complete and the photographer finished with snapping the humiliated losers, orders were barked in English for the formation of ranks of three. They were to march out at gunpoint and leave the hellhole ruins for good.

Hugo noticed that once the photographer had finished,

the GIs stopped attending the wounded. The photography was a publicity stunt and nothing more. The wounded would have to march with the rest, however uncomfortable, flesh wounds notwithstanding.

*

20TH JUNI 1963, 11.22 PM
GUEST BEDROOM, OBERWINKEL

The last image in Hugo's mind before sleep overcame him was that of marching past lines of American artillery: large howitzers and smaller field guns. Here was the cause of the bombardment. Had they continued, the cellar would have been turned into a mortuary.

Tomorrow's reunion would be in the schoolhouse. He would show Rene, Hanne, and Marco, too, where he had sat and learned. Maybe even his old chair and desk would be there. Perhaps the blackboard?

*

"We have forgotten the age-old fact that God speaks chiefly through dreams and visions."

C.G. Jung

*

Their teacher – Herr Fischl – had not turned up, and his classmates were quickly taking advantage of the lack of authority by running wild around the classroom, upsetting pots of ink and paint deliberately as well as accidentally.

Two boys were throwing pieces of chalk at a third boy and abusing him with racial insults. One girl was being very provocative with some of the boys in a way that none understood. A book was thrown that narrowly missed Hugo's ear, landing on the floor, then kicked around as a football.

In desperation Hugo calls out: 'Where is the teacher?' to which his good friend Anton replies, 'He isn't coming anymore. He's a Nazi in the Nazi Party and he won't be coming back.'

Anton mimics the teacher by goose-stepping around the room, raising his arm in a fascist salute as if he were a dictator in the making.

'No one is going to teach us,' he tells Hugo with relish. 'We're alone.'

Hugo stands up from his desk where he has sat quietly and approaches the window with its view over the village square. Outside, standing on the cobbles, a group of people have gathered. They are strangely familiar to him, yet he doesn't recognise any of them. Their dress is remarkably colourful and styled in a way that is completely foreign to anything he has ever seen before. It is as if they are not of the world at all, but aliens from some other time and place that he cannot comprehend.

The group total some fifty in number, from tiny infants in pushchairs to more mature members of a large family. They are so remarkably familiar to him, as if he has known them all his life, yet he cannot identify any of them. He watches for some while as the group poses for photos. He can't hear them for all the noise in the classroom, but he can see them laughing and enjoying themselves.

Turning back to his classmates, he declares boldly: 'Don't worry – there will be no war. My English family is here. We'll never have to go to war again.'

A senior boy grabs him by the shoulder and shakes him violently. 'Don't be stupid, Mauer! You're not a priest; you're not even a Catholic! You're not English and you're not even German. You're a wretched Jew boy who just wants to make money!'

Suddenly, Hugo is surrounded by the class. Someone shines a light into Hugo's face; the force of the big boy's grip causes a reflex in Hugo and he lashes out blindly.

'Hugo! Hugo! Wake up, for heaven's sake!'

Gripping her husband's wrists in a desperate attempt to prevent him thrashing out at her, Rene, gasping muted shouts, brings him back to the reality of 1963.

'You were dreaming – calling out. You wouldn't wake up, dear. Sorry, but I don't want to wake up the children or your mother. I know it's all this travelling we've been doing and you being back in your old home. That's all it is – a dream. Don't worry, you're safe now.'

Uncharacteristically, with a firm hand he pushes her away then rises to his feet, pulling at his pyjama jacket.

'Let me get up. My pyjama is sticking to my back – very warm. I will take it off.' Casting the damp jacket to the floor, sitting on the edge of the bed for a moment, trying to make sense of his experience, trying even to place Rene because at this moment she is a stranger to him.

'I had forgotten how warm the nights can be here in summer. The air is always moving in Cornwall, nah? Not here.'

'Are you all right, dear? I hope you're not coming down with a sickness like the children.'

'Of course not! I'm fine – I'm fine. This is a very important time for us – very important for our children. Switch the light off and go back to sleep.'

Hugo, however, didn't want to go back to sleep. He wanted to think, to remember, and the darkness of the bedroom provided the ideal environment.

Physically, he lay in Germany, in the very room he was born in, though he didn't know it. Mentally, he returned to a Cornish field.

Tuesday 28th August 1945, 9.47 am

The Cornish fields were claustrophobic in Hugo's opinion – small and surrounded by hedgerows. The trees atop the hedgerows were not much either, scrubby little oaks that didn't grow particularly high but leaned to the southern sky in devout worship to the sun, their canopies like umbrellas against the northern winds.

The people, too, were not particularly tall and also seemed to lean in the direction of the south as if the coastal winds had that effect on all living things.

Hugo did not have the eye of an artist. He did not – could not – look at the countryside and see a pretty scene. Sentiment was not his to possess. Instead, he saw the countryside with a businessman's eye. Land could be profitable. All land had its advantages, he thought, and a man could make the most out of any environment providing he had imagination, and Hugo had imagination aplenty.

Bringing in the harvest that summer of 1945, he could see the potential of this "foreign" land. If he were to stay he would grow flowers; the soil and temperate climate were ideal for flowers. For now, he could only bide his time and scythe someone else's corn, but upon release he could try the idea of growing something somewhere in his native Bavaria rather than labour on his mother's farm.

By ten o'clock that morning, a bright, blue, cloudless sky had established its authority on the day and a new shift was coming his way. He'd volunteered to go out at dawn so that he could finish earlier that afternoon. Karl and Thomaz – never early risers – were coming out for a later shift with others on board the lorry.

From the back of the lorry, Karl's familiar face appears, bellowing familiar German tones: 'Hugo! No post, Hugo. No post.'

It must have been the expression on Hugo's face that caused Wally Johns to drop tools and approach him. The son of the farmer to whom Hugo and the others were assigned as prisoners of war, Wally had, since their arrival some eight months previously, been trying to establish his own friendly relationship with Hugo.

Wally was roughly the same age – the same generation. He'd been exempt from military service, told to continue on his father's farm in a reserved occupation of farm labourer. Like Hugo, he'd wanted to join the Air Force, to do his patriotic bit for King and country, but his parents had requested that he remain with them due to certain abnormalities thrown up by a medical shortly after his 18th birthday. His eyesight test showed him to be colour-blind; he was also under the height requirements for military service and underweight – in fact, the ideal physique for a steeplechase jockey.

It was agreed by a weary panel that none of the British armed forces were missing anything by not having him on the parade square. His mother, Meg, had been nanny to Sir Giles Paton – Lord Lieutenant of Cornwall – a letter from whom suggested that young Master Johns could better serve his country as a dairyman and tractor driver on his home farm rather than become a Bevin Boy – the alternative fate for British youth at that time.

Now, with the war over, some villagers were suggesting that Meg had deliberately starved her boy to avoid the draft, as he was growing into a man of sound stature – quite solid around the trunk, though he was never likely to be tall.

Hugo particularly fascinated Wally. Hugo was everything Wally wasn't – tall and powerfully built. Though not blond or even fair, he was the type of Aryan the British propaganda unit had been warning about – tall, athletic, broad shoulders, with chiselled features. In Wally's eyes, Hugo looked strong enough to be able to pull a wagon on his own without the need for a horse or tractor.

Wally had grown up hearing tales of the Kaiser's war, as it was known in those years, and the remarkable reputation for stamina and honesty of German prisoners. No farmer from that period had ever complained of a theft, wilful damage or any other such crime involving a "Jerry". Not so now with the Italians, where things would go missing, get broken, or some maid would complain of sexual shenanigans. God forbid if it rained, as no work would be done in the rain unless at gunpoint. Such was the "Eyetie".

'Hugo?'

Hugo hears the call but chooses to ignore it. His work is fine.

'No post, eh?'

Wally edged closer.

'*Nicht post*, Hugo? *Nicht post?*'

'*Nein*. No.'

'Never mind, boy! Tomorrow maybe, eh?'

*

'Tomorrow never comes, it's always today.'

Hanne Mauer, aged nine.

*

21st Juni 1963, 5.18 am
Guest bedroom, Oberwinkel

Leaving Rene to slumber, Hugo rose early with the previous night's visions of bizarre dreams and recollections crystal clear in his mind.

Today, he would walk the old haunts. He'd been looking forward to it, and now as the sun was climbing would be the best time. He didn't want Rene with him on this occasion, or either of the children selfishly demanding at least some or most of his attention. He'd had quite enough of that over the past few days.

Looking out from the landing, he could see his mother already busy in the yard below feeding chickens and looking so much older than he remembered. It had been… what? Eighteen years? *Now she looks like an "Oma"*, he thought.

Reluctant to engage her in conversation for fear that there was nothing in common between them, he slipped out the rarely used front door, taking with him the ornately carved walking stick – his late father's pride and joy. She wouldn't notice it missing.

His father, Joseph, had survived the First War only to die at a neighbour's house fire, or rather as a result of that fire. Isolated villages such as Oberwinkel provided their own fire services, with a wagon and pumps stationed in the village for those very occasions when a fire broke out.

Joseph Mauer answered the call at around 10 pm on the night of 3rd September 1933 when a fire that had begun in a barn threatened to engulf a neighbour's house. Eyewitnesses recalled a heroic effort from all who turned out, and in particular Joseph Mauer who entered the house on several occasions to rescue valuable property for the owner.

Joseph's lungs – already compromised due to the gas

attacks suffered on the Western Front – were severely affected by the smoke. He collapsed exactly two weeks after the fire whilst sawing timber in a nearby wood. Coughing – severe coughing – probably aggravated by sawdust did for his heart. A search party found his body some time later, his hand still grasping the handle of the cross-cut saw, with that very ornate walking stick laid out beside him.

A boy of eight years when Joseph died, Hugo, together with his elder brother, worked alongside their mother to maintain the family farm until their own call-up for war number two. Hugo had likened the "new" war to a bus – a bus that had taken their father but had not completed its journey, so it had to return to pick them up as well in order to reach its eventual destination.

Today, he wanted to walk to the spot where his father's body had been found – the father he'd barely known. He'd been at school when they'd brought the body down from the wood to the village. He recalled watching a small party of the most able-bodied men descending the steep grassy slopes, straining under the weight of the stretcher, while the priest waited in the village to receive them.

Hugo had discovered the exact spot his father died some days later when he and his brother came across the clear signs of sawing – the lengths of freshly cut timber stacked awaiting transport, and a heap of sawdust. The shepherd, Manfred Arnold, had solemnly returned the saw and stick to the family. He'd been a member of the party who'd fetched the body, and as a contemporary had fought with Joseph in the same Bavarian regiment. He'd also been a fellow in the same brigade – though the night of the fire he'd been tending to his flock grazing some kilometres away; a fact noted and not forgotten by Hugo's mother.

Hugo wondered whether he might bump into Herr

Arnold on this visit and, if he did, he would thank him as an adult for the care and consideration he had shown to the family over many years, helping as he always did with harvests and such like.

Manfred's nephew, Anton, had been Hugo's best friend in the village. The two had been inseparable since their very early years, only going their separate ways at call-up: Anton into the Heer and Hugo into the Luftwaffe.

With the passing of the years, finding the place where his father had died was more difficult than he'd expected. Almost two decades changes a place, and although the largest tree under which Joseph had been found still stood, it was no longer the largest tree. A good way to identify it for certain was by finding the initials that he and Anton had carved into its bark. They'd played here so often before the world changed, before the war that took them away, before Gondorf, before Holland.

He'd had a belief – aged eight – that there were spirits here, his father's among them, but such a belief was nothing but a distant memory.

Nonetheless, as the English say, it wouldn't hurt to try.

Under the tree, the tree that knew his father, the tree that bore witness to the old man's demise, Hugo gripped the walking stick tightly, as if strangling the life out of a snake. *How hard can it be? Think of Papa's face, remember his old jacket, and focus on his shoes – no, they were boots! Always boots. Remember what Mama did with those boots? No? What was it now…? She gave them to someone? Who was it? Maybe it was Herr Arnold.*

It was difficult conjuring up the image of a man he'd last seen as an eight-year-old. *Don't think of words, think of his face. What face?* He hadn't even seen a photograph of him in many a long year. Hopeless, but he kept at it for a few more moments. With eyes tight shut he summoned all his cerebral energy into conjuring up a vision of...

Metz.

Metz stood before him. In uniform all buttoned up and looking resplendent, smiling at Hugo as if to say: "Thank you! I know you cared." Hugo turned away in horror. Metz disappeared.

Nearby, a hunter had erected a deer lookout – something Hugo wanted to climb to enjoy the elevated view but refrained for fear that its builder might consider him frivolous or a poacher, so he walked on, breathing in the fresh mountain air and loving every breath he took.

With each step he gathered energy and pace, and by mid-morning he was feeling elated in a way that he had not felt for many years. Swinging his father's walking stick, his feet as light as air, rapidly advancing beyond the parish and into open country where his troubled mind emptied with every kilometre.

Turning a corner, coming towards him was a woman in the traditional Bavarian dress of Dirndl. She appeared to be about the same generation as Oma and every bit as deliberate in her rolling gate as she negotiated the twisting, rocky path.

Not wanting to seem foreign or strange, keen to be polite and wondering whether she is someone he might have known, he steps aside for her to pass, smiling warmly, trying to engage her acknowledgement in the hope they might have known one another.

Carrying a candle and rosary, the woman's demeanour is sad and lonely. She slows her pace to look at him, acknowledge his gesture, before stopping abruptly in the track to stare at him in disbelief.

Hugo, too, stops abruptly. 'Frau Witt?'

'Hugo?'

In Hugo's eyes the woman has aged considerably since he

last saw her. She, in need of glasses, squints at the mature man of thirty-eight who stands before her dressed in the most un-Bavarian style of Marks & Spencer casual trousers and open-top white shirt.

The rosary and candle in her trembling hand, her demeanour, her black shawl across her shoulders. The cemetery is ahead of her by some kilometres yet.

'Anton?' he asks tentatively.

She nods, before bringing her trembling free hand up to cover her downcast eyes, and begins to weep.

Hugo, too, turns away, and for the first time in his life weeps openly.

*

Chapter 3

Homecoming

Later that morning, Hanne found her own way to the deer lookout as if instinctively drawn to the spot. This will become her very special place over the next few weeks. No qualms about her being considered a poacher. From here, she can see the village below, the fields where her father and grandparents had worked. This was her new, unknown horizon. At home, she knew all the horizons.

God must also have a deer lookout from which to observe his creation, and if she is quiet she might even see some deer.

Deer lookouts are wonderful! Children at a loose end can fill their time away from parental demands, and younger siblings who are just too young to be good company. A nanny Hanne is not. From this day forth her ambition is amended, as now she will become a naturalist like David Attenborough or Sir Peter Scott, and so to sit patiently waiting for wildlife to appear is a most important discipline to attain. Mumbling, she narrates to an imaginary BBC audience of many millions who, sitting in armchairs of a summer's evening, hang on her every word.

Hopefully, the two girls approaching her position from the meadow have not seen her lips moving while she narrates into the microphone. Don't they know a documentary is being made?!

Cut! Return to the studio. There are cousins to meet. Inconvenient, but it's become uncomfortable, and she knows just who they are as only a nine-year-old can know. Looking beyond to the red rooftops she imagines that the whole village houses her relatives: aunts, uncles and cousins both close and removed by several generations. The village is her tribal home and she is more at home here than she is in Cornwall where she stands out as a foreigner and even worse than that – a "Jerry".

Rene is always telling her how German she looks, how much like her father's side of the family. Marco is different; he is still in the making and could go either way.

How silly! I'm Anglo-German, which is a contradiction because the Angles were German. Well, Danish Germans.

She'd only just learned that spring exactly how the Angles, Saxons, Jutes and Friesians had settled Britain after the Roman Empire, where they'd come from and where they'd settled. She knew because her Celtic Cornish teachers and classmates knew better and were always reminding her of *their* pre-Roman heritage.

Heidemarie, placing her foot on the first rung of the ladder, was the first to speak in her native German. '*Was machst du?*' ('What are you doing?').

Hanne misunderstood "du" for "doing", but understood the gist and replied in English. 'I'm looking for deer.'

And so the English–German dialogue began, with the cousins seemingly communicating in two different languages as if it were the most natural thing ever.

'Come with us. We want to show you something,' invited Heike in English.

'*Kommst du!*' said Heidemarie, which Hanne took to mean, 'Come you!'

Stepping down from her tower, Hanne surrenders her isolation to her new best friends. She loves them immediately though refrains from putting her arms around them, thinking the gesture is not at all German and far too forward and unnecessary. After all, they are not strangers in her eyes; they are as one – all granddaughters of Oma – Oma Hanna Mauer. They need no introduction.

The trio set off across the fields, en route to a destination that Hanne cannot imagine. Fanciful thoughts fill her head, of treasure and dragons and even German TV stars on the other side of the hill. Maybe a herd of rare Bavarian deer await her. It's exciting!

Wherever it is they are heading for, a dog awaits them – a big dog. She can hear distant barking so it must be an Alsatian as this is Germany and Germans only keep Alsatians and dachshunds. The French keep poodles, the Danes have Great Danes, the British have bulldogs and the Canadians have Labradors and huskies. There could be no other explanation.

She even wonders that this might even be the rehearsal for the family reunion, which is on Saturday. Surely all the community must be involved in its preparation?

It seems to her they are walking a long way, but it is only because Hanne is unfamiliar with the lie of her ancestral home; the gentle bluffs and wooded valleys conceal many things of which she has no experience.

When at last she catches sight of her cousins' goal, she can't quite make out just what it is they are taking her to.

'What is this? Is it an army camp?'

All across the horizon a large chain-link fence stretches for as far into the distance as anyone can see, interspersed with a tower here and there – much higher than Hanne's deer tower. The towers rise so high into the sky that she can imagine the occupants looking out to the next country: Austria or France perhaps?

So many towers!

Perhaps the cousins have mistakenly interpreted her interest in towers. With the exception of the deer tower, she's never been up a tower in Cornwall – not even Smeaton's Tower on Plymouth Hoe where she'd gone once with her English grandmother.

Heike, pointing at the fence and with a sweeping gesture, explains in English: 'This is the border,' and pointing at two distant figures standing in the observation post of the tower and barely visible, 'Those soldiers are from the East. Some are Russian. Come on!'

'Is it safe?'

Heike, understanding her cousin's concerns, reassures her: 'Don't worry! They're our friends.'

'You speak English.' Hanne was most surprised.

'My Dad is an American – an American soldier. Nobody likes him.'

From the observation room of the tower, the approach of children heralds an event in an otherwise tedious day. Twenty-nine-year-old border guard Erwin Seidel is particularly keen for a diversion in an otherwise monotonous shift. A family man with young daughters of his own in East Berlin, Erwin harbours an ambition to be a rock star, but is painfully aware that he is on the wrong side of both twenty-one and the fence.

His father, Joachim, a musician and fan of Rachmaninov, had been a reluctant guard in the last war stationed at various Stalags, including the infamous Colditz; and it was Joachim who'd written to him that very morning with news that was going to break his only son's heart in two.

For this moment, Erwin simply folds the white envelope with the Berlin postmark and places it in his breast pocket unread. He suspects its content to be awful, convinces himself that it cannot be positive news, that events over which he has no control have gone against him and there will be no turning back. He says nothing to his comrade Rollo Roth. It's Roth, with binoculars pressed firmly against his eyes, who spots the girls approaching. 'Our friends are coming to see us again.'

'I'll go down and see them. They know me.'

'You shouldn't be encouraging them!' warned Roth.

'The Party encourages them. "Win hearts and minds", remember? Besides, what harm can it do? I like to see people – lonely, stinking outpost that this is!'

It is this last utterance that concerns Roth. Border guards in the *Grenztruppen* were chosen specially for their ability to cope with the duties of protecting the border. A variety of measures ensured that men chosen for their stamina, marksmanship and Party loyalty prevented lapses of personal frustrations and desires. Guards were frequently rotated so that they wouldn't become over familiar with a particular location or colleague. Roth and Seidel had only met for the first time two days ago and it was likely that they would be replaced by the end of the week and probably never see one another again.

The place was getting to Seidel and this was still a new assignment, so what would he be like in a year's time or the year after? A border posting required considerable patience, but there were the benefits, such as the country patrols, which in the summer were at least more pleasant than a nerve-racking city posting such as Berlin.

To Seidel, the fear of having to shoot or arrest a fellow German concerned him more with every passing day, with its monotony of constant parade-like bullshit of uniform coupled with the blind obedience to serve the mundane orders of superiors and the ever-watching Party. Out here, they were almost self-employed security guards who could admire the view, read magazines, books, take walks, exercise the dog, even catch sight of beautiful women that might pass near.

Twenty-four-year-old shop assistant Sylvia Munch was one such local beauty who would tease them by sunbathing on a knoll in clear view, spreading out on the grass a tartan wool rug before stripping down to her underwear, unclipping her bra strap if she lay on her front. Just reading, nothing subversive. She had their full attention and seemed to be acting as the West's secret weapon in testing the strength of the border, as an entire division could cross at this point when all eyes were on her.

Each day there were radio tests, of course, and visiting patrols from both East and West. The Americans would turn up in a Jeep comprising infantrymen, together with a German civilian dressed in a suit and tie, and often a local police officer or two – the Bavarian *Grenzpolizei*. Somebody would usually have a clipboard for note taking. Notes were also taken in the tower, describing everything from the registration of the vehicle to the appearances of the men – cap badges, if they could be deciphered. There was a chart on the wall showing all the various American and British army regimental badges, a chart that Seidel believed originally dated from the last war and had been adapted from *Heer* to *Grenztruppen* use.

Games would be played during such observational visits. Seidel and his fellow guards, despite a mistrust of each other, were not without a sense of humour. They would wait until such time as they knew they were being watched and then act out some charade to measure the reaction of the visitors on the other side of the fence. They would taunt by gesturing imaginary coffee invitations: 'Come on, Joe. Come and have some coffee. We've just made a brew!' Or by gesticulating a phone call: 'Joe? It's your Uncle Sam! We have him on the phone. Come and talk to him. He wants you to go home, Joe.'

It was their own side, East German *Grenztruppen* patrols and Stasi visits that bothered them the most. Questions, questions, questions: 'What have you seen?'

'Where?'
'When?'
'Why are these record sheets out of sequence?'
'What do you mean, the visibility was poor?'
'Why haven't you shaved this morning?'
'Do you think this is a holiday?'
'We can send you to Berlin at a moment's notice!'
'Remember your family at home.'
'Remember you could serve five years in a Gulag!'

Seidel fancied the idea of approaching an American patrol just to chat and pass the time. Only the fear of being carted off to a Gulag prevented him from doing so. He didn't speak any English apart from memorising a few lyrics from favourite songs, such as Buddy Holly's 'Peggy Sue'.

Pretty, pretty, Peggy Sue, oh, Peggy, my Peggy Sue – ooh hoo.

He'd nicknamed his wife "Peggy Sue". He imagined that the Americans might have a few words of German – they'd been in the country long enough, after all. He wanted to talk about rock and roll, and motorbikes like Vincents and Triumphs and BSAs, not realising that these were in fact British machines. His ambition was to own a big BSA twin cylinder machine like a Gold Star and wear a black leather Marlon Brando style jacket. His favourite film was *The Wild Ones* starring Brando – a film he'd seen because it was shown as an example of how society falls apart if left to the corrupt, degenerate, democratic system of the West. It had been shown as a warning in barracks in 1960 and accompanied a shorter film on the perils of VD.

In his possession was an English language book entitled *Who's Who in Showbusiness 1961*, which he thought was American but was also in fact British. He'd found it by chance in the long grass, as if deliberately tossed onto his side of the border. He suspected that it might have been thrown by the sexy Fräulein Munch; that she had thrown it over to taunt them and show what the decadent West of the early '60s was all about, and maybe to get someone like him in trouble if it was kept and discovered.

The annual was full of facts about British and American screen and rock and roll stars. He had no idea that Cliff Richard and The Shadows were British or whether Lorne Greene was an American or Canadian star. He just loved staring at the glossy pictures and imagining himself as such a star pictured astride a powerful motorcycle.

Heike and Heidemarie remind him of his own children and he makes sure to have some chocolate ready to welcome them. He fetches guard dog Ilsa from her run, as the children like seeing her and she would only bark until such time as she was confronted with them. Her barking drove him to distraction, but like all the dogs he worked with he was fond of her nonetheless. He trusted her because he could trust no human being. She was another distraction in an otherwise boring world of duty.

Heidemarie can't wait to see him. 'Hello!'

'Hello!' replies Seidel, strengthening his grip on Ilsa's already tight lead. She whimpers. He opens the inner gate and walks out into the compound to meet them at the outer fence.

Heike introduces their new friend. 'This is our cousin, Hanne. She's from England.'

'That's nice! I have some chocolate for you.' He fumbles in his pockets, feigning a puzzled expression, pretending all the while to have left it elsewhere – an act he performs for his own daughters whenever he takes them home toys or sweets.

Producing three bars of chocolate no less, he breaks them into strips and passes them through the wire links, smiling broadly as they accept his gifts.

'Thank you!'

'Yes, thank you!'

'Can the dog have some?' asks Hanne in English.

Seidel is puzzled until Hanne breaks off some squares and gestures toward Ilse, who sits impatiently on her haunches.

'Yes, she can have some,' he assures Hanne. 'She's a good dog.' He gives the squares to Ilse, who is indeed a good dog, but not good enough for her masters in East Berlin. Her days are to be spent in the quiet of the Bavarian hinterlands.

Seidel glances up at the tower where Roth is watching them, god-like and disapprovingly. 'Well now, you'd better be running along or I'll be in trouble for talking and not working.'

Rising to his feet, Hanne thinks how tall he looks, even taller than dad. She thinks that he looks like her TV cowboy hero, Clint Walker, and that he has a very kind face and his whole manner is warm and welcoming. She imagines that he will go home each evening whereupon, like Clint Walker, he will hug his wife and family and tell them how much he loves them. She imagines that he might have a daughter very much like her and probably also called Hanne.

'*Auf Wiedersehen!*' He waves with his free hand before tugging on Ilse's lead; it is time to follow her master and return to the safety of the inner sanctum.

'*Wiedersehen!*'

'*Wiedersehen!*' calls Heidemarie, waving frantically.

'Bye! Thank you! You have a nice dog!' calls Hanne in English. Erwin stops briefly to acknowledge her, turning to smile – a smile she will capture and keep all her life.

'Goodbye, little English cousin. Come on, Ilse.'

Begrudgingly, the dog follows her master's heels away from the chocolate donations and the little English girl who'd shown an interest in her. The cousins had not walked far from the fence – perhaps a hundred metres or a fraction more – a lazy, carefree amble through the long grass, their goal accomplished

– when the crack of a shot rang out behind them. The crack was sharp enough to make Hanne jump and glance back, much to the amusement of Heidemarie. Nothing can be seen of the fence now that they're deep in the valley, but they can hear Ilse barking frantically.

'What's happened?' Hanne asks.

Heidemarie is reasonably confident. 'He's probably shot at a bird. They do that sometimes.'

They conclude that there is nothing to worry about. The idle stroll toward the village will continue unabated, with the exception of frequent stops to lie in the grass and pull at the wild flowers. Heike and Heidemarie know that the border is all about strange things and that no one should enquire too much on either side of the fence. Hanne the foreigner knows no such thing and feels an overwhelming sense of insecurity because of it.

*

Footnote: Bureau investigation concluded later that year
The official reasons behind the shot discarded suicide and concluded that it was an accident: that Border Guard Comrade Erwin Seidel had taken out his service pistol to either check or clean the mechanism, whereupon it discharged accidentally. Roth claimed it as an accident, that he'd watched Seidel all the time as was his duty and that apart from Seidel's descent of the inner staircase he'd not lost sight of him for one moment. The letter in Seidel's pocket had been opened, but its contents had not been officially recorded. Filed away in Stasi HQ, the letter was eventually returned to Erwin Seidel's family in 1990, a month before his father Joachim died aged seventy-eight.

*

Mittwoch 26th Juni 1963, 6.10 pm
Oma's dining room, Oberwinkel

Sitting around Oma's long dining table that evening for tea, Rene, frustrated with the lengthy silence, could bear it no longer.

'Hanne went with her cousins to the border post today.'

'Be careful! The guards shoot children, you know!' Hugo was deadly serious.

'We heard a shot as we were walking away.'

Sitting opposite one another, both parents exchange concerned glances, which Hanne notices, as does Oma at the head of the table.

Hanne desperately wants to explain how it had not been like that at all, how wonderful the guard was and his beautiful dog. How he'd come down to meet them from his lofty tower armed only with chocolate and a winning smile.

*

A gusty day in Berlin is seen by Cornish people in Bavaria

After tea, it is Hanne, with her accustomed cheek, who suggests they put the television on for the evening because now they've recovered from the long journey and feeling quite normal again, Clint Walker just might be on, with his voice dubbed into German, or even better there might be some news relating to the border post that she'd visited that afternoon.

To Hanne's delight, Oma has an eye-catching television – a very modern state-of-the-art Grundig that makes all competitors look ashamedly Stone Age even though it is already five years old. Both Hanne and Rene had been most impressed on first seeing its wondrous design and wooden casing that could only have come from the future. The "box" was a shining example of what the British papers at home were raving about – the new German manufacturing powerhouse. This, however, would have been a revelation to Oma, who was quite unaware of her nation's newfound reputation overseas. She still used oxen to plough the fields and, with the exception of electricity, the farmhouse remained just as it had done in the days when her husband had set off to fight a fire and her sons had set off for war.

Oma only tolerated the TV because some relative insisted she have one just in case a national emergency was about to break and then she would need all the information she could get. In her defence, she said that if the Russians were to come she would be one of the first to know about it – television or no television.

Hanne had to know whether Germany also had a "Children's Hour" and whether they had any British or American programmes that she could understand. She pestered her mother with this request rather than her father as she was still shy of Oma and suspected that dad would only say something like, 'We have not come all this way so that you can watch television, young lady.'

Hugo passed all responsibility when Rene suggested that they ask if the "box" could be put on. He wanted nothing to do with it and told Rene she should ask Oma herself and that he shouldn't act as interpreter all the time. The family should communicate directly with Oma, language or no language. She wouldn't eat them alive despite appearances to the contrary.

Caught perilously in the no-man's-land of her daughter's pestering and her husband's reticence to communicate with his own mother, Rene summons her courage. She can at least point and gesticulate at the box, deftly articulating the thumb and forefinger of her right hand to demonstrate switching on.

'All right if we have television on, Oma?' and then just in time remembers to say in German: '*Bitte?*'

'*Doch! Bestmont!*' replies Oma, nodding.

'*Danke! Danke!*' Rene, genuinely grateful for the exchange, scrutinises the "box" carefully if she is to pull or turn the correct switch that will bring the set to life. There appear to be only two, but then it also functions as a radio and a record player.

Hugo suggests that as it is nearly seven o'clock they should see the news. Mindful not to concede too much in the way of choice to his beloved daughter, he is keen to impress his own mother of his worth as a father; that it may be 1963, but he won't be walked all over.

The bulletin is already underway as the set warms, the sound coming through first and eventually a grey, though clear, picture, which impresses everyone. Hanne's interest in the border is rather prophetic to say the least, as the lead item is all about it, only on telly the border is the Wall in Berlin and President Kennedy is visiting the divided city and making a speech. Even Oma stops long enough to listen to Kennedy address the crowds, his English speech immediately translated for German viewers by subtitles and the growl of a correspondent. There's rampant applause when he addresses the crowd in German: '*Ich bin ein Berliner!*'

'He's a doughnut?!' queries Oma in German, not sure that she'd heard him correctly, her reaction causing Hugo to smile for the first time since leaving Cornwall; not that she notices.

'I wonder if the President will come here and meet our guard?'

'I don't think so, dear. Germany is a big place,' says Rene, hugging her daughter.

*

Donnerstag 27th Juni 1963, 8.50 am
Oma's meadow, Oberwinkel

The following morning was too humid even for Hugo. The cool coastal breezes of Cornwall that kept the air moving and made it so palatable for working in had, over the years since his arrival in the Duchy, somewhat softened his ability to cope with high summer humidity in Central Europe. A Bavarian summer could be very warm. Today was no exception.

Stopping briefly to wipe his dripping brow, he came under the glare of Oma, who, despite advancing years, seemed more than able to till the soil of weeds – hacking at them with a vengeance. The last time he had seen such an expression was when he'd been ordered along with Karl and Thomaz to dig graves for American servicemen killed in action.

*

Mittwoch 4th Oktober 1944, 9.10 am
A field somewhere on the Dutch/German border

Then the GI had glared at him for momentarily stopping to wipe the sweat from his face. In Oma's disdainful expression, Hugo could clearly see again the soldier's face: his gaunt, skinny figure, his smart khaki blouson and trousers freshly pressed. He remembered the man as being what he had always expected an American to look like – a mongrel mixture of fifty-nine varieties that he and his fellow prisoners nicknamed "Heinz". A man of European, Asian and African descent, and thinner even than the bolt-action carbine he carried at his side.

It was the arrival of another truck that distracted Heinz from his hate-filled glare. It was loaded with bodies, mostly American but some German too.

'Okay, listen up! You guys did this, so you can do the honourable thing.'

Heinz – as he was to be known by the prisoners – was about to take the digging detachment, that included Hugo, Thomaz and Karl, and give them a lesson in preparation prior to the deceased being laid to rest. With a body already on a stretcher laid across the broad bonnet of a Jeep, he demonstrated just what he wanted the POWs to do, together with his ability to instruct a captured enemy using little more than numbers and instructions taken directly from the US military manual.

'One – *eins* – you remove all personal items starting with the boots.' Unlacing the mud-splattered, blood-stained boots, he pulled them off the feet of the corpse but only with some difficulty, before holding them up by the laces as lesson number one, tying them together, then unceremoniously dropping them into a large, round receptacle into which they fell with a thud.

Karl desperately wanted to lighten the mood by joking that Heinz had a poor bedside manner and would be charged extra for that sort of clumsiness in an Amsterdam brothel. He sensibly kept his joke to himself.

Heinz then started to fumble in the various uniform pockets of the dead soldier, pulling out a packet of cigarettes, a chocolate bar, wallet, stubby pencil and a Woolworths notebook. Collecting the various items in both hands he held them aloft as if he were a triumphant winner showing off his prize.

'Two – *zwei*. Personal items go into a bag like this one.' He put the items down and lifted a large polythene bag wherein he placed the objects that the dead man had hoped to carry across Europe before returning home.

Opening the wallet, he took from it several dollars in cash and a small photo – the image not of a beloved fiancé or wife, but of a dog lying in long grass, panting and seemingly grinning – grinning for the loving attention of his master. The photo and cash were replaced with greater solemnity and dropped into the bag. 'These are returned to the man's family. If you take the money, or any personal item of a soldier, we will shoot you! Be sure of that,' he warned, patting the holster of his sidearm just so there was no possible misunderstanding.

'Three – *drei*. Cigarettes, condoms, whatever, go into the garbage bin.' He threw the pack into a nearby bin without caring to look whether there were still cigarettes in it.

'Four – *vier*. You tie the bag with the man's ID tag – that's dog tag,' he reiterated, in the belief that his captive audience were bound to understand the term, but checked nonetheless. 'Do you understand?'

Exchanging looks, the POWs nodded in unspoken agreement that if they didn't *they'd* be joining the corpses.

'Then get to it!' barked Heinz, removing himself from the impromptu class with a backward stomp of the feet as if demonstrating to the young "savages" a proper lesson in US military drill.

Physically, the task was so much easier than digging the graves. All they had to do was work as a team removing the boots and going through the pockets, but it was a nightmarish, grisly task. The waxen cadavers sometimes appeared to be still alive – groaning, farting and sighing as the final draughts of air expelled from lifeless bodies.

Others were badly mutilated, as if a mad butcher had hacked at them with a cleaver. Their deaths must have been agony, Hugo thought. Yet others seemed simply to be asleep, slumbering peacefully as if slapping their faces would bring them round.

'My God!' exclaimed Thomaz as he delved into his first pocket and withdrew a large pack of condoms. 'This one was looking to screw his way across Europe!'

Karl had found a wad of cash in a pocket of another corpse. 'Yeah, and this one was planning to pay for it with hard cash.' He glanced immediately at Heinz who was watching them with hawk eyes. 'Yeah, yeah, I know. Don't even think about it,' he whispered.

'We can keep the cigarettes and condoms though,' said Thomaz. 'Watch Heinz – he turns a blind eye.'

*

DONNERSTAG 27TH JUNI 1963, 9.03 AM
OMA'S MEADOW, OBERWINKEL

Opening his eyes to the present, Hugo glanced down at the hard, dry soil he was tilling. He was so keen to show his mother how he'd grown as a man. He'd been a boy the day he left, tall and gangly, proclaiming silly promises to protect the Fatherland.

Was she proud? She never said and he never asked.
He felt like asking now: Were you proud, Mother?
Did I do the right thing, Mother?
Are you proud of what I've done?

I've lived, I've come through all this and I'm here again now. So many are not. The boys I buried while I lived – the American boys, the German boys.

I went through their pockets.

Can you believe that, Mother? I went through their pockets like a thief! I lifted their only possessions and placed them into bags.

Their mothers collapsed; they fell to the floor. I know they did. Enraged and bitter, they cry every night to this day, I know they do. Their nightmares came true.

In Cornwall I grow flowers, Mother; and each flower that I grow and care for I pretend that it's a boy. I pretend that I can grow all those lives again, that I can bring them out of the soil and give them life again.

And when my field of flowers is grown and their heads open and turn toward the sun, I salute them. Did you know that, Mother?

*

Mittwoch 4th Oktober 1944, 6.57 pm
A field somewhere on the Dutch/German border

The six Germans were each wrapped in parachute silks before being lowered into the trench. It was the last duty of a day that drained the surviving detachment of any residual energy that they'd had following the battle.

Thomaz felt that another day of this "slavery" would be enough to cause him to join the dead by jumping in the graves with them. 'I feel like we're abandoning them!' he blurted out before weeping.

The sun was within moments of setting. Hugo, Karl and Thomaz agreed; they would come to attention and salute their comrades whatever the circumstances, whatever the threat.

Hugo in particular was eye-balling Heinz; and Heinz – itching to raise his rifle – was not about to let such insubordination go unnoticed, so he referred the matter upward.

'Sergeant? Do we let them salute like that?'

'Relax; it's not a Hitler salute. They're burying their own. Besides, we're handing them over to the British tomorrow, so it's not our problem.'

*

Where Hugo had once glared at Heinz in defiance, now he glared at Oma, for in his damaged mind she had momentarily become Heinz, but there was no greater earthly authority for her to appeal, so she glared right back.

He came to as if awaking from a dream to see her stern expression meeting him head-on.

'He who doesn't work, can also not eat,' had been her oft spoken critique of any idleness when he was a boy. Now he muttered her words under his breath as he resumed his labour.

*

Zaterdag 2nd December 1944, 8.42 am
The Dutch coast – exact location unknown

Born and raised in landlocked Bavaria, Hugo had never seen the sea or a seagoing vessel other than in picture books and magazines; nor had Thomaz or Karl for that matter, and not one of them really cared that much. Karl joked that if they had wanted to see the sea, they'd have joined the Kriegsmarine.

The sea as witnessed through picture books, photographs and the newsreels is a very different place to the real thing. The North Sea, viewed in all its unpredictable rolling reality for the first time, both intrigued and unsettled them.

They had travelled across France prior to the Allies landing in Normandy but had gone nowhere near either the north or south coast. So now, like rabbits transfixed by an unfamiliar object, they stood mesmerised by the water's enormity and temperament as it swelled, pulled and slapped the pebbled shore.

Parked on the shore was one of the largest seagoing vessels they could imagine.

'It has to be American!' exclaimed Thomaz.

'Nah, British,' argued Hugo, not because he knew better; he didn't.

'Whatever it is, it's brought in vehicles – tanks, lorries, that sort of thing. And it's going to take us out of here.'

'Take us to New York, Karl. You'll like that!'

'No, Thomaz, not New York for me. For you maybe? I'm a European and I intend to stay a European.'

Behind them by some 10 kilometres, the camp of tents that had been their cold, infested home for three weeks and four days. Forced labour had not been the problem there; it was the lack of something to occupy mind and body as they waited to be shipped out to England.

They had chased rats, and some wag even confessed that a rat had actually chased him back. They had bet all manner of currency on rat racing, or the fastest earthworm that could disappear into the soil, the fastest snail and the slowest snail – anything that you could wager on. Fortunes would have been lost if fortunes had been available to any of them; but those who have fortunes don't normally find themselves in a POW transit camp betting on rat racing, or kicking their heels until a boat takes them away. Dysentery had threatened the camp and no one had escaped that save for the guards. It wasn't a critical thing, just another endurance. Their British guards were efficient in keeping discipline and a tight perimeter, whilst mercifully lacking the hate that could be seen in the eyes of some of the Americans who'd taken them prisoner. This would change, however, in the New Year with the discovery of Nazi death camps such as Bergen-Belsen, Buchenwald and Neuengamme.

In the East that summer, the Soviets had already liberated camps such as Auschwitz, Sachsenhausen and others in the Baltic states, and news of atrocities were spreading, but for now the British were even-tempered. That would soon change, of course. Hugo did not know about such things, nor did Karl or Thomaz. The Führer had told them nothing. They would find out later; but one thing: they had witnessed crimes but passed them off as war.

So they shot her dead?
  She was an enemy agent.
  It's war.
  Those prisoners are all communists – that's why they're in rags.
  They'd do the same to us. Worse even!
  He tried to kill a soldier. That's why they shot him.
  There was always an excuse of some sort. Excuses, excuses and more excuses.
  We have an explanation. We can give you an answer. Our answer is: this is not murder or uncivilised behaviour because we would have been their victims.
  Do you understand, soldier?

Do you comprehend the reasons behind hanging those children?

When you have been in the Wehrmacht as long as I have been...

Excuses were the currency of atrocities. They absolved you of crime; they were passed around and juggled like balls in the air. If you were an ordinary foot soldier, you could load excuses into your magazine along with bullets. Easily done.

How odd it was to see the British at close quarters now; so different to the Americans. The language was the same, but they were nothing alike.

The Americans, for example, comprised several distinct kinds. There were the Northern European Yanks who seemed resigned to the fact that it was a job to be done but it wasn't personal because there was some family connection there. Then there were the Southern European Yanks who hated the Germans; but their hatred was as nothing compared with the Jewish Yanks or the Eastern European Yanks who were itching to kill every Kraut they encountered. They would spit, kick and punch a prisoner whenever the opportunity presented itself, and the opportunities frequently presented themselves.

Thomaz had been a particular target of a man whose sadism knew no bounds. Thomaz had the face of a man with a target between his ears. Or rather, he scowled back and that infuriated the sadist.

The British were different, or rather indifferent. Their attitude was simply one of disdain. They didn't hate the German prisoners because the prisoners were nothing to them. There was no feeling of animosity because the game was over – Britain 2 : Germany 0.

Beaten, the Germans were no more than a duty that had to be completed. Guard them, process them, put them on transport and deal with the next job, whatever it might be. Nothing personal. Jerry tried, Jerry lost. There was never going to be any other outcome.

The British had been winning wars since the dawn of time. It was part of British life – a heritage thing. King Alfred beat the Danes; the Normans beat everyone; the Plantagenets beat the French for a hundred years; Elizabeth I beat the Spanish; Wellington beat Napoleon; and now Churchill had beaten Hitler. Britain's history books were full of victories, and the total score was well into double figures.

Jerries? Huns? Poor buggers! Tried twice and lost each time. Give 'em a cup of tea, have 'em clear up the mess and send the buggers home. Nobody takes on the British Empire and wins.

No, with the British, it wasn't personal.

Karl had been telling anyone who'd listen about his uncle Heinrich. How he'd been captured during the Kaiser's war and sent as a POW to Scotland where he'd worked as a farm labourer and been taken in by the family who came to treat him as one of their own.

'They'll look after us!' exclaimed Karl. 'You'll see!'

'I'd rather be going to America,' said Hugo. 'I have cousins there. *They'd* look after us.'

Interrupted, craning their necks, a vast armada of heavy bombers some five miles high, emitting con trails against the fleeting patches of blue in an otherwise laden sky; a mighty force of avenging angels of death eastward bound, their mission of imminent destruction little more than an hour away.

The landing craft that was to remove them from their native continent was the largest vessel of its kind that they could imagine. It had come in with vehicles and fresh troops aboard. No wonder the Allies had landed in such force if the landing craft that had brought them were so big.

Like some beached whale with its wide mouth open, gasping for air, waiting for an incoming tide to refloat it. This was not just a landing craft, it was a landing ship – gargantuan in scale and capable of carrying hundreds if not thousands of troops.

Onboard, the mixture of diesel, urine and vomit combined to create the next element of torture that lay ahead. Each man was handed a life vest and told to sit down and be patient. The tide was still some hours away from floating the craft, meaning that the voyage to captivity – once it was underway – would be long and arduous.

Patience ebbed and flowed that afternoon. The sea did not.

Obedient Germans, they sat still for what seemed an eternity, until some individual got up and moved, and nobody reprimanded him or shot him, so others got up and moved around and grumbled. Those quieter ones like Hugo remained sitting in whatever space they'd found for themselves, their heads bowed into what little privacy and shelter their uniform coats could provide, while others leant on the cold, grey fo'c'sle and stared out towards a new and uncertain horizon.

Even when the tide eventually floated the huge vessel off the beach – underway for England – progress was slow… interminably slow. Diesel fumes blew back into their faces and reached down their throats, causing men to retch and writhe with each roll and pitch of the flat hull on the agitated open water. Vibration through the cold, flat, grey-steel surfaces and the perpetual rocking motion took its toll. This was every bit as bad as a battlefield. Surely, by the time they reached England, no one save the helmsman would be left alive.

Karl was the first to succumb to seasickness. Protesting in gasps to both God and man he considered his condition terminal and that these minutes were to be his final moments: 'First dysentery, now seasickness! There's nothing left in my guts to throw up! If we survive this it will be a miracle.'

Seasickness it was, but there was more to Karl's deteriorating condition. Despite his bravado, his faith in a British welcome, he was perhaps the most fearful of the three friends. Whilst he had stood on continental soil, he had felt close to home, close to his family. He could have walked home had the chance presented itself.

In the transit camp, the thought that occupied him each and every day was the desire to escape. Beyond the wire he would throw away his uniform, bury it and steal some clothes from a washing line. Pretend to be a civilian – the British and Americans wouldn't ever suspect because they wouldn't realise or wouldn't care. He could speak French quite well, and with his dark hair and brown eyes he could be a Walloon, so the Allies would be fooled. Without a uniform nobody would know.

Okay, he had no papers, but a lot of people would be on the move home again as the Allies advanced. He could always bluff his way by saying that the Gestapo had captured him and imprisoned him. During interrogation they took his papers, then released him as the Allies were advancing quickly and he wasn't important enough to hold. That happened a lot; he had heard that it did. He would then begin a new life with a new identity, but he would still get word to his family that he was well and that he would be with them just as soon as the war was over.

A beautiful young woman would take him in and hide him, feed him and clothe him. He'd heard of this happening, too; German deserters and Russian slave workers on the run. He'd heard many stories based on real incidents.

What lay ahead scared the living daylights out of him. What if the British weren't so receptive? What if they kept the Germans – for good this time? They'd tolerated his uncle because that was war number one; this was war number two and there had been even more casualties, especially among civilians who'd been bombed.

The Germans had lost again; no one was going to show them any respect. Children would spit at them and throw stones and dirt; women would hit them with sticks. They might be paraded through towns and jeered and beaten. The British hated Catholics and they were bound to hate German Catholics even worse.

He knew a good deal about British history; how wars had been fought against the Catholics. He believed that the British hated Catholics in the same way that the Nazis hated Jews. His uncle had written quite recently and included in his missive this line from an old British friend: "I'd hoped Hitler had come in 1940 just to do to the Catholics what he's [doing] to the Jews!" In pre-war years, his uncle had maintained his connections, remaining in touch with many of his British friends.

In Britain, how would his parents – Matheu and Inge – know where he was? What if he died in captivity? Why should the British treat them fairly when there was little enough food for anybody let alone wretched POWs? If they were to be released then it wouldn't be until at least 1954 or '55 at the earliest. No authority would let them go earlier than that! They would be made to clear up all the damage – rebuild what had been destroyed and make proper amends.

The Nazi Party members would all be killed; they'd have to be eradicated once and for all; hanging and shooting all of them. Good riddance! If Britain and America didn't do it, then Germany would. Hang the bastards from street lamps and leave their wretched bodies to rot as an example to others. Do unto them as they had done to others. In London, they might even behead the scum and put their severed heads onto spikes as used to be done.

Children would have to understand the hard way that Nazism could never be tolerated ever again. Thankfully, Karl was no Nazi in principle, but he'd known plenty who were, and others who were cajoled into the most barbaric acts. Some very ordinary fellows had claimed (some even boasted) of murdering and raping civilians – even children – and they weren't SS or die-hard Party members. And if they admitted this to the British and Americans, then every damn one of them would be condemned by association.

For a fleeting moment on that wretched ship, he swore that on lifting his sorry head he could see his parents standing there in plain view. Yes, there on the very same deck as he, arm-in-arm, watching him, so very concerned but rooted to the spot as if unable to reach him. Fighting disbelief, for he could see them every bit as clearly as he'd ever seen them. It was only when he tried to get to his feet that the phantoms evaporated as if into a mist. Propping himself up he looked around in vain, convinced that their presence had been within his reach, but by now they had vanished. Loneliness at that moment overwhelmed him.

He knew ghosts when he saw them, and this was his first sighting – ever.

Almost two years later in the calm of 1946, Karl was informed officially that his parents had been killed in a bombing raid. News sent in the form of a press clipping by a cousin he hardly knew. The raid in which Matheu and Inge died took place on the very day and at the very time that he saw their apparitions on the ship.

*

Freitag 28th Juni 1963, 7:12 pm
Oma's dining room, Oberwinkel

Hanne stifled her need to giggle. Stupid giggling is an act of nature that's brought on by something silly or something that looks silly, and this was silly. She thought it was very amusing to see her father nod off at the dinner table halfway through a meal. How silly was that?!

To begin with, because his elbows were on the table with the palms of his hands cupped around his long nose and wide mouth, she immediately thought he was about to sneeze, but when the sneeze didn't come she thought he was praying – saying Grace silently, thanking the Good Lord for all they were about to receive – because this was a very religious house; but no, he was sleeping, and right under Oma's gaze.

If Oma had noticed, she wasn't letting on. Hanne glanced between the two with the utmost discretion, not wishing to draw attention to her father's state. She did, however, glance at mum, but if Rene had noticed she wasn't letting on either. Oma would not be pleased if she realised. She might even slap him around the ear. Now, that would be something to see.

*

Dienstag 18th Juli 1933, 11.05 am
The bakery at Oberwinkel

Hugo's subconscious had transported him away from the table, back to a time immediately following his father's death when he and his close friend Anton would push and pull the handcart across the village and out of the parish to the bakery of Herr Gustav Mencken.

The baker was a rotund, chubby faced, kindly sort, giving them each a glass of milk whenever they turned up for their task: to either deliver grain or collect bread. He was never a moody or difficult man, and the boys enjoyed their meetings with him because he treated them as responsible adults rather than children. He never spoke down to them and they liked that.

They liked his wife too, a very attractive young woman – quite tall, with a full figure, moon-faced with flowing red hair and large green eyes. Much younger than her middle-aged husband, her stunning appearance elicited in them feelings that they didn't quite understand.

Spying them from the back room, she would beam a smile, wave or call out to them in greeting as if, somehow, they were important to her. They thought she was like a film star even though they'd never seen a film in their short lives. Their concept of a film star was that of heavenly beauty. Like a film star, she remained out of reach – never coming into the shop but always remaining in that dark, busy back room, her delicate hands and slender forearms immersed in flour.

That particular morning was memorable for this reason: there was an atmosphere when they arrived; something was not right. A painfully thin woman and a stick-like young boy stood in the shop looking anxious – the boy was about their age but half their weight.

Pale, shivering and dishevelled, as if the two of them had been sleeping wild in the forest. The boy appeared not to acknowledge the arrival of Hugo and Anton, staring fixedly down at the cracked and scuffed black leather that had largely parted company with the soles of his second-hand shoes.

Between shivers the mother was trying to negotiate a deal, but the baker was having none of it. 'What use have I for a promissory note? It makes no odds to me, *fräulein*. The empty basket you carry is worth more to me.'

Hugo and Anton's arrival provides a welcome diversion for the baker.

'Now then, boys, you have my grain?'

'Yes. Have you got our loaves?' asks Hugo.

'Yes, I have your loaves.'

For a brief moment normality returns to the bakery – all is good here. Hugo and Anton look toward the back room hoping to glimpse Frau Mencken. She is not visible this morning. Never mind! The baker, relieved to have an excuse to break away from the woman, absents himself with a gesture to get the boys' bread from the depths of the mill.

'What do I have to do to get bread?' the woman calls out after him, almost crossing the counter line. 'Do I have to grow my own wheat, too?'

It was only when she spoke that the boys recognised just who she was – Frau Gruber – widow Gruber as she now was. Her husband Otto – like Hugo's father a veteran of the Kaiser's ill-advised war – had only recently died aged forty-four; his "poor lungs still full of British mustard gas" was the local take on his premature demise, and that apparently was straight from the housekeeper of none other than Herr Doktor Liebermann.

The frail woman stood hunched before them bore little resemblance to the carefree individual they remembered going about her business in the village. Such a happy lady, Frau Gruber; she wore her happiness in the way other women might wear a pretty frock. Why, she defied Earth's gravity and danced when she walked and sang when she spoke. Every other woman in the district was insanely jealous because really Gruber was nothing but "a strumpet" in their collective opinion, bending and curving all over the place as soon as she saw a man.

They had seen with their own eyes how once, in the presence of a man she hardly knew, she sucked provocatively on a boiled sweet until it was small enough to remove and then placed it into her child's mouth of all things! Right in front of his gaze! She would even invite men to dance with her and kiss them on the mouth when it was over!

She had come to Oberwinkel to work as a piano teacher and to marry her beloved Otto – a local boy. They'd met in Frankfurt just as the First War ended and fell in love dancing to Satie's 'Je te veux' – a live performance. Abandoning her ambition to be a composer she left the city to marry her "country soldier boy" as she called him. The women of Oberwinkel considered this to be her biggest mistake.

Despite always having a good word for everybody, despite always being friendly, this joie de vivre of hers was never likely to endear her to those of her own gender. The village women were of peasant stock, broad backs, heavy breasts and hands like shovels. She was nothing like them and, worst of all, she was of no discernible standing whatsoever.

'Look at that hussy. Nose in the air!'

'She should have stayed in the city – that's her place. The elevated princess dancing with us common folk and laughing in our faces? How dare she!'

That's what Hugo remembered people saying as his mother went about her business whilst making sure he was in tow; but he well remembered how the children of the village loved Frau Gruber and she, in turn, adored them. 'The village children might all become musicians one day,' said headmaster Herr Fischl so admiringly of Frau Gruber's remarkable teaching abilities.

Far less was known of Otto. The son of a reclusive wood carver, Otto was rarely seen in the village and was viewed like his father as something of an outsider, living in his late parents' cottage high in the south hills. Whatever he thought of his pretty wife's ventures into the village no one really knew. He seldom accompanied her, and the view was that she insisted on going alone to teach piano, shopping and entertaining herself in the village. Some claimed that he was homosexual and that his marriage was nothing more than a sham that left his pretty bride constantly in search of fulfilment.

One thing that people were absolutely sure about the couple was that "Gruber" was not Otto's family name – it was hers. She referred to herself always as Frau Gruber not Henning, which should have been her name on marriage into Otto's family.

Other rumours persisted that she was a Jewess, and that belief made perfect sense to the villagers because she had Jewess written all over her smug elfin face. She was never to be seen in church.

She was everything they weren't, in dress, deportment and demeanour – ability, too; and any amount of friendly greetings from her were never going to change such entrenched opinions.

Clearly, now, her fortunes had taken a disastrous turn. Otto was dead and Frau Gruber was not only bereft, she was completely unable to care for herself and her only child, Claude. Had she been a peasant of the village, they might have come to her aid as they had done with Hugo's mother when his father had died, and others, too.

In answer to her question, the baker replied: 'Yes, *fräulein*, it would help if you could grow your own wheat. These are difficult times for everyone, don't you know.'

'How can I grow corn with just my boy for help?' she pleaded, lifting the child's bony hand. 'His father is dead – killed eventually by that dreadful war. I have no other family here!'

'Your husband was gassed on the Somme, wasn't he?' asked the baker.

'Yes,' she replied timidly.

'Was he awarded a medal?'

'Yes – no! I don't know.'

'A medal would be worth more than this IOU. I know someone who could melt it down.'

'But we need bread now!'

The baker was adamant. 'If I gave you a loaf, every villager in the district would be banging at my door. I'm sorry.'

The briefest of smiles in acknowledgement to the baker was the sign of Frau Gruber's resignation to fate. The once effervescent young woman who had skipped through life as if it were a game was now teetering on broken heels. The baker gestured to the boys to get a chair – quickly – but instead Hugo came forward with a better proposal.

'I can give you a loaf, Frau Gruber.'

*

The bread under his nose had been warm – straight out of the oven. Now it was stone cold, but it didn't matter. Warm bread was a luxury.

'That loaf I lost – I gave it to the widow Gruber. She needed it – I didn't lose it – I'm sorry. I lied.'

The very same expression of incredulity that he had seen all those years ago on Frau Gruber's pale, gaunt face was now etched on the leather-skinned, craggy face of his mother.

*

Saturday 2nd December 1944, 4:53 pm
An English beach on the east coast

The hell of crossing the sea in a flat-keeled landing ship had seemed eternal. If the Allies had intended to torture their enemy and exact reparation then this was definitely the most effective method.

The sensation of the ship's pitching remained long after disembarkation on the beach. Those who could stand and walk looked – to those gathered on the quayside to gawp – like drunks staggering after a drinks binge, whilst others less fortunate were carried off on stretchers.

In respect of fortune, good or otherwise, Hugo envied the British Tommies assigned to guard their new charges. No bullets flying past the heads of these boys, no ordnance to blow their limbs off. No entrails burbling out of stomachs split open by hot metal. No. These lucky lads appeared to be soldiers in every respect except that real experience of war that he, Karl and Thomaz had come through.

They might be prisoners now, but that experience of battle had changed them – changed their spirits so fundamentally. They hadn't fought for Hitler or some ideal; they'd fought for one another, for their brotherhood and their own survival. Nothing to come in the years ahead would ever scare them or affect them as that battle had done. They had been children when they had first donned their ill-fitting uniforms – clueless and arrogant – willing puppets of an unbalanced dictator. Here on some English beach, the uniforms were still in place, but they covered the shoulders of men who had not only broadened physically, they'd actually survived hunger, sickness, slaughter, capture and confinement. Their friends were gone forever, buried in foreign soil, their eternal souls trapped in purgatory.

A broad slipway led from the beach onto a promenade. Herded onto a quayside it seemed as if they would then await another boat. Very little was said or even whispered among the new arrivals. Perhaps it was resignation, but the Nazis had been most adept at disciplining all Germans to such a degree and for so long that individual whispers had long been subdued.

Hugo thought the guards looked like characters from history dressed in their leather jerkins, especially those with broad-rimmed helmets. They reminded him of the illustrations he'd seen of English soldiers – longbowmen and pikemen who fought the French at Agincourt. He'd learned of the famous Hundred Years War between France and England only a few years before at school in Oberwinkel. The teacher who had replaced Herr Fischl had emphasised that the English and French were sworn enemies who would always be on opposing sides, and how the English had so regretted taking the side of the French in the Kaiser's war that the Germans and English were kindred nations of superior stock whose bloodlines were one and the same.

The scene was reminiscent of the time they were captured by the Americans. Every time they feared being rough handed, such fears were unfounded. The guards were not being nasty or rough with their charges, but perhaps that was because the proverbial photographer was on hand to record the scene with his camera and tripod. There was a cine cameraman shooting film, too.

English was such an unfamiliar language and here it was all around them. He'd got used to French and even knew a few words. Maybe he could try them on the guards. All around him Tommies chatting and laughing about God knows what, as if they'd been here on the quayside all their lives, gutting fish and processing prisoners of war. It was a strangely formal yet also informal procedure in that the guards chattered quite freely amongst all the commands.

Hugo didn't understand the commands – few of them did. The lance corporal with the beret and spectacles and armed only with a brass spray gun offered a simple procedure communicated by repetitive gesture: 'Open your jackets and get sprayed like tomatoes with fruit fly. Tonight you'll have a chance for a bath and get some fresh clothes.' He said this to everyone. No one thanked him.

From the quayside waiting lorries ferried them to an enclosure some miles away. Gone were the civvy-like "leather jerkin guards"; the men here were a much tougher looking bunch armed with machine guns and sidearms.

Crouching awkwardly on his haunches, a peak-capped RSM – stocky, middle-aged and clearly experienced in this specific role – was searching a prisoner's trouser pockets while the man held his coat open. To Hugo, the RSM looked like a schoolmaster who'd been seconded back into uniform for this very purpose; all those years spent confiscating catapults from the pockets of naughty boys. Perhaps he'd earned his stripes in the First War? Now, stiff in the joints, portly and world-weary but with an understanding of the predicament of *his* captives. *Maybe he'd been a prisoner once?*

Eventually – Hugo's turn. 'So, your name is Mauer?' the RSM asked as he went through Hugo's meagre belongings. Not quite pronounced right. Hugo nodded.

'My name is Mower,' said the RSM.

Hugo understood enough to reply: 'Hugo Mauer.'

'Alfred – Alfred Ronald Mower,' he mumbled, knowing that really he was speaking to himself and that it was his way of keeping some sanity in an endless line of duty. He barely looked up at Hugo's face: 'Stupid, isn't it – fighting? Still, almost done now – soon be over.'

Raising himself up to look at Hugo for the first time, he apologised: 'I'm sorry I can't speak your language. Maybe one day, eh?'

Aware that he too was under the scrutiny of other guards, the RSM nodded to Hugo and beckoned him to enter the compound in the manner of a bored manager welcoming a hotel guest.

*

Freitag 28th Juni 1963, 10.10 am
Oberwinkel

Hugo had promised Hanne that he would go walking with her that morning and, true to his word, after breakfast he reached for his late father's walking stick and beckoned his daughter to join him.

They would start off by walking up into the meadow to the west of the village and to the edge of the wood. Hanne was already familiar with the meadow and the wood as she'd discovered it on only her second day in Oberwinkel – it was the place with the deer lookout and it commanded a splendid view over the village.

Hanne hated any gradient; she expressed her concern that some farmer might own the land and be angry with them for trespassing, or that the border guards might be patrolling and tell them to return to the safety of the village as war was surely imminent. Otherwise why would the American president be in Berlin?

She, of course, had already trodden this path. That was different: *she* could not be trespassing as she was a child and therefore invisible. Farmers and landowners would not see children stomping across open ground, but an adult of well over 6 feet in height and weighing in at… ooh, had to be 15 stone… was a prime target for a telling off. Big feet could do a lot of damage and leave a marked trail for anyone to follow.

Hugo reassured her that he had been playing and working in these fields since he was much younger than Hanne was now, and that providing they were respectful to the countryside no one would mind. This only confirmed her conviction that children *were* invisible. They stopped to catch their breath at the foot of the deer lookout ladder.

'You like it up here, nah?'

'I watch the deer from the lookout, and when I'm not doing that I'm collecting wild flowers.'

'When I was a boy, I came here every moment I had.'

Hanne was thrilled to realise that she had gravitated naturally to the place her father had loved when he was a child. Clearly, it was a hereditary thing.

'Look, I will show you something.' Hugo beckoned her to come and see a particular tree – an ancient sycamore that he believed stood guard over the village, sentient and unchanging.

'This tree is very important to the village. It protects us and watches us as we go about our business. People used to say that the spirits of all those who ever lived in the village migrate to the tree and watch over us. Look at this.' He points to the faded initials H.M. carved into the bark.

'These are my initials carved when I was a boy – not much older than you are. Carved into the bark forever, nah?'

Hanne bent forward to touch the grooves left by her father's historic handiwork.

'Posterity,' she said, taking care to pronounce it with particular emphasis on the first syllable. (Another word learned and noted earlier that year.)

'Boys had tree houses in the woods, nah? We build them high, nah? Nobody was allowed, that is how special it was.'

Hanne wondered just who was not allowed to do what but kept the question to herself, lifting her head to the sky, not to look for the remains of a tree house but at the patches of warm light filtering down through the branches and bathing them in luminescence like two actors caught in the broad spotlights of a stage play.

The canopy of trees afforded some welcome shade from the rising temperature. 'It's so hot here in the summer. How does Oma sleep at night? The blankets are really heavy and hot.'

'*Federbett* – not blankets. Different, nah? In the winter it is very cold – much colder than Cornwall.'

Hanne couldn't imagine just how cold – she thought Cornwall was plenty cold enough, especially their draughty old farmhouse, which she hated. For a rare moment, she was quiet and still, thinking about that chilly house and its ghosts awaiting their return. In the momentary pause that had overcome Hanne, Hugo stole an opportunity for her attention.

'This family reunion is very important for you and Marco, nah? It will be a tradition that you must keep long after I have gone. You can bring your children and your children's children – it will be good for them. You must keep the ties you make here, Hanne – with your cousins. *Willst* – Will you do that for me?'

Hanne nodded and carefully considered the very meaning of "tradition" and what it entailed. She knew it would mean many more visits to Oberwinkel in the coming years and she was more than happy with that. She just couldn't imagine that there might ever come a time when her father wouldn't be with her.

Hugo was already on the move. There was something else to show her.

Their next stop was a wooden bridge spanning a narrow, but clearly deep, brook. The old footbridge was somehow different. Hugo ran his palm along the handrail just to be sure. It felt new, and why shouldn't it? The old one that he had known must have been replaced at some time – maybe washed away in a storm? Or rotted enough to make it unsafe? Or perhaps it had been deliberately destroyed during the war?

This was a sturdy and strong replacement whereas the old one had been rickety, but then he and his mates had thrilled to its dangerous condition, believing themselves to be adventurers crossing a great ravine.

The river meant a lot to Hugo. It wasn't much to look at now through adult eyes; sedate, narrow and unassuming. Back then it was a wild border crossing filled with all sorts of dangers, including crocodiles and flesh-eating fish. To fall in was to die. No one got out alive.

Further downstream was different. Friendly waters were to be had there. It was wider, the current was not so fast nor so deep or dark or swirling, and in the summer it was ideal for swimming. There were fish too, for catching. Nice, friendly fish, but this particular spot was different. Here there *were* monsters and demons to drag the unwary below.

This was the very spot where Anton and friends had saved his life. Now he could pass on his story – just this story, nothing else – because this was purely a children's story and Hanne might identify with it or certainly learn something from it. How he and other children had been skating on the frozen river sometime after Christmas that year and all had been fine until the ice gave way and he dropped into the freezing water.

'Winter can be hard, nah?'

Hanne, still uncharacteristically quiet, nodded while watching a maple leaf swirl around like a rudderless boat before disappearing under the narrow bridge.

'When I was young, the winters were so cold the water here would freeze to ice so hard you could skate on it.'

'Did you skate on it?'

'Yes, yes. I was a good skater, nah.'

'I knew you would be.'
'Yes, but very foolish.'
'Why?'
'Because I did not know to stop. I thought the ice good and hard. Good for a skater like me. But it broke. The weather warmed and the ice gave way under my feet.'
'Did you drown?'
'I might have. My friends pulled me out.'
'Did they have to revive you with artificial respiration?'
'My friends rescued me – yes. They helped me out the freezing water, but they did not know artificial saving – no.'

There followed a silence as they watched the river flow beneath them; a silence filled with many conflicting thoughts. Hanne's thoughts were of a heroic dad defying death and nature to re-emerge from the dark depths a triumphant survivor. He must have been a very strong boy.

For Hugo, another vivid memory.

The shock of the water. The ice like a glass ceiling above his head as he kicks, but he has weights on the end of his feet – skates. If the current pulls him downstream away from the broken ice he's doomed. There is a chance if he unties the skates. He pulls at a lace but it knots immediately. This is no time for struggling with stupid knots. He pulls at the heel of the boot, but it's too tight. He tries the other lace and that undoes, but the lace is so long and he's very quickly running out of time. Panic will finish him so he has to keep his nerve. Above him he can see shadows, and some part of him gains hope from that.

Just as he feels he can't hold his breath any longer, he sees a stick coming down through the water. He grabs it like a hungry fish taking bait. Someone is pulling him up – someone very strong. Then nothing. He concentrates hard, but memory is a funny thing. Anton tells him later that a man passing that very spot pulled him out and lifted him onto the bridge. The man slapped him and got him to cough up water. They don't know who the stranger was or where he'd come from, but without him Hugo would most definitely have perished.

There and then the silence ended.

'Was Oma happy that you didn't die in the water?'

'No, she beat me. But I was never such a fool again.'

'Is this why we've come to Germany in the summer?'

'Yes, so do not complain about the heat.'

'Perhaps for the reunion we should come in the spring or autumn?'

'Then how would I grow my flowers in Cornwall?'

'You could tell Wally what to do. He's good at planting flowers.'

Hanne was quite right. Wally was good with flowers just as he was good with people.

*

Wally Johns – a little aside

He could so easily have ignored Hugo all those years ago – treated him in an offhand manner as some did. And if he had been unfriendly, then Hugo wouldn't have stayed in Cornwall. He would have bided his time until release then made his way somewhere else; only not here to Oberwinkel.

He might have tried his hand in America or Canada, but that's not to say it would have worked out as well. People there might not have welcomed him at all, and the chances of buying just a small patch of land, as he was able to do in Cornwall, might have been very slim indeed. Land over there sold in hundreds and thousands of acres. Most importantly, there would have been no Rene. No Wally, no Rene.

Monday 15th April 1946, 8.21 am
Cornwall

It's the little things, like waiting for news, that made captivity so difficult. What news of home? Had the Americans destroyed Oberwinkel? Had the Russians taken it? Would there be anything to go home to?

They knew he was waiting for news and it was infuriating, until one morning the call from the back of the truck was more hopeful. 'Hugo! Hugo! Post for you!'

Throwing the hoe into the hedge, Hugo ran after the lorry like a champion sprinter chasing a baton in the relay. Leaning out over the tailboard of the army truck, Karl waved the long awaited envelope as the POW contingent cheered Hugo on. Such was his speed on uneven ground that he tripped and stumbled but quickly regained his balance to the sound of an almighty roar from the back of the truck as his fellow inmates urged him to catch up. Within moments he'd gained the ground needed to grab the letter from Karl's outstretched hand.

Exhausted from the sprint he cursed Karl for not having just tossed it onto the ground. 'You need the exercise; you're getting fat!' was Karl's witty retort. 'And besides, we had money on whether you could catch the truck!'

Having chewed his fingernails to the quick, Hugo had no way of getting his thick fingers under the tape of the broken seal. All correspondence to prisoners of war was opened, checked and usually resealed with sticky tape or gum. This one had been opened and it was sealed even tighter than it had been when it was first posted from Oberwinkel.

He had to be careful as he didn't want to tear the letter inside, but it had to be opened now because who knew what it might contain by way of news? It might say that the family were starving or they'd been taken by the Ruskies. Maybe the Allies had flattened the village by way of reprisal. Maybe all of these things.

("Ruskies" – a term picked up from Cornish co-workers who in turn picked it up from US soldiers stationed briefly in Falmouth prior to D-Day.)

He prised off a length of blackthorn from the hedge and used that to open the envelope, then skimmed the text looking for disaster.

This was not Mama writing; this was Hilda, his sister. Good for Hilda. It actually didn't contain much by way of information – just a page – but it was communication at least. The family were fine – everyone was okay and the Russians had stopped short. Oberwinkel was now in the American sector.

Hugo stuffed the letter into his top pocket and returned along the track to locate the hoe he'd so quickly discarded. Wally – also working in the field – had watched the whole episode and was now grinning broadly as Hugo returned.

That evening, Hugo sat at the long oak kitchen table reading his letter over and over as if there were something in it that he'd missed; that really it can't have been such good news and perhaps it contained a hidden code that he needed to decipher.

By the time Wally came in Hugo had just read the letter for the fifteenth time. 'Good news from Germany, Hugo?' But Hugo didn't respond so Wally tried his basic German.

'*Gud noyse?*'

'Maybe…?' For want of using his own language Hugo gesticulated with a shrug of the shoulders.

'Well… you can always stay here, you know.' He sat down next to Hugo, looking him straight in the eye whilst pushing his forefinger onto the tabletop to affirm what he'd just said in case there was any misunderstanding. 'Stay here…' He paused for a moment, desperately trying to find the words; then, with one final affirmative tap of the tabletop: '*Schtayensie* here! Yah, dat's what you can do.'

If Hugo understood then he didn't show it, so Wally persevered. 'That girl – *das fräulein sie met* – Rene – the Land Army girl? You like her, Hugo – she's almost as tall as you. She'd like you to stay. You're good here on the farm, and if the Ruskies have taken over your home you're better off here with us.'

'Maybe,' said Hugo in reply to a sentence he barely understood.

Wally picked up a glass cruet, tapped its base on the table and mimicked moving a pawn. 'What say we play chess tonight?'

'Good!' replied Hugo – putting to use the only other word in his new and expanding vocabulary.

*

Freitag 28th Juni 1963, 1.46 pm
Oberwinkel

Descending the steep meadow Hanne was now back in full chat mode talking about anything and everything that came to mind. Hugo simply had to be there.

Above the chatter he looked for a roof and chimney to reveal itself as it had always revealed itself on this particular descent down the meadow. It was the roof of Herr Professor

Rupert Swan's house – or rather, the white-painted gable end of the house that had always stood out so vividly on sunny days such as this.

Had it not been for the professor teaching him chess as a boy then perhaps Hugo's life in Cornwall might not have been so productive. Chess had opened so many doors – introduced him to the great and the good of his new adopted community.

Professor Swan had once been a newcomer to Oberwinkel so he'd known something about the problems of being an outsider – a foreigner – coming into a small, narrow-minded, rural community. A Flemish-born academic, Swan had studied chemistry in Frankfurt at the turn of the century and in 1910 married a Bavarian woman who worked on the campus and spoke highly of the tiny Bavarian village of Oberwinkel. Her actual connection with the village was never fully recorded by local gossip, especially as she never came to live in the village having died of tuberculosis in 1919 aged forty.

Intrigued by his late wife's adoration of the place, Professor Swan retired to the village as if in tribute to her wish to reside there. Oberwinkel had never had an academic in residence before and the avuncular old man was made most welcome. Some thought he would attract other notable academics and assorted famous people and that could only be a good thing for the village as such people would undoubtedly bring money and prestige. Some warned, however, that an influx of odd city types – such as Frau Gruber – would bring about the end of Oberwinkel as they – *the villagers* – had known it. 'What can an academic bring to us? Can he repair a stone wall? Plough a field? Sow a crop? Milk a cow? Shoe a horse? Deliver a newborn calf?'

Others argued that it might bring about – in time – township status.

Others simply mistook him for being English.

Hugo skilfully broke into Hanne's latest monologue to tell her how, at age twelve, he was for a while the youngest member of Professor Swan's Chess Club and how the old professor had made it be known to the headmaster that boys would be most welcome in his newly formed chess club that met every Thursday evening in the school classroom throughout the dark, winter months.

The boys who joined – Hugo and a few close friends – took it into their heads that the professor had been a chess grand master and that he'd played and beaten Europe's finest players. To them, he was a professor of chess and a grand master.

The club was an ideal training ground for the boys, who were encouraged to play the professor and other adults – though few locals were actually able to play. As word of the club spread across the district, chess players began to arrive on Thursday evenings from distant neighbouring parishes: two schoolteachers, a Jesuit priest, a librarian, a town clerk, a grocer and a woodcutter.

Matches at the club would have continued quite happily had the school's headmaster – Herr Manfred Fischl – not been replaced by an unqualified National Socialist called Haas.

Haas had no time for chess or any social clubs that diverted people from their work and the National Socialist cause. In his view, foreign-born academics like the professor had no place in German society and the boys would benefit more – he insisted – from physical training. He would oversee that – personally.

And so Professor Swan – having invested so much of his time and money in the chess club – collected all the boards, clocks and pieces and retreated to his house with a view to keeping a low profile until such time as Germany came through this "fearful time of National Socialism" as he called it and returned to its senses.

The last time Hugo had seen Professor Swan must have been 1942 just prior to his call-up. The professor had been tending his garden and even then had looked quite old and frail hunched over a spade; but his was a hunch he could no longer straighten. The chances of seeing him still in his garden were slim indeed. Shame, thought Hugo, as the professor had always been a kind and friendly man who was well known for calling out to people whenever he saw them pass.

'Are you keeping up your game, Hugo?'

'Of course, professor! I remember everything you taught me.'

That was twenty-one years ago. The old man could still be around. Maybe Hugo would see someone to ask.

*

Thursday 31st July 1947, 7.16 pm
Cornwall

It wasn't until his time as a POW was nearing its conclusion that Hugo played chess again. Albert Rowe the beekeeper asked him one evening whether he played. 'A little,' replied Hugo, which was his stock response to virtually any question. The response was enough to get an invite to tea one evening and play chess.

The significance of the visit was not lost on Hugo. Although still officially a prisoner of war, he'd been invited into somebody's home as an honoured guest. How wonderful was this?!

POWs had been invited as groups to meet local communities, with displays of singing or to play a team game, but to actually be invited as an individual into a family home was something else altogether.

Albert Rowe was not only a keen chess player, he was secretary of the Penzance Chess Club – a coveted position he'd held since 1931. Hugo would be an ideal opponent – new blood, new moves probably. What a challenge! It would almost be like having an international match.

Hugo was most impressed when on bending to enter the stoopingly low-ceilinged, paraffin-lit sitting room, there awaiting his arrival was a posh little rosewood chess table set with ornately carved ivory pieces. Professor Swan also had an ornate chess table and countless other wooden chessboards dotted throughout the house in case a game should break out at any time in any room.

"Aunty" Rowe – as Albert's wife was known to all and sundry – was very welcoming and suggested the men get their first game underway whilst she prepared tea. As conversation was going to be very limited, this was an excellent suggestion. The game got off to a spirited start with both players throwing caution to the wind as they tested each other's mettle with aggressive moves, before quickly, and diplomatically, the game was conceded by Hugo.

The second game was more cautious and interrupted only by Aunty bringing in a trolley of tea, coffee and saffron cake baked to such an excellent standard despite rationing. This caused Hugo to bring out his phrase book in order to compliment her most highly that it was the best cake he'd ever tasted – and he meant it.

The third game was the best game of all as the two men brought to the table all their experience. Professor Swan had taught Hugo well and the advantage was Hugo's in this game, but he did not intend to spoil the welcome his courteous hosts had afforded him and so offered a draw. It was a tactful and entirely diplomatic move that was to pay remarkable dividends.

*

Freitag 28th Juni 1963, 2.13 pm
Oberwinkel

'Hanne? Do you play chess, nah?'
'A little.'
'Then properly I will teach you. I was taught by the best teacher, nah.'
Hanne quickened her pace to catch up; she liked the idea of her father teaching her to play chess – properly.

*

Tuesday 19th August 1947, 6.48 pm
Penzance, Cornwall

Just what sort of reception a lanky young POW would get in the Penzance Chess Club – a hallowed place for sure – Hugo dare not think. A callow youth who just happened to be a former enemy, and a monosyllabic one with limited language ability, was surely not likely to be made welcome by the intelligentsia of West Cornwall that met every Tuesday evening at 7 pm in a reception room at the town hall and had done so for more years than anyone could remember.

Albert Rowe's invitation to Hugo that evening to come along to the club was a rare honour, particularly for a former enemy combatant. There was much to learn and the first lesson was that the "intelligentsia" were nothing more than a cross-section of townsfolk ranging from a commanding officer in the local yeomanry to a bank manager, a hotel concierge, various teachers, a stationmaster, a council road sweeper and a trawler man – all of whom showed delight in meeting their new opponent and teammate for upcoming matches.

To the club members, Hugo was an exotic find; an actual continental European from across the water who must have surely been weaned from the cradle on Bach, Mozart, Beethoven, Strauss, Mahler and, most importantly, chess; he was bound, by the very dint of his heritage, to be a match winner.

He might not have been so welcome in Plymouth or Exeter, Bath, Bristol, London, Coventry or Manchester, but Penzance had never been bombed and that in itself eased Hugo's passage into the chess club and beyond.

It wasn't long before he was being invited to play matches at home and away, with some of those matches even taking him out of the county to Exeter. Whether it was sheer luck, natural ability or Professor Swan's excellent teaching, Hugo couldn't be sure, but despite terrible pre-match nerves he was managing to defeat all comers. Even the most gifted of university academics were capitulating in little more than thirty minutes of play. Hugo had never considered for a moment that the eminent Professor Swan was anything less than a grand master and that he had learned at the master's feet.

Over time, he actually looked forward to Tuesday evening sessions in Penzance as an established player working his way steadily up the board ranking while still officially a POW whose limitations included the proviso that he should not travel further than one mile from the farm to which he was assigned.

He was also frequently invited to the homes of club members for Sunday tea, where he mixed with the great and the good: commissioned army officers, merchant navy captains, harbour masters, hotel directors, local nobility and gentry – all of whom were opening their doors to a former Luftwaffe soldier who'd never flown because the Third Reich had run out of money, but played a damn good game of chess!

Wally, too, was something of a chess player, though too shy for the mighty Penzance club. Winter evenings would find him and Hugo busy making chess pieces – Wally turning the pieces on his father's crude lathe whilst Hugo carved the intricate features of each piece.

His acceptance by the community was causing him to consider staying beyond his forthcoming release. Summer was swiftly drawing to a close and it wouldn't be long before the authorities opened the gates for those POWs who, like Hugo, were not considered a threat and were able to demonstrate beyond reasonable doubt that they had had no association with the SS and any ongoing murder investigations. At least 20,000 of their number could apply to remain in the UK if they wished.

Both Karl and Thomaz had made up their minds to stay for at least another year – Karl happily admitting that his worst fears had been unfounded.

*

Freitag 28th Juni 1963, 2.44 pm
Oberwinkel

'You have all the time, nah?' asked Hugo of a dawdling Hanne, who didn't seem to want to come off the path and back onto the main road that led to the village.

'No ... Maybe?' she replied, picking at a long stalk of rye grass from the bank. 'No, but I like it up in the meadow. I can see everything.'

'Your mother and Oma will think we've been captured by the border guards.'

'We're on holiday, aren't we?'

Hugo had not considered the return as a "holiday" as such, but to Hanne it most certainly was. He sat down in the long grass and beckoned her to sit beside him.

'The first time I came back... This is not the first time, nah? I came back here long before you were born – 1947. I had not seen Oma since 1943, not my brother or sisters. My brother – your uncle – had been a POW too. We all came here in 1947 and it was a happy time for us. We'd survived – it was good. Yes, but Germany was sad – people were starving, life was hard. Oma had black hair when I left in 1943. When I came home she had white hair like snow!'

'Did you recognise her?'

'Yes, but Germany I did not recognise. The cities were destroyed: rubble not buildings; thousands – millions – without homes, without shelter. People dying on the streets – hunger and disease. The living working hard to build again. It made us sad. My friends lost families. I was lucky.'

'Did you cry?'

'Yes, we cried.'

'Is that when you went home to Cornwall?'

'Yes, I went "home" to Cornwall.'

'I'm glad you did or you might have starved.'

'You need to know what happened – you, and your cousins and brother, so that it never happens again, nah? You must keep meeting here – maybe every two years. Bring your children and they will bring their children and you will keep a reunion that we have started – our little family – and then no one will starve again or leave their homes. *Willst* you do that, Hanne?'

Hanne assured him that she would always come back. Always.

*

Mittwoch 10th Dezember 1947
A full moon through a train window

'Why don't you send Wally a postcard? A German postcard – a genuine German postcard. He will be more than pleased, I can assure you of that.' Karl could be very convincing.'

'He was very good to me, nah,' replied Hugo. 'He deserves something better than a card, but for now it will have to do. I'll get one at the station while my mind is on the job in hand. Tomorrow I will have forgotten.'

'How can you forget Wally of all people?'

'No! Not forget him, but I will be almost home and my thoughts are with the family.'

'Ah yes, the famous Oberwinkel. A village with a mad priest, a crazy nun and a worn-out old nag of a horse.'

'Laugh all you want, my friend!'

'You gave me the storyline long ago, comrade. I know your abode as well as you do if not better!'

'Then come along and see for yourself when Christmas is done. We will make you welcome and show you the *real* Bavaria. You'd like that, nah?'

'I am a terrible houseguest, Hugo. I would taunt your brother and enrapture your sisters.'

'Imagination is cheap and requires no audience. You would be a most welcome guest, providing you didn't mind bedding down with Gertrude and Gilda – our oxen.'

'Luxury! We have slept in worse places and don't we know it.'

Brakes hissing, the train was beginning to slow; passengers walking along the corridor braced themselves on hand rails. Hugo wiped the condensation from the window with his sleeve, though there was little to see now the sun had set. The red sky reminded him of Cornwall – POW days stood on the cliff top watching the sun sink into the Atlantic. How could he be nostalgic for a place where he'd been a prisoner? But nostalgia it most certainly was.

Frankfurt-am-Main. Behind schedule this evening by eight minutes. Hitler was no longer running the railways. There were other plans underway – American plans. This was going to be the new capital of Germany. Berlin was ruined, largely Russian and isolated like an island in the middle of a sea of communism. Frankfurt was the obvious choice.

Only, for Hugo and Karl, it wasn't. It was clearly a ruined city, bombed to hell and controlled by American soldiers who demanded to see papers and to roll up their sleeves to bare forearms that would show telltale signs of SS indoctrination.

'We've been through all this many times!' protested Karl in his best English.

'And you'll go through it again! Many times!' barked an Afro-American infantryman who was no more happy to be standing on a bleak Frankfurt platform on a cold, dark evening challenging any amount of incoming passengers alighting from the 17:32 express.

Satisfied, but nonetheless pissed off with his lot, the tall, bulky NCO wasted not a second more and with the palm of his hand slapped their shoulders as if they'd been errant kids caught scrumping by the farmer.

'We didn't get a greeting like that at Lostwithiel, did we?'

'Or St Erth. This is our welcome home, Karl. Better get used to it, nah?'

Picking up their meagre luggage, of Karl's two suitcases and Hugo's canvas rucksack – luggage donated by well-wishers in Cornwall – they made their way past travellers and the wretched dispossessed to the station entrance, where outside its glass roof darkness shrouded their return.'

'My God! Hugo, look at Kaiserstrasse!'

'How can this be Kaiserstrasse?'

Ahead of them, in the murky gloom, rows of varying shapes that at first they could not quite comprehend: a jagged landscape of darkness where shadows melted against the day's weak, winter light. In the air, the sound of steel on stone as if some ancient mason were chipping away at the Earth's core.

'Some of them will work well into the night,' came an unexpected, whispy voice from out of the darkness, causing them both to jump a little. 'They won't stop until they've rebuilt Frankfurt.'

'Who won't?' asked Karl, unsure as to who or what he was addressing.

'The women, of course.'

'What about their men?' asked Hugo.

'Men? What men would they be? There are no men here save for the Americans and they won't help.'

The voice emerged from the shadows of the arched station entrance: a short, emaciated figure, her sunken features immediately causing them to step back in repulsion.

'My beauty offends you?' she demanded.

'No!' snapped Karl, losing his cool.

'Then I am yours – and yours,' she said, pushing a bony finger into each man's chest. 'But I ain't cheap. Don't you think that I am cheap, because I am a fine lady of Frankfurt who has dined at the richest tables – tables you cannot imagine the like of.'

Her mood began to darken with every utterance. 'I was born of nobility I'll have you know. My kin were the most famous in the land until the Nazis came and stripped them bare. They stripped me bare too, but I'm still here. You won't find me breaking rocks with that sow herd down there!'

She pointed into the distance toward the sound of hammering, then paused to gauge their reactions. 'You are fine German men, I can see. You've come for a good time, I can see. I am reasonable in my price, but my body is that of a royal and you should respect that.' She grabbed Hugo's hand to bring him close to her emaciated chest, but he pulled away shocked.

He reached for his pocket. 'I can buy you some bread, not much but it will be enough.'

'Let's get out of here, Hugo!' urged Karl.

Panicking in his retreat, coins spilled from Hugo's trouser pockets, and the woman dived to the pavement to gather what she could like a gull in a fish market swooping down for the guts cast into the gutter.

Running away from the station entrance they left her foraging in the cobbles, fearing that she would pursue them. Karl glanced back over his shoulder.

'My God, Hugo, we ran into Hell itself in 1944 and now we're running from a woman!'

'It's not funny, Karl!'

'Do you see me laughing? Where is Germany? Where's the Germany we knew?'

Blowing steam in the cold air of early evening, there was enough distance now to stop and relax a little.

'Look at our breath, Hugo – steam! I haven't seen steam in my breath since… since… I don't know. Since we were last here in that other lifetime of ours!'

'Cornwall is so warm and the air is always… That's…'

'What is it, Hugo?'

'My rucksack! I must have left it at the station!'

'You idiot! She'll have gone through everything. Was your wallet in it?'

'I'm going back for it.'

They had not run so far, and there was a chance that it would be okay, but if the woman had found it she would demand a high price for its return.

'Better to let her have it, Hugo!' Karl called after him.

As he reached the entrance there it was in the very spot where he'd dropped it, straps still buckled tight, the canvas bulging with Christmas presents bought in Penzance and a carved chess set he'd made with Wally in their spare time.

The plan was: he would snatch it up like a thief before dashing out into the darkness, keeping an eye out for the pitiful woman and other lost wretches who were now gathering under the rare lights of the station entrance.

The rucksack was untouched – mercifully, as he must have left it a sure five minutes ago if not more.

On the ground nearby, a heap of clothes – black rags it seemed. And spilling out onto the cold, dirty concrete from the black rags was black hair. Hugo's assumption that somebody else must have run off and left... but then he knew the smell of death only too well. Rather than run, he knelt down and pulled at the bony shoulder to reveal the sunken, staring face.

Around her lay the coins Hugo had dropped – some *pfenigs* clasped tightly in death.

Then, unexpectedly from behind, a stern man's voice: 'Did you kill her?'

'No! Of course not!' Hugo turned to see a large man standing over him – a porter, judging by his uniform.

'I saw you talking with her only a few minutes ago!' the porter accused him. 'You and another man!'

'I didn't kill her!' Hugo picked up his rucksack and ran into the darkness, narrowly missing a tram and some cars in his haste to get away from the scene. Karl was waiting for him.

He could hear the man shouting after him and maybe the word *"Polizei"*.

'Run! Run, Karl! The woman is dead; they think I killed her!'

'That's all we need! Come on, we'll keep to the dark streets.'

They doubled their pace, but keeping speed was difficult with two laden suitcases and a rucksack. Hugo suggested they dump the cases and return for them when things died down a bit. They could already hear a distant siren approaching – the exact type of two-tone siren they'd last heard being used by the Gestapo. Then, it was never a consideration, now it was a siren heading straight for them. The headlights of a car picked them up in the blackness and they knew they'd been spotted – hopefully not a police car.

'Stay calm, Hugo, it's just a car. Let him go by. We're not doing anything wrong.'

They slowed to a walking pace; Hugo slipped his hands into his pockets – no hurry here. 'If it stops, we tell the truth, Karl. I'm telling the truth. If we start to lie, they'll find us out.'

'I can't lie – I wasn't there. I didn't find her. You did.'

'Why's he slowing down? It has to be the police!'

'Let's take this side road, Hugo. Now!'

Into the black street they ran at full pelt, kicking up their heels. Every loud step reverberated off shattered walls; shouts ricocheted. They could hear the car stop so there was a hope that its occupants had not seen them clearly enough and were not inclined to follow on foot. Their only way out of this predicament was to stay in the dark areas and get out of the city by morning. No buses, no trains, stay calm and use their military training to avoid capture. Travel under darkness, put some distance behind them and avoid contact with anybody.

The street was a dead end. There was no way out other than to retrace their footsteps. They'd lost their pursuers, whoever they were, and the siren had gone on elsewhere to some other incident, so best to turn left back onto the road they'd been travelling. It had to go somewhere and particularly away from the station.

'We're okay, Hugo. We'll just walk.'

'I'm starving! All I wanted was a bed for the night and a meal.'

Suddenly, they were illuminated from behind. They hadn't spotted the car that had stopped short of the lane and waited for their return. The engine started; it was difficult to ignore its presence, but that was Karl's advice, and in the absence of a better idea it seemed sensible until some other escape route appeared. The car began to move, quietly matching their pedestrian pace, creeping behind them like a tiger about to pounce on its prey.

'We're done for!' exclaimed Hugo, turning defiantly to face into the headlights. Surrendering, he raised both hands; the game was up, he'd come clean.

In response, the car – an American Chevy – pulled up alongside him, the driver winding down his window.

'Better jump in,' urged the German voice behind the wheel.

Was this an arrest?

'Where can I take you and your friend?'

'You're a taxi?'

'Of course! Did you think I was the *polizei?*'

'Yes – we did!' said Karl, bouncing into the vacuous American back seat, mightily relieved.

'Why would I be *polizei?* Have you done something wrong?'

'No, but we have a guilty conscience,' said Hugo.
'About something that happened back at the station.'
'Where do you want to go?'
'A hotel. Somewhere affordable and away from the station.'
'I know just the place. What happened at the station, my friends?'
'This woman was dead on the floor when Hugo went back, and somebody thought he'd killed her.'
'Is that all? She was a prostitute?'
'She was offering her services.'
'People are dying here all the time. It's a good place for an undertaker. The Americans keep people hungry; it's a crime, but who's going to do anything about it? The station is full of corpses and they bring in more desperate bastards by the planeload every day. Fly them in, bus them out to the tracks and let them find their own way. Turks, Sudeten Germans, Czechs, Poles… Germany's a graveyard. So what are you doing here in Hell?'
'We were POWs. We've come home for Christmas and to find work.'
'What was your unit?'
'Luftwaffe – in support of the 3rd Parachute Regiment.'
'I was Kriegsmarine. We're the lucky ones, eh? The Royal Navy sank my ship and sent me to Canada. What about you?'
'They sent us to England – Cornwall.'
'Where's that?'
'Near Canada.'
'What say we eat together, my friends? I know a good place, the food is okay, nothing special.'
"The Chicago Café" illuminated in neon, its shop window covered in condensation, its inside lit with warm, yellow light; outside, steam venting like some ship waiting to embark on a voyage, the little building was a bountiful oasis in a sea of

wrecks, quite ethereal but so very welcome. The car glided to a halt. The driver swung out of his capacious seat, and cool as could be tipped back his American peaked cabbie's cap, adjusted the hem of his leather flying jacket, opened the back door for his passengers and bade them welcome to his pride and joy.

They emerged from the cab cautiously, glanced over their shoulders, fearing a trap of some sort.

'Did you smell Frankfurt when you arrived?' he asked.

'Yes, we smelt it.'

'All the bodies are in the rubble. They get pulled out each day along with the rats that grow fat on them. The Amis brought in cats and dogs to get the rats, but people were so hungry they ate the rats *and* the cats *and* the dogs.'

'Amis?'

'Amis – Ommies. Americans. They don't like me much because I'm a Canadian.'

'How are you a Canadian?'

'I stopped being German when my ship sank. I stopped being a German when they opened the gates to Bergen-Belsen, Auschwitz, Treblinka. That's why *they're* starving people – because of the camps.' His outstretched arm gestured that paradise awaited them inside.

'What will you have, my friends?'

Through the plate-glass door it was obvious there was everything to have – everything American: an American counter lined by American barstools; smoky grey walls from which hung American artwork – black and white pictures of glamorous Hollywood stars, even a grinning President Truman alongside colour adverts for Coca-Cola and Chrysler automobiles.

Behind the counter a statuesque blonde woman of around thirty-five years stood ready and grinning, her large breasts full of American welcome, and *so similar to the baker's wife*, thought Hugo. All around her work area sizzled meats grilling by the ounce, pounds of raw mince straight out of the fridge, eggs on a griddle, sliced giant tomatoes, onions, pineapple; hissing, steaming water for any amount of coffee. This was manna from heaven for two weary ex-prisoners on the run from the law.

'All fresh today!' she enthused in American English. 'Flown in direct from the United States. What'll it be, gentlemen?'

'I'll have everything!' exclaimed Hugo in his native tongue.

'Bring them two Milwaukee Specials with coffee and the works, honey.'

'Sure thing, Ted. Same for you?'

'Sure.'

He bid them to sit down on a bench seat similar to those in the Chevy cab and of a kind that Hitler would not have approved of because it was so comfortable you could conceive children on it. Thick foam covered in red plastic, its back reached up to their heads and proved beyond doubt that a new world of luxury had just dawned.

'Nice place!' exclaimed Karl, mightily relieved to be feeling safe.

'You like it? It's mine – *ours*, in fact.' He pointed across to the now busy blonde preparing their meals. 'Kathy – she's my woman. She's from Albuquerque. Her old man's a colonel. Rich man, long story. We met in Canada and she came home with me. Wonderful woman – wonderful! We set up here earlier this year – spring; yeah, wonderful woman!'

'You're from Frankfurt?'

'Was. The old Frankfurt, not this hellhole. We're going to rebuild this place, Kathy and me. Going to be something to see when it's finished – Germany's new capital. Berlin is history, my friends, history.'

Kathy called out from across the counter: 'How do you like your steaks, boys?' Hugo and Karl looked at one another perplexed. Hugo was still struggling with English.

'She means, well cooked and tender, or maybe you prefer tough and chewy with a little blood easing out. Some people like that.'

'Whatever comes, it's good.'

'Make it tender, babe!'

'Who supplies your food?' asked Karl.

'United States Army Air Force. They fly it in direct every day. I tell you, this is the place to be if you're of an entrepreneurial spirit. The Americans have plans for this place. This is the new Germany – right here.'

'What about the people who are hungry? Don't they come in here?'

'They can't afford it. Maybe in time when the economy picks up, but that's a way off yet.'

'Then, who are your customers?'

'You'll see.' Ted slipped a cigar out of its tube, put it to his smiling lips and seemed to wink as if giving a signal. Within seconds Kathy was at his side, lighting the cigar with a solid silver lighter that had smoker Karl desiring the object even more than he desired *her* at that moment.

'You smoke? Here, buddy, have a cigar.' Taking another tube from his breast pocket, he proffered a cigar to Karl. 'Kathy, do this boy a favour and light that up, would you, honey?'

Non-smoker Hugo turned away to stare out of the dripping window at the parked up Chevy, still worrying that the authorities were hot on his heels for murder. Karl would be okay; he'd see to it that he wasn't incriminated.

'You boys got some accommodation for the night?' asked Ted.

'Not really.'

'You took a chance, huh? That's no problem, we've got a room upstairs – cheaper than any hotel still standing – if you don't mind sharing, that is.'

'We don't mind.'

Just as the steaks were being served by an ever-smiling Kathy, a morose figure suddenly appeared at the door slapping the glass with the palm of his only remaining skinny hand. Hugo, who'd been staring fixedly into the darkness, visibly jumped with fright. Ted, furious, leapt to his feet and charged across the room at the would-be intruder, pulled open the door and in English shouted: 'Get out of here, will yer?!' before pushing the one-armed man away. 'You can't afford this place. I've told you before. NOW, SCRAM!'

Composing himself, he returned to his seat, smiling broadly because he'd repelled the invader.

'Problem?' asked Karl.

'Nah, every night or so we get some joker trying it on. They think we're Switzerland. They think we're some kind of charity. We're not, we're a business same as any other. Can't afford to give stuff away or we'd be bankrupt if we did – yes sir.'

Ted drew hard on his cigar before turning his head to blow the smoke away from the food. 'These people are the last remnants of a city that's about to change forever. The old city's dead – gone forever. The new city – of which *we* are the vanguard – will have no place for people like that – beggars. Yeah, it's sad. Yeah, I cried tears along with the rest of them, but tears won't rebuild this place. The Amis know how to do it – no sentiment, work hard, ambition, make something of yourself. That's how you survive. Yes sir, it's sad alright, but sadness never got nothing done. Am I right?'

'I'm sure you're right,' said Karl, chewing his steak and sensibly taking the path of diplomacy. They were too hungry to argue themselves out of a meal.

Hugo looked out again, this time to see a Jeep pulling up alongside the Chevy. Hell! Now what to do? Run through a back door and bring the US Army down on them for the second time in five years? This time would be the last time. Alternatively, stand and surrender, or better still sit quiet. Let *them* make the first move. Then run!

Hugo watched the men alight, exchanging banter, casually approach the door to the café. Okay, perhaps this wasn't official. Through the door strode five of the largest GIs that either he or Karl had ever encountered. He was about to choke on the best meal he'd ever tasted. *Why now?* he thought. Such was the way of things in the past few years. He would stand up and make a clean confession. Karl was in the clear and they'd have to understand that.

'Hey, Ted!' The largest of the men feigned a limp finger salute in the direction of the owner – the kind of salute learned from the movies, not the parade ground.

'Hey, boys! How yer doin'?'

'Good, good. How you doin', Kath?'

'Good! You boys want your usual?'

'Sure thing.'

Settling themselves down in an adjacent booth, they flung their olive-green caps on the tabletop, revealing severe crew cuts and – for Hugo and Karl – an air of menace. The newly arrived civilians were strangers in the café that night and they weren't listed on the menu. The broad-shouldered NCO showed a particular interest in Hugo, who remained staring fixedly out of the window while surreptitiously watching their reflections.

'You like Jeeps, boy?' But Hugo didn't respond.

'My friend is not an English speaker, sergeant,' Ted replied.

'Is that a fact?'

'I speak better English,' said Karl, speaking out of turn and instantly regretting it.

'I wasn't about to speak to you, son. It's your friend I want to speak to.'

Suddenly, Hugo turned to face his inquisitor. 'I speak English okay.'

He was about to get up to surrender to the inevitable, but Ted put his hand out to stop him. 'What is this, sergeant? The boys are just trying to have a meal. They're our guests – we're friends.'

'I don't mean nothing by it, Ted,' said the sergeant, raising his hands and grinning a Cheshire cat smile. 'I simply wanted to show the guy my Jeep if he was interested. That's the little vehicle that won the war, you know. You Germans could learn something from it.'

This remark set off a chain reaction of hysterics, the stock comedy of a bully.

'You were in the war?' asked Karl as soon as the cacophony had died.

'No, but we're here now, son.'

'We were in the war,' piped up Karl.

'Karl, please!' urged Hugo.

The Cold War was within fierce glances of kicking off that very moment and would have done had it not been for the intervention of Kathy with dextrous hands full of white china cups, saucers and – incredibly – an aluminium coffee pot all finely balanced. 'Now, boys, let's have no squabbling, if you please. Consider this Canadian territory and I don't want no diplomatic incident. Besides, if you look out of the window, you'll see the MPs have pulled up and they're looking for an easy time of it tonight. Coffee's on the house.'

Kathy was never one to exaggerate her abilities or just what she could see with her own two eyes. Three Jeeps loaded with MPs *had* pulled up, a sight that unnerved Hugo even more, but there was nothing he could do except nudge Karl.

'We'll settle with you and be on our way.' Karl fumbled in his wallet, but Ted was having none of it, especially when he saw the colour of money being offered.

'Enjoy your food and coffee. There's no problem here. The sergeant is always checking strangers out whenever he comes in here. Thinks he's a big shot who has the ear of the President himself. You'll stay with us tonight. We'll talk about the old days and you can tell me how you think you're going to pay for things with Reichsmarks.'

'What's wrong with Reichsmarks?'

'Nothing except it's no longer legal currency. We use Deutschmarks, my friend – Deutschmarks, dollar bills and American cigarettes. This is a different country to the one you and I fought for.' Ted coughed and blamed it immediately on the poor quality of the cigar. 'If only I could get decent Cuban… Never mind. Enjoy your meal, boys!'

Upstairs in the apartment, the schnapps flowed freely even if the card game wasn't quite up to the standard Ted had hoped for.

'Safer up here, my friends. Never get into a fight with the US Army – you won't win.'

'I think we might know more about that than you realise,' said Karl, sucking happily on his third cigar. 'Where did you learn to play cards?'

'In the Kriegsmarine and then in the camps – bridge, poker, jacks; it filled our time. I dreamt of a place like this back then, and my ambition doesn't stop here. There are hotels to be built in this city. A man like me could start an empire. It's a time for new beginnings, and not many generations get that opportunity.'

Discreetly, Karl looked around him at the mess that was Ted and Kathy's humble abode. Messy, dirty even: old newspapers covered the floor in place of carpet; smoke-stained paint on the doorframes and ceilings; strategically placed tin buckets ready to catch leaks; a blood-stained mouse trap; a single brass tap that wouldn't stop dripping into a large white enamel sink full of unwashed pots; frayed lace curtains that hadn't seen a washtub since before the war. The idea of a hotel empire appeared a long way off.

The apartment was in complete contrast to the uber-clean establishment downstairs from where the smell of ever more steaks, burgers, frankfurters and coffee wafted up on invisible clouds of temptation.

'If you are still hungry there is more food downstairs that can be brought up. Don't hold back, my friends. We know what it's like to be hungry.'

'Hugo is always hungry.'

'That's why I joined the Kriegsmarine – so that I would never be hungry. Sailors always eat unless they're on a lifeboat, and I didn't think that would be my fate, but eventually it was. Shot out of the water by the Royal Navy and dropped off in Canada. How lucky were we?'

No one answered that. For a while there was a silence between them – an awkward silence: thoughts of those who could have been with them that night enjoying the food, the schnapps, the smoke. The war had been a very personal place and no man wanted to think his story of conflict and survival was worth less, or greater, than that of a comrade-in-arms. Ted would not elaborate for fear that his new friends could trump him easily with tales of hardship and torture; and likewise, Karl and Hugo kept their shared experiences to themselves.

'My brother and my cousin were not so lucky. It was very bad in 1945. They survived the war, but not the peace.'

'What do you mean?' asked Hugo.

'I'll answer your question with a question – when were you captured?'

'October 1944.'

'And when did you arrive in England?'

'December '44. Exactly three years ago this week.'

Ted exhaled like a man taking his dying breath, and for the second time that evening his cheery demeanour changed. Earlier Karl and Hugo had noticed how quickly he'd flown into a rage when the starving beggar tried to enter the café, and now again his face had taken on a very grim expression.

'How did they treat you as prisoners?' he asked.

'It was difficult at first, waiting to be shipped to England. We all had dysentery—'

'That was a common ailment. Did you have shelter?'

'Tents.'

'Tents? You were lucky. Albert and Joachim had nothing – no shelter, no food, an enclosure built for hundreds of men that eventually accommodated thousands. They dug holes with their bare hands for what little shelter they could make for themselves. The Americans killed them through neglect.'

'The Americans?'

'Oh, don't get me wrong! No, it wasn't only the Americans – the French, the British, they all wanted to get rid of the Germans. You were prisoners before the death camps were opened – all those Jews, gypsies, Slavs. So they did the same to us, only slower. No one wanted to be held accountable by pulling a trigger or dropping a gas cylinder. So, they kill through neglect. The effect is the same.'

Ted stood up from the table wiping his eyes, before fumbling in his trouser pockets for cigarillos; fumbling desperately to smile again; fumbling to be the amiable cab driver who now had it all, the entrepreneur in the making. Entrepreneurs don't break down.

'If you'd been captured in 1945 you wouldn't be sitting here now with me, sipping schnapps and licking the tomato ketchup off your lips. You think it was just the Russians? The Russians *still* have our POWs. The Allies killed those captured in the West – no, not with bullets or gas, but with exposure to the elements, disease through lack of sanitary provision, and minimal food.'

'We have heard nothing of this!' Karl was particularly concerned as he too had relatives in the wider family unaccounted for, but he also remembered the fears he'd had on that sick-making sea crossing to England, about how this time the English might not be so hospitable.

Ted rounded on him, stabbing an unlit cigarillo into smoke-filled nothingness in an effort to drive the point home.

'Why would you hear anything? Would the British press come up with stories of Allied atrocities? Of course not! But that doesn't mean it didn't happen – it did. And it happened to the civilian population, too. Now you see only a few of these wretches haunting the dark places, scratching a living among the dirt and rubble. Most are dead.

'When we came here from Canada just over a year ago, Frankfurt was a very different place. You know, when the Amis dumped their food they put it into trucks for driving to a garbage dump, but women threw themselves onto those trucks to grab whatever they could grasp. And the Amis laughed at them and drove through them! But it's true – I saw it.

'My woman – Kathy – she saw it. The people I knew, the people that I had known, if they didn't die in the bombing they died in the starvation that followed, and the Amis stepped over their bodies. Eisenhower hates Germans! De Gaul hates Germans! Roosevelt is gone. Churchill is gone. They want to eradicate Germany forever and that process is still underway. You will see it for yourselves.'

'But how do you know about the POWs?'

'I'm a cab driver. My fares are Amis – Amis of all ranks.

They talk freely in my cab about all sorts of subjects you could never dream of, but it was the talk of a Red Cross man that interested me the most. He had just landed in Frankfurt, from exactly where I don't know. He was Swedish and he was in the company of a high-ranking Amie – a general or somebody really high up, I couldn't be sure. And he was asking the general about the POW camps in France and in the American sector, talking about how none of the POWs had survived in 1946. They were all dead. And the general was saying that that was no concern of his as he had "other fish to fry" as he put it.'

'Why would they say this in front of you?'

'They were not in front of me! I'm the nut behind the wheel; they only see the back of my head; they don't know whether I'm German, Canadian, Swiss or Amie. To them, I probably don't even speak English, so they talk freely.'

'Maybe you misheard?'

'I don't mishear with my own eyes, my friend. This city is littered with corpses that starved to death – buried under all that rubble out there. And where are the men of my generation that I knew? This was a big city. They didn't all go to the Russian front. And I saw with my own eyes the women leaping onto those garbage food trucks, pleading for them to stop so that they could have something for their children at least. Don't you think the Amis could feed all these people? Of course they could. But they didn't.'

'I can believe it,' said Karl. 'I'd expected them to treat us worse this time. Two world wars! But the British have been good to us.'

'The British and Canadians have behaved in a better way. The British, however, do what the Americans tell them now. They're in debt. That's why I'm a Canadian. Do you know that the people who survive here are the ones who pretend they aren't German? Don't be German whatever you do – they'll kill you. Even now, look over your shoulders! Be Dutch if they ask, Swiss, Czech, be whatever you like, but don't admit to being German; and even if you do admit to it, don't be proud, be humble.'

'I thought the Geneva Convention protected everyone?'

'Eisenhower doesn't give a fig about the damn Geneva Convention! Germany doesn't exist anymore – we are a "non-country". That is why the Geneva Convention doesn't apply because "we" don't exist. Here, we are in America. Over there, in the north, you're in Britain. And over there, in the west, you're in France; but there is no more Germany. What you see out there is the skeletal remains of Germany.

'Soon, people won't even speak German. That is how much they fear us. Eisenhower and Truman are the ones writing the history books as we speak. There'll be no mention of the disease and the starvation. I heard that a million POWs have died in captivity in Allied hands – a million! That includes the boys and old men, but that doesn't include all the civilians. Perhaps several million if you include the civilians – including those poor wretches lying in the rubble out there! To the Amis, we're just Nazis, while the real Nazis are taken to America where they work on missiles and atomic bombs ready for the next war.

'When you leave here tomorrow morning and you go out into the wider Germany, speak to those who, like me, know the truth of it. Speak to those who are homeless, without work, without income. Speak to the priests – they know. Some have spoken out; I've heard that myself many times. Some Amis speak out too, but they are silenced – told to shut up by their superiors. Other Amis say, "Who cares about you Krauts! You did this to others, now it's your turn!" They're right, I understand their anger, but the last thing Europe needs is more Nazis only this time dressed in American uniforms.

'The war may have finished for you in England, in America

and Canada, but here it continues. The shelling and shooting may have stopped, but the bloodletting goes on and on without end. You may be free, my friends, and I may be free, but our comrades are to this day locked up behind the wire and dying still.'

Having slept in his clothes fully prepared for a quick getaway should the café be raided, Hugo wiped the condensation from the upper storey window with his sleeve and stared out at the ruined remains of what had been a vibrant, living city.

There was no sunrise. Grey merely replaced the blackness that had replaced the previous day's grey. Overnight, Berger Strasse had been littered with a light covering of wet snow that by morning was already melting into blocked gutters and broken downpipes. Directly below, a scruffy child of indeterminate gender held out a saucepan to catch the flow of dripping water.

Hugo's nightmare, which was still vivid at that moment, was becoming ever more frequent. In it, he is haunted by the deranged woman in the burning village singing her mournful song, only last night she was joined by the spectre at the station – the two having become one. In the nightmare, she spies him lying in the dirt. He crouches deeper and deeper into the grass, but she comes closer until she is standing over him. In her skeletal hands is a shovel; grinning, she proceeds to heap soil on him, burying him alive. Paralysed, he can do nothing; he chokes and, in an effort to wake, calls out for Karl as the soil impedes his windpipe, but Karl can't hear him.

Eager now to get the remainder of their journey underway, he looks back at Karl sleeping soundly – snoring like he always did. It's a true comfort to see him.

Outside, he is mightily relieved to see that there are no Jeeps waiting to take him away. The café is not surrounded by MPs ready to break the door in, no shouts fill the air, just a steady rumble of assorted traffic on cobbled streets; and it just may be that they can depart quietly and without fuss into a city that at least appears to have some normality as the inhabitants begin the business of another day.

Of all the people who have died and continue to die, why should he blame himself for a murder he didn't commit? It probably wasn't even murder; just one more slow death like another leaf fallen from a dying tree. Maybe someone else killed her in those minutes when they left the station. Maybe she just died of starvation, heartbreak, or even the effects of that final rejection, and there was nothing anyone could have done. She was a casualty whose passing no one would record, for no one cared, and in that respect there was just one more thing for him to do. He would leave flowers as a tribute – that's if he could find some.

*

Freitag 28th Juni 1963, 3.03 pm
Oberwinkel

Stealing glances at Hanne. He wanted to be proud, he wanted to open up to her, but the barrier was still in place – the barrier he'd been building, the barrier with deep foundations. Nothing on earth could shift it. There wasn't a bulldozer or any sort of tracked vehicle big enough to break it down.

Tears welled for a moment. He looked away, certain that Hanne hadn't noticed anything. The idea that one day in the far distant future this child might die on the streets of wanton neglect horrified him. Surely hell was safely under lock and key. There was a certainty that he preferred to consider: that one day, way, way into the future, he would tell Hanne about his "wanted man" status, and that somewhere in a Frankfurt police archive was his description in a folder; but that could wait. A family reunion would be a happier occasion without a ten-year-old girl from Cornwall telling everyone in confidence, and in English, how her father was really a fugitive from both American and German authorities – wanted for questioning in respect of an unexplained death.

It also occurred to Hugo that without chess Hanne might never have been born.

*

Saturday 15th July 1950, 1.51 pm
Cornwall

Wally's invitation to play chess in the village hall had introduced Hugo to Rene.

'You are, what we would call in this country, a natural chess player,' remarked Wally of his good friend's ability. Despite the compliment Hugo barely glanced up, although this was probably more to do with his lack of understanding the language than any determination to concentrate on the game in hand.

An inter-village match had brought a group of supporters and other interested parties together in the great hall of Aubyn House for want of something better to do that afternoon. Among them a couple of former Land Army girls now in service at the big house insolently leaning against a wall, inadvertently leaving grubby palm prints on 200-year-old plaster as they propped themselves up while telling jokes and other whispered tittle-tattle.

The older, rounder, stout village women, there to support

their menfolk whilst making tea, whispered their own suspicions that these "girls" were simply in attendance for a bit of a laugh and to ogle the tall, handsome former POW who was proving to be a wizard at chess.

They were not entirely wrong in their suppositions.

London-born Rene – herself so noticeable by her amazing height of 6 feet tall and not an inch less – *would make an ideal friend for Hugo*, thought Wally.

'I see you have an admirer,' he remarked, spotting the appreciative glances of the taller of the two girls, her attention clearly focussed on Hugo. She wasn't a stranger to Wally as he had been the first person she'd met on arrival in Cornwall in the summer of 1942.

She was billeted – as she had been since 1942 – in the converted stables of Aubyn House. Her employers – the Valdean family – re-employed her, after the Women's Land Army was disbanded, to be a nanny to the family's three small children; a post that brought some perks as the East End of London, like Frankfurt, was in a mess, so there was no going home.

Hugo raised his eyes from the board to see Wally gaze across the room at the two girls and acknowledge them with a smile, a discreet wave, whilst silently mouthing, 'How are you? Long time no see.'

Fearing it might be some sort of ruse in order to distract him for an illegal move on the board, Hugo was mightily suspicious, but then another glance. It was true: Rene caught his attention, smiling right into his eyes as if admiring his every move. Shyly, all too briefly, he reciprocated – a rare smile for the former POW.

Quickly resuming his attention on the game in hand, he could now spot the move that would put Wally in check and soon thereafter into checkmate.

'I'll have to watch you,' warned Wally. 'Soon you'll be

playing at county level.'

It was also Wally's idea that Hugo settle into British life by participating in a good British pastime, such as playing the football pools. Hitler and his "disreputable staff", as Wally called them, would never have thought to institute such a wonderful socialist opportunity as Britain's own football pools, and this surely was their overall downfall, in his opinion.

Playing the pools was, according to Wally, a great opportunity for a working man of meagre means to better himself without having to rob a bank and all the consequences that that might entail. And Hugo, being a keen football fan, was only too keen to better himself with what appeared to be a sure-fire gamble. It was also a good way to learn English, and Wally was his primary English teacher in return for learning some basic German. That was the trade-off because Wally had an ambition to visit Berlin one day to see for himself just what had happened.

Hugo's lack of progress in learning English was probably down to the fact that he now shared a farm cottage with old friends Karl and Thomaz, and together after work the talk was German. The few words of English he'd started to learn were now rarely uttered, but even in his native tongue there weren't enough words in the national vocabulary to express his delight on opening a very official looking brown envelope addressed to him alone and marked "Strictly Private" and "If undelivered Return to Sender".

'I don't believe it!' he exclaimed on tearing open the envelope and taking out a cheque made out in his name.

'What is it, Hugo?' asked Karl.

'I've won seven shillings and six pence on the football pools!'

'You bugger! I didn't win anything,' cursed Thomaz who,

along with Karl, had also entered into the draw.

'Luck is for the brave!' Holding the prize-winning slip above his head like a cup-winning football player, Hugo was triumphant. Not only was he winning chess matches, but now he was winning cash prizes, too.

'I put down my four home wins as Wally suggested – my favourite four. All four teams won their matches. This is a postal order from Littlewoods.'

'That's more than enough to buy Karl and me a good meal and a lot of drink,' said Thomaz. 'Don't forget your friends, Hugo. We wouldn't have forgotten you had the fortunes been in our favour.'

It was the word "friends" that sparked an idea in Hugo's head, especially as he now had some money to play with.

'I have another idea! I am going to take Rene to the pictures.'

'The tall girl who works at the big house? They say she has poor eyesight!' joked Karl.

'Laugh all you like, but this is my opportunity.'

'It just might be if you could speak the language,' Thomaz reminded him.

'She'll understand when she sees the colour of my money!'

But Karl was not convinced that Hugo would be ready to walk out with an English girl. 'Better still we teach you some basics. You're going to ask her to come with you to the cinema – yes?'

'Yes.'

'In Penzance?'

'In Penzance,' Hugo confirmed.

'So, say it in English – say it to me. I'll be Rene.'

Hugo concentrated, trying to recall and then arrange in their English grammatical order the words he needed. He began: 'Would… like…'

'That's good,' said Karl, encouraging every faltering step.

'Would… like… you come to…'

'No, Hugo. The grammar in English is very different. You should say: "Would you like to go to the fucking cinema?"'

'Okay,' said Hugo; 'Would you…'

'like…' prompted Karl.

'like…' repeated Hugo.

'to go…'

'to go…'

'to the…'

'to the…'

'fucking cinema.'

'fucking cinema.'

*

For Rene, the invitation to the cinema gave her an opportunity to get to know this equally tall, shy young man who had intrigued her for months. The first time she ever saw Hugo he was waiting for a bus in the Market Square to take him to Penzance. Despite being dressed in civilian clothes, he was clearly not local, nor was he – she thought – particularly German.

He was very dark in hair colour and skin tone, and she assumed he must surely be a Pole or Czech. Germans were very blond and blue-eyed, weren't they? And, if he was German, why was he still here after the war?

She didn't see him again for some months, although his image remained clear in her thoughts. He intrigued her; she'd never seen anyone quite like him and that was unusual considering that as a city girl she was used to seeing hundreds and thousands of people and never gave one of them a second look – until now.

Perhaps it was because there were so few people in this far southwestern corner of the world. Unlike the East End, there weren't crowds of people to pass on a daily basis, just five or ten at most, and these were the people she lived with and worked alongside.

If she ventured into a town like Penzance or Helston there were people, but it was all so much more intimate. Everybody seemed to know everybody else. In the big house there were just the staff and the family going about their business, so everything seemed magnified somehow. Strangers seemed to have a very different sort of presence, she thought. Would she have looked twice if the tall foreigner had been waiting for a bus in Charing Cross? Of course not! London in wartime was full of foreigners.

The very idea of working in the countryside, too, had been so alien to her; a strange but wonderful place that she had only ever seen represented in books and paintings. Cornwall had been completely off the map in her imagination and she'd had no idea where it was or how to get there. She knew of a distant aunt in Dorset, but that county, too, was far off and unreachable for a naïve, inexperienced East End girl.

She might never have ventured far beyond the East End had it not been for the direct hit on the engineering factory where she worked.

*

Just one more (important) little aside…

Rene's story:

Wednesday April 8th 1942
Walthamstow

Aged nineteen, Rene had narrowly escaped death when a 500 lb bomb crashed through the skylight of the factory she was working in, blasting machinery and an entire shift of operatives into the four block walls and bringing down the ceiling to bury any survivors from the initial blast.

Rene, by sheer good fortune, had taken two minutes out of her shift to visit the toilets situated in an annexe adjacent to the main shop floor. The blast burst her eardrums and in a cold panic she called out, unable to hear her own voice, until such time as she realised she was alone.

Pushing her way through tangled metal and climbing over rubble, smoke and dust filled the air while a broken electric cable sparked and spat at her like a venomous snake.

Suddenly, she felt someone grab her shoulder from behind, forcibly pulling her back onto her heels and away from the carnage; it was the gateman, Reg Ormear, his black uniform now grey with dust, his anguished face barking some unfathomable order in an effort to make her understand.

Safely placed on the grass she tried to focus as Reg bravely returned to what was left of the building. As her unsteady vision cleared moment by moment, she could vaguely make out a man's head facing her, his eyes staring fixedly at her, appealing for assistance.

She tried to stand, but her lanky legs would have none of it; so she crawled to reach him; tugged at an iron bar that seemed to be trapping him. It came free easily as if she'd found an inner strength she never realised she possessed. Pushing her fingers deep into the rubble, chucking brick after brick over her shoulder, she dug for all she was worth.

Suddenly, loose masonry cascaded, tipping her backwards. She screamed for fear of being buried alive. Mercifully, the avalanche stopped as quickly as it had begun. Momentarily pinned down, not daring to look then slowly opening her eyes, there in her lap was the man's severed head.

Doctor Mervyn Pritchard was a pipe-smoking, war-weary Welsh Presbyterian in late middle age, who frequently coughed and openly criticised the Catholic Church in the presence of all his patients; and those who were not easily offended paid no heed as he had a good reputation and otherwise excellent bedside manner.

The Whiteshaws were not Catholic and so took no notice of his customary enquiry whenever the front door was opened to him: 'You're not Catholic, are you?' No, came the reply. 'Good! Then show me the patient if you'd be so kind.'

As the days had passed since the bombing, though safe at home in the suburbs, Rene's shaking body had refused to settle. 'She can't stop shaking, doctor!' Agnes Whiteshaw was beside herself. 'She's been shaking all week long. What are we to do?'

Taking Rene's hand, Pritchard held it gently for some moments, examining each eye in turn. She returned his kindly glance and tried to smile but her trembling lips couldn't maintain the expression, so she looked away at the bay window, sunshine beaming in through dirty cross-taped panes that caused a lattice shadow effect on the bedroom wall. It wasn't just her hands that were shaking it was her whole body from head to foot, and consequently the metal-frame bed on which she lay shook too; so much in fact, that it would travel across the floor. It was the first thing Pritchard heard upon entering the house, thinking that it sounded like some frenetic passion in full flow upstairs.

'You worked in the polymers factory, didn't you, Rene?' She turned to acknowledge his question but couldn't answer him.

'She was a lucky girl, doctor. All her shift killed – everyone on that floor – every single one. She were in the toilet and that's what saved her. It were a direct hit. A young girl of Rene's age shouldn't be seeing things like that, now should she?!'

'They produced engine mountings and bushes, I seem to remember? Definitely a target for Herr Goering and his mad Austrian puppetmaster. Catholics, you see. Can't trust the buggers. How old are you, Rene?'

'She's nineteen, doctor – just turned nineteen – haven't you, luv?'

Fiddling with the strap of his tin hat, the doctor mumbled to no one in particular as if thinking aloud, until such time as he'd released the strap that attached it to his gasmask case. Momentarily checking to see that her attention was elsewhere, he tossed it onto the linoleum floor where it crashed with a dull thud. Not much of a noise to anyone except Rene, she leapt off the bed, violently pushing Pritchard and her mother aside before diving under the mattress springs from where she whimpered like a small child terrified by a nightmare.

'It's shell shock,' said Pritchard, picking up the helmet and strapping it back onto the bag but all the time watching his patient cowering under the bed.

'Shell shock? But she's a civilian. Now, civilians don't get shell shock, do they, doctor?'

'They do when there's a war on, Mrs Whiteshaw. And in this war the Germans are bringing it right to our doorsteps. I saw plenty of cases in the last war as a young subaltern in the medical corps.' He wagged his finger to bring home his point. 'In the trenches, mind, not on the home front! I've seen worse – much worse. Very debilitating, but this is quite mild, you see.'

'Is there anything you can do?' asked Agnes, wringing her hands.

'Ideally, I'd like to get her into a hospital that deals with this, but quite frankly there's nothing for civilians. She'd recover quicker in the peace and quiet of the countryside. Have you got a relative or friend in the country that might be able to take her in?'

'An ageing aunt, but she couldn't cope with this! Besides, it's a ramshackle cottage and in her present state Rene would shake it to its foundations.'

'I'll be alright, doctor.' Rene, her voice trembling, spoke for the first time in the doctor's presence.

'Could you not give her a sedative to calm her, doctor?'

'I don't want to sleep – the nightmares are horrible!' With immense effort Rene crawled out from under the bed and valiantly tried to get to her feet, but the severe shaking made it impossible without assistance. Spontaneously, mother and doctor went to her aid, lifting her back onto the metal bedframe, which started to rattle again.

'The shaking will subside in time. I'd like you to find peace and quiet, young lady, but in London you're going to find that difficult.'

Perusing the bedroom décor from his perch on the side of the bed, Pritchard removed his spectacles and polished them with a corner of the bedsheet, the procedure giving him a moment to think. On the wall he spotted a picture – a framed print of a daffodil field in full bloom, its once rich colours faded by two decades of bleaching sunlight.

'I have a nice painting of daffodils like that one in my surgery. National flower for us Welsh, isn't it? Maybe you've seen it? One of my patients is a local artist who used to live in Cornwall and was a member of the Newlyn School. Have you ever heard of the Newlyn School?' Rene shook her head.

'No, well that doesn't matter, but he was a veteran of the First War like myself, and he had shell shock, and the doctor who originally treated him in Civvy Street sent him off to the West Country where the effect was most positive.

'In Cornwall he learned to paint and that's where his involvement with the Newlyn crowd led him to becoming a very successful artist. Like you, he shook, and the condition went on for the best part of a year before he eventually stopped shaking, but I think we can do better than that if we get you away from here soon – that's if your mother is happy to release you?'

Replacing his spectacles, he glanced up at Agnes, who smiled and nodded approvingly.

'Very well. Now, my old neighbour, Mr Bevin, the Minister of Labour, has been recruiting young women to help with the war effort…'

'I don't want to go back to a factory!' protested Rene.

'And nor shall you! This is not factory work; you'd be working on the land – in farms and woods. It would be hard work and I can't promise you a posting in Cornwall, but there's always Wales. The Gower Peninsula is beautiful! Very beautiful and quiet – yes indeed.'

'I'd love it!' Almost instantly and for a brief moment the trembling voice and shaking limbs seemed to subside as Rene beamed, but Pritchard warned her not to be too optimistic; there were no instantaneous cures for shell shock.

'I'll write a note for the authorities, explaining your condition and how I think life in the country might be the ticket for your recovery. Be sure you keep me informed of your progress.'

'I will, doctor.'

The sticker on the hat case read in print: "With care", then underneath neatly handwritten in blue ink: Miss R. Whiteshaw, 24 Rosemary Avenue, Wanstead, E11, via Chelmsford.

'You won't need a nice hat here,' barked a brusque female voice. 'Quite superfluous indeed! We'll give you a uniform.'

The bus driver handed out an assortment of cases and bags of luggage to his passengers as they alighted onto the gravel entrance drive of the once great country estate of

Whitley Park. 'It's not a hat, just a case with some clothes in it,' explained Rene; 'my Mum gave it to me. It's all we've got.'

Her explanation meant nothing to the welcoming committee comprising Mrs Audrey Chambers and Miss Marylyn Williams who were already impatient with their new intake and keen to usher them into the vacuous grand hall of Whitley House, the requisitioned home of Conservative peer Lord Marchant.

The whole process – from Doctor Pritchard's house call to arrival for training – had taken just three weeks. Rene, still shaking, was at the commencement of a six-week training course in the basics of agricultural working. Now a proud member of the newly formed WLA (Women's Land Army) she was to take her seat along with an intake of some eighty girls from all over the southeast.

The stern Mrs Chambers, in the traditional manner of a headmistress, climbed three wooden steps to claim an elevated position on a platform covered by cheap carpet offcuts, from where she could see the entire ensemble. She clapped her hands to gain the attention of the chattering rabble before her, cleared her throat and bade her contingent of new recruits welcome before giving a potted history of the organisation, the sound of her own cultured tones giving her a deal of pleasure as it reverberated around the packed hall.

'Can you hear me at the back…? Yes? Your parents may well have told you that the WLA was first formed in 1917 – so nothing new under the sun. Reformed most recently in 1939 just prior to the outbreak…' – by which point Rene's attention span had reached its limit, in part due to the splendid surroundings of the hall with its magnificent Renaissance murals and medieval carvings that Shakespeare had probably touched, or at least might have seen. Through immense concentration she tried to consign to memory snippets such as: '… a quickly growing citizens army that will reach over 70,000 strong by this time next year… introductory training… placements… committees… gangs… haymaking… harvests… tractors and horses… muck spreading… early mornings… late nights… not to take bad language to heart… fieldwork… skills… potatoes… greenhouses… enough mud to drown in.'

Twenty minutes later, once the speech was over and the polite applause subsided, Rene turned to her neighbour and whispered, 'No shopping for us for a while, then.'

The next morning after a breakfast of cool porridge, she was dispatched again by bus to the nearby Midlands village of Hopthorne and Jersey Farm for lessons in how the countryside worked and what was expected of her; it was all very outdoorsy and pleasant and she was loving it already.

Looking around at her fellow classmates, they seemed to come from all corners of the social divide, with names like Shirley, Rosey and even Lavinia. She'd never been in a room with anyone called Lavinia before.

The six weeks were hard work, but the long days were also a lot of fun with some good friendships made in the process. Rene might never have left the Midlands or seen Cornwall had it not been for a near mutiny instigated and led by her over the serving of kippers for every breakfast at her lodgings.

Kippers – her landlady insisted – were a staple for British people from the Scillies to the Shetlands and the best start to a working day for everyone regardless of creed or class and therefore would be served daily. Rene, along with several colleagues, could not agree and so the breakfast renegades were summarily dispatched by express train to the far southwest for tractor training.

Before her factory was bombed, Rene, who'd been working since just after her fourteenth birthday, had never raised so much as a query with anyone regardless of how she towered above them and how through sheer height alone she could have been intimidating but never was. Now, following her narrow escape from death, a brave and confident young woman was emerging, though her incessant trembling showed no sign of abating.

Night-time brought the most horrendous nightmares: screaming, visions of animated corpses emerging from the rubble, with all too familiar faces of colleagues chastising her for surviving, severed heads rising from the floor then floating in the air; visions that conspired to torment her no sooner had her weary head hit the pillow. Years later, she would compare notes on these nightmares with Hugo, both praying that a disturbed night would not be experienced by both at the same time. Thankfully, over the course of their long marriage, the bringer of nightmares respectfully acquiesced.

Her days, however, were more peaceful and joyous than she could ever have hoped for. The train journey from Birmingham to Penzance filled her with wonder for a country she had not realised existed beyond London. All along the south coast of Devon she stared out of the carriage window transfixed at the sight of so much water and so many boats of all sizes and shapes. She even heard someone say of her, 'That young lady smiles all the time! How wonderful to be young!'

To Rene, the journey was more like that of a cruise on an ocean liner than a train meandering down the Devon coast. Worried about missing her stop she would harangue the guard every time he passed through the carriage. 'Don't worry, miss,' he'd assure her, 'the train goes no further than Penzance. It's a terminus, see.'

Her instructions were to meet a man called Albert Wallace "Wally" Johns, who was to be her instructor for tractor training. In the farming community of the West Penwith area, he was highly regarded as having a natural ability for the modern world of mechanical technology and had even completed an engineering apprenticeship in Camborne. 'No good with horses,' his old man would tell folk, 'but he can pull an engine apart, repair and replace it before your tea gets cold.'

Wally was set to meet Rene in Penzance and together they'd catch the bus to Nancepean Farm. Little did either of them know that they would not only become life-long friends, but that Wally would encourage and inadvertently introduce Rene to her future husband, who at this moment in time was ensconced on the Continent as the enemy across the water.

Billeted with two other Land Army girls – Angela and Madeleine – Rene settled into her new accommodation safe in the knowledge that the bombers couldn't reach her so far west; and even if they could, they surely wouldn't bomb a stable block that belonged to a country house. This part of the world, unscathed by the war, at least seemed secure by its remoteness.

The following morning, the three girls – already firm friends – gathered in the tractor shed for their first lesson. Wally – not one day older than any of the girls he was about to teach – appeared a few minutes later than his pupils with the intention of making an entrance, and sucking on a pipe that clearly didn't suit his baby fresh face and tender years. Dressed in heavy denim, navy blue overalls that were clearly too wide and too long for his short, skinny frame and having abandoned his cheery meet-and-greet persona of the previous day, Wally's attempt at a more authoritative demeanour failed to impress his new class – particularly Rene.

'This, ladies, is a Fordson Model N tractor, and the first thing you need to know about tractors is that like horses they need feeding.' Wally's voice sounded alien to Rene. To her ears, he was more like an American or Canadian than someone British, and as they were so far west perhaps this wasn't surprising. She'd never met anyone from Cornwall before, but she did her utmost to concentrate and understand as much as she possibly could without a translator.

'What do you feed these tractors on? Hay and carrots?' she quipped. Like traffic lights his face turned from a pipe tobacco induced novice green to flaming bright red almost instantaneously. She hadn't meant to be mean and felt rather ashamed when he stumbled with embarrassment rather than roll with the silly joke as a Londoner would have done.

'No. You feed them on Tractor Vaporising Oil, which is known as TVO, and engine oil for the engine itself. Without proper fuel, the tractor doesn't work and will be nothing more than a lump of metal taking up space in the yard and be no good to no one.'

'Then the tractor has nothing to fear,' retorted Rene. 'We know exactly what it feels like to not have the proper fuel!'

The joke meant everything to the girls but left poor Wally bemused and wishing they were anywhere other than in his beloved workshop. The desire to run out the door and join the Royal Air Force was never more appealing than now, but it wasn't an option so he put the kettle on.

With tea on the go, the morning was spent demonstrating how to fuel the tractors with a hand-operated pump, how to check oil levels, the technique of starting the machines with a starting handle and, if the wretched thing didn't start, he taught them how to change plugs. That's when he noticed Rene's trembling hands.

'There's nothing to be nervous of – it won't bite you.'

'I'm not nervous, I've just got the shakes.' She was tempted to explain how her factory had been bombed and how she'd survived, but the truth was she felt guilty for having survived. She was afraid that people would think her a coward and that she must have hid when the air raid siren sounded.

For his part, Wally didn't push his enquiry any further. The war was causing the most severe reactions in folk and he knew better than to try and make a conversation out of it. Everyone had their story to tell, even him.

Ironically, the first ploughing job the girls undertook didn't even involve a tractor as the farmer they were assigned to insisted on using a pair of horses. 'No good will come of tractors,' the old man informed them. 'Waste of time! I know horses better than anyone, and besides there isn't enough petrol to run tractors. There's a war on, don't they know, fuel's hard to come by. Horses put back into the land what they take out.'

They couldn't argue with his logic, but the effort of trying to hold a horse-drawn plough for hours and hours of ploughing was almost too much. Even the horses were in bed before they were, and bed itself offered little comfort when every muscle ached.

'Aren't you even going to take your boots off?' Angela asked. 'The farmer's wife will kill us if we get mud on her bedclothes.'

Barely able to lift herself, Rene put her feet on the floor and bent to untie the laces. It was Madeleine who noticed first.

'Rene? You're not shaking… you're really not shaking.'

'Too tired to shake.' Rene fell back onto the bed exhausted, but this time, for the first time in three months, the bed didn't shake.

Another week another farm another plough another horse until eventually she got to drive her first tractor. So this was agriculture; this was the country life, and the only bugbear now was occasional chauvinism from farmers and farmworkers who saw the end of the world rapidly heading their way in female form.

'Don't take any notice,' Wally told her. 'It's not that you're women, it's that they're too old to do anything about it.'

Problems were solved between the girls whenever the men took it upon themselves to be busy elsewhere. Wally was always dependable even if the tractors were not, and even on those occasions when he couldn't be found there were always the maintenance handbooks and a small booklet entitled *Tractor Ploughing in War Time*, issued by the Agricultural Advisory Department.

Madeleine left to join the ATS the summer a photographer from *The Cornishman* newspaper came to take pictures of Angela and Rene sitting behind the wheels of their tractors. Haymaking was underway much to the chagrin of the men who'd never witnessed such tomfoolery as two uppity city girls posed, grinning like a pair of Cheshire cats into the lens, as the photographer snapped away with an antique bellows camera that looked as if it had been used to take Queen Victoria's coronation portrait. In all fairness, the photographer's assignment was taken most seriously. He insisted on their utmost concentration over the next hour and a half as he painstakingly took their pictures in a variety of poses for use in that week's local edition and for the Dig for Victory campaign posters. 'If you're really good, these might make Fleet Street,' he warned in all seriousness.

'Hollywood next stop, then!' joked Rene.

From the field's edge, crude and jealous remarks blighted what was otherwise a perfect day in both weather and activity.

Later that evening, and long after the photographer had packed up his tripod with the sun falling headlong toward the horizon, Rene was struggling to engage reverse gear – a not uncommon problem with this particular tractor – when a man's voice yelled: 'JERRY BOMBER! TAKE COVER! TAKE COVER!'

Switching off the tractor's engine, only the sound of birds and the breeze whispering through the woods could be heard.

It took a moment, then, sure enough, in the distance she could hear the distinct hum of an aeroplane – maybe in trouble or at least very low. Trying not to panic so as to get off the tractor without catching her denim trouser leg in one of the pedals – she'd done that once too often and almost broken her leg.

Glancing above the treeline of a nearby wood she could see a bomber heading toward them in a shallow dive, black smoke trailing from one of its engines and worryingly on course for the very field they were in.

Leaping clear of the seat she dived underneath the tractor just as the belly of the aeroplane ploughed into the field barely 50 feet away. She could see the agonised face of the pilot behind the tinted, Perspex windscreen; his expression like that of a rodeo rider desperately pulling at the reins of his bucking, uncontrollable bronco. As the plane skidded across the grass its propellers churned up the freshly mown ground, batting clods of earth and stone across the field that showered down on the haymakers like shrapnel – some of it impacting the tractor under which Rene was sheltering.

Shaking again but determined to keep her nerve, she scrambled out from under the tractor expecting to see yet another terrible scene. The aeroplane had come to rest and was still largely intact, though black smoke was billowing from the hot engine that had been on fire prior to the crash. Certain that there was a crew onboard she sprinted toward the wreckage shouting to the others: 'IT'S AMERICAN, NOT GERMAN. SOMEONE GIVE ME A HAND!'

The bomber was a US Navy Liberator returning to its base at St Eval on the north coast having completed an anti-submarine mission in the Atlantic.

Entry to the aeroplane seemed hopeless but she noticed an aperture in the fuselage. Maybe it was for a large gun – she couldn't see a gun, but whatever it was it was the only way in. Clambering inside, reaching out in the unfamiliar, claustrophobic environment of the fuselage, pulling her way forward to where she had seen the pilot before realising that her progress was blocked by a steel bulkhead. It wasn't the way to get to him.

Retracing her footsteps she climbed back out of the same aperture from which she'd entered, only instead of dropping to the ground she now climbed onto the roof of the fuselage. Below her someone was shouting encouragement.

Stepping along the spine of the aeroplane she thought of a film she'd seen as a child – Buster Keaton walking along the top of a moving train carriage trying not to lose balance. Silly thoughts in precarious moments! Unlike Keaton, balance was never her thing.

Dropping to her knees, peering down into the gunner's turret; nobody in there. Onward now to the cockpit – just a few more steps. Yes! There! The pilot in clear view, still strapped in his seat, dazed and confused, talking into his throat mic as if in direct contact with his base.

Glancing up at his would-be rescuer, he gesticulated and shouted: 'Get away! It'll blow in a minute… Get away.'

Someone tossed up to Rene a heavy club hammer with which she could smash the Perspex. Breaking through to him she could now reach down with her long arms to release his seat harness then pull at his flying jacket with all her strength – strength that had come through months of pulling against shire horses, cajoling them, lifting heavy potato sacks, starting tractors with starting handles. Her remarkable strength caused him to reciprocate, pushing upward, holding onto life. This was no place to give up; life wasn't going to end here – not today.

Slipping to the ground, Rene once more grabbed the dazed pilot by the collar and continued to pull him until they were both safely clear of the wreckage. Laying him on the close-cropped ground of the hayfield, kneeling she took his hand and held it firmly between her own. He, too, was shaking.

'Where are the other men? Your crew?'

'All bailed out – just me.'

Rene was awarded the George Cross and consequently merited a mention in *The London Gazette*, which thrilled her London family. She couldn't have known whether the plane would have caught fire or not, so she was rightly recognised as a true heroine and consequently feted as the girl who saved the life of a US airman on the very day she'd posed for a poster.

To the magazine editor, she was a heroine in two respects: the hardworking Land Army girl and the fearless rescuer of an Allied airman. But in an age of heroes and heroines, her day in the limelight soon passed, and by the time she met Hugo in 1948 her bravery had faded from the collective memory as people made a concerted effort to return to a post-war normality.

This attitude was not unwelcome as it suited the city-cum-country girl who much preferred her life to be ordinary. Always modest, she never mentioned the crash or her award – the highest decoration for a civilian – to anyone, preferring to remain the lofty Land Army girl in dungarees.

The incident also brought a temporary respite to her shaking, though for many years afterwards the condition would return to affect her for various reasons. The pilot whose life she saved, Lieutenant Terrence Deforrest Robbins, remained such a good friend that he travelled at great expense from his home in Idaho to England for Hanne's christening in January 1954 at which he was made an honoured godfather.

*

Freitag 28th Juni 1963, 4.19 pm
Oberwinkel

Hugo glanced at his watch; it was getting late and tea would be ready. Oma would not be at all pleased if only half the family were in attendance; she couldn't abide empty places at the table; and what of poor mum all alone with her mother-in-law and not a common word to exchange between them.

He knew only too well what it was like to be in the company of a mother-in-law who was distant and unwilling to build bridges. He could understand how Agnes – Rene's mother – had resented *his* presence. Marrying the enemy! Breaking the family apart! Just what was Rene thinking of?

*

August 1950, the exact date forgotten; Hugo didn't record it.
Cornwall

From that very first outing to the cinema in Penzance to see David Niven and Kim Hunter in Powell and Pressburger's *A Matter of Life and Death*, and from the moment he gently placed his left arm around her shoulder during the picnic scene, Hugo had known that he would never – never walk away from Rene. There could be no German bride for him.

In his head, he was David Niven's character – Peter D. Carter; and he knew beyond a shadow of a doubt that he had fallen head over heels for a former English Land Army girl and there would be no power on earth or in Heaven that could separate them.

Agnes, like his own mother, was a widow – Rene's father having died of leukaemia in 1930. Agnes was convinced that his service as an artillery gunner in the First War had brought about his premature demise and it most probably had. Such a common denominator cemented the bonds that linked Hugo and Rene.

With Rene's help he learned English quickly. Each and every date was also an English lesson. Now, thanks to Rene, he only had to hear a word once and he would remember it, though his pronunciation left much to be desired. She was a natural teacher and a keen student of grammar and, for his part, Hugo was a willing and intelligent pupil. He had so much to say to her and desperately wanted to understand everything she said. He wanted to know who she was and where she was from, why she'd agreed to meet him – an "enemy" – when there were so many returning British servicemen.

It wasn't until just a few weeks before Hanne was born in 1953 that Rene was able to explain to Hugo the reasons that had brought her to West Cornwall, and only then because she started to shake uncontrollably and the doctor had to be called one evening.

*

Freitag 28th Juni 1963
A very warm evening in Oberwinkel

Hanne knew that her godfather – Uncle Terry – was an American, but had no idea as to her mother's role in saving his life or the great award bestowed upon her, though she would discover their story many years later. For now, all she knew was that it had been a smashing walk with dad and that it was getting hot – very hot indeed.

When the heat of the day had subsided, Oma agreed to babysit whilst Rene took her turn to walk with Hugo through the village, or "promenade" as she called it. She wanted to see the village and meet the community, so the prospect of linking arms and chatting without kids or mother-in-law in attendance was an opportunity too good to miss.

'Did you enjoy your walk with Hanne today?' asked Rene.

'Yes, it was a good walk.'

'Talks, doesn't she?'

'For England, I think.'

'You need to bond, both of you.'

'She is… What is that word?'

'Inquisitive? Curious?'

'Yes, curious. She asked about Uncle Terry.'

'Did you tell her how we met?'

'Her mother the war hero? A job for you to tell her one day, nah?'

'She doesn't need to know. I don't shake anymore and that's all that matters.'

'Maybe her uncle Terry will spill the beans one day.'

'It was *our* war, Hugo; they don't need to know. Their lives are different – *will* be different.'

Hugo as tour guide knew each and every house in the village. 'So-and-so lived there,' he would say; 'she was the oldest woman in the district – probably in Bavaria. Her grandson was a convicted criminal and joined the SS. The Russians executed him. Just as well.

'Cousin Jurgen lived in this house. He was a builder. He did not come home after the war. Nobody knows. His daughter lives in Berlin. She will come to the reunion. You will like her.'

Rene, the George Cross heroine, had been too timid to venture out alone, fearing that someone might try to engage her in conversation, find out that she was British and then spit at her for having been on the side that had beaten Hitler and ridiculed his ridiculous promises. The war was only yesterday after all. Eighteen years was nothing in people's memories, and it wasn't simply that Germany was a beaten nation – it was the indignity of it.

Saying nothing to Hugo, in her head she was prepared; just in case. Her thoughts were thus:

They'd raised their right arms to blindly follow a complete and utter maniac to disaster; a corporal with a Charlie Chaplin moustache! A pavement artist who could barely sell his own work! The insane man who'd taken control of the legitimate government when he should have been locked up in an institution! What nation on God's green earth would blindly follow a maniacal former corporal-cum-failed street artist who bore a resemblance to the twentieth century's most successful clown? What's more, he'd done all this damage to Germany when in fact he was Austrian. He even instigated a policy to rid Europe of people who were dark just like him, whilst favouring a fair-haired, blue-eyed race – a group with whom he bore no resemblance and was clearly no example.

No, Rene didn't want to retaliate, but if push had come to shove then she'd have let the offender have it with both barrels. With Hugo beside her, she had no such worries.

'I love the cobbled streets and the houses! It's like a fairy-tale village. I keep expecting Hansel and Gretel to come skipping down the street.' She pointed to a large monastic building. 'Is that building your old school? It's magnificent – for a village.'

Hugo nodded. 'It is an abbey to Saint Margaret. You know why my mother wanted me to be a priest, nah? Here is the "factory" right here in the village. It might have been my fate had the Nazis not come when they did.'

'Better a priest than a Nazi, Hugo.'

'We would never have been together,' said Hugo quietly, in a rare expression of sincerity to his English wife.

People passed them and initially politely exchanged greetings, until such time as someone recognised the mature, post-war face of Hugo Mauer.

'Good evening! ... Hugo? Is it...? It is you! How are you, my friend?'

Another was more formal: 'Herr Mauer? How pleased I am to see you again! Your mother said that you were a prisoner? Is that true? Did they treat you well?'

Some enquired as to whether he'd returned for good. Others were strangers who had come to the village in the post-war years and had no idea as to who he was, but they spoke anyway; but at least two people chose to ignore him completely. Didn't matter, he'd known *them* to be Nazi Party workers employed in what had been the Gauleiter's office, so to hell with them. In all, it became a busy "promenade" as the villagers stepped out into the cooler evening air to partake of the fine summer weather.

He asked someone about the Nazi headmaster Haas who had taken over the school from the gentle Herr Fischl. 'Haas is in America now, working for the CIA. I hear he is doing very well and the Americans reward him very well indeed.'

Hugo didn't really know why he'd enquired about Haas as he cared not one jot, but the man to whom he made the enquiry had also been at the same school at the same time and it was just a way of making conversation in a world where so much had changed. 'And Fischl?'

'Fischl was not so fortunate. He died in prison defending his anti-Nazi credentials.'

At the narrow bridge that crossed the river, where Hugo's grandparents had first entered the village looking for work in the 1880s, Hugo told Rene of the epic battle that had ensued on that very bridge: 'My great-grandparents were not welcome. My great-grandfather was a cowboy…?'

'Cowboy?! You mean "maverick"?'

'Yes, maverick – a fighter who had a way of things… Doing? Nah? He did not… What is the word?'

'Endear himself? Meaning to get along with…'

'Yes, "endear". He was Bavarian. Bavarians are stubborn, nah?' remarked Hugo as he proudly recalled how his "maverick" ancestor had fought a vicious "battle of the horsewhips" on the bridge when the family's wagon encountered another midway across. 'Each man held their ground. Each had a whip.'

According to Hugo, the encounter had entered village folklore, and various stories of his grandfather's legendary anti-social behaviour – stories that had been told to him as a child by Oma – were also known throughout the district.

'Sounds like you're a chip off the old block!' replied Rene, squeezing her husband's hand. 'I wonder how I would have coped had I been taken prisoner and brought here to work, unable to speak the language and far from home.'

'You would have coped,' said Hugo.

'I couldn't have started a business or bought land as you did.'

'Maybe with me here? I would help you.' Hugo stopped and looked not at Rene but off into the distance as if to utter such a thing was too emotional for a Bavarian of his generation to confront. He'd become *too* emotional in recent years, he felt.

Emotion, so often frowned upon when he was at school, even during Herr Fischl's tenure as headmaster, and later removed in its entirety under the Nazi doctrine. His school friend, Jacob Schultz, had been badly beaten by Haas for crying in the classroom – crying for the loss of his pet dog who had died the night before. Haas had even recommended to Jacob's father that his son be removed from school and his family in order to be sent to Berlin where the Hitler Youth would cure him of self-centred sentimentality.

Rene, however, was thrilled with Hugo's sentiment. Sentiment was a word that the Nazis had all but removed from the German lexicon and so Hugo had not easily understood its meaning as he grappled with English vocabulary. It had shocked her that he appeared not to be able to comprehend its meaning.

Now she waited for him to turn to her, look her in the eyes and hold her gently, telling her how much she meant to him, but she realised that the German in Hugo had returned and his aloof demeanour was strengthening again in this environment. His sentiment had been a fleeting exposé that he could cover up in an instant.

'I see no ships?' she asked.

'We should go and see this fence that Hanne and her cousins saw.'

'Not tonight, Hugo!'

'Tonight? No, but before we leave for home again.'

At the cemetery gates on the outskirts of the village they stopped to stare at the various headstones, polished and in shining contrast to the historic Cornish headstones of granite, weathered and uncared for.

'Are your ancestors here?' she asked him.

'Some. My ancestors came from villages to the north and west. When no longer the grave can be maintained also the stone is removed, unlike in Britain.'

'Would you want to be returned here?'

'Do not worry – I will live forever!' he laughed.

She'd asked him the very same thing some thirteen years earlier as they'd walked around a Cornish cemetery. 'Would you want to be buried here in a foreign land?'

'I will not die,' he'd replied then. 'I should have died a hundred times, but death does not want me.'

She had thought it a very sad thing to say at the time, but had let it drop because then there was a new business to talk about and a new cottage – "Roseveare".

*

Monday 5th May 1952
A hamlet between Hayle and Penzance

Hugo had taken her on the bus to see Roseveare Cottage.

'Splendid in its isolation!' he exclaimed when they eventually arrived at the garden gate. She was sure he'd learned the expression verbatim and most probably from Wally, but whatever, he was quite right; it was indeed "splendid in isolation".

Roseveare Cottage was not on the market; it was a tied property owned by Rene's employers the Valdeans and vacant to a young family employed in agriculture. Hugo and Rene fitted the requirement in every respect – Hugo now in the employ of Mr James Hubert, tenant dairy farmer, and Rene employed as a live-in nanny for the Valdeans. They simply had to keep the place tidy and make themselves available for milking duties three weekends out of four. Hugo would continue in the employ of Mr Hubert, but the large garden offered a unique opportunity to begin an enterprise – market gardening.

Hugo had learned from day one in Cornwall that the soil combined with a temperate climate in the far west of the county was ideal for growing produce – anything from cabbages and potatoes to daffodils. The cottage garden was too small to grow daffodils but it would be ideal for smaller blooms such as anemones and hyacinths.

There were already roses climbing the front walls of the cottage and it was clear that the previous residents had loved the place and treated it well.

'It could be home – not much,' said Hugo. Rene assumed "not much" meant no amenities.

'It'll do fine,' she said.

'Water no, electricity no. Needs paint and paper, but rent no.'

'We'll manage, Hugo.'

'The garden will make a fortune.'

'Fortune?' exclaimed Rene.

'Flowers – anemones, hyacinths.'

It took a moment for the penny to drop, Rene had become so used to trying to interpret Hugo's true intentions. 'People around here won't buy flowers because—'

Hugo interrupted her, 'No. The flowers we put on the train for London. Up the road is the station, a walk of twenty minutes. The farmer makes a living – we make a fortune, nah?'

'It'll take a lot of time and effort.'

'Time and effort we will find!' Hugo assured her.

'Yes, we'll find effort all right!'

*

Now strolling in Oberwinkel, Roseveare Cottage seemed such a long way away in both time and place. Rene felt that they'd come such a distance in little more than thirteen years when full of hope they'd taken on the little cottage with its damp walls. Despite having no water or electricity, by the time Hanne was born in the autumn of '53 they had at least got some wallpaper up, and between them they'd made a success of the garden having banished every weed.

Working on the garden every spare moment they had, their first crop of flowers sold to a London agent for £150 net, and the following year their net income increased to £350 – more than a year's wages earned as a farm labourer.

Reinvesting the money in poultry, Hugo and Rene added eggs to their produce; and not just enough chickens to produce an omelette, but a feathered battalion of 120 hybrid layers that would give them an additional source of income with profit.

By the time Hanne's younger brother Marco was born, Hugo and Rene had secured a loan for their own property – a five-acre smallholding. Proudly running his own business from his own premises, Hugo was at long last master of his own destiny.

*

Samstag 29th Juni 1963, 11.24 pm
Oberwinkel

The morning of the reunion found Hanne in her favourite place: the deer lookout. She'd been there since just after nine o'clock, convincing her mother that the reunion wasn't due to take place until midday and so there was plenty of time because deer and other Bavarian wildlife prefer the cooler mornings to being out in the midday sun. She promised faithfully to be back in good time.

'No later than a quarter to eleven!' Rene warned her.

'But the school's only a minute's walk away.'

Rene would not be swayed and insisted on the curfew, although she preferred to keep Hugo oblivious of his daughter's absence. He was already in the school and had been since just after breakfast seeing to last-minute arrangements together with his brother and sisters. This would be an historic occasion to begin all family reunions, creating a tradition that would cement Anglo-German relations for centuries to come. Vital if another world war was to be avoided.

The siblings speculated that the tradition of a family reunion would continue well into the next century and beyond, and that it was imperative that the young cousins got along, as they were the post-war generation on whose shoulders so much was expected.

It was good to converse in his native tongue again with those he had known all his life – Lennart, Martha and Kirsten. This newfound ability seemed strange indeed: he could translate in his head every word spoken, though his German vocabulary was far greater than his English and he didn't sound silly speaking German. He felt a fool when speaking English in front of native English speakers. Sometimes they would smile at something he'd uttered incorrectly or inappropriately, and he really hadn't meant them to smile if he was being very serious, and often he *was* serious in his comments. And those moments where he'd meant to be funny, people remained resolutely unmoved. So, speaking English, he felt he couldn't win; his inherent shyness would get the better of him. He didn't want that either.

Wally put him at ease and had done from the moment he'd first greeted Hugo off the truck in 1944. Rene, more than anyone, had helped him with the language, whilst Wally had wanted to learn German and considered Hugo to be *his* teacher.

Now Hugo was bi-lingual, his linguistic ability confused him to the point of near madness. Lennart, who had also been a POW, had picked up a few words of Italian because he'd fought alongside the Italians at Monte Cassino, but he'd never been exposed to a foreign culture in the way Hugo had.

If they were at all impressed by Hugo's ability or by his business success as a British entrepreneur, they didn't show it or say as much. There were no questions; in fact, no inquisitiveness on their part at all concerning the past ten years, and not a word was said by way of approbation. To listen to them, or to watch their progress that morning as they arranged chairs, tables, flowers and decorations, it was as if nothing had happened in the past twenty years; as if no war had taken place, no Führer, no battles, no imprisonment, no waiting for news. Maybe in the years to come it would all come spilling out. Someday, someone just might ask: what happened to you when the Allies overran your lines? Did they treat you well? Did you have to bury your friends? How did Mother cope? How did you cope when he didn't come home? How did you sustain yourself when the Russians came? Did they hurt you? What about the Americans? Do ghosts haunt you when you sleep?

For now it was all locked away to be held deep inside where the sun didn't shine. The colours of the flowers were more important today, the length of the table. Would there be enough room for everyone? Were there enough chairs? Would they be comfortable? Would there be enough food and drink? Shall we take pictures afterwards?

Hanne had taken a sketchbook, a pencil, some coloured crayons and an I-Spy book of European flora and fauna. By eleven o'clock she was busy sketching and making detailed notes of everything she saw from the deer lookout; it could all be part of her school project, which she would present to the envious class upon her return in September.

On her wish list to see: an eagle, a capercaillie, a marmot and an ibex. Seeing a wolf or a wild boar would be the greatest achievement of all, though the prospect of seeing such wild beasts also scared her somewhat. In windy old Cornwall she'd be lucky to spot barn owls, foxes and badgers, though there were plenty of rooks, wood pigeon and jackdaws, but there was certainly nothing dangerous.

A doe grazing in the near meadow was at least something. If she were to remain quiet and still then it might come a little closer, but she was already quite stiff and sore having been sitting patiently on the wooden slats for almost two hours. She would have brought a cushion from the van had she thought about it. Not a cushion from Oma's, of course. Oma's cushions were not for removal. Not that Oma had ever stated the rule, nor was it written down as a notice, it was just understood that Oma's cushions were not for removal in 1963.

Maybe, in the years to come, long after Oma's departure, children would be able to take cushions from the houses of their grandparents, but for now – certainly not.

Hanne could see herself clearly in the role of "*Oma*" one day. She would be a kind and helpful *Oma* to her grandchildren and would most certainly approve of cushions being taken for use in deer hides such as this one – provided it wasn't raining. No grandchild of hers was likely to want to go out in the rain anyway.

In Hanne's vision as "*Oma*-to-be", *this* would be her home – Oma's house in Oberwinkel. It would pass to her quite naturally so that she could continue the "family role" in its rightful place. She would preside over future family reunions, she would be matriarch of the Mauer family and her tenure would take them all well into the next century!

For now, she would wait and bide her time until being called to take over the role of matriarchal *Oma* – as it might be some years away. There was, however, a call to be heard – a call that disturbed the doe from grazing, lifting its head to get a direction on the sound – a human sound. It wasn't her imagination working overtime, the doe's reaction confirmed it; someone was calling – someone English.

Oh, no! Mother! Of course! It's time to get out of here and get ready!

Descending the timber-framed lookout as quickly as she could possibly descend anything so awkward, a German word filled her thoughts – *schnell, schnell, schnell, schnell!*

She loved the word and the sound it made, and now it had entered her head to the exclusion of all other words. Every day of the holiday she had learned a German word and today this word was the word to use.

She ran full pelt down the grassy slope of the meadow, full pelt into the village, her heels clopping loudly along the cobbled road to Oma's whilst repeating over and over, '*schnell, schnell, schnell*', under her laboured breath.

Rene was feeling vulnerable. She was in a foreign place and her guard was down – one of her children was seriously overdue.

'Hanne's on her way,' she assured Hugo despite not being able to base her assurance on fact.

'Time is difficult for that girl!' Hugo growled. 'You should not have let her wander off.'

'Well, the reunion is only across the road in your old school, and Hanne does love it up in the wood looking out from the tower. Isn't that where you and your brother and sisters used to play?'

'Yes, but my mother would have beaten me if I kept people waiting. She still might beat me if we are late. This is very important for Hanne and Marco and their cousins – a tradition is begun that they must continue. People would not go to war if they know one another. Only strangers fight wars.'

No sooner did he utter the words, much to Rene's relief, and not unlike a diva arriving late for her curtain call, Hanne breezed into the room certain of what she had to do. 'I'm back!' she triumphantly proclaimed between wheezes.

'Just in time, young lady! Your little brother is ready to go, nah. We went almost without you.'

Reaching out, Rene ran her fingers through her child's thick, auburn hair. 'Oh, Hanne, you're in a state! Just look at you!'

'Yes, I'm in a German state – called Bavaria.'

'Come here, we'd better tidy you up.'

Rene had laid out a pretty floral-patterned frock ready for Hanne – also a hug followed by a kiss on the cheek. Utter relief. Glancing up at a rather infuriated Hugo, his eyes focussed on the wardrobe mirror, tying his best Windsor knot, cufflinks glinting, white cotton shirt lovingly ironed, his trousers immaculately pressed, she hadn't seen him look so well turned out or as handsome since their wedding day twelve years ago. His black leather shoes were so polished as to almost reflect the bedroom ceiling, and she wondered just when he did all this preparation. Or was it Oma at work in the background? Of course, it didn't matter.

Once out in the bright sunshine of that afternoon, away from the steps of the house, Oma, standing in her doorway, bid them make their way the short distance along the road to the school. She promised she would follow soon, but for now she wanted them to walk together as a family hand in hand in order that she could take a photo of them walking and looking back at her. For the first time, Rene, and Hanne, too, glanced back to see a woman they had not seen before – a proud and loving matriarch.

***

Chapter 4

The Reunion

Climbing the newly installed pine stairs to the classroom, yet opening the same old familiar door that must have been in place when Hugo was a boy, there they all were inside: milling, chatting, catching-up, waiting patiently for the moment when they would all sit down together. The long tables – each neatly covered in taught scarlet tablecloths – placed end-to-end spanned the length of the hall. The cutlery shone in the midday light and was so precisely laid out as if carefully measured by an English butler's rule; the red napkins, the decor – it was wonderful!

Just as Hanne had envisioned.

Emmi – tiny, three-year-old Emmi resplendent in purple track shoes with Velcro straps and flashing lights – was the first to run across the floor with arms outstretched to hug her cousin. Hanne eagerly swept her up in her long arms, hugged her and kissed her on the forehead whilst adjusting the child's pink, plastic hair clip with a free hand.

'You've made a friend already!' smiled Sandy, keen to remain out of his wife's limelight for this was *her* family day and all eyes would be on her and Marco – the English family.

Hanne spoke to Emmi in hushed German tones, stroking her fine dark hair, which caused the child to relax and beam a smile that melted Hanne's heart.

'Oma's great-great-granddaughter. What do you think, Hanne?'

'She's an absolute sweetheart! You must be so proud.' Hanne handed Emmi back to Heike who was waiting patiently to greet her cousin with a hug and a kiss.

'Yes! I am a very proud *Oma*! That is true. What about you, Hanne? Are your children married?'

'Well, Freddie was with a lovely young woman, but they separated last year. And Christof is working hard as a systems engineer and doing extremely well. He's so well thought of by his employers, but I don't think he has any time to… lead a life – you know? These youngsters have to work so hard to get anywhere these days.'

It had been such a long time. She had made a few visits over the decades, but the reunion had remained a diary entry for so long and now today it was real once more. Sandy had never been, though he'd met some of the cousins when they had visited Cornwall and liked them a great deal.

Hanne had been lax in keeping her father's wishes. Marco was the true keeper of the reunion and without his effort then maybe the dream of unity between the two family branches might well have been lost.

Once the baby of the family, Marco had been about the same age and size as Emmi on that first visit – that very first reunion in 1963. Hanne had been too old then to confide in him or have him as a playmate, and he didn't remember a great deal about that first time other than feeling dreadfully sick when travelling and then upon arrival at Oma's.

He remembered Oma fondly – apparently. *Well, perhaps that's because he was a toddler,* thought Hanne, a toddler whose language was neither English nor German and was therefore neutral in the eyes of his German grandmother. Hanne never enjoyed such a relationship with her namesake despite having returned on occasions in order to try and cultivate a relationship with Oma and the German cousins.

On a visit in 1973, Heidemarie had been rather disdainful of her "idiot" English cousin, especially as Hanne was then struggling with the language, so Heidemarie made her pay for it, thinking maybe that her remarks would not be understood by such a "gawky, spotty, self-obsessed English *dummkopf!*"

As Hanne glanced along the table to see Heidemarie deep in animated conversation with her grown-up children and their spouses, she inadvertently caught her cousin's attention. Heidemarie immediately beamed a smile that was reciprocated by Hanne, but even after the passage of some thirty-seven years such an expression was not likely to mend the damage of that earlier visit.

That was the year she had thought to surprise Oma with her presence; the year that she stayed to find work and learn German properly by working as an assistant in a small hotel where she could interact with native speakers; but the awful truth had been that she was not welcome in either the family or the hotel.

Hugo's idea of creating a regular family reunion did not – initially – survive the '60s. Hanne's post-war generation saw no value in maintaining links in a stuffy get-together organised by the older generation. How much better it was to simply turn up and say, 'Hello!' rather than wait for an occasional family gathering.

By 1973, the drag of the years was doing nothing for Oma's well-being. She didn't appreciate the modern permissive age nor did she appreciate the untimely arrival of an overly tall, sexually mature young woman covered in barely enough dress material to make an adequate dusting rag. Gone was the ten-year-old inquisitive child in jeans and ponytails. Oma was shocked at her demise, especially as the replacement bore little resemblance to her innocent predecessor.

To make matters worse, upon her departure from home Hugo had given Hanne a large denomination Reichsmark for spending that had last been in circulation in Hitler's Germany. Trying to cash it in almost landed her in severe trouble with the authorities in the form of two *Polizei* officers flagged down by an irate shop assistant. Hanne had been trying to exchange the note for a new electric toaster that Oma just didn't possess. Hanne needed her English breakfast.

Mixing a combination of very basic English with a spattering of O-level German and French, Hanne did her level best to assure the monolingual officers and shop assistant that her father was a devoted German citizen living in England and that he would have given her the note in good faith not realising how things had changed as he had been a prisoner of war and deprived of any news by the British authorities. In fact, he'd always used the term "Reichsmark" and never referred to the Deutschmark.

She later wrote home on a postcard: "Oh, by the way, Dad, Oma sends her love and that Reichsmark you gave me almost landed me in a cell overnight." On receipt, this simply caused Hugo to smile very broadly, particularly when she related the story in person some months later.

The only positive outcome from that summer of 1973 was that Hanne eventually got a handle on the German language, enabling her to become reasonably fluent in the basics at least. She could now communicate with her father's family, but it was always so much easier speaking English to her favourite cousin Heike – the daughter of another wartime liaison.

Heike's father had been a US Army sergeant who had met and married her mother, Kirsten, in 1951. Heike had learnt English from the cradle and as a pupil of a US forces school.

Cousin Manfred could also speak English because he lived and worked in New Zealand and had married a Canadian woman, Janine – who, like Sandy, was also attending her first Mauer reunion.

There were other cousins who could speak English to a greater or lesser degree, and certainly the younger generation were nearly all bilingual.

Hanne thought that Oma would not have recognised this reunion – this bilingual gathering. It didn't take too much imagination to visualise the old matriarch sitting at the head of the long table with that dour expression of hers. It would have been nice to talk to her, find out what she thought of the proceedings and whether she was pleased or even proud of them. Concentrating as hard as she might amid the chatter and noise of dining, Hanne did her best to visualise her grandmother and communicate her feelings.

She would tell Oma how her great-grandchildren and great-great-grandchildren might take the reunion well into the twenty-first century just as Hugo hoped they might, but the name Mauer would mean little to Emmi – now scooting around the floor on her bottom – as the family name diminished with a lack of male heirs. Marco's daughters were English and, as young adults, felt no German ties, despite having been regularly brought to reunions as children.

Yes, the irony of it, thought Hanne: a Mauer family reunion, but the only Mauer here by name was English born and bred – Marco.

Dinner completed, outside in the sun various family photographers were marshalling the family into a group shot for posterity just prior to the walk that would take in the cemetery and Oma's grave.

It was while Sandy was taking his group photo that a distant, lonely figure caught Hanne's attention. Glancing up she saw a teenage boy staring at the assembly through an upper window of the old schoolhouse; chin cupped in hand as if he was bored of the whole event and would sooner be elsewhere.

First impressions were that he might be a young member of the family, especially as he looked most familiar to her. Perhaps he was too shy to come down and partake in the group photograph; but no, all the family were assembled here with no absenters. Everyone had elected to come out and enjoy the sun.

Maybe, she wondered, he was the son of one of the catering staff who'd been looking after them that afternoon. Before she could turn to mention her concerns to someone – purely for clarification purposes – he'd disappeared.

She mentioned it to Heike as they walked. No, Heike hadn't noticed a face at the window but promised she would ask later when she saw the caterers. She would be seeing them to settle up and thank them for all their hard work.

Heidemarie made a point of joining them and reminding them of that "summer of 1963" when they were so "young and carefree" that they wandered far and near with gay abandon.

What about 1973? Remember me? Dummkopf? Hanne thought better of it; and besides, the German words she needed were eluding her. Her head was full of Spanish, Italian and French, all of which she'd learnt in recent years and could speak to a basic degree.

'It seems like yesterday when Uncle Hugo and Aunt Rene would bring you and Marco to stay for the summer,' remarked Heike, gripping her cousin's arm as if to reinforce their bonds.

'That summer was over forty-five years ago. My goodness, Fredrick is thirty-five and Christof is thirty-three!'

'In your father's book they're just children in school uniform.'

'He wrote that twenty-five years ago. He had a thousand copies printed and I'm still selling them on Amazon and at the local post office. We didn't have room for all the boxes – they were taking up floor space everywhere!'

'I have it on the bookshelf and one day I'm going to learn English and read it; but I just don't have the time!' said Heidemarie, keen as always not to be left out of the group.

Hanne suspected that "Busybee Heidemarie" would never have the time, but that hardly mattered. 'Believe me, you're not missing out by not being able to read it.'

'But he was our most accomplished relative. He wrote that book to bring people together. We're all so proud of him here.'

Heike agreed: 'Yes, we are. A prisoner of war, who stayed in England, learned the language and became a millionaire and was even decorated by the Queen! How wonderful is that?'

'My relationship with him wasn't always easy, and there were things that both of us might have handled better. Who knows? All I know is that this reunion was important to him, even though he didn't care for Oma. He thought that if we kept on having the reunion there would be no more wars in Europe.'

Heike squeezed her cousin's arm. 'He was right. There hasn't been another war in Europe.'

'There was the Balkans,' said Hanne, 'but that had been brewing for a long time – long before Dad was born. And you know, I'm not naïve about my father. Had Hitler invaded Britain, my father would have pulled the trigger along with everyone else who put on that bloody uniform.

'If a high-ranking officer had been killed by the resistance and if my father had been ordered to round up the local population and shoot them – all of them – entire communities of men, women, children, babies, dogs and cattle – he'd have done it. Because like all the rest of his generation he was held tight in the grip of Hitler, Himmler, Goebbels and the rest of that stinking crowd.

'They told Germans to jump and the Germans replied: "Of course! How high would you like us to jump? We can jump higher than anyone!"

'My father didn't refuse his service call-up. He didn't question anything – not to my knowledge. He didn't try to escape. He didn't hide Jews or help Slavs, gypsies or gays to escape. His name was not von Trapp. It's only when you lose and you become the captured rather than the captor. That's why my father changed. He wasn't innocent and he wasn't anyone's victim. He chose to follow his masters.'

All of a sudden, the tone became too sombre. Heidemarie never questioned her father, Lennart. 'They were boys, Hanne – kept in the dark. They didn't know. It was the SS – the Waffen-SS. They were the ones who committed those awful things. And even if the regular boys were told to do horrible things, *they* would have been shot and their families imprisoned. They *had* to obey.'

Hanne was not so sure. 'I'd like to believe that, but I find it difficult.' Her comment sparked a memory of a special Christmas when Hugo presented her with a wooden toy that he'd made just for her. How she loved that toy; how she cherished that memory of him beaming with pride on Christmas morning 1962.

'Dad was different when I was younger... When I was older and his business was better established, I probably expected too much of him and I didn't show him the gratitude he felt he deserved. And I think I reminded him too much of Oma.

'At least he wrote about my mother in that book. She was a hero awarded the George Cross for rescuing an American airman from his burning bomber when it crashed into the field where she was working as a Land Army girl. That pilot became my godfather.

'She met Dad later, after the war, but if it hadn't been for the bombing in London and the factory being hit – the factory she worked in – then I wouldn't be here today. Such is fate.'

'I read that about your mother,' said Heike. 'Horrific! That man's severed head falling into her lap! And when she shook and shook and they couldn't cure her!'

'Yes, the doctor diagnosed "shell shock". So she was packed off to Cornwall as a Land Army girl. She was only nineteen.'

At the gates of the cemetery the various family groups that had separated during the half-mile walk came together to stare through the gates at the large polished ornate stones and crosses set into the shady, wooded grove. Oma's stone was quite central and easy to spot from the lane.

Heidemarie pointed out that Hanne even shared her name with Oma.

'Yes, Father always put great stock in gestures, and my name is a gesture to his mother, I suppose. It's odd to see my name on a gravestone – gives me the shivers!'

'I expect it won't be long before they remove the stone and then—' said Heike.

'And then there will be nothing to commemorate she was ever here.' Hanne thought it an odd thing to remove gravestones and reuse the plot. 'It's tradition, isn't it?' she asked.

'Yes, but not in England?'

'Not in England, which makes it good if you're researching your family tree. The old stones remain forever. Or at least, that used to be the way.'

Strange to think of Oma being removed from history – the history of the village. Just as her memorial stone seemed so central in the cemetery, in life she had occupied a very central place in Oberwinkel. Geographically her farm was centrally situated, and in the hierarchy of the parish the Mauers were neither the poorest nor were they the richest.

In the eyes of her granddaughters, Oma Hanna Mauer had been such an historic presence, like some deep-rooted oak tree that had stood for a thousand years. Now, standing there on a bright, cool autumn afternoon, along with all the other grandchildren and great-grandchildren, it was hard to feel any emotion. Hanne had tried to connect to the old matriarch all those years ago in 1963 and again in 1973, but it wasn't to be.

Today it might be different; today they would be contemporaries.

'I don't think Oma approved of me – not when I was a young woman,' said Hanne. 'Do you remember when I worked over here for a time – in the hotel? Oma thought I was outrageous!'

It was the memory of Oma's expression at catching her "outrageous" English granddaughter standing admiring herself before the long mirror, vainly flattering her physique. The granddaughter who didn't go to church; the granddaughter who wasn't even Catholic; the granddaughter whose German language ability wasn't an ability at all. There she was, nineteen and not even able to speak her father's native tongue. What had Hugo been thinking?

Today, it would have been so very different. Today they'd have spoken in German and compared notes on all manner of things; they would have been friends for sure.

Heidemarie knew the story, as Heidemarie had never been anywhere else in her life and Oma must have confided her thoughts to those closest to her; if not to her personally, then to Lennart, who must surely have told Heidemarie or discussed it at the dinner table. No wonder Heidemarie thought Hanne such a *"dummkopf!"* All these years later the thought was enough to make Hanne shudder.

This afternoon, Heidemarie was more concerned with memories of 1963.

'Tomorrow, let us walk back up to the old border post – the three of us – like we did all those years ago when it was new.'

In need of a distraction, Hanne readily agreed. 'Okay.'

'Just us three. The men can amuse themselves.'

The idea of a walk always appealed to Hanne, but in reality she always found it a struggle – especially the hills; and there were plenty of hills surrounding Oberwinkel. Hanne preferred talking, and so mixing the two was difficult, though it did help to take her mind off the inclines. It had all seemed so effortless aged ten in that summer of 1963. She'd forgotten much of the route over the fields and meadows and that wasn't surprising, yet it was all very familiar territory. The memories cascading through her head were very clear, though Hanne wondered whether she needed them. Returning to see an old border post didn't really seem so significant except that it was a bonding exercise for her and the cousins. She was happy in the knowledge that they were all clearly related and that they'd probably grown more alike as the years had passed. They could have been sisters, a thought shared between the three of them.

Heidemarie was not at all slowed by the passage of the years. She was the most excited that morning, as excited as she'd been as a nine-year-old, even now racing ahead to look over the next brow as Hanne and Heike chatted in English, both in agreement that Heidemarie was always the organiser and motivator, whether it was the reunion or a place to visit like this. But then she always exacted a price – a small price, but a price nonetheless.

'How old is Heidemarie?'

'A bit younger than you, a bit older than me.'

'Only she runs ahead like some manic rabbit. Where does she get her energy from, for goodness sake?'

'She lives here, Hanne. She walks these hills all the time.'

Had Heike not stopped to point out the border post on the next ridge, Hanne might well have continued walking never having noticed the remnants: the bare, concrete posts; the rusted remains of twisted wire, chain link, bolts; and the tower. She'd have walked on with her eyes to the ground simply talking of all manner of things.

'Is that it?' she asked incredulously.

'The remains, yes.'

But Hanne could only remember that summer's day, when it was so still; that warm, deep blue sky; the dog panting, drooling for chocolate.

This was a very different place altogether.

If Hanne wanted to talk in confidence to Heike, then she would speak in English. It didn't seem so rude as Heidemarie – now well out of their orbit – had already reached the post hundreds of metres ahead of them, ferreting around as if looking to find something that would connect her with the past; something someone might have dropped and mislaid all those years ago.

'I didn't think you'd want to come up here,' said Hanne.

'I didn't – particularly. Heidemarie doesn't understand; I suppose because Bruno's still alive she thinks no permanent harm was done. But she doesn't understand what it was like living in East Berlin.'

'What happened exactly? Your letters stopped. Last we heard he'd been in some sort of accident, but we were never quite sure what had happened.'

'He was a boy playing a silly game – not unlike his father and uncle.'

Heike turned her gaze toward a distant bluff; she seemed reluctant to say any more and Hanne wondered that it might be too painful, but she was curious about the photos Heike had sent her not long after settling in East Berlin.

'Those photos of you and Roland when you were first married...' asked Hanne, her voice trailing off, fearing that she was maybe probing a little too deep.

Heike, always polite, reassured her, 'I was so naive – so idealistic then.'

'There was a photo of you standing in front of your car – in the street? I think it was a Trabant or something like that?'

'A blue Trabant with a white roof. Me leaning against the bonnet dressed in black, with sunglasses that I'd brought with me from home – here in Bavaria. How cool was that?' She looked away into the distance as if avoiding Hanne's scrutiny. 'I thought... I don't know what I thought!'

Heike's demeanour reflected a distinct change in tone. Hanne silently cursed herself for being too inquisitive. Best to lay off for a moment, but a door was beginning to open.

The brief silence between them prompted Heike to continue as if she were answering her own questions as much as those of Hanne: 'Stupid little girl from the West who believed she could be a communist, too. Communism was better. Yes? The opposite to fascism – that awful history on our shoulders. I couldn't bear it! Remember what I thought? I was suspicious that everyone was a fascist. Remember?' But Hanne didn't remember; this was all a revelation.

'Then I met my man – Roland the great writer, the great journalist. The hero in a post-Stalinist, post-fascist state! He was the son of a hero – a man who had rescued his mother-to-be and fled Berlin, with the Russians hot on their heels. That's what we thought we were, or could be – some sort of folk heroes who would change something. You know, things were good when that photo was taken. Roland had been promoted and Bruno was a happy boy at school.'

Hanne smiled, desperately trying to recapture a lighter mood. 'It was a lovely photo – the sun shining, the street looking lovely with the trees in the background. And you looked like a film star!'

'We'd only just got that car – for Roland's work. It was a good time: we had our apartment – flat, as you call it in England – and that funny little car...'

'Do you miss it?'

'The car?!'

'No! The life you led?'

'Yes, always I miss it. That was Bruno's home. That was the street he grew up on. It was a nice street. One day I might go back to live... Who knows?'

'You sent a picture of the apartment block and of Roland working at his typewriter.'

'They must have checked it – checked those photos I sent you. The censor checked everything.'

'It's not like they were photos of the Wall or soldiers or policemen or Stasi headquarters.'

'They watched us all the time, Hanne. That's what *this* place was all about – watching, listening, making copious notes. We liked taking photos. I'd have sent you more, but...'

They would have talked more, but they'd reached the old fence and Heidemarie was eager to see their faces. She could barely contain her excitement.

'Do you remember it, Hanne? Do you remember when we came here all those years ago when we were children?'

'I remember it clearly.'

'Now you see it is a monument preserved for future generations. There is a signboard telling you the history. I brought my children here and I will bring my grandchildren. We were part of that history, Hanne.'

'I remember the guard coming out. He was very friendly. Do you remember the shot that rang out as we were walking away?'

'Ah! They were always doing that – testing their weapons. You surely didn't think they were shooting at us?'

'I wasn't so sure at the time.' Hanne exchanged glances with Heike, who was keeping a discreet distance from Heidemarie's enthusiasm.

They agreed that it was strange to be able to walk and explore where they could not back in 1963. Now they could walk all around the tower examining it from every angle. The dog exercise area had gone – the large, brick-built kennel and the extensive grass run.

'Do you remember the guard dog?' asked Hanne.

'Trude? Yes, she was a lovely dog.'

Of course, Heidemarie remembered the dog. She would! That's just the sort of thing she'd know, and commit to memory – the dog's ruddy name!

Heidemarie was already beginning to irritate Hanne. She wanted to talk to Heike again without Heidemarie, and the only way to do that was to be rude and speak only English and, for the sake of a few hours on a windy hill, that was not going to happen.

Instead, she replied in faltering German: 'Father had one just like her – "Tascha". She would guard the money he paid to the flower pickers. No one would go near the van when Tascha was in there – only Father. He loved that dog maybe more than he loved us.'

'Look at the view, Hanne.' Heidemarie had moved on, leaving the dog subject behind. 'You can see everywhere from here.'

'It must have been so cold in winter,' remarked Hanne, pushing her hands deep into her coat pockets and thinking it was already cold enough for an autumn day. The sky was a low, heavy grey, so unlike the cloudless blue summer sky of 1963 when the guard had greeted them. Then, the tall grass had been blowing in the breeze and Hanne had thought it all looked like a wavy green ocean.

Today was cheerless, the soaking wet grass causing her feet to be horribly wet, and that fact alone caused her to empathise with the men who had been sent here – like the kindly guard. What had been his fate, she wondered? *Poor man sent out to this outpost of the Soviet empire!*

She remembered him as a handsome man – tall and dark, not unlike the Hollywood star Clint Walker, whom as a child she had watched every week and adored.

Pre-pubescent feelings had been stirred all those years ago yet she hadn't been able to make sense of it then. Now she could; it made perfect sense. She'd met in real life a "star" and that was probably Heidemarie's memory too. Not the dog – fine though she was – it was the dashing man behind the dog. Unobtainable, remote and utterly safe behind that gigantic, endless chain-link fence that went on and on forever.

She'd imagined that all the many hundreds of posts only ended (or began) once they reached the Baltic.

Suddenly, Heike dropped to her knees near the base of the tower, her eyes scanning the long grass as if she too was searching for something. Looking up in desperation she cried out: 'This is a sad place!'

'What do you mean, Heike?' asked a startled Heidemarie.

'I mean it is sad – full of ghosts. We were children then. Times change.'

The walk back to Oberwinkel was, to say the least, sombre. Gone was the sense of adventure. Heike was subdued whilst Heidemarie tried too hard to chivvy the group along; but something had spooked Heike. *This is one for the memoirs,* thought Hanne – three daft, middle-aged women climbing a hill in the wet to relive their past.

Sensing the change, Heidemarie was clinging to the group, afraid that it was something she'd done to upset the status quo, so there was no opportunity for Hanne to get Heike alone. Hanne sensed a story was beginning to emerge, a story she didn't want to leave until she knew the full facts of Heike's time in East Berlin.

Heike, too, would be leaving for home and had a long way to go – Lubeck. Soon the reunion would be over for another two years. Much of the family had already left Oberwinkel; it was always a brief get-together, an opportunity on just one day to say hello and exchange notes, update contact details, realise just how quickly time was passing for the "children" of the war generation. Where it would go in time, no one knew.

Nobody attending, with the exception of Marco, was a "Mauer" by name. Oberwinkel was a very pleasant little village, but it was merely a stopping-off point for an ancestor. With the exception of Heidemarie, the "family" were not to be found here anymore. Even Oma's grave would soon be gone.

Heidemarie was the motivator – the power behind the reunion – and though she showed no sign of retiring from her role, there would come a day when it would all be too much. Who would come then from England, Canada, Austria or the Baltic to remember a gathering of a Bavarian family that had, by name, at least, become so rare in their native homeland?

Maybe it didn't matter. Maybe the job was done. Connections had been made and fostered over these past fifty years. The Wall was gone and history marches on regardless. The Western powers had found common goals and new objectives for their commercial expansion. The likelihood of them ever turning in on themselves for a third time was simply implausible. "British PM embraces German Chancellor" ran the front-page headline of a Bavarian newspaper that Hanne had picked up on her arrival two days ago in Frankfurt and was now spread across the rear floor of her black Opel hire car. She didn't care for politicians of any nationality.

She wasn't sure just how many more reunions she'd attend. It was always interesting to see the cousins, but it was only Heidemarie and Heike who regularly kept in touch, sending cards at Christmas and the occasional email. Her sons had no interest in the reunion; though one day they still might, she thought. And there were so many places to see on the Continent – why come back here all the time?

She'd keep an open mind.

For now, her thoughts were of the journey home. Drive back to Frankfurt, drop off the car and catch the train for Brussels. She'd be home by the middle of the week. There was just one more day to enjoy, so she wanted to fill it with a variety of little activities. She wanted to take a walk by herself this time to the haunts she'd established as a ten-year-old. She particularly wanted to see the deer lookout where she'd loved to climb and sit for hour upon hour. Hopefully that would still be in place. She'd look at the stream, too, where her father had almost drowned as a boy. Hopefully that wouldn't be diverted or polluted.

Sandy wouldn't be with her; he'd already gone – pressing business, not at home but in Provence, followed by a week in Andalusia. His job as a sales consultant now working in a freelance capacity gave him more freedom but required more of his time; both of them resented the need for money, but his retirement drew ever closer and that's what kept them going.

She had the rental house all to herself that evening and maybe Heike would be able to join her for dinner so they could resume their conversation.

The house, or "cottage" to use an English term for that's how it would have been described had it been in an English village, was relatively easy to find due to its round tower annexe situated on a bend in the road that climbed away from the medieval village toward more modern residential estates that were no less pleasant but lacked the character of the old village. Either the tower had been added to the house or the house had been joined to the tower. Hanne wasn't sure as to the history of the building, but it was a feature that helped to secure rentals – a fairy-tale Rapunzel tower that would have appealed immensely to the ten-year-old Hanne. If only Oma had lived in a tower in Rip van Winkle all those years ago. She'd have taken home scores of photos as proof to the kids in Cornwall who might otherwise never have believed it.

Hanne also thought it very novel to be playing host to her German cousin in a German village in a German house. She would cook a German meal, pour some schnapps and be German for one last evening.

***

Chapter 5

Heike's Story

(Landshagen, Bavaria)

A pleasant enough hotel set at low level so as not to disturb the view from a popular spa town, it was quite modern and well equipped, but nothing special. The postcards could remain in the desk drawer – not worth taking. Ironically, it was very close to where Heike had grown up; her mother's home was a walk away, or would have been had history played out differently.

Getting ready, having accepted Hanne's invitation, Heike fussed over what to wear, which wasn't like her at all, and she was in two minds about what she would say if Hanne wanted to pursue the Berlin subject.

How silly to even mention it! Hanne didn't even know that much. For a moment that afternoon everything flooded back because of that wretched visit to the monument. Perhaps it would have been good, even cathartic, to tell Hanne what was in her head, but now that time and feeling had passed. She'd buried it all again, locked it away in the glove compartment of her mind.

It had been nothing more than a "moment" and now that moment had gone.

She no more wanted to go there than look at the old family house just up the road. In one respect, she appreciated Hanne's interest, but this was ancient, personal history and talking about it would open old wounds. If she did open up, then Hanne would want to analyse it, chew it over with her, look for a solution, recommend someone to see or some well-meaning organisation. That was the kind of person Hanne was: she facilitated such things for people; helped them to find answers. But most of all, she didn't want Hanne to take it home to Cornwall and discuss it with Sandy and the "boys".

Heike hardly knew Hanne's children; they'd only met on a couple of occasions, the most recent being when Hugo died and Heike attended the funeral. From Cornwall it would spread across the wider family and be discussed by Heidemarie and Heidemarie's in-laws, who were close. It would be discussed in Canada and South Africa and God knows where else.

Like Hanne, she saw little of the wider family, and that was something of a self-infliction because she preferred the distance that Lubeck offered her – a distance from her past. In Heike's mind she was the rebellious black sheep – the half-American communist who turned her back on the "Fatherland" to embrace the cause of communism because she was so vehemently anti-fascist.

Where to begin with this one? Not everyone was so anti-fascist. Start with the lipstick – lipstick for fair skin and hair, so nothing extravagant. Hanne was so fortunate with her thick, auburn hair! The mirror is a good listener. Start with the mirror. The mirror will reflect everything...

*

Donnerstag, Januar 6th (Epiphany), 1972
Landshagen, Bavaria

Heike couldn't bear the post-war legacy; the weight on her young shoulders she felt was too much to bear. Her intolerant

American father, absent for much of the time and becoming more absent by the day, had raised her to believe that the only way was the American way – this, from a man who was spiteful and intolerant.

He hated communism in all its forms and therefore was as good a recruitment sergeant for communism as anyone could be. To rid the world of communism was his stated aim as a military man and it was the only thing keeping him in the military. Without it, he'd have hightailed it out of "Krautland" on the first transport heading Stateside – wife and children or no wife and children. He applauded American involvement in Vietnam and cheered loudly whenever a "gook", as he and his chums called the Vietcong, was pictured in the media either dead or captured.

Heike had seriously considered taking a heavy hammer to his collection of handguns in a bid to render them useless, but most of all with a view to letting off steam. It infuriated her that he would clean them on the kitchen table as if they were cutlery, yet he never polished the cutlery. Mama was too easy-going, too tolerant.

So communism was retaliation. She embraced the East like a Victorian orphan brought up in the workhouse who longed to return to their natural mother.

That New Year, she was in the midst of hatching a plan: a plan that would take her across the Wall and into East Germany – forever.

The plan involved packing two cases, buying a train ticket for Berlin then somehow taking a city train into the Eastern sector; if that wasn't possible then she'd present herself to the guards at Checkpoint Charlie and request asylum. It was a given that she'd have to cross some heavily guarded barrier, and research (through membership of the DKP – the German Communist Party) had shown her that some Germans *did* go the other way and that they were "most welcome" on the other side. She wasn't naïve, she wasn't expecting to receive a heroine's welcome, but she was sure the authorities would be honour bound to accept her application just as soon as they realised how genuine she was.

Her plan did have consequences; it wasn't going to be a victimless flight. Mama was going to be heartbroken. If Heike were to tell her, then that would be the end of everything because there was no way that Mama would let her go. Once behind the Iron Curtain, the curtain would come down. There would be no turning back.

A well-meaning lie might just soften the blow. The lie was this: she had a job to go to – an appointment with a prominent West German employment agency that would find her secretarial work. After all, no young woman could stay in a backwater such as Landshagen all her life. Move with the times; people are mobile; youngsters are expected to move onward and upward. What's more, she was bilingual – any city agency would give their eye teeth for someone with language ability. Who knows where she might end up? She might even be assigned to an embassy of all places.

Since leaving school she'd worked as a waitress and a receptionist – small town jobs for those who were content with their lot – but the infrequent arrival home of her American father, often unannounced, meant that she was rarely content. He never said 'Hi' or even 'Goodbye'. He'd just turn up with a dark menacing cloud hovering over his close-cropped square head, demanding this or that; it was all too much for a young woman who was now old enough to go her own way.

"Operation Lie" would be acted upon at the very first opportunity. First, she would apply to a genuine agency, as it was vital that Mama should see for herself a written invitation. Mama was no fool.

Operation Lie would be the utmost secret. Not even Peter, her younger brother, with whom she shared everything and protected like a mother hen, would be informed of this one. Sad, too, that she would have to leave him behind, as he'd be good company and, like her, showed every sign of becoming a good communist. Maybe, when she was settled in the East, she could sponsor him to join her.

Peter's belief – from which she drew much comfort – was that their real father was in fact a Russian soldier – Valentin Petrick – a mysterious friend of Mama's who had remained in contact. They knew that Mama thought highly of this old friend, that she'd visited him on occasion before the Wall went up, and that they weren't to mention his name in the (rare) presence of "Papa" aka "GI Joe".

It was Peter's opinion that "Joe" had taken their mother on in the years after the war because he'd got her pregnant but the baby was stillborn. Under pressure from his superiors he'd reluctantly married Kirsten. They were allocated married quarters until such time as he bought the house at Landshagen with the intention of housing his new wife well away from camp.

When asked how he might know all this, Peter simply said, 'Oma hinted at such; and when I asked Mama whether we were Papa Joe's children, she wouldn't answer.'

For the wider family, American blood in the Mauer line was one thing; it had brought food and some money during desperate times of hardship; but Russian blood was not acceptable under any circumstance. Russian blood would have resulted in suspicion and being ostracised, and these were just the good points.

It had not been an easy life for young Kirsten Mauer during the war, fearing for her elder brothers, trying to run the farm along with her widowed mother, and then the stinking, savage bitterness of the post-war years with all its scarcity of basics: food, clothes, essential materials, and all without a man to support them. Kirsten's war had begun in May 1945.

Heike had always suspected that her mother had married out of necessity, not love. She often wondered who on earth could love the obscenely gruff and dirty GI sergeant who made no attempt to learn a word of German and whose language was peppered with cursing and contempt for those around him.

He openly hated the Germans but actually hated the British more. 'At least you're not an Limey bitch!' he'd shout at Kirsten during some of his more "colourful" moods. He would claim to anyone who would listen that he'd "rescued" Kirsten from "Hitler's rat-infested garbage dump". That Eisenhower should have "nuked" Germany and later Britain, then marched into Russia to finish off the commies. That the US should have gone to war against the British Empire in 1935 when the time was right and then none of this "godawful stink would ever have happened".

None of this did Hanne know, and Heike preferred it that way. Uncle Hugo might have suspected. He was never an "admirer" of Sgt "GI Joe" Savers.

Heike had originally tried to find excuses for her American father — if father he was. According to his account, related solely by Mama, he'd been a witness to the uncovering of the Malmedy massacre. He, and he alone, according to his story of that bitter Ardennes winter of 1944, lifted the frozen bodies of no less than eighty dead comrades from the snow and ice.

Later, with the war over and those guilty parties brought to book, Joe had blown his top when the commanding SS Officer responsible for the massacre, Obersturmbannfürher Joachim Peiper, escaped the death sentence along with every other participant — spared, it is said, because the US needed the support of anti-communist Germans in a divided country and the support of German-descended Americans at home.

Joe also claimed within the family to have been photographed surveying the tragic scene and to have witnessed dead children also massacred by Peiper. By sheer coincidence, Heike had seen the photo he referred to in *Time* magazine many years later while she was waiting for a doctor's appointment; and yes, remarkably the man surveying the awful scene did indeed look like Joe.

Why not? Why would he lie? The dark, grainy, stocky figure in the photo looked just like him, stood like him. The facial features were not so clear, but the stance of the man was Joe to a 'T'. His weight characteristically shifted to his right foot while the photographer snapped the scene. Joe did that in photos. Heike considered it a very American pose – laid back – whereas a German would stand feet spread apart with his hands clasped behind his back as if ordered to stand easy. Germans stood at ease, they didn't relax.

She wondered whether perhaps this incident had been the catalyst: Malmedy created the monster that assumed the role of father. Maybe prior to that discovery in the forest, Joe had been a very different human being? Maybe that whole disgusting view of hell and the lack of justice following removed the gentle and considerate man he might otherwise have been?

He never once made reference to any relatives, living or dead. He seemed to be an orphan whose only true family was the US Army. She didn't even know exactly where he was from: Texas? Wyoming? Detroit? If he was indeed an orphan, no wonder he couldn't relate to a family unit. Yes, he provided food and a place at a US Army school and he brought them up to speak English, but love to him was patriotism, not a personal feeling for another being. Joe loved his country – the flag, the President, the Constitution – but cared not one jot for any common man, woman or child.

Particularly, there was no love for Kirsten; it was as if he'd taken her prisoner and deprived her from then on of any affection or happiness. For a man who freely admitted that he'd never seen any action, least of all been in a position to capture the enemy, Kirsten became his ideal captive.

Joe's "war" had been at the tail end of the Allied advance, witnessing, but never doing. Dutifully, he cleaned and oiled his weapons daily but never so much as fired a shot in anger, and it bugged the hell out of him.

Deprived of an outlet for his emotions, Joe and his company formed the "mopping-up" brigade, always a week or even a month behind their advancing comrades, and it drove him CRAZY!

*

Sonntag 23rd Oktober, 6.40 pm
Hotel Room 218

She looked deep into her reflection. Joe wasn't there. Thank God! Nowhere in her skin, in her design, in her structure, demeanour, hair – either texture or colour – he wasn't there.

Peter was right all along. If Joe were their natural father, he'd show in some respect by now, even in the odd quirky mannerism that comes with middle age, some indicator of genetics. Genetics never lie. Kirsten was there alright, looking back through those small, hooded, pale blue eyes, the tendency toward short-sightedness, the stubby Bavarian fingers, the round shoulders and, most of all, the voice.

'Is that you, Kirsten?' people would answer the phone to Heike even after her mother had died.

Peter was not like Joe either. Tall as a giant, thin as a stick and as fair as summer corn. He was no more Joe's descendant than she was. There was a grandchild now – Emmi – but again no signs of Joe anywhere to be seen.

Two generations: they were in the clear; it was like being declared innocent of a crime they hadn't committed only it had taken well over half a century to prove their innocence.

Like Kirsten, Heike didn't normally make an effort when it came to going out. Nobody ever made that effort in the East because it was bourgeois. She wasn't like Hanne in that respect (Hanne was very bourgeois), but tonight she'd take the time and make herself presentable as she appreciated the invitation and genuinely liked her English cousin a great deal; it was a reciprocated true fondness. They so rarely saw one another and it could have been left with a: 'Well, *auf wiedersehen*! See you in a couple of years. Take care!'

If she'd been at home, she'd have looked for some old albums, picked out some photos – the Berlin photos – photos that would have helped to describe things. Yes, that bloody old rust heap of a Trabant. Loved it to begin with, hence the photo with its missive:

"Dear Hanne and Family, Everything is fine here in Berlin. I am sitting on the bonnet of a car that is known as a Trabant. Do you have Trabant cars in England? We also have cars called Skoda and many Trabants. We love driving here. Love, Heike"

Also staring back at her: the *young* Heike, still recognisable in some respects but much diminished. Heike the idealist, the naïve, misguided communist.

At home in Lubeck, she could have shown Hanne pictures of Roland, at the typewriter, their apartment, strolls in the park – all captured with the indestructible Praktica 5TL SLR, their beloved camera taken by the Stasi and eventually recovered by Roland in the milieu that was the ransacking of Stasi Headquarters in 1990. Liberated in triumph, it fell out of its case as Roland climbed the stairs; falling like a brick it could so nearly have killed someone, dropping three floors down through the stairwell before landing with a bang on a tiled floor, miraculously missing the heads of the surging masses that had invaded the building with him – all in search of answers.

Roland went everywhere with that camera and even kept it on a shelf in the living room for anyone to see, as if it were some sort of trophy. His father had often said to Heike that the beauty of growing up with nothing means that when you have something – however small – you love it and cherish it all the more.

Official permission to carry the camera and use it as a card-carrying journalist was almost a government permit to be happy in your work, and how rare was that? Senior colleagues had chastised him: 'You wouldn't have been allowed to carry it in my day, let alone take family snaps!' or 'You're lucky, young comrade. There was a time when the government would have locked you up or at least sent you out with a minder.'

Only Heike knew that Roland wasn't so lucky. His job was "minded" very much indeed. Whatever he wrote or photographed was carefully checked and double-checked by any number of "minders". They followed him, too.

Sometimes he'd be aware of their presence, most often he wasn't. There was no freedom to seek out a story. Stories were given to him by a desk chief saying: 'Run an 800-word piece on the steelworks at so-and-so. Take some nice pictures of the production process. Talk up the employment side, productivity, you know. Don't mention the foreign workers. Find a positive angle – exports, good working conditions, that sort of thing.'

Roland knew all about "that sort of thing"; it didn't need explaining. He knew to toe the line from the moment he began the job as an editorial assistant. Good East Germans did not question; it went without saying. It was Heike's Western influence, her ideas of free speech and her explanation of the role of a Western journalist, that's what made the difference to Roland.

She actually began to question him: 'Well, why don't you do this or do that? Why didn't you question him/the process…', whatever. She couldn't help herself because she was *really* a Westerner.

*

Samstag 29th April 1972, 10.38 am
The moment of Heike's defection

The door slammed shut on Heike's life as a West German at precisely 10.38 am. It was the door of a detention cell; it was every bit as stark and grey as she'd been expecting so there were no surprises.

It was an indignant arrival in the East. Gripped, pulled, pushed, cajoled and stripped. Then: 'Wait! Wait until you're fetched.'

'When will that be?'

'Shut up! We'll tell you when.'

It was a long wait, a very long wait – over a week – a week of cold, heavy, grey metal imprisonment. Only when that time was complete did the panel convene. Eventually, somewhat reluctantly, *they* (the panel) convened. They didn't know what to do with her because she was clearly an individual. Here was a girl from the West, telling them that she was a good communist, but they knew she was missing the point – she was thinking for herself. She'd made up her mind and had therefore committed a selfish act. In trying to be, she'd failed. No one was supposed to "think" in East Germany. Thinking was dangerous.

To the panel, she insisted: 'I am a true patriot, that's why I'm here.' But the panel found this rather nonsensical. She talked in-depth of the manifesto, the "glorious socialist revolution", to the very people who themselves were filled with doubts because Ulbricht had brought his own doubts to the table just a few years prior to her arrival.

'She thinks this is 1953!' someone whispered.

'Isn't this where the best of the real Germany can be found?' she asked boldly, her words recorded and paraphrased in the following week's ministerial meeting.

On the third day, she requested, and received, a large notepad on which she could write down all her thoughts about why she was defecting, which she had to admit was extremely unusual for someone who wasn't escaping justice in the West.

I admit I have no real concept of what being a communist is really all about. I believe it is about an ideal; about fairness and equality; that a socialist world is one that would never, ever tolerate the detested fascism ever again. The communist state, to my mind, forms a bulwark that protects those inside the vessel from fascism. The "real" Germany is east of the Wall, not west. The West has been corrupted by capitalism – American capitalism; and I loathe it. I hate everything American and I am convinced they will destroy Europe. The rich will get infinitely richer, while the poor work and suffer.

I hate America because Americans have recruited Nazis for their own nationalistic programs. These men they call "the good Nazis". Werner von Braun is a case in point; Speer, too. Their murderous, bloody-handed comrades have escaped thanks to sympathetic clergy within the Catholic Church. I hate that institution with all my being. It is the way the disappearance of leading Nazis from Germany has been so orchestrated, so easy and unhindered. The attitude has been: Let them fly, let them flourish; we don't care! The Jews cared, the British and French seemed to care, but their debt is to the United States, so they look the other way and in this respect they too are complicit. Only Simon Wiesenthal seems to have the will to bring these murderers to book. I believe Simon Wiesenthal will reclaim justice for mankind.

(Heike adored Simon Wiesenthal as if he were a pop star. She confessed that her interest bordered on the obsessive and, had she lived in Israel, she would willingly have been an acolyte.)

I consider the "real" Germany – the "real" Fatherland – to be here in the GDR not the West.

I see no reason why I can't apply for citizenship in the GDR. Some have done it, and I know they are relatively few. In the West it is called "defecting". I am following my heart.

Heike Savers

This was all highly suspicious. Panel members wrote down their feelings on a daily basis and filed them away for reference.

"You want to live in the East? Are you for real? Go home, child. Grow up, why don't you?"

This is clearly a new CIA tactic: send in a child who claims a hatred of all things capitalism. No more back-door 'spies'; walk right in and denounce the West because the GDR will welcome you with open arms. And what's more, this one is right out of the American military establishment and admits as much. Put her back on the bus! She's wasting our time"

"She's not CIA or any Western agent – she's clearly Red Army Faction. It's as plain as the nose on my face. She's on the run from the authorities."

" We could send the little cow up the line to Moscow. Let the KGB sort her out!"

"Play their game. If she is a plant - a sleeper - let's be dumb. Why not? If she's Red Army then she'll break cover at somepoint. Whoever she is, this little cow could be a cash cow, leading us into a whole new network. Put her in the hands of the Stasi. I know just the man..."

Some days the panel would summon her; other days, she was left to stew in her cell – a prisoner of her own making. With nothing to read, she slept to pass the time and in sleeping dreamt of the days that awaited her. Her "Sandman" reassured her that: "It will be good eventually. Stick with it, because once you leave here the early days will be the best and then you will establish yourself with the help of others and everything will be alright."

Depression was never far away and would generally kick in upon waking; the continual light, no window on the city surrounding her, no morning, no night-time, no birds to sing.

Throughout incarceration they watched her every move. She invented her own games, such as "guessing the time" as her watch had been removed. Another game was guessing who was in the corridor – male or female? Young or old? She would give "names" to the anonymous busy feet of people going about their business. *That's Hans today. Oh, that's sounds like Ilke – she's so light on her feet*. In return, they listened for her silence.

The panel: a diverse collegiate of the communist school of world affairs hurriedly convened because a girl had turned up unexpectedly of her own volition to a dull party where no invites had ever been issued. If this were to become a regular occurrence, they could put a procedure in place.

The panel consisted of: a high-ranking Stasi officer; a high court judge; a politburo man come all the way from Moscow by slow train; a retired army general; and assorted Party professionals both male and female chosen for their unfaltering allegiance. Some of these had been Nazi Party officials many years previously in their youth, but Heike never suspected.

Faces came and went: some fiercely stern, others just curious. There were those who were quite animated and human, while others seemed as pallid, stiff and lifeless as shop mannequins.

Each time the panel sat in that draughty, vacuous chamber, there was great rubbing and wringing of hands and fingers. Their constant fidgeting unsettled Heike, who had naively imagined that the GDR would have been ecstatic in their welcome of a wannabe citizen. They were not.

Files were ordered and brought in by underlings who scurried in and out, depositing each file for minute examination before it was taken away again by another underling.

Conspicuous by her youth, a thin, very pale young woman in a knee-length plaid skirt took copious notes and refrained from uttering a single word in all the time that Heike saw her. Altogether, this miserable bunch of granite-grey, largely middle-aged Party members, who would have seen themselves as anything but jailers, held the keys to the anti-kingdom – the only place Heike wanted to be.

They sought to know everything about the nineteen-year-old defector. This was in itself most welcome; Heike had no intention of holding anything back as she was in need of unburdening her soul. She told them about GI Joe Savers, carefully detaching herself, claiming that he most probably wasn't her father; that her father was very likely Russian.

She told them about her "English family; her English cousins" and "Uncle Hugo". Nothing derogatory. She had to tell them everything she'd ever experienced and everyone she'd ever known – especially non-Germans. She was to leave no one out, however boring, however inconsequential.

Some of the panel were experienced interrogators. They'd interrogated some notable British, American and German defectors whose double-agent status was suddenly compromised or because they were on the run from law enforcement as terrorists or criminals. Heike was very different; there was no precedent for someone simply arriving unannounced; it never happened.

In Bavaria, East German sleepers were given a brief to report back on Fräulein Heike Savers. Education, family, work experience – anything they could find. Kirsten received a very friendly visit from a young couple armed with clipboards saying they were simply following up on Heike's application to join "their" company in Berlin. They needed to ascertain a few facts. Kirsten – wholly oblivious – was only too happy to oblige with whatever information they needed.

Even in faraway Cornwall, Hugo Mauer was visited by a couple claiming to be Bavarian tourists trying to find the right road for St Michael's Mount. He later recalled their visit as pure happenstance that such a nice couple, coincidently well acquainted with Oberwinkel, should be touring in the area. Unwittingly, he spoke proudly of his Oberwinkel connection and his Bavarian family even though the couple were complete strangers to him. He was by nature a very discreet individual, but such was their easy manner that he even invited them to drop in for tea that evening and stay the night, which they did. On leaving, and after complimenting him and Rene on a fine bed and breakfast, they promised to keep in touch. He never heard from them again, though in later years he remembered them fondly: 'They were such friendly people – typical Bavarians.'

There was just one more nocturnal dream for Heike before she was eventually released. It was a particularly graphic dream that both disturbed and enchanted her. She dreamt that the entire building was a camera. Inside its casing, she felt lost and vulnerable; she didn't know how to enter or how to leave the giant camera. She was both inside and outside the mechanism, clambering over its cogs, looking in and looking out through its lens. That was the last visit from the "Sandman" – he never called again.

On release, it was arranged that she meet a newspaperman. He was going to run her story, as it was so fascinating. His name was Roland, and he was also going to take some pictures of her – didn't matter that she didn't look her best; he thought she looked wonderful! That was the first time she looked into the lens of the Praktica and saw beyond to the face of the man she would marry.

For a few weeks at least, the sun shone on her "Fatherland". She believed she had been welcomed as a "lost daughter", and even made the paper – Roland's paper. It was good to begin with. That can be the way of life; the early days are sometimes the best.

*

My God! Am I going to tell Hanne all this?

In the original copy that Roland wrote, Heike claimed not to be an affiliate of any organisation; she had no criminal record, though she joked that she might have had, had she killed her father. It was a nervous joke and not really appropriate for a GDR Berlin readership. In all, she really did believe she was in a better place than rural Bavaria or a USAAF base.

She asked for these words to be emphasised: 'America has used the atom bomb in anger – the only country to do so! We must all defend ourselves.' Then insisted that this be stated, believing it would impress her panel.

Naively, she talked about her debriefing and that it had seemed interminable; that she was genuine in her resolve to be a good East German and that she would not break under any circumstances. Nor would she run home to the West crying her eyes out.

Heike was not free to roam. She was offered a job immediately, a post she couldn't turn down as freedom of choice was something she'd left on the train in West Berlin. Her role: full employment as an interpreter, making best use of her bilingual skills. Her office: within the same acreage as her incarceration.

She'd passed countless checks with the security services, she was free to enter the system, but they were convinced she was a "plant" so they assigned a mentor – a tall, slim, charming Prussian gentleman with an aristocratic background. He would oversee her work and lodgings and anything she might need. She would know him simply as Herr Comrade Frederick Wendt, a seemingly harmless, kind individual who bore no resemblance to the stony grey panel members who'd been her jailers and interrogators for the last month.

Wendt had been assigned because, like her, he was a defector. The only difference being that he had been a big fish in the pages of mid-twentieth century European history.

Wendt had been known in pre-war years as Norbert Weber – Germany's champion tennis player. He had won Olympic gold, shaken Hitler's hand and beamed into the Führer's smiling face.

In 1941, he'd held the rank of Obersturmführer as a famed member of the National Socialist Party, but the end of war brought his glory days to an abrupt end. Captured, interrogated and imprisoned briefly by the Allies, Weber was released into a defeated land of raped women and fatherless children. "Kicked out into the pitch blackness of hell!" he later recalled in his autobiography. By 1947, he was a celebrity has-been without purpose, rank or money, so leaving reinvention as his only saviour.

His talent, however, was purely limited to knocking a tennis ball across a court, yet he tried on several occasions to forge businesses, but failed disastrously each time. The year that Heike was born, 1953, saw him emigrate first to Argentina and later to Brazil and Ceylon, before eventually returning to Hamburg in 1957 where he was arrested for embezzlement and various tax irregularities.

Narrowly escaping a prison sentence, Weber defected to the East that very year where he was soon employed on East Germany's newly formed Olympic Committee. The famed athlete who had won Wimbledon and shaken the hand of King George VI was to find a new appreciative audience amongst the communist nations of the East.

For his services to sport he would later be awarded the Olympic Order, and his new nomenclature of Frederick Wendt ensured his former Nazi past was never questioned again.

Heike knew nothing of his past, nor did she suspect. He was simply the tall, slim, erudite gentleman with white hair who spoke softly and extended his hand in friendship. He was the gift for her month of cold isolation.

Afraid that her mother Kirsten would see the Berlin newspaper article, she wrote a letter that would explain something about the past month.

… the stern faces I'd expected initially, but I began to fear the worse after the monotony of each day of interrogation was leading me to believe they considered me a spy and would either incarcerate me for good in a Gulag or even shoot me. I would disappear and no one would be any the wiser. No one manhandled me during my questioning. The food was okay, and the guards kept their distance. They seemed neither to like nor dislike me. They made no reference to my name, just: 'Come with us now!' or 'Stay there until we say otherwise.' And: 'Don't speak until you're spoken to. Understand?' But now the awful transition is complete, I've been assigned to a good man who treats me as if I were his own daughter, and I so badly need a father. He is my ideal of a surrogate parent, sometimes speaking fluent English

to me in an attempt to gain my full confidence I think, suspecting that something I utter just might reveal some hidden agenda or identity.

Please don't be offended, Mama. I've wanted to be here for so long...

She never sent the letter, and for a while Kirsten remained oblivious as to her daughter's true whereabouts.

The Sandman was absolutely right – things got off to a great start. Yes, the job was monotonous, her colleagues not particularly friendly and the "DDD" (Dirty, Draughty, Dank) accommodation was less than appealing, but there was Roland – her first East German friend.

Not that they became friends instantly; or rather, Roland tried a little too hard. The professional interview was fine. Roland was experienced enough to treat the assignment as he would any other – put the subject at ease, ask the right questions, place the subject in an appropriate setting for a photo. For this, he used the backdrop of the Wall itself and a tower, his angle being that Heike was now safely on the "right side" of the Wall.

Heike, for her part, was a willing interviewee only too happy to express her side of things, blissfully unaware that her individual thoughts and needs counted for nothing here.

Roland was barely twelve months older than Heike but seemed much more world weary – she thought. Not bad looking, probably married with umpteen children, as he was clearly not single because he had no pride in his appearance whatsoever; drowning in that ratty, oversized pullover, and he even turned up riding an old bicycle that was too small for him. She approved of the bicycle: *Communists ride bicycles, or should do* was her belief.

He asked all the pertinent questions, which were easy-peasy because she had graduated straight out of the "University of Inquisition" having spent the last month answering every question that could be put to her about her short life, so this bit was a doddle.

That was followed by the photo session: 'How should I stand? Or maybe I should sit?'

'Both.'

'Do you want me like this?' she asked mischievously, balancing on one leg her arms outstretched.

'No. You're not a model. You're a... You're a...'

'Traitor to the West?'

'Well...'

'Defector?'

'Defector – yes.'

'So how would I...?'

'Just turn now to look at the lens.'

'Like this?' She flicked her head provocatively as if she were Marilyn Monroe or Audrey Hepburn.

'No. Just be...'

'Be what?'

'Natural.'

'But you're taking my picture. I have to do something!'

Roland was not losing control of the shoot, as he didn't have command of it. He tried a new tactic.

'Do you like my camera?' he asked her. 'It's a Praktika – very strong, very robust. The results are excellent if you use the right lens.'

'Have you used the right lens?'

'I think so – a wide angle, as I want to include the Wall and the tower behind you. If I want to photograph you close up, I'll use a different lens – like a zoom, I think.'

'You know about photography?' Too late! Roland's gentle smile had crashed to the ground with a bang. 'Silly question – sorry! You're a journalist – of course you know about photography.'

'Not that much, actually – I'm a writer first and foremost. I haven't had the camera long so I'm still experimenting with it, finding out what it can do. I'm teaching myself to process film, too, but the lab at the newspaper does most of that. I can use it for my own purposes, which is a rare privilege here in the East.'

This was better. The more they talked the less Heike posed. He snapped her from all sorts of different angles – profile, close up, ultra-close up, mid-shots.

'Do you know of famous photographers in the West?' he asked. 'Like Cecil Beaton? Or Lee Miller? Or maybe David Bailey?'

'No, I don't,' she replied, the keen breeze softening her voice. 'I've left the West behind.'

Looking back on this episode, she cursed herself for having been prickly with him, not quite trusting what it was all about. She couldn't know for sure, and the last month had been particularly hard. Hindsight is a wonderful thing. In that moment he could so easily have been yet another Stasi man playing with her emotions. All she wanted was to be left alone to be a good citizen; she didn't need all the crap that went with it.

Roland promptly shot off thirty-six frames, whilst adjusting focus and shutter speed and making a mental note that the more he talked the better everything seemed to be. She relaxed whenever he talked, and as things were going so well he suggested loading a new film and shooting more with a different lens, that's if she didn't mind.

The only thing she minded was the presence of a heavy-set man sitting on a bench some 25 metres away supposedly reading a newspaper but clearly watching them.

'Who's that?' She nodded in the man's direction.

'Don't bother about him.'

'Is he your editor?'

'No, of course not. He's just reading a paper – that's all.'

'Can't you tell him to go? Tell him that you're press – that you're being put off by him?'

'But I'm not. Seriously, he's fine. He's not bothering us.'

Roland would have loaded a third film had it not started to rain a little. The timing was just right. Seventy frames was more than enough for this piece and he knew it, but the pretty girl from Bavaria was too good a catch to never see again.

'I'll let you know when we run the piece. It might not be for a day or so, but this is a big story, so who knows. It's not every day someone walks into the GDR from the West. I'll be in touch – bye!'

*

Wikipedia
Heike's Entry

There was a time when people spoke of having fifteen minutes of fame. Today, people's actions are immortalised on the Internet; so there was no need to tell Hanne of any of this incredible story. Heike was there on Wikipedia for all to see, along with all the other infamous defectors to the East – all the traitors, spies and terrorists.

Perhaps it didn't matter; the memories were flowing freely now.

*

Uncle Frederick

Somebody had left a carefully folded note on her desk. Its spiteful message was this:

STUPID LITTLE BITCH! We're all trying to get out and you just wander in. People have died making a bid for freedom. Their graves line the Wall that you walked through to get here. WE WONT FORGET YOU WHEN OUR TIME IS COME!

Suspecting that whoever had written the note was watching, she re-folded and discreetly placed it under a paperweight. At least now the chilly atmosphere had a voice, though not a signature.

Before leaving that evening she smuggled it into her handbag with the intention of presenting it to "Uncle" Frederick when he arrived at her apartment. He was under orders to keep regular contact with her, to charm and befriend, guide and watch over her; his remit was to talk openly, giving her all sorts of information just to see how she might use it. If that information was relayed to the CIA or MI5 and it came back to them, then they had their mole.

She welcomed him in, happy and somewhat relieved to see his beaming face. Embarrassed that she could only offer him just one hook for his rain-sodden mac, but there was a pastry put aside in the tiny fridge that they could snack on and also coffee, nothing extravagant, but this was the Eastern bloc. She poured him a cup and showed him the note.

'Ah! Well, I don't think that's anything to worry about. People are by nature mischievous. Someone is trying to get a reaction from you. Don't give them the opportunity, my dear. You've made the right choice in joining your brothers and sisters in the East. It was the best move you could have made – you must have no regrets. Would you like to work in a different department? I can arrange that, but I can't promise that it wouldn't happen again.'

'No, thank you! I don't want to be seen as a quitter.'

'Good for you! Respect is won and quitters are never respected.'

Uncle's words resonated completely with Heike. These were the words she'd been missing all her young life – the rhetoric of a father who advises, praises and guides his children. GI Joe Savers had only ever chastised her. Even at Christmas, if he'd been at home, which was rare, he'd chastised her.

Over the next couple of days, glancing out of the office window she saw Roland twice – not to speak to, but in the distance, circling the vicinity, stopping his squeaky, rattley bicycle to talk to someone. He looked quite determined; maybe looking for something or someone? Perhaps this was simply his "patch" and he was just going about his journalistic business as always?

She asked a colleague about him but was brushed off with: 'I don't know! Why would I know? We mind our own business here and you'd do well to do the same.'

He really didn't look like a Stasi man, she thought, *but maybe the best Stasi are clever like that.*

*

If instead of being in a hotel room she had been at home, she would have found for Hanne the second letter that she wrote to her mother, Kirsten.

It read:

Dearest Mama, Having reached Berlin, I decided to cross the border into the East. I know this will come as a shock to you, but I feel I must live by my principles. I could not live in a country that sheltered former Nazis and even gave them positions of power.

I am happy and employed here in the GDR, though I cannot tell you exactly what I do because it is important work. Maybe one day, when Germany is reunited again as a truly socialist country, we will all be able to talk about many things, but it is better because of the pressure put on us by the West that for now discretion is the key.

Hopefully we can meet soon — somewhere. For now, please know that I am safe and well and in a happy place.

This second letter was never sent either.

*

Kirsten wasn't sleeping for lack of news. She would have registered with an organisation that put family in touch with relatives in the East, but she had no reason to suspect her errant daughter was in the East.

'I've been looking all over for you!' he gasped in triumph, propping his lanky stature up against her doorframe.
'I didn't think I was difficult to find.'
'I was hoping to bump into you.'
Between laboured breaths, Roland would glance beyond her to the centre of the small, sparsely furnished apartment and particularly at its central light fitting as if he were trying to spot something hidden. This unnerved and offended her, but he couldn't seem to help himself. He continued to scan the

flat, staring in turn at a flower vase with the same intensity and then a light switch.

When he'd finished staring into her apartment he asked matter-of-factly: 'Would you like to go for a walk?'

'With you?'

'Of course with me!' He sounded desperate yet also very familiar, as if he'd known her since school days.

'Okay.' So they walked out into the dull light of an autumn evening that was still quite mild, Heike retaining a respectful sideways distance that would have accommodated a passing tram.

'Where are we going?' she called across the chasm.

'I thought that being new here you might like to see some things you don't know are here.'

'What things?'

'Things that I know because I've always lived here and I've always wanted to show an outsider but never had the chance.' He smiled, but clearly there was another motive and it was writ right across his face.

'I wouldn't have done this in the West,' she said, facing him again; 'not just walked out with someone I really didn't know.'

'Then you have given me a compliment!'

'I like this time of year when all the leaves are falling. I like spring too, with all its colours and new grass growing. Do you li—'

Before she could finish her small talk, he gestured her to stop still and listen carefully.

'There! You hear that?'

'What?'

'That rumbling below our feet. That's a train – the Stadtbahn directly below us. It runs all around the city, East and West, but it doesn't stop in the East anymore.'

He glanced at her to see if she was paying attention. She wasn't looking at him at all but staring at the ever-revolving

Mercedes star on the Europa-Center, its lofty tower so tantalisingly close, so out of reach in the Eastern sector.

'There are nearly 700 fluorescent tubes that light that star. Did you know that?' Heike shook her head.

'Funny how we look across at their bright lights whilst they look across at our security towers and factory chimneys.' He patted his jacket with both hands, feeling for an elusive cigarette packet left on an office desk. She thought he was either so Stasi that he was actually frisking himself or he was trying to locate a hidden microphone.

'How did you get here?' he asked.

'Me?'

'You're the only one here, aren't you?'

'I told you before! I gave myself up at the border. Asked for asylum. Is this what you wanted to show me? The sound of a train and the view of the West?'

'I'm surprised you didn't want to stay in West Berlin. All the wonderful shops and bright lights. I'd like to go there.'

'It's full of fascists. Not a nice place; it isn't what it appears to be. That sign proves my point. Hitler loved Mercedes. It's all still in place – the whole rotten structure. This is the *true* Berlin – the *true* Germany.'

She meant it, but felt guilty when he offered no response. Glancing across the chasm, he even looked quite crestfallen, as if she'd ruined his evening.

Only she could break the moody silence that followed.

'We could have spoken in my apartment, you know.'

'Are you crazy? Walls have ears!' he snapped.

'Not my walls,' she insisted.

He reached into his trouser pocket and pulled out an envelope. He passed it to her as if handing her a birthday card. 'Open it,' he said, smiling. Inside was a newspaper cutting: his piece on Heike's defection.

BAVARIAN GIRL FINDS HOME IN THE EAST

Fräulein Heike Savers, a twenty-year-old unemployed former waitress, has sought sanctuary with the authorities in East Berlin after having become disillusioned with life in the West. Fräulein Savers gave herself up to Border Police last month having travelled to West Berlin from her home in Bavaria. She has told our security correspondent that she is keen to settle in the GDR and make a new life for herself. It is understood she has no close relatives resident in the GDR.

'That's it?' she asked. 'After all I told you about my motives?'

'Do you like the photo I took?'

'What sort of journalist are you?'

'One who reports what he is told to report. I wrote more, including much of what you told me, but my editor cut it. I have no other say in it.'

Embarrassment flooding his cheeks, he looked away at the star on the Europa building.

'There is more.' He took out another press cutting and gave it to her to unfold.

'This is from a paper in the Western sector.'

SUSPICIONS OVER RECENT DEFECTION

A twenty-year-old Bavarian woman who defected to the GDR last month is most likely a Red Army Faction (RAF) member, says West Berlin Security Chief.

Fräulein Heike Savers, the daughter of a US serviceman, worked as a waitress before leaving her job and family home to defect to the East.

'My God! Mama will never forgive me!'

'She doesn't know?'

'What have I done?'

'I suspect you've done more than you realise.'

Fifty metres away, snuggled tightly into the womb-like

branches of a sweet chestnut tree, a sniper squeezed his trigger and shot off a round that hit Heike squarely in the chest. He yells: 'That one's from GI Joe Savers – just so's you know!'

She spun around on her heels, its velocity so great that only Roland could catch her before she hit the pavement. That was the first time he held her.

'I think I'd better find you a chair. Come! Come!'

Just metres away, a dirty café would do for now. He pushed open the door and lowered her down into the moulded orange plastic of the bucket chair.

'Can I get you something?' asked the female proprietor.

'Two coffees, please!' Roland gasped, before adding: 'And a cigarette. Get me a packet of cigarettes.'

'Sure. Any brand?'

'Any brand, I don't care.'

Devoid of any discernible circulation, Heike leant across the table and shook for all the world as if she were haemorrhaging life like a punctured balloon.

'Why would they write such a thing?' she sobbed.

'Is it true? Is that why you came here?'

'They think I'm part of Baader-Meinhof? Who would think such a thing?!'

Roland was loath to offer an answer. Better to appear pious, stay quiet; wait for the coffee and cigarettes.

'You're one clever man, I'll give you that!' she spat like a wounded cat.

'I don't understand. How do you mean, clever?'

'You're secret police. This week you play the good cop. Next week you play the bad cop. That is what they did to me last month in jail. Good cop, bad cop. *You* know how it works. *I* know how it works. Well, Mr Policeman, you got your story out and ruined any chance I have of ever going to my mother. She will never speak to me again; the family will ostracise her and – and – and…! I don't know! I don't know!'

'I'm not a cop. I'm a journalist – that's all. I did what I am employed to do, nothing more.'

He wanted to reassure her by covering her trembling hand with his, but such a gesture wasn't going to do it for Heike.

'It isn't just the family who will ostracise her – the whole neighbourhood will shun her and all because I wanted to be East German.'

He fought retaliation. *It's not so great,* he wanted to say, but East Germans born and raised know better than to be anything but discreet, so he kept his opinion tightly closed as he had been brought up to do.

Sure enough, news of Heike's defection reached home and, yes, the neighbours did shun Kirsten – in Landshagen, not Oberwinkel. Somebody just happened to spot the article and the surname. *Savers? Wasn't there an American sergeant with that name? Used to keep himself to himself? Anti-social! Didn't he marry a local woman? They had two kids? A girl and a boy – younger brother – you know? It's the girl – she's the one who defected! Can you imagine?*

Oberwinkel was different. Perhaps no one recognised the surname. Or maybe no one bothered to read any papers that day, so word never made it to Oma or anybody else in the Mauer circle. International papers did pick it up, but nothing "front page", just a few bylines under International News on page 18. Not many people read those pages.

It was in a few English language broadsheets aboard the early morning paper train – tightly bound news bundles thrown out unceremoniously onto the platform at Penzance for the vendors to pick up at the very moment Hugo was standing waiting patiently to load early daffodils for Covent Garden. Often, he would pick up a paper to read then save for fire lighting. That particular morning, he didn't bother.

The New Plan

The new plan involved more lies, including:

> *"Dearest Mama, Initially, I did move to West Berlin, but I met this wonderful East German journalist called Roland... I have fallen in love and moved with him to East Berlin. Hopefully I will be able to come and see you soon..."*

Not that Roland was aware of his amour at this time, especially as she gave not the slightest clue of any interest whatsoever. The nearest they'd come to dating was the walk to the café where she'd collapsed.

This time, however, the letter was posted; only it landed on the floor of an unoccupied address. Kirsten had already left for Xanten, leaving most of her furniture behind in the rush to get away. The letter was not forwarded but returned to sender by the letting agent.

Why Xanten? It was a long way from Bavaria and Hugo had mentioned it once and made it sound fascinating because the Romans had been there.

*

The List

Heike made a list of ten people she would invite to dinner. These were in numerical order:
1. Simon Wiesenthal
2. Karl Marx
3. Friedrich Engels
4. Horst Buchholz

5. John Lennon
6. George Harrison
7. (left blank as a space to be filled. M. Delon was an '8' not a '7'.)
8. Alain Delon
9. Serge Gainsboro (or Jacques Cousteau, depending on availability)
10. Hardy Krüger

The idea was to invite all of them together, providing dates didn't clash, and simply provide them with an opportunity to talk, talk and talk. Lennon and Harrison would improvise with a musical interlude every now and then, Serge Gainsboro would sing and read poetry (Harrison strumming an accompaniment), and it would all be interspersed with much laughter.

Heike's regret was that in coming to East Berlin she had probably turned her back on the chance of bumping into Horst Buchholz doing his shopping in West Berlin. Never mind. However, it did intrigue her to think that he might have read about her in the newspaper and wondered just who she was. He might even make a cutting of it and encourage someone influential, creative and connected to turn her story into a play or film.

Her story, of course, was still very much in the making.

When all her guests had turned up and were enjoying themselves, glass of wine in hand (or beer for some), smoking pot and pipes and cigarillos, Roland would turn up unexpectedly. She would invite him in through the smoke and the perfume of wine with the proviso that he behave himself and that he take plenty of photos of the group for posterity. She would title them the '73 Group, after the year. The '74 Group might be different for whatever reason depending on who could attend.

When everyone had left come the early hours, she would encourage him to stay a little longer – not too long though.

*

This list was bound to amuse Hanne! Maybe she had a list, too?

*

Odd to think that there had been a time when she'd wondered how best to meet Roland again. She hadn't exactly endeared herself to him, as she didn't really know who or even what he was. If only she could be sure that he was a real journalist and not just a Stasi information officer.

Not that she held any grudges against the Stasi. *They were doing a difficult job* – in her opinion. *So what if he was Stasi? He would be ordered to be a certain way by someone, and that's okay because if it protected the state from those that would do it harm – fascists – then what's the gripe? They're simply doing an impossible job and most likely with limited resources.*

Heike's choices had been hers and hers alone. No one invited her to come. Who can blame them for being suspicious? On a positive note, the sun was shining in East Germany and it was warm and energising!

*

Would Hanne really understand this?

*

It was the little things that were beginning to mount up: the odd pen or pencil that had been put away so securely; a pencil sharpener and so much else that seemed to walk whenever she turned her back. No one asked to borrow anything. They could have done, but no one ever did.

Sheets of paper that were pristine in her handling became marked and creased if she left her desk unattended. Manuscripts would be returned from other departments with the complaint that the sheets were out of order or that there were pages missing.

Her chair had a mind of its own: sometimes too high, sometimes too low; frequently loose in its construction, it would sometimes collapse, much to the amusement of those around her.

Typewriter ribbon would quickly fade and the miserly storeman would berate her for wasting valuable state resources. He'd always been so quiet. At least he was speaking to her. Many didn't.

From the toilet cubicle (which was only slightly smaller than her work place), she would hear exchanges such as: 'What's that awful smell?'

'Don't you know? It's a terrorist!'

She thought now would be a good time to buckle under and surrender, but most strange of all was GI Joe's voice calling from way down the long corridor: 'Don't let them get the better of you, kid! Damn Krauts! Show 'em what you're made of!'

*

Crime and Punishment

People were not easily engaged. However hard she tried smiling and saying hello to anyone passing or stood within earshot, the result on the streets or in the office was always the same: a look of shock followed by a scurry to safer ground.

Maybe, she thought, *it is because Berlin is a city and city folk are like this the world over: London, New York, Paris. Every capital is like this because there are just too many people, so don't take it to heart.*

She called them "hermit crabs" because their scurrying reminded her of the little crustaceans. There *were* rare exceptions – very rare and not always welcome.

Her walk home from work had always been uneventful, until one evening she responded to a young man's voice calling: '*Fräulein?* Please come! My friend has hurt himself. Please come!'

Willingly, full of enthusiasm, even though it was dark and devoid of others in that very narrow street. Problems happen and in a good socialist society people help one another.

'Of course!'

She ran towards two young men clearly with a problem. There, on the wet, shiny pavement, was a man lying on his back gasping for air, his companion kneeling beside him and deeply concerned. 'What is it? What's happened?' she asked.

'Here, *fräulein*! Can't you see?'

'See what?' She crouched down and peered hard through the darkness at the desperate youth whose eyes longed for assistance.

'I can't see anything.'

'My friend has fallen on his knife and cut himself badly.'

'Knife?' Her eyes searched the darkness for the glint of a knife but could see nothing untoward. Satisfied that he held her full attention, the prostrate man arched the small of his back as if tensing, his laboured breath now subsiding, his pained expression easing into a grin. If he was about to die, there was nothing she could do.

Turning to his companion she cried: 'Get an ambulance – quickly!'

'No need for an ambulance, *fräulein*.'

Raising himself like Lazarus, the prostrate youth reached out and grabbed her hair with one hand, pulling her tight towards him. His accomplice pushed the point of a small knife into the nape of her neck. Two hermit crabs had overpowered their prey.

The larger of the two clapped a fat hand over her mouth whilst the knife's point pressed deeper against her flesh. Instinctively, she surrendered to her fate.

'Take off your jeans!' ordered the kneeling companion in hushed tones.

She hesitated then struggled, until the crab tightened his grip.

'DO IT!' he demanded.

She unbuttoned the waistband, pushing the jeans down to below her trembling knees.

'All the way! Take them right off!'

She obediently did as she was told, slipping off her shoes and jeans.

'Hand them over – NOW!'

It was the shout that turned her. The demand was too much. Dropping the jeans to the floor, she suddenly became aware of some greater presence – aware that she was the great-granddaughter of the man who would not give way on the bridge leading into Oberwinkel.

From out of the darkness *he* stepped forward, taking her hand in his and clenching it tight. 'Now hit him, child! Hit him hard!'

She hit her assailant with a force that came direct from her ancestor. She could feel his strength and resolve pumping through her muscles.

A punch to the eye, then a knuckle against his nose, then to his ear, followed by a storm of fists lashing out at a speed that the youths had not expected and could no longer handle. She was hitting out at *them*, she was hitting out at GI Joe, she was hitting out at the Stasi; she was hitting out at all those colleagues who shunned her, stole from her and called her a terrorist. Within seconds she had all of them against the ropes; she had them on the run.

'We only wanted your jeans, you bitch!'

'Don't think we wanted you! You're not worth anything, slag!'

They retreated, fading into the darkness, as did her great-grandfather. He was no longer needed, but she thanked him nonetheless.

The walk home to safety and sanity was at first quick and easy as Heike the fighter revelled in victory, her stride swift and determined; but soon the glow of the elevated victory walk turned to agony as the adrenalin wore off to reveal painful wounds.

By the time Uncle Frederick happened by her apartment that evening, she was in a state of shock – pale and shivering, she had limped the last 200 metres home.

At least his easy company soothed her. 'I'll make us both some coffee.' He glanced back at her shaking head. 'You don't want some? But you must! I insist! My coffee is the best you will taste.'

'But it's *my* coffee!'

'It's not just the coffee, it's the way it's made. Sweet biscuits, too – very important.'

She tried to stand, but he motioned her to be still. 'Sit back and relax. I'll take care of you.'

She showed uncle the puncture wound to her neck. He agreed that it was very nasty – very nasty indeed. 'Not as nasty as that swine's broken nose.'

'Where did you learn to fight off attackers?' he asked.

'You mean like a cat? That's easy! I have a brother and I grew up with boys – German and American. Some of them were big tough kids, you know.'

'You'll be more careful next time. Avoid walking in the shadows and the quiet places.'

'I hadn't considered…'

'What? Considered the possibility of crime here in East Berlin? You must be careful of foreign workers. They come here from across the world to take advantage of our industry and our education, but their habits die hard.'

'Uncle – these men were German!'

'How can you be sure? Didn't you tell me it was dark? That you couldn't see their faces clearly?'

'Yes, but their voices were German – Berliners.'

'Come now, child. All our citizens are provided for and have no need to steal. People with psychiatric needs are helped throughout their recovery, so why would you have been attacked by Germans?'

'They were after taking my denim jeans. There is a black market for Western clothes, isn't there?'

'Is that something you've read in the West?'

'Maybe I did. Perhaps I was stupid to walk around like some spoiled brat. I know I should be more discreet. I'll find something more fitting.'

'We're not China,' he snapped; 'we don't wear uniforms or sackcloth and ashes.'

There followed a brief, slightly awkward silence in which Uncle Frederick sought to change the subject to something lighter. Over the next two hours he talked of many things, all of it mundane, while she listened, nodded, then instantly forgot because her mind was back on *that* wretched street.

Just as he was leaving, he muttered something about having found a new department for her. She almost didn't hear him; it came out of the blue – a giveaway statement, along with: 'It's turned cold again. Don't let the draught in.'

Odd that they'd talked about so much that evening, but nothing about her job. This was suddenly tossed into the black night air like an afterthought with no care as to where it landed. She wondered whether it was actually the reason for his unannounced visit that evening, but her condition had diverted him and he'd almost forgotten until he was leaving.

At the new office doing the new job, not everyone was unfriendly, or rather, standoffish. There was a would-be friend – a young woman who introduced herself simply as "Melissa". Melissa was only too keen to share her own experiences.

Ten years older than Heike, Melissa was for all to see a mature and worldly young woman who seemed out of place in the deep, vast bleakness of the canteen. Her aristocratic bearing would be more likely found in Vienna's marbled halls than here amongst the mildew of East Berlin; her soft tones drowning in the cacophony of base, sweary chatter, she was an exotic fish poured into a stagnant pond.

Elegant in her approach, she wore her cigarettes like a glamour model, her roll top and skirt caressing her long, slender form. Heads turned for Melissa's entrance. Now, having observed her subject over many weeks, she sought to become a canteen buddy occupying the always-vacant seat at Heike's regular table.

'May I join you?'

'Be my guest.'

'I've seen you from across the room always sitting alone. You're the girl from Bavaria – the American sector – yes?'

Determined to show her peasant credentials, Heike continued chewing, answered with her mouth full – most irreverently. 'I'm here to be a good citizen.'

'Of course you are!' Melissa reached for her cigarettes in order to graciously offer her friendship. Heike shook her head: 'No thank you. I don't.'

'Do you think that it's important we have a philosophy in life?'

'I think we should have something to believe in.'

'Such as?'

'Communism.'

'Communism? You say all the right things.'

'Then what should I say?'

'You should say what's in your heart. That's important, isn't it?'

'Then, I think communism *is* in my heart.'

Melissa leaned back, her easy smile as charming as that of a TV host adeptly interviewing a member of the dim-witted public, her broad pouting lips sucking the fire out of her West Berlin cigarette.

'Communism is in my heart, too. But there is more… How shall I say? There is more to communism than Marx, Engels, Lenin, Trotsky or Mao.'

'I don't understand.'

Melissa leaned forward across the table. 'Communism is in the heart and soul of the citizen – the worker – like you and me. But the leader is beyond such naivety; he is open to contamination. All leaders are open to contamination regardless of their naïve, original stance.

'Capitalism corrupts because it is based on power – the power of the few. Let me explain… Let's say that Fidel Castro sees the President of the United States in his Cadillac. Idealists are like children; they must possess what they see. They must have a Cadillac. Then Castro sees that the President has a wife and numerous mistresses. So he must have a wife and mistresses. Then he sees the White House. So he too must have a palace.

'A castle is always a castle whether it's a capitalist castle or a communist castle. The building remains the same; its inhabitants are the powerful. We are always the weak, the subservient ones maintaining the status quo.'

'Are you testing me?' Heike demanded.

'Testing you? Why would I test you?'

'You want to see that I am who I say I am. You want to see that I am a committed communist. Don't you see? I came through all your tests. I will always come through your tests whatever you throw at me.' Heike glanced away toward the large canteen clock in an effort to disengage her new "friend".

'Now, I'd be happier eating alone. I don't need your friendship. We have that freedom at least.'

'Of course you do. I didn't mean to impose.'

Gracefully, Melissa retreated, but only for a while.

That sentence, "We have that freedom at least", haunted her for many days and weeks after its utterance. Why did she say that? She was in Utopia, wasn't she? But here was proof of an inner admission that freedom wasn't here. She hadn't found freedom and, realistically, nor did she expect to find it. She'd exchanged a controlling "father" – if that's who he was – for a confinement in an alien place where she had no family connection whatsoever.

Melissa, having made an introduction, continued to court her with beaming smiles if they passed in a corridor, or with a cheery wave from a distance. She never passed up an opportunity to greet Heike, acting as if they were really soul partners who were on the verge of reconnecting for yet another life together.

Perhaps she's mistaken my sexuality? thought Heike. *Better get me a boyfriend!*

She consulted her dinner guest list. There was only one name – at the bottom in brackets – a name without any ranking, but unlike Lennon, Harrison or Marx he stood a real chance of making a difference in her life – Roland.

The new job had many advantages: one of which was that it took her each week to Roland's newspaper offices. She could now add to her resumé not just the title of translator but also that of courier, picking up financial information and handing over translated newspaper cuttings from the world's press that could be used for an East German readership. After all, there were no East German correspondents in any English-speaking country – not official journalists anyway – so her job was to translate certain English language news stories for East Berlin.

She was, in effect, a writer of bylines, but the credit was never going to go to her. The byline was always credited to "our foreign correspondent".

Each afternoon between 4 and 5 pm, Monday to Friday, she would pull a large four-wheeled trolley loaded with boxes and packages to the basement entrance where she would exchange her load with that of outgoing documents held by the storeman and his security officer. It was an opportunity to try to peek in beyond the loading bay, but it was impossible to see anything or gain access to the inner sanctum.

Then one day she was given special permission to hand deliver a package to a sub-editor. This was the opportunity she needed and had hoped for.

'Follow me.' She could barely contain herself. The security officer was opening doors for her, doors that led to the future.

'That's his desk,' said the officer, pointing to a bespectacled, perspiring young man of barely twenty who was carrying the world on his narrow, hunched shoulders. His desk looked no more important or busy than her own, she thought, yet for some reason she felt most inadequate.

She handed over the package before brazenly asking for a pen and notepaper upon which she hastily scribbled a note. 'Do you know a journalist called Roland?' she asked.

'Roland? Yes.'

'Would you give him this note please?'

The sub wasted not a moment in reading it first: "Hello Roland! Hope you are well? Haven't seen you in a while. Did you know I come by every so often in my new job? Maybe see you sometime? Regards, Heike."

How embarrassing! *Was nothing confidential here?* Scanning the vast newsroom she thought she could see the back of Roland's head.

'That's him over there.' The sub pointed to the head she'd already recognised. 'Give it to him yourself. He won't mind.'

She couldn't leave now without completing her objective – a mission for which she had to be resolute or forever embrace the idea of spinsterhood. This was her chance to redress their so far silly relationship. Navigating the maze of desks and swivel chairs, avoiding the busy bees on their feet – who paid her no heed at all – Heike soon lost her momentum, juddered to a shocking halt.

Within a breath someone had beaten her to it – an earnest young woman who playfully ruffled the tan-brown hair of Roland's nape as she bent forward across his desk. Grabbing a seat to draw up next to his, the interloper was engaging Roland in business with no idea that the girl who haunted his every waking thought had anxiously parked a mere couple of metres behind him.

Hopelessly turning in retreat, Heike determined to put the "idiot Roland" to the back of her mind. For now, she needed to get her trolley back to base packed with a new consignment of information. Her bosses would be wondering what was keeping her and this was a position she didn't want to lose.

She was within a door's swing of walking out of the newsroom forever. 'Wait! I'm glad you're still here. I need you to take something back to translate.' It was the sub-editor.

He fumbled for some minutes looking for something important that she couldn't begin to imagine. She felt awkward – angry. How stupid to think that Roland was waiting around for her to make up her mind. *Dummkopf!*

Now in a panic, the sub mumbled whilst urgently pulling out every drawer and evacuating every pigeon hole in his otherwise meticulous open-plan office space trying to locate the all-important document that had to go back with Heike that evening. She wasn't going anywhere until he found it. Patience was not the easiest of virtues for her, but this afternoon it would pay off. A looming shadow behind her caused her to turn. 'Hello! I thought it was you!'

'Hello Roland!'

"Uncle" Frederick was particularly encouraging of Heike's relationship with Roland and even urged them to tie the knot sooner rather than later as it would be easier for him to find them an apartment – his gift. 'Perhaps in Rheitzenstrasse?' he suggested. He would even take the place of her father and give her away on the chosen day. Since her defection, she had come to adore her adopted uncle, little knowing that he was recording her every move *(of which I played a significant part)* and reporting daily to his masters. Not that there was much to report. From day one she had confounded her Stasi hosts by appearing to be just who she said she was – a committed communist.

This did not cause them to look away; they were not fooled. She was clearly biding her time, putting them off the scent. It would only be a matter of time before she would be heard or seen contacting her CIA controller.

To the Stasi, she was clearly a new generation – well schooled in the art of subterfuge. The Americans had obviously learnt from past mistakes and were now more careful in their selection of just who they would send in. And what could be better than a German-born idealist under the cover of being an ardent communist? The Stasi were convinced this would be the outcome; and when it surely came, they would fall on her like a ton of bricks.

Uncle Frederick greenlit her communications with the West – encouraged them wholeheartedly: the photos she took and wanted to share so naively with her distant relatives in Cornwall of all places. He positively encouraged her freedom of expression by encouraging Heike to post frequent letters. 'Don't forget your poor Mama, Heike. She'll be fretting. Write to her. Call her.'

All the while he was her censor and he, more than anyone, was the reason that Hanne and other distant relations had happy photographs to put into their family albums. However, neither Hanne nor Hugo ever noticed that they too were the subjects of occasional observation: the car parked in the farm lane; the happy couple with a picnic basket enjoying their holiday, enjoying the Cornish scenery.

Kirsten was watched from a distance. Working as a doctor's receptionist in her newly adopted home of Xanten, in reality she knew very little. Not one of Heike's letters had reached her. Convinced that Heike was punishing her for marrying GI Joe, taking whatever advice she could find she registered with various organisations that specialised in finding relatives in the East and keeping those family members in touch with one another. It wasn't much, but it was something.

Heike, oblivious to all these observations, remained naive and innocent, a willing participant in a land of suspicion.

Now that Roland was on board, sharing a bed, sharing meals, Melissa became easier to deal with. Heike, with a ring on her finger, was less reticent and would now respond to the greetings with a smile, or a wave at a distance, and eventually friendly exchanges: *How are you? I'm fine! Do you fancy a coffee?*

Lieber Melissa. Turns out, that in getting to know her she wasn't bad at all. She was, in fact, remarkably good company. Her smile lit up the coldest of East Berlin rooms; her gentle laughter warmed the soul. Her luminescent beauty enchanted all those who fell under her spell. She could talk with authority on almost any subject: history, maths, science, religion, philosophy, Oriental religions, even international politics. It was Melissa who claimed to the point of insistence that the man behind President Kennedy's assassination was none other than his successor, President Lyndon Johnson.

'He stood to gain most. He hated the Kennedys; they hated him. JFK had placed him in the impotent position of Vice President, a position you give to your closest enemy and rival. Keep your friends close but your enemies closer still.

'In Texas, Johnson was on his home ground when Kennedy was shot. He was surrounded by friends and associates, who together sewed up the whole bloody affair, murdered those who knew too much and were about to blab – Oswald, Ruby and many others who disappeared and died in mysterious circumstances.

'*They* pointed the finger at Khrushchev and Castro and anybody else they considered a legitimate enemy, and they didn't stop with JFK. They killed Martin Luther King and Robert Kennedy.

'By the close of 1968, Johnson's mission was accomplished. He'd got his war in Vietnam; he'd got rid of the family he hated most in the world. In time, the West will acknowledge Johnson's guilt, but it won't be for a while yet.'

It was a theory that Heike was only too pleased to hear. She remembered clearly the evening of 22nd December 1963 when GI Joe had cheered like a maniac on hearing the news that President Kennedy had been assassinated in Dallas.

'Serves that effing son of a bitch right!' he'd balled at the TV screen while stamping his feet in glee. He even threw his beer can at the living room wall and Joe was not one to waste beer – such was his ecstasy that evening. He was also a Republican by nature who thought Johnson the only decent democrat, and now the way was clear for the USA to rule the world and destroy communism once and for all. Undoubtedly, it was Joe's happiest day in what was otherwise a thoroughly miserable life.

The Johnson/Kennedy subject opened a door that Heike had not expected to open again, not since those days of primary interrogation in Stasi Headquarters. She'd laid Joe to rest, but yet again here he was bursting back into her life and demanding attention.

Melissa's questions came thick and fast:

'Is your father still in the army?'

'Where was he based?'

'Did he ever confide in you?'

'Are you still in contact with him?'

'Who cares? He never cared for me! He never cared for my mother or my brother, and he probably isn't even my father.'

Melissa backed off immediately. 'I'm sorry, Heike. You're right, I shouldn't be so inquisitive.' She paused theatrically, taking a long drag on her cigarette. 'It's just… you see, I think my father was a GI, too. I didn't know him, but I'm curious as to who he might have been, where he came from, what he did in the army, and there's no one I can ask. My mother is dead; my adopted parents are not approachable in that respect. They won't talk about my real parents.'

'What happened to your mother?'

'She was killed in a road accident when I was a baby. Silly! Survived all the horrors of war only to die in 1946 crossing the road. That's death, you see. Always busy; always on the lookout for souls.'

Roland summed it up with consummate ease, surprised that Heike hadn't also made the connection.

'Melissa sees you as a sister — that's what the attraction is. You're both German on the maternal line, but American on the paternal. It's a tribal thing and that's the attraction.'

'That's ridiculous! I'm not even Joe's daughter! My father was a Russian.'

'Melissa doesn't think so. She sees you as she sees herself — a lost mongrel in need of an identity.'

'There's nothing "mongrel" about Melissa.'

'Maybe she's just lonely. And you're another loner.'

'Yes, I think that's more the truth of it — two loners — two outsiders. There is, however, a difference between us.'

'What is that?'

'I may be a loner, but I'm no longer alone.'

She sank back into the arms of Roland as if he were a big comfy mattress in which she could at last sleep the sleep of the saved.

At least Melissa was friendly. Many people weren't. They kept themselves to themselves, carefully keeping their own counsel because in a closed society people were watching one another and making notes for higher people in higher places whose jobs relied on compiling those notes.

Some people became friendlier when Heike married Roland. Now they could see that she was perfectly serious; she wasn't passing through the neighbourhood; she really did mean to stay.

They became friendlier still when Heike announced her pregnancy.

Whilst they became friendlier, Melissa began to cool. It wasn't an overnight thing, but it did become noticeable to Heike that the relationship was under strain for some unknown reason. At first, Heike put it down to jealousy: marriage, a baby on the way. Melissa was feeling left out. The cheery smile wasn't so evident, the exaggerated wave across the crowded room was replaced by a nod in acknowledgement; and when they did get together, the talk was distant and quite forced.

'I'm sure that you could find someone like Roland. There are plenty of eligible men—'

'What makes you think I'm in need of a man?'

'I… just thought…'

'It's good that you're happy, it's good that you're expecting a baby, but it's never been my goal. I don't want to fall in love with anyone – men or babies. I am, for the most part, happy. I have my work, I have my friends – you included. But there are greater things in this world.'

Having snapped she allowed herself a brief smile, but the old Melissa was missing, sadly missing, and whoever this was who'd replaced her was no fun at all.

'What do you want out of life, Heike? Are you waiting for something to happen? Is there something that wants to make you reach out and achieve something?'

'I wanted to be here in East Berlin, to leave my old life behind. And I've done that. Maybe that's an achievement? Now I have my family and that's an achievement. I won't make the mistakes with my child that my mother made with me and my brother. Even if something happened to Roland, I wouldn't compromise my child by taking up with someone who didn't love them or love me. That's what my mother did.'

'Your mother was a girl in different times, Heike. People's choices depended on their survival.' Melissa's irritability was pulling her away. 'I've got to go. We'll catch up some other time?' Heike nodded. Melissa had never had to be "elsewhere" before. This was something new.

*

If Heike didn't get a move on, Hanne would be back in England.

- ✓ Pick up the handy,
- ✓ switch off the lights,
- ✓ place room key in handbag and
- ✓ set the satnav.

*

All of a sudden Melissa was gone. For two weeks, there was no lunchtime rendezvous, no distant sighting across the courtyard, nothing. Enrica was a friend now because Enrica was also newly married and pregnant; Ute was a friend now because she'd been pregnant; and Sylvia was a friend, too. None of them knew Melissa other than by sight, and they certainly didn't know where she lived or, in fact, anything about her.

'Somebody must know her. She can't just have vanished?' Heike exclaimed over another Monday lunch.

'She was stuck up.'

'No! She was friendly!'

'Really?'

'Never said a single word to me.'

'Or me.'

'We talked about all sorts of things. She was very knowledgeable,' Heike insisted.

'I think she thought she was above us all. Such a madam, but I heard she hung out in some dark places.'

'You think she was a prostitute?'

'Why not? She could earn good money that one.'

'No, I think she was just another Stasi plant. She's gone because she's done her job. Mission accomplished. She'll be somewhere else now. She was friendly to you, Heike, because you're the girl from the West. They'll watch you; it's only natural. Forget her. Put it down to experience. Providing you didn't say anything to incriminate yourself, you're safe. It's just policy that keeps people safe.'

'Why would I incriminate myself? I've nothing to hide.'

'Of course not! It's just routine, the way things are. The authorities are paranoid that the Americans will invade at any moment, so they'll keep tabs on you because of where you came from.'

No one shakes off their past – certainly not in East Berlin. Heike realised that.

Probably, if she hadn't been eight months pregnant, and not suffering the most debilitating back pain, Heike might have reacted very differently. Roland was late home, and the knock at the door was worrying for that reason alone. Nobody knocked in the evening – nobody.

There, standing on the step like an orphan in need of shelter, was Melissa – anxious, impatient, drawing on yet another cigarette like a condemned woman about to face the gallows. For the briefest of moments Heike didn't recognise her, such was the change in her demeanour.

'Are you okay? I haven't seen you in a while.'

'I'm fine. Can we talk?'

'Of course, come in.'

'No. Come to my car. It's there.' She gestured toward a blue VW Beetle just beyond the gate.

It crossed Heike's mind that if Melissa was Stasi, then she might regret getting into the car, but an arrest would be much more official and high powered than this.

Not without some difficulty, Heike manoeuvred into the passenger seat whilst Melissa fumbled in the glove compartment for some papers.

'You know, we conceived in a car. Now I can't even get in one!' joked Heike. Melissa didn't hear it and continued her search until she found what she was looking for – a map.

'You see, I've been doing some research. That's why you haven't seen me. I've discovered something about my father. You remember me saying that he was an American GI like your father? Well, he was here at this base. Is this where your father worked?'

Heike studied the improvised map of a US Army base somewhere in the American zone. 'No. Joe was, and may well still be, at a base in Frankfurt. It's a big place and it's where I went to school as a boarder.'

'I've discovered that my father was in the small arms wing at this base. He was an instructor. What about your father? What did he do? Would he have known my father? Could I contact your father? Could I say I know you? I'm so desperate to meet my father, Heike. I know he wants to see me, but it's so difficult.'

'They say you're a Stasi informer.'

'The Stasi watch me like they watch everyone else. Why do you think we're talking out here in the car? I'm not in their pay, Heike. I just want to make that connection with my father before he's too old. Would you help me?'

Of course Heike would help. Without giving anything a second thought, she described in detail whilst sketching a rough map of the base at Frankfurt, listing names and places, departments and the entire layout of all the buildings she could remember. She didn't stop to think about why a woman who needed to find her father needed such an elaborate map, but she wasn't doing it so much for Melissa but for herself: confronting her past in an effort to try to lay some ghosts. And when it got too dark to see, they switched on the interior light and continued until such time as Roland made them jump out of their skins by tapping on the steamed-up window, by which point the map was as complete as could be.

'Sorry! I was delayed. Shall we go in? I'm quite hungry.' He never asked why they were sitting in a Beetle in the near dark drawing up maps. He was an East German and knew that it was better never to ask, even when your profession is all about asking questions.

Melissa thanked Heike profusely and politely refused the offer of a meal, insisting that she better get home because her cat would be waiting for her. In reality, there was work to be done. She had all she needed.

Strangely, the very day Johann Bruno arrived, weighing in at a very healthy and cuddly 3.5 kg, Neues Deutschland announced the capture of Melissa Engel, notorious terrorist member of the June 2nd terrorist movement. Her involvement in the audacious bomb attack on a US Army air base at Frankfurt had left one man dead and thirteen injured.

It was in all the newspapers; there was no getting away from the headlines. For a week, Roland hid the news from his housebound wife, knowing that she had most likely played an unwitting part in detailing the camp for Melissa. She had not for a moment considered that Melissa was anything other than a lost soul looking for her real parent.

She knew that feeling – the feeling that *her* real father was "out there somewhere". Whenever the opportunity presented itself Heike would spot some middle-aged man in the crowd going about his business: *Could that be him? Is he here? Does he know I'm alive?* And each day she would shake herself out of such silly dreams. *Don't be stupid! Don't be sentimental! Of course he's not here! He's Russian! Not German!*

Then with each new day she would look again, convinced that he was waiting to be found.

One day, she followed a man across town for quite some distance. He was most definitely Russian because he had *that* look – the look that her brother had: a Slavic look. Everyone who had ever known Peter said that he had the look of a Slav.

She followed the stranger in the way a Stasi agent would, jumping onto trams, hiding behind a newspaper; pretending to fiddle with her shoe if he gazed back in her direction. She only broke off the surveillance when he entered a tower block. It had to be him, of that she was sure.

She waited for some time in the chill, damp, polluted air, smoking, coughing and blowing her dripping nose, but he didn't re-emerge. She was no spy, but if the man had been aware of her presence he might well have suspected her.

She never saw him again, but for several years she continued to haunt that particular neighbourhood armed with a packet of expensive Woodbines that Roland had picked up on the black market, her idea being that she would proffer the man a cigarette by way of an introduction. He would understand.

Roland was right to protect Heike. He knew only too well that when she found out about Melissa it would break her heart. Not that she was so fond of Melissa, but the thought that her carefully sketched map had enabled a terrorist group to kill and injure innocent people would shock her to the core.

The print news wasn't difficult to hide. Heike barely glanced away from Johann for a moment. She watched over the child's antics constantly, sleeping by his cot and often almost forgetting the fact that Roland was there too. And she adored Roland.

Roland knew only too well that a day's news is soon forgotten, but then there was the TV and the radio, both of which were always "on" in the newsroom. It was all over the media. Party officials interviewed on radio analysed the bombing for hours, talking about the perpetrators, the victims, the role of the US Army in Frankfurt.

The TV was no better; and worse, there were the West Berlin channels with their own "experts" analysing every nuance of the outrageous attack. So-called experts and pundits speculated that the following week there would doubtless be another terrorist attack in the West and then another and another because the Red Army Faction was also beginning to leave its bloody signature along with that of the June 2nd movement.

Roland was only too grateful that at home they had so far never invested in either a TV or a radio.

His biggest fear was that the authorities would make a connection between Heike and Melissa, that at any time there would be a vicious thumping at the door and it would be the Stasi, but such a visit never came and for a time he relaxed. The Stasi were not interested in terrorist activities on the other side of the fence, maybe because they had a different interest in the outcome; maybe they colluded?

A destabilised West was no bad thing for the East, and it was a possibility that the terrorists had popular support among the ordinary folk on both sides of the Iron Curtain.

Eventually, Heike did find out. On her return to work, Ute, Sylvia and Enrica couldn't wait to tell her all about the terrorist who'd been in their very midst.

*

Looking back over those years, the memory of that news sent a shiver through her. She was convinced that from that moment on, her time in purgatory had begun; that she and she alone was guilty of the death and the injuries sustained in that explosion. It was a heavy burden and one that she'd never spoken about to anyone other than her beloved Roland. Tonight, she would tell Hanne.

*

Kind Uncle Frederick

Johann's initial effect on his mother was that he strengthened the maternal bonds she felt for Kirsten. Up to now Heike's life in East Berlin had been a selfish existence: all was fine, and often wonderful when the sun shone.

Heike loved her mother; or rather, the good and considerate Heike loved her mother. There was another Heike whose burning resentment of GI Joe laid the blame firmly at her mother's door. Kirsten had made it too easy for Joe; Heike's self-imposed exile was the result and the punishment.

But now there was a baby and Heike wanted to show him off to his grandmother. Why, Kirsten would be bound to sweep him up; adore him; coo and cuddle and cradle him till her arms ached with love. Arranging a visit seemed perfectly reasonable; but that was the Westerner in Heike's thinking. She still hadn't quite cottoned on to the fact that she wasn't free to cross the border whenever she wanted to. The Wall wasn't there to protect her from the fascists in the West; it was there to keep her amongst the communists in the East.

She appealed to Uncle Frederick.

'I need to find Mama, to make contact again. She doesn't reply to my letters and I know she must feel so hurt by what I did… The baby's old enough to travel now. What do you think? He wants to see his grandmother!'

'My! What a clever boy he is! Only five months old and already he's expressing an opinion. It really isn't practical; it would be too emotional for all concerned. Better to stay put and avoid the hurt.'

'Hurt? How would we be hurt? Is my mother okay?'

Uncle didn't answer.

'I'm asking… Is she okay? Tell me please!'

'Why do you ask, my dear? Don't you know? The Americans will keep you if you try to go home. They'll interrogate you and take the child and make your life a misery. They won't even let you stay in Bavaria or Xanten or wherever you want to go.'

'Xanten? Where is Xanten?'

'It's where your mother now resides. She left when she found out about your life here in East Berlin.'

Uncle stood up and walked to the single-pane apartment window as if something outside had caught his attention, tapping a cigarette out of its packet, placing it to his thin, aristocratic lips before turning back to Heike.

'They will arrest you, you know. You're a traitor in their eyes. They'll fly you to the US where you'll be imprisoned; your child will be put into a foster home. And once they have you, they'll never let you go. They would tie your name to that of your colleague – the terrorist who was arrested shortly after the Frankfurt bombing – Fräulein Engel. You'd never see Germany again. They might even slap a terrorism charge on you if they could connect you with the bombing. We could not guarantee your safety, you understand? We cannot help you if you leave.'

Uncle was quite right and Heike knew it, but she wouldn't accept it. This wasn't a rational thing; she had to return home with the baby because there was something deep and primeval stirring her innermost thoughts – the need to return to her tribe. Heike the Westerner, born and brought up to be as free as a bird, free to do as she pleased whenever the mood took her. She was now a long, long way off understanding that those freedoms she'd once enjoyed had been left behind forever. That evening as they promenaded in the park she told Roland of her need to see her mother again. 'She'd adore him! I have to go, Roland.'

'Why?'

'Because I understand now – I understand what being a mother means. Before Johann, I was living for myself.'

'I see. Did I play a part?'

'Of course you did! I wouldn't go anywhere without you – you know I wouldn't, my love.' She grabbed his arm and pulled him close, burying her nose deep into his tweed jacket sleeve – sniffing back tears.

'What's the matter with you, my little Marxist? It's not like you to be so emotional. Are you suggesting that we jump the Wall? Because these days, that's impossible.'

'No, I haven't lost my senses – not yet at least. I thought maybe you might have a privilege as a journalist? You've worked for your newspaper a long time now and maybe your editor could see his way to sending you on a working holiday?'

'To a neighbouring Eastern bloc country – yes. In the West our authorities would fear me defecting, or they'd insist that

I spy for them. Everybody who goes to the West on business is ordered to spy, there is no choice, and if you do spy then they'll ask you again and again – they never give up. So that's not possible and may never be possible.'

'Do you mean we're stuck here forever?'

'I am not stuck! I've always been here. You're the one who used your democratic choice. Were you so naive as to think that they'd let you wander home again whenever the whim took you? My God! Heike, what were you thinking?'

Heike took her face out of his sleeve, dropping the grip on his arm as she did so. 'This stupid old tweed jacket of yours could do with a clean – it stinks!'

'Don't be angry with me! You're scaring the baby. I was different then. I didn't have Johann or you!' He looked for a reprieve in her face, but found only stubborn determination.

He tried to offer some hope at least: 'There is talk of an accord being reached soon that would enable people to emigrate to the West officially, but it's only a rumour. Much will have to be ironed out before anything is agreed.'

'I don't want to emigrate, Roland. I like it here – really. I just want to see my mother with Johann.'

'I know you do, but it isn't possible. Comrade Wendt is right – the Americans would detain you and take the baby. The only alternative is to bring your mother here.'

'But then she couldn't leave either and she's too old to find work here in Berlin. She likes the quiet life, small out of the way places. She's not a city girl.'

'No, but she can visit West Berlin and you could see her across the Wall. There is a vantage point for Westerners—'

'I don't want to wave to her, Roland! I want her to hold Johann in her arms – her grandson.'

The remainder of their walk might have concluded with them metres apart and observing an awkward silence, not unlike their very first outing together, had it not been for the interaction of an elderly couple who approached them – Herr Wilhelm Bakker and his wife of forty years, Traudel; a friendly couple now retired from the civil service but in receipt of a decent stipend for services to the state. Near neighbours, they lived just a few houses away – their instruction being to keep a discreet eye on the young couple.

The encounter was not a first. The Bakkers had introduced themselves very soon after Heike and Roland had moved into the neighbourhood and so it was not unusual to stop for a moment and exchange pleasantries. That particular night, the encounter helped to lighten the mood.

'Good evening! How are you both? How is your beautiful little boy?'

'He's very well, thank you! Always a handful, of course!'

'Aren't they always – especially boys. May I pick him up?'

Traudel Bakker phrased her request in a way that to refuse would have been churlish in the extreme, but Heike was only too pleased to show him off. Johann was in a very sociable mood and made not a murmur as the seventy-two-year-old former concentration camp guard lifted him from his pram and lovingly caressed his chubby flesh.

'I love babies!' she told them, looking into the distance. 'We would have had grandchildren by now, but my son was killed on the Russian front – long before your time.'

Heike reached out, gently placing her hand on the woman's cold, bare forearm as if there were still a need to comfort her all these years later.

'He was born in 1924, you see. Every boy born in Germany in that year died on the Eastern Front. I don't think a single one survived. The other years were more fortunate, but not that year. I still see his old teacher, Frau Abeln. Her whole class of boys from that year perished.' She hugged the child close to her chest. 'Oh, but you're beautiful, aren't you? Life will not be like that for you, my love.'

'Not unless the Americans break through!'

'Ah! Wilhelm. Enough! Don't frighten the young couple. So, he likes to joke, you know.'

Heike held her hand out to the baby so that he could grip her finger. 'I want his grandmother to see him, but there is a problem.'

'A problem? Why so?'

'She lives in the West – in Xanten. He is her first grandchild…'

'My dear, where there is a will there is a way. My man and I are convinced that one day soon the West will pull out of Berlin – they can't afford to maintain it forever, bringing in food and materials all the time. And when they pull out of Berlin they will soon pull out of all Germany.'

This was just the sort of response Heike wanted to hear from somebody, and the old lady was not about to disappoint. She continued: 'The Americans are isolationists by nature. They're here to spread the dollar and cause inflation – that's what they did when we were younger – but in time they'll realise it costs them more than they gain. They will pull out because they're ruled by financial gain, not by nationalism – certainly not by socialism. As soon as their shares start falling they'll be out of here, I'm sure of that.'

'You're so right,' replied Heike; but Frau Bakker needed no encouragement to continue her tirade against Western imperialism: 'Vietnam has not gone their way and they're running from there with their tails between their legs. They'll do the same here. They won't risk a nuclear war. And when they go, the British and French will go with them because without the Americans they are nothing! Take my word for it – you and your baby have nothing to fear!'

For a while, the two women pulled the West apart, and particularly America, while their husbands looked on patiently and politely, keenly aware that they shared not one common thing other than to be citizens of East Berlin and a certain passivity in the company of women.

Johann eventually broke up the party screaming, perhaps when he realised that his mother had seemingly parted company with him forever; or maybe he glimpsed the shivering, wretched ghosts that clung to the woman who had once shoved, cajoled and whipped their living bodies in Treblinka.

'I want to see Mama pick him up,' she later told Roland: 'I want to see her pick him up and cradle him in her arms, and I want to see that more than anything in this world.'

It wouldn't be long before she got that opportunity.

Making a plan

Just two weeks after their walk in the park, Uncle Frederick came forward with a plan – a plan that would help in her quest to reunite with Kirsten. It was really someone else's idea – someone she didn't know and would never meet. The plan involved the following: firstly, she should write to her mother in Xanten and invite her to West Berlin where she could indeed meet with the baby. Uncle had fixed it; he understood her needs. Heike would be free to cross over into the Western sector, but with the proviso that she rendezvous with a man who would make himself known to her in a certain place at a certain time.

He would pass to her a package – an innocuous package, nothing nasty, but something that he couldn't cross the border with because it would set unnecessary alarm bells ringing in the West and his family would be compromised.

'What if I'm searched?' she asked.

'Oh, you'll be searched alright,' Uncle replied; 'but they won't find anything other than a new wristwatch that your mother will have given you. That's what is in the package, and you will need to open it and put it on as soon as you receive it. Even if you have to stand in your underwear for a few moments the watch will be of no interest to their security people. Should they question it for any reason, you will have the packaging with a receipt and a small note saying: "With love, Mama".'

'I already have a watch.'

'Then you leave it at home. I will collect the new watch from you just as soon as you return.'

'What if they arrest me?'

'Arrest you for what? On what charge? We're not asking you to spy, simply to bring home a very important article.'

'But, Uncle, you told me that they would know me if I returned. The girl that defected – remember?'

'If you were crossing under your identity, then yes, it would be more risky. But we'll give you an extra identity so that they won't make any connection.'

'It sounds very dangerous!'

'You won't be there for long. You have a time limit of just two and a half hours.'

'And if I refuse?'

'Child, it's the only way I can think of that will enable you to meet with your mother and show her the baby. I have racked my brains trying to come up with another idea, but this is the best I can do. There is no alternative.'

'Should I tell Roland?'

'There is no need to tell him. You will only be gone for a few hours during the middle of the day – as much time as it takes to stroll in the park. Tell him when you're home again.'

The kindness of Uncle Frederick seemed to know no bounds. He was the one who'd found them an apartment in a quiet, professional district; he was the one who encouraged her links with her British cousins, the man who cleared the family photographs; the man who'd found her a new job and with it a loving husband. She would not have survived in East Berlin had it not been for Uncle Frederick.

Now, he was calling in the favour.

The British Café

It was all meticulously arranged: they would meet in the British Café for tea and cake, or scones, whichever was preferred. Prior to their meeting at 11.17 am, a man would make himself known to her. It was all very James Bond. He would hand her a package, they would kiss each other as if cousins and then he would depart. Nothing could be more simple. Kirsten need know nothing.

How exciting to even think that soon she would be seeing everything she'd left behind – her mother, the bright lights in the shops, no queues, the colour in people's clothes and even the colour in their faces.

Johann would need to look his very best; it was tempting to pack his entire wardrobe. Baby formula is not so easy to handle when your hands tremble. Hugs are tighter, kisses more pronounced. 'What's the matter with me?' she called out in frustration at trying to do up a button on the baby's woollen cardigan; all this to a husband yet to leave the house, a husband quite unaware that his new wife would soon be on her way to West Berlin with his only son.

The last time she had trembled like this was when she left home for a new life in East Berlin. That whole episode seemed a lifetime away.

'What's the matter with you this morning?' he asked, never having quite seen her like this.

'I'm fine!' she lied. 'It's just one of those mornings when nothing goes right.'

He completed the task for her, only too happy to help out. It would have been so nice to tell him the truth – tell him that his mother-in-law was in town and that she was just popping out to see her; just passing through the Wall and the gates for a coffee and a sandwich in that "other" fortress.

Kirsten would most certainly take to Roland; Heike was sure they'd make a great family. And who knows, maybe the old lady in the park was right; maybe the Americans were close to pulling out of West Berlin and even West Germany. The Germans would get along just fine if left to their own devices.

Roland was one for the clock – the precision of time. He knew that if he left their apartment at 8.10 precisely his walk to the tram would be a leisurely one; he hated having to hurry. East Berlin trams were always on time; *he* was always on time. Heike could count on him being out of the door and on his way, and sure enough this morning was no exception.

Well, it might not have been an exception had he not realised that he had left behind a document that he'd worked on quite late the previous evening. The document was a boring information sheet on an out of town glassworks that had cost him at least three hours' homework and faded his typewriter ribbon, so the fact that he'd paced a good hundred metres or more by the time he realised was infuriating to say the least.

He stopped and turned, knowing that he'd have to go back to get it because his editor insisted on having the wretched paper that morning by 9 am. The editor wasn't a bad boss; Roland had a good relationship with him, so better to remember now than at journey's end.

Turning the corner back onto Meyer Strasse, face down anxiously contemplating his polished black shoes getting wetter and wetter splashing through copious puddles while cursing his stupidity. By the time he might be able to get to work, he was going to look a right mess from head to foot. *Won't this rain ever stop?* Roland hated getting wet. Maybe if Heike hadn't been acting so oddly he'd have remembered the wretched document, but such was family life. Single life was simple before marriage; as a single man, he'd never forgotten anything. Whatever, Heike was a very different person now the baby had arrived.

He was within 25 metres of the apartment when he eventually lifted his eyes from the pavement. What he saw stunned him. There was Heike with Johann in her arms climbing into the back seat of a black limousine – a broad man in a black suit holding the door open for her like some sinister chauffeur. Slamming the door, he then jumped in and the car sped away in the direction of Heinrich Strasse.

This was always Roland's greatest dread: a foreigner like Heike was always going to be under suspicion whether she realised it or not. Now he feared that she and the child were on their way to prison and there was nothing he could do about it.

Editor Karl Tibitz was at least grateful for the document, despite giving it scant attention. One of life's natural journalists, he prided himself on his observations, claiming that he never missed a trick, and dropping into conversation his belief that the police force had missed out on a great detective when he chose journalism over state security.

Roland knew that if he asked Tibitz for confidentiality, he would get it. Tibitz was perhaps the most trustworthy of Roland's small circle of colleagues that could be relied upon in an emergency; and this was an emergency.

Tibitz gestured Roland to follow him, to move away from the phones and walls and lamps and ceilings, and well away from those colleagues who might loiter nearby. 'Let's have a cigarette, shall we?'

Outside, the two men found a very open space where they could light up and chew the fat, safe – they hoped – in the belief that to be overheard out here in the open yard with a background noise of distant traffic and construction work would be nigh on impossible.

Trembling slightly, Roland was clearly agitated.

'What's the matter with you, my friend? You look like you've seen a ghost,' said Tibitz.

'What do you know about Hohenschönhausen?'

'Hohenschönhausen? That's an area some kilometres northeast of here. What about it?'

'There's a prison there.'

'Really? Who told you that?'

'I heard it somewhere. It's been there since the war but the authorities pretend it doesn't exist.'

'Then I'm sure it doesn't exist.'

'I think my wife has been taken there.'

'Your wife? What's she done?'

'She's been telling people that she wants to see her mother in the West. She's been saying that she won't take no for an answer. I think someone's informed on her and so the *Polizei* have picked her up.'

'My dear Roland, I'm sure there's a perfectly reasonable explanation. Do you know for sure that's why she's been apprehended?'

'I saw a man bundle her into a car this morning – the baby too. They'll take the baby away from us! I was stupid to let her talk like that to strangers – so stupid!'

'If that's all you saw, then there could be any number of reasons. Was she struggling with the *Polizei*?'

'No, but she had the baby in her arms.'

'Did they see you?'

'No.'

'Perhaps I could make a phone call on your behalf? I have contacts. I won't mention any prison, and I strongly advise that you do the same.'

'I'd be grateful for anything.'

The air was no fresher in West Berlin; to a degree, it seemed worse, but then again there were more cars. Big cars, brightly coloured cars – Mercs, BMWs, VWs, Opels, Fords, Audis, Porsche. She'd never before in her life given a car a second glance, but now as they streamed past her they seemed to form quite a spectacular parade of bright colours.

She looked around at the people to see if anyone was looking at her, pointing her out. She felt more exposed now than at any time in her short life. Someone was bound to recognise her and draw the attention of the *Polizei*, who would in turn hand her over to the American authorities.

Hey! It's that girl! The one who defected. She's the traitor!

She's a terrorist! She's the one who masterminded the bombing in Frankfurt!

Like a premonition, as if on cue, in the near distance someone shouted out – a man's angry voice. She was too far away to make out what was being shouted, but she wasn't going to risk anything, and picking Johann up out of his buggy she walked into the nearest shop and pretended to be a customer.

Through the shop window she could see two uniformed *Polizei* running towards where the shouting had come from.

'That'll be another angry shopkeeper after a shoplifter, you can bet,' remarked a female staff member on her knees restocking the store's hair care range. She didn't look up at Heike or the baby; her attention was solely on pricing the new products. 'We've had them in here – foreigners up to no good. Berliners didn't steal even when they were starving to death! Send them to the East, I say. Honecker knows how to deal with them!'

Wondering why she wasn't getting a response, she glanced up at Heike: 'Can I help you with anything?'

'Erh, I was wondering what you'd recommend for my baby's hair?'

'All the Johnson's baby hair care products are in the aisle marked "For Baby". This is all adult hair care.'

'Thank you, and… do you know where I might find the British Café?'

'It is here on Invalidenstrasse. Turn right when you leave here and it's down the street – just a minute's walk – on this side of the road, on the corner of Hessische Strasse.'

'Thank you!' Heike was about to walk out, but the assistant stopped her.

'Wait! I thought you wanted to buy some baby shampoo?'

'Yes, I do – thank you!'

'Be careful in the British Café. It's full of soldiers – British soldiers. They can be… rude, you know.'

'Why?'

'They see too many German blue movies and think all of us are sex crazy.'

As Heike walked out clutching Johann, who in turn was clutching her purchase, the assistant turned to her colleague. 'Another shoplifter, I bet. Dodged in here to keep out of trouble, but I was watching her. They use babies now to hide what they've stolen and for pleading innocence. They ought to be ashamed! A life in the East under Honecker would put her right!'

On the other side of the Wall, not so many metres away, Roland was chain-smoking; his head full of visions of prisons, of a baby being brought up in an institution and the eventual return of a broken wife – beaten into submission and a shadow of her former self.

The British Café was a tiny outpost of Empire, its walls adorned with old framed photographs of Churchill, Montgomery and, of course, Her Majesty Queen Elizabeth II. Illustrious portraits framed, as were their various letters to one another: correspondence between Churchill and King George VI; and correspondence between Churchill, the King and Montgomery.

In the corners of the room, the colours of those regiments that had been stationed in the British quarter since the war stood like so many giant parasols, along with various union flags from Continental battles, all torn, faded and redundant.

'Tea please!' asked Heike in perfect Anglo-American. There was no need, the waitress was one hundred per cent Berliner born and bred.

The assistant in the pharmacy had been quite right, there were a number of soldiers frequenting the café noticeably in civilian dress. Off-duty soldiers always stood out, with their short hair and immaculate casual clothes, as if the '60s had never happened. A group of women sat across the room in a haze of smoke – clearly not Berliners, though their English was not at all like Hanne's or Aunt Rene's speech.

They were discussing babies in the most base way, grumbling to one another about the cost of nappies, the problems of potty training, all the while inhaling cigarette after cigarette; it didn't take Heike long to realise that these women didn't like children at all, nor did they like their husbands or the army or "bloody Berlin".

'When I married my old man in Aldershot, he said we'd be in Malta and then Cyprus and then Belize. Then he'd come out, he said. What did we get? This stinking shite hole for the past four years! We were in Sennelager for two years! We either froze to death in winter or sweltered in summer. His next posting is Tidworth and that'll be it! So much for joining the fookin' army and see the fookin' world – pardon my French.'

'Annette's old man left her for a Jerry! Left Annette high and dry on her own out here and not knowing anyone on camp. She'd only just arrived. He'd been here for months, and when she arrived she found out he'd shacked up with this cow in the nearby town. She had to fly back to Brize Norton and begin divorce proceedings. And do you know what? That Jerry cow was the town bike! Didn't matter what regiment came in, she slept with every bloke who bought her a pint in the Naafi.'

The men, supping their off-duty lunchtime beers, took no notice of the women. The only thing Heike noticed about them was that whenever one of them ordered another pint of beer, it was ordered in German – albeit very basic German – and that their comments were focussed entirely on the waitress.

She was beginning to wonder about the possibility that the stranger who was to rendezvous with her just might not turn up. If that was the case, she feared that Uncle would somehow blame her for not being on time or for being in the wrong place. What if this wasn't the only British Café?

'Excuse me?' she called the waitress over. 'This is the only British Café, isn't it?'

'Yes. There isn't another with the title. The British frequent all the cafés and bars in their sector, but this is the only one with the title "British Café".'

'Thank you!'

A youngish man, around thirty years of age, breezed in looking rather uptight. *Could this be him?* she wondered. He took no notice of her and made his way to a table where he sat down, stowing a bright orange plastic sports bag under his chair as if fearing someone might trip over it or even take it. He looked like a German, she thought; definitely not a British squaddie.

For a while, she wondered whether he'd make a move towards her. She was tempted to smile or nod or wave at him just in case he hadn't recognised her. What if he hadn't been as well informed as Uncle had suggested? Maybe he was a novice and this was his first assignment. After all, he wasn't behaving in the way that Uncle had said he would. According to Uncle, her contact would arrive very businesslike, go straight up to her, reach out and kiss her like a relative, hand her the package and then depart, making his apologies.

And then there was Mama. What would she make of a strange man coming up to kiss Heike before passing her a parcel containing a gift for unwrapping that very moment?

Mama was the other unknown. What if she was angry or moody – distant and unresponsive even to the baby? The more the minutes ticked by the more her fears began to overwhelm her.

Thank goodness for Johann's smiling face. He seemed to be able to take everything in his stride with hardly ever a murmur or outburst. He was her constant pleasure. No mother could be more proud of this young man; he never complained, and not one sleepless night in all these past eleven months.

She could already picture him in the years to come – tall, athletic, with a happy disposition. Like his father, he would probably be a wordsmith, having done well at school, of course. Roland would love and nurture him in all the ways that GI Joe didn't or wouldn't do with her or Peter. Theirs would be a tightknit family unit with maybe another baby in a year or so: a daughter perhaps next time round.

And perhaps the old lady in the park was right in her forecast: that the two Germanys would become one again once the Americans and their allies pulled out. After all, they couldn't stay forever. By the year 2000 Johann would be twenty-eight with a family of his own perhaps.

She looked back at the soldiers and the group of loud, complaining women, then bending down to Johann gently whispered: 'Whatever you do, don't ever become a soldier.'

It was at that moment that another man strode into the café alone – also young, not bad looking in Heike's opinion. His eyes scanned the room before he noticed Heike; no one else seemed to notice him.

He strode over to her table, his face beaming with mock delight. 'My dear cousin! At last, we meet again.' He put a small parcel onto the table beside her. Nervously, she rose to greet him and they embraced and kissed as arranged, much to Johann's amusement.

'With my sincere apologies please accept my gift and wear it immediately – it will help you to get home. Forgive me, I can't stay.' His beam fading, the stranger turned on his heels and left the café, the doorbell clanging behind him as he disappeared into the maelstrom that was West Berlin.

Thank heavens! She relaxed. *Was that all it was about? At least that bit is over.* She tore open the brown wrapping paper to reveal a jewellery box. Inside the box was the most delightful Swiss-made watch, its blue and red dial furnished with chrome hands and even a figure for the date. What's more, the strap was real leather! This was no cheap watch from a department store.

'Very '70s, perversely ostentatious, very West Berlin.' She dangled it in front of Johann's searching eyes; he seemed fascinated by the gift. 'Do you think Uncle will let me keep it? I hope so! Don't you?'

As she strapped the elegant watch to her wrist, she looked across to where the lonely young man had been sitting. He wasn't to be seen, but his bag was still under the chair – the bright orange plastic sports bag.

She was just about to alert the waitress to the fact that he must have left it behind—

*

Flying glass and wood and metal punctures and tears fragile human bodies. You need to be in just the right place if you're to survive.

*

Even in the newsroom, the blast was enough to send a shockwave through the building. Windows shook. Roland and many other East Berliners stopped what they were doing to wonder just what the hell had happened. Even the mighty Wall couldn't diminish the moment a West Berlin café was blown out into the street. Then came the sirens – the endless sound of sirens.

Heike eventually awoke to find Kirsten staring down at her, clasping her weak hand tightly. The room was so extremely brightly lit and she had been in the dark for so long. The dream from which she had just awoken with a jolt was that of being lifted from the tarmac of a cold street by a man so strong that he picked her up as if she were nothing more than a rag doll. He'd said, as if speaking through a tube: 'This one's alive! Be gentle now.'

All of a sudden, the conscious world to which she'd been returned made sense. She was back in the delivery room – aching in every muscle. She turned her head for an answer.

'Have you seen the baby, Mama?

'Have you seen my baby?

'Have you seen your grandson…? I will call him… I will call him… I called him Johann!'

A SHADOWY MAN AND BRUNO

Roland could make no headway with his wife's recovery. Her battered and bruised body was taking time to heal, and whenever he tried to place a loving hand on her she flinched and retreated.

The apartment was unbearably quiet. Sometimes, in a nearby room, he would overhear her talking to someone. Curious as to who it might be, he would peep round the door to find that there wasn't anybody else at all. Heike would be on her knees talking to Johann, conversing with his spirit as if she could see or sense the boy in a way Roland could not. She would speak to Mama Kirsten, too, even though she was safely settled back in Xanten; her physical absence seemed to make no difference.

Kirsten had been delayed in reaching the café that morning; a slow train from the west had necessitated an unscheduled change of train, then her inability to find the café had led to her arriving shortly after the bomb had detonated. Standing among the gathering crowd, trembling, she watched the emergency services go about the rescue while the *Polizei* tried to usher them away.

'I think my daughter's in there!' she pleaded, though she couldn't be certain.

In the crowd, voices speculated as to whether it was a gas explosion – it was a café, after all – or whether it was terrorists.

Exactly an hour after the bomb went off, the Red Army Faction called a West Berlin newspaper admitting responsibility, claiming that the bomb was planted specifically to hit British service personnel for their occupation of Northern Ireland and the killing of innocent lives during the Bloody Sunday riots. The café was an easy target.

Heike was conscious as they loaded her into an ambulance.

Kirsten, having recognised her, pushed through the cordon, heard her mumbling something about having to be back in the Eastern sector because Roland needed her and the Americans would capture both her and the child if she didn't get home immediately.

For two days she sat at her daughter's bedside as Heike's condition swung from initial improvement to decline. At one point it looked as if she was losing her battle and a priest was called with the utmost urgency, only for her to rally, much to Kirsten's relief.

During her long bedside vigil Kirsten would talk to her of many things, much of which was of no real consequence, but she repeated this line many times: 'I saw my two brothers go to war and I was there to welcome them home. I'm going to welcome you home, child.'

Of course, she could do no such thing; but she was determined to be there when Heike regained consciousness.

The wristwatch? No one in West Berlin gave it a second thought and it was returned to Heike with a scratched face but otherwise undamaged, its Swiss mechanism as precise as ever.

Once she had recovered enough to face him, she handed it solemnly to Uncle Frederick, who commended her most highly for the part she played in receiving it. The placing of the bomb had been tragically coincidental. No one East or West could have foreseen such an attack.

The irony was that the watch was of no significance to anyone whatsoever. It was all a device to test Heike's loyalties. A sleeper – as they suspected her to be – might well have attempted to inform her superiors of the transaction or try to find out if the watch contained anything. Of course, the bomb went off shortly after it was handed to her, so the test was void. She remained a suspect in the eyes of the Stasi, but at least they had no evidence to confirm that she was an agent for the West.

*

In the car that evening, she would tell Hanne all this – at last. One thing: she wasn't going to talk about was the depression following bereavement. Hanne could not understand it; no one could. The cold, the sleepless nights and days of black, black depression. Those days when she so longed to walk to the Wall in order to try to break through so that someone would shoot her dead. Oh yes, that was a way out for sure, and the only thing that stopped her was the thought that whoever shot her would be someone else's son – a beloved son. No son of any loving mother deserved to be her executioner.

*

Peter's timely arrival in East Berlin brought her back from the brink: his motivation being to save his big sister.

He'd taken the same route, entered through the same gate and said much, much the same to his inquisitors as his sister had done thirty-six months earlier. The very same (welcoming) committee, in turn, treated him with equal suspicion. They came to the conclusion that he too was part of a newly emerging information-gathering operation, that was curious to say the least because it was actually beyond their collective imaginations to even consider that in heart and spirit he was a motivated idealistic youth who railed at those unpunished Nazis who were again in charge of West German affairs.

Following ten days of fruitless and cruel interrogation, Uncle Frederick delivered him to Heike and Roland's door with this introduction: 'I think you know this young man?'

She didn't, of course. The tall, skinny, unshaven youth standing trembling and hunched on the doorstep bore little resemblance to anyone she knew or had ever known. She glanced back at Uncle's face as if to say, *Who's this you've brought us?* The youth seemed vaguely familiar. He appeared to be under arrest as Uncle, with stern demeanour, was holding him close with a firm grip around the bicep. It was as if he'd been caught stealing apples and now the farmer was returning him with a reprimand.

She looked deeper into the miscreant's face, which was partially obscured by the evening's grey shadow and ten days of stubble growth. Only at that moment did the penny drop: her eyes glistened, a faint smile of recognition; it was the *last* person she'd ever expected to see standing there on Held Strasse.

'Peter?' Her timid question faltered on the evening air. Was this really her "little" brother on her very doorstep?

The shadowy boy nodded so gently, so submissively, whilst Uncle pushed him over the threshold before doffing his trilby and turning back toward the waiting black limousine. Heike gently took the stick of an arm that had been gripped so fiercely and led him into the warm kitchen. 'You must be cold and thirsty. I'll put the coffee on. Or do you want tea? Are you hungry? You must be hungry.'

Roland stopped himself from asking stupid questions of Peter. He was sure that he knew exactly why he was here; but at least Heike was talking and, for the first time, actually smiling. Now was the moment for making up a bed. He left them to talk, but Peter was beyond talking to anyone.

It was easier – slightly easier – the following morning over breakfast. There was porridge and fresh bread, coffee all laid out before him and, most importantly of all, warmth. He hadn't felt warm since arriving in East Berlin. The last week and a half had unnerved him horribly, and even in the comfort of his sister's modest apartment he was having difficulty relaxing. She wanted to say something reassuring but couldn't think of anything so she asked bluntly: 'Did you honestly think they'd welcome you?'

'I don't know. What did *you* expect when you came here first?'

'I was a very naive child.'

'Oh, come on, Heike! You did an amazing thing – got away from all that crap, and you did it on your own. You knew what you were doing. I wanted to follow you, but I was too young. I was the naive one, not you.'

'So what changed your mind?'

'I had to come when Mama told me what had happened to you. We thought you were safe and happy until then.'

'I *was* safe and happy. I just wanted Mama to see him. It was a bad thing in the café, but it could have happened to us anywhere. It could have killed Mama, too. Thank goodness she was late!'

'You lost your baby!'

'I didn't lose him!' Heike was momentarily incredulous that he should even imagine such a thing: 'He is still here – we talk all the time. Johann is always with me.'

Peter the realist, the little brother who'd always taken a delight in bursting his elder sister's balloons, the child who'd refused to believe in God or Father Christmas, could only glance down in silent tribute. Even Roland had not heard this from Heike, though he had suspected as much.

'The Red Army Faction are crazy! It's not the way to achieve their aims.'

'Would you have thought the same thing if Heike hadn't been there?' Roland asked him.

'I don't know. They have a lot of support you know,

especially among our generation. Germany needs to listen – West Germany needs to listen. The fascists are all still in place running government over there. Local government has been infiltrated and the big industries are controlled by them. Someone has to stop them.'

'But not with bombs and bullets!' snapped Roland. 'Our baby is dead because of those Baader-Meinhof bastards. I nearly lost my wife, too.'

Heike slammed the table with her fist. 'Roland – PLEASE! Your baby is not dead!' For a moment there was another deep, anguished silence.

Peter continued: 'I'm not an apologist – I'm just saying what is happening.'

'The boy who planted that bomb knew I had a baby with me,' whispered Heike, wiping streams of tears from her cheeks with the back of her hand; 'I saw him come in… He saw me, he saw Johann. He could have said to me – something? Made an excuse for us to leave. But he didn't. He walked out, leaving us to… He knew what our fate would be and he didn't care!'

She collapsed to the floor in an uncontrolled heap, shaking, heaving, gasping for breath between sobs as the world fell in on her. Roland dropped to his knees beside her, embracing and absorbing as much of her misery as he could take upon himself: 'Let it out, darling… let it all out… Cry for Johann… cry for him, darling… cry for us all.'

Talk of the bombing or the reasons behind it infuriated Roland. He was not entirely sure that he wanted a brother-in-law under his roof at that particular moment in time. He turned to shout at Peter, shout at him to get the hell out of their lives, but the boy had already disappeared from view.

During the days that followed Peter's arrival, Roland had to admit to himself that for the first time since Johann's death

Heike was finally gaining strength and was even animated again. She was now able to share their bed; and for that, he would always be profoundly grateful for the boy's arrival. Hopefully, the days of talking to ghosts were behind them.

Heike, the good citizen

The Stasi were never far away from the couple. This was not unusual, of course, in a totalitarian state, but Roland and Heike Bermann were special cases – she being a defector from the West.

Now, with Peter having defected as well, there was even more reason for those tasked to watch and listen as the little family tried to pull itself back from the brink of despair and back toward cold, grey reality with all its daily frustrations.

Every so often they would hear shots being fired as someone tried to get through or over the Wall, but the Wall had grown so immense in height and breadth that only the very hardy and foolish attempted to actually cross it. Anyway, safe to say that apart from those occasional outbursts – shots followed by shouts – nothing remarkable happened in that apartment on Held Strasse to give the Stasi cause for concern.

The apartment was bugged and had been from the beginning of their occupancy. Listening devices placed discreetly here and there. Even when the couple felt it was time to move to something larger and more rural, especially now that an additional family member was living with them and, most wonderfully, another baby was due, Uncle Frederick dutifully stepped in to convince them that the apartment was a far better environment in which to bring up a newborn; his argument being that should NATO forces invade, East Berliners would come under the immediate protection of the state, something those living in more rural areas were not afforded.

Heike the good citizen never saw those who watched her, and they watched her daily. The bearded man across the street with the friendly dog, the old lady upstairs who always smiled and talked, the busy young woman who ran the laundrette and offered cigarettes, even teachers at the school and, most especially, *me*.

We all watched her.

You see, *we* watched because *we* had to, as someone was watching *us*.

From the pages of German history came those professional spies who had forged their credentials as communists during the struggles of the '30s. Others had been street fighters openly engaging the National Socialists of Hitler and Röhm with whatever they could bring to bear. They considered themselves "survivors" of a regime that had all but wiped out their comrades. Driven into the woods or neighbouring countries, these communists had been the first inmates of the concentration camps – the first to be worked to death, to be executed; the first to have no marked graves or memorial to their struggle for existence.

The younger "watchers" fell into two distinct camps: those who fancied themselves as worthy citizens of the state (ironically, Heike might have considered that she belonged to this vanguard); they would do as they were told; individuality was, in their view, a dangerous thing and resulted in people getting killed. Then there was the second group of watchers. This group watched because the state had something on them. Work for us and we'll reduce your son's prison sentence or get him the comforts he needs. Work for us and we'll turn a blind eye to that misdemeanour. Work for us and we'll get your mother to the top of the waiting list; she'll need that eye surgery; she needs a roof over her head. Work for us and you'll get that promotion/ house/holiday. We just need you to watch someone, make some notes, that sort of thing. We'll look after you.

Nobody asked Heike to watch anybody. *She* was the watched, but not the watcher. It never occurred to her. No suggestion of impropriety was ever made. This was an idyllic state, after all; and yes, she was still naive.

In a godless society, there were no godfathers for children, but Uncle Frederick played his part in stretching his mighty wing of protection over Heike's newborn – Bruno Johann. Should Heike be found to be an active spy and therefore imprisoned, the child would be accommodated and treated well. The papers and plans were drawn up and ready; all it needed was for Heike to put a foot wrong, then the allocation could proceed with due haste.

As the years flew by, Bruno's playground was the neighbourhood. He could go up to the Wall, but not too close; don't cause anyone anxiety, and do what the guards tell you – always!

School was fun but hard work. Children in the East were better, he was told; stronger, more capable than their cousins in the West. That was a particularly difficult concept: the idea that the people on the other side of the Wall were known as "cousins".

'Are you good citizens?' the children were asked every morning. 'Of course!' came the reply. What other answer could there be?

Bruno was unremarkable and unaware for the most part that he was something of a special case in the East Berlin educational community. His mother's file flagged up the fact that she was a defector from the West and therefore under the close scrutiny of the authorities. Quite often, when Bruno's name came under discussion by teachers, youth workers, or whoever, he would notice them conspire and glance at him for a moment or two.

'Is that *her* boy?'

'Yes, he's a good boy, but just keep an eye out, would you? Make some notes if you have to. Talk to me first if he says something a little odd, you know the sort of thing.'

Bruno never did oblige anyone with something a little odd or anything else. He was to all intents and purposes a very happy child, content in the narrow world in which he found himself.

The Wall fascinated him. He found it endlessly interesting to watch the guards at work, marching, smoking, watching with their binoculars, shifting their machine guns from shoulder to shoulder. Binos would make a good birthday present because he and the gang could play at being guards and spies. Lengths of copper pipe were fashioned into toy machine guns that would annihilate those trying to "escape". They would mimic goose-stepping and changing guard, and they were good mimics – barking orders at one another, swearing, checking papers. Any girl who wanted to play had to be a spy and would be searched and roughly pushed and cajoled. No one seemed to object to this game, although female interest soon waned.

The first time Bruno was shouted at by a guard to stay well away it scared the hell out of him and hurt his sensitivities: 'But I'm on your side!' he shouted back. The incident simply fed his curiosity all the more. He told his mother and in turn she told him the story of how she and her cousin Heidemarie would visit the border post to talk to the nice guards when she was his age. She told him, too, about her English cousin and how they took her along one day and how deep in the Bavarian countryside it was so very different. Everyone was more relaxed and friendly, but here in the city tensions were always high and the guards were much more nervous as there was so much more at stake. Best to stay well clear.

It concerned Heike that in Bruno's short life he had never walked in the grass. Whereas she had grown up playing in the summer meadows, climbing hills, rolling down hills, climbing trees, falling out of trees and swimming in the river, Bruno's playground was nothing more than Held Strasse and its surrounds.

The nearby parks had weedy, short, patchy grass that a hundred thousand rubber soles turned to mud in winter; it could never be the expanse of rural Bavaria.

For the most part, she spent much of her time picking Bruno up off the concrete and the dust, washing his wounds, disinfecting the bloody open gashes before sending him back out with a plaster. All too frequently he would fall on concrete, brick, rubble, timber pallets and planks with rusty nails.

Every other week, every other year, there would be some near catastrophe involving Bruno, yet the older he got the more robust he seemed to be and to all intents and purposes indestructible, which was a relief to his doting parents; but his neighbourhood was also his zoo.

He liked school; he was a happy pioneer, and before too long he would be in the FDJ (Freie Deutsche Jugend). Accidents apart, he didn't give his mother serious cause for concern, for which she was extremely grateful.

With each passing year, Heike considered herself content with her lot. Her "escape" from the West – her defection – seemed, in hindsight, to have been a beneficial move. Peter had long since moved out of their apartment having found work in the steel industry, again, under the directorial guidance of "Uncle" Frederick. Once employed, he distanced himself until there came a time where they no longer heard from him at all, much to Bruno's chagrin, as he adored his uncle.

*

Twenty-first century car radios infuriated Heike. Pressing "Search" was nowhere near as easy as turning a dial. Why did everything have to be so complicated? Eventually, it settled on a station playing British hits from the '60s, '70s, '80s and '90s. Very apt considering she was on her way to see her British cousin and in her head she'd already made the journey back to the '70s and '80s.

*

Nordmende Minibox

They had a nice apartment – a rare privilege in East Germany – and, most importantly, they were a family. Promotion eventually came Roland's way and brought with it a car (another rare privilege). Even a lowly second-hand Trabant was a great asset for the family; and the apartment secured by Uncle Frederick was a gift indeed. Few East Berliners – the proletariat – lived in such spacious accommodation.

By Western standards, it was nothing special, but on the Eastern side of the Wall such an abode suggested a citizen of rank. Roland was by no means a citizen of rank, merely a jobbing staff reporter – even after promotion to Chief Industrial Correspondent.

Someone suggested there might be further career advancement if he learnt English, and who better than Heike to fill the role of Roland's English teacher? He was a keen pupil, his belief being that if he could speak English he would get better assignments – be sent to international conferences even if only in the Eastern bloc, China, Vietnam, that sort of thing.

Little by little she taught him, starting with the common similarities between German and English, and before long they were tuning their little used transistor radio into English language stations and digesting the news broadcasts and the music. It wasn't always straightforward.

'The idea is to listen to English being spoken, not music,' she chastised him.

'But, darling, I love Erik Satie's music. My father loved Satie. *Gnossienne*. Don't you just love that piano? Haunting, isn't it?'

'Creepy, in my opinion. Gives me the shivers. Come on, Roland! Let's find the BBC or Voice of America or something.'

Listening to foreign broadcasts was something that East Berliner Roland had never before considered because it had always been against government wishes. As a schoolboy and member of the FDJ, he'd been encouraged to "out" those he knew to be tuning in to Western broadcasts. Previous generations of FDJ youth had even been sanctioned to break the aerials of those who had set them to pick up "subversive transmissions". The authorities actively blocked reception wherever possible, but the airwaves were a force of nature, and with advancements in broadcast stations and receivers the days of holding back the tide of Western influences were coming to an end. Now, under Heike's influence, he was exposed to a new perspective coming in over the airwaves of the little Nordmende Minibox. It amazed him that people would argue in the West about all sorts of things – subjects that in East Germany were never open for debate.

For every argument heard there was a counter argument and it fascinated him in much the same way as Bruno was fascinated by the Wall. Politicians even expressed their views to journalists who in turn seemed quite free to ask whatever they wished.

Ironically, it was not Roland but Heike who was somewhat unsettled by the broadcasts that she initially translated for her husband. She had spent years convincing herself that East was best; that the West was not only corrupt but also fundamentally flawed in so many aspects. Now her ideals were being challenged: not by some government organisation but by the BBC.

She didn't really know anything about the BBC or Britain. All she knew was that her cousin and uncle lived in the far southwest of England, but beyond that she had no concept. This was due largely to the fact that Joe hated Britain and the British with a passion unmatched by anyone else she knew. For him, Britain was number one in his list of hated countries and yet he never explained just where his vehement reaction had its roots. He would cite the misdeeds of King George III in the Americas and tell the family how lucky they were to be dual nationality citizens with free choice and not subjects of "a mad king" like those damn Limeys.

He wasn't alone in his hatred of the British – she'd known other Americans who could be very derogatory of "the Limeys", and the consensus seemed to be that if you were American you either hated Britain or at best didn't give a fig about the skinny little island.

She thought about censoring the programmes so that they only tuned in when a programme was unlikely to be broadcasting propaganda, for that's what the political content had to be, she was sure. Roland, however, was eager to listen: 'Come on, Heike! If I'm to speak this language, if I'm to understand the culture, then I need to listen – *we* need to listen – together!'

Roland was not a communist in the sense of idealism, he simply saw himself as a hard-working East Berliner, essentially a German and nothing more than a citizen of a state that had erected a vast barrier supposedly for the protection of its own people; naively, that it wasn't the Wall that held him captive but his own lack of ambition and ability.

Some of Roland's family had fled to the West in 1961 – those few from his mother's family who had survived the war: a distant aunt, uncle and two cousins. He remembered that his parents had also been tempted into going before the Wall was constructed. 'They were of two minds,' he would tell Heike. 'It was a very near thing. We were so close to making that move. We even started to pack, but caution prevailed. They had no one to go to, no job.'

His father, Niklas, feared that if Khrushchev were to push the Western powers out of Berlin – and it would only take a half hour at most in his opinion – then those who'd gone to the West would be caught and punished. And so reluctantly they stayed.

Listening to the radio – BBC World Service and very occasionally Voice of America – Roland and Heike grew increasingly aware of their own vulnerability. For the first time, it began to dawn on the couple that the East German state was actually watching them more than they'd ever dared to consider. This realisation was brought on not so much by a particular incident but by a discussion programme one evening where a former KGB agent in London was discussing how Moscow spied on all its citizens, but that that paled into insignificance when compared to East Germany.

'The Stasi,' according to the agent, 'were masters of surveillance having inherited the skills and tools necessary from the Nazi state. Nobody is more paranoid than the East German state,' he claimed.

'Sounds like a treacherous defector to me,' said Heike, 'a man with scores to settle and money to be made from the West. They'll pay him highly for having said that.' But Roland wasn't so sure.

It wasn't long after that programme that someone asked Roland how he was getting along learning his "new" language. This was unnerving. Who had been told? Had someone said something? Had Bruno talked at school? The boy came under suspicion for a while and a rift opened between father and son.

Then, one night in May, Roland noticed that whenever the radio was on there was a background hum – quite faint, but audible nonetheless. The hum remained whatever station he tuned into, but would fade somewhat if he took the radio out of the living room and placed it elsewhere. Something electrical was interfering with the reception so he tried isolating various electrical appliances, from lights to the refrigerator, but none of these actions made any difference. So he wrapped the radio up, placed it in a box and took it out in the car.

He drove out of the city for quite some distance until he reached open countryside north of Pankow. Worried that he'd been followed, fumbling inside the box like some guilty thief fearing that he might expose his illicit haul, he switched it on and, sure enough, there was no hum – just a clear signal.

It's probably something in the building, he thought. *Something in the building interferes with the radio reception? Maybe it's the local substation. How stupid!* Driving all the way out here, drawing attention to himself, and for what? This is what paranoia does to people. *Bloody hell!*

Uncle Frederick had not been shown the radio. Like naughty children hiding a guilty secret, Heike and Roland would hide it whenever Uncle visited. Silly, perhaps, as there wasn't a law against owning a radio or a TV, but they didn't want to talk about it so they put it out of sight in a linen cupboard. That's what East German families tended to do – hide things; pretend they didn't exist. Better not to have it or show it, especially as it was tuned to an English-speaking service; that way, nothing need be explained if anyone asked.

It was Heike who didn't want television and this was a reaction to her upbringing. GI Joe had brought the television into the family home sometime around 1962 and initially it was the most exciting thing ever. Neighbours from all around the district would drop in just to marvel at the picture set in that wonderful mahogany case. Nothing was allowed to be placed on its table-like top – no flowers, no photo frames. If it went wrong, he was able to fix it. It would pick up American programmes transmitted from a nearby base, and as bilingual children both she and Peter would translate the content to their friends, which, in the eyes of their peer group, made them geniuses. It was only later – some years later – that she realised that GI Joe used the television to demonstrate American culture and dominance.

He would plonk himself down in his personal "Ezee" chair as if lord and master, switch on the TV and tell them how they should learn from the westerns, especially about how civilising the American influence was.

'Look,' he would announce during a western adventure series: 'where there had been desert and savages, now there is a great nation of homes and gardens and towns and cities that is today the biggest and most prosperous nation in the world.'

'So what are you doing *here*?' Peter would whisper under his breath in German. Joe never heard, or if he did he pretended not to.

Worst of all, Joe insisted they watch an American TV series called *Combat* because, in his words, it captured the "reality" of the war he'd been in and "demonstrated the American ability to triumph over the evil of the Nazis".

In their apartment, Heike and Roland feared that they had to be the only ones listening to the English language stations and if anything was going to get them into trouble then it was this habit. But it was a habit they couldn't break.

Week after week, day after day, they were beginning to learn about the neighbourhood they inhabited. It seemed an irrational fear at first, the realisation that they were coming under scrutiny from all sides – from the state itself and from the West.

They had assumed that the West had no interest in the communist East other than it blocked free movement for their citizens. To the contrary, they learned that the BBC had little interest in Western Europe but considerable interest in the Eastern bloc. It dawned on Roland that the average Briton probably knew more about the citizens of East Germany than they ever did about the citizens of France, Belgium, Holland or Denmark.

Every day they would pass Westerners on the street – often Americans and British who came across to gawp at the "poor" Easterners going about their business – locals clearly identifiable by their drab, old-fashioned clothes; visible by their very reserved demeanour; visible because they so patiently waited and demanded nothing from anyone.

Roland didn't give a second glance to any of the tourists, though Heike despised them. 'I'm not an inmate!' she barked at one woman who was glaring at her and clearly paying her too much attention.

*

Thirty years later, she felt guilty about that flash of temper, the very thought of it made her squirm.

She knew the small town that Hanne was staying in but keyed in the address to the satnav as it might be difficult to find.

Fed up of hits from the '70s, she pressed "Search" and there, as if on cue, was Erik Satie's *Gnossienne*. You couldn't make it up. Maybe God *is* a DJ?

Should she mention politics to Hanne? If this conversation were to go ahead, what would Hanne think about her cousin's politics? 'You defected? We were told you fell in love with Roland in West Berlin and went to live with him in the East! How could you have been a card-carrying communist? How could you give up what you had in the West? Were you mad?'

It would be an impossible conversation. Most of the family didn't know the truth. They believed that Heike had gone to work in Berlin, fallen for a visiting East German and decided that she couldn't live without him and so joined him for love in the East. That's what all the cousins, aunts and uncles believed because that's what Kirsten had told them.

Heike would tell Hanne about Joe; his eventual separation from her mother was barely noticed by anyone in the family, particularly Kirsten. He just went off one day and never returned; never said anything or left a note – just didn't ever come back. He never so much as filed for divorce. As far as anyone could guess, he was most likely living bigamously somewhere in some log cabin that he'd always talked about building. That's all he ever talked about if he was in a talkative mood, but no one ever believed he would because there was nothing in his multi-mixed lineage to suggest that he could use an axe let alone build with it. It was more likely he was holed up in some trailer park and most likely in the southern Midwest where guns and ropes were still allowed to dictate the course of local disputes. That's the sort of man they believed him to be.

For a few years, cheques would arrive in the post for small amounts, nothing substantial but regular payments. No message was ever attached and Kirsten showed no care whatever.

Hanne would have no such secrets. She would be dumbfounded – dumbstruck. Hugo had been such a success. He hadn't even renounced his German citizenship, yet the Queen had honoured him. How proud could a child be of their father?

Concentrate on the road. Forget about saying anything. People have their secrets for whatever reasons – good reasons, often. Nothing need be said or at least ventured. Yet she did want to talk. She wanted to unburden herself. The years were moving on swiftly and the war generation was all gone. They couldn't be hurt. What did it matter now?

She practised how she would begin this. She would start off by saying: 'You won't think bad of me, Hanne, will you if I tell you everything? Tell you the truth. Tell you what I was, what I did. How my first son died and…'

She pulled the car over to a field entrance, turned off the engine and put the hazard flashers on. Sobbing, she fumbled around for a packet of tissues from the glove compartment and dabbed at her soaking wet face. Sniffing back the tears, she fixed her stare in the mirror and continued her rehearsal.

'You see, I thought I knew better. I thought it would be a better life, and for a time it was. The fact that I lied does not sit easy, I can tell you. You loved your father, but I hated mine – hated him with a passion. I'm not sure that he was my father.'

It occurred to her that this field entrance might be a good place in which to turn around. She had Hanne's mobile number, so she could ring and come up with some excuse, but that didn't solve anything. She thought of the visit to the grave – Oma's grave – with all the family in attendance.

Visualising her own demise, her grandchildren gathered at her graveside might say something like: 'Oma Heike the communist. Where so many escaped she walked right into the thick of it. But you know the worst thing about Oma Heike? She couldn't tell anyone the truth. Everyone was fooled into thinking they knew her, but they didn't. Oma Heike took the truth with her – to her grave.'

This vision shocked her. She must carry on to Hanne's rented house, tell her whatever had to be said even if it took all night. She would tell her about Roland's involvement with the opposition movement that would put them all in jeopardy and that her own brother may well have betrayed them to the Stasi.

*

Old acquaintances

Unknown to Heike at the time, Roland had renewed a friendship with an old school friend: production worker, Mikael Zech. They had been close at school – enthusiastic Young Pioneers of the Socialist Youth Group – but had drifted apart as adults.

Zech had been a talented electrical and technical engineer but had come under suspicion and was arrested on more than one occasion for "unpatriotic behaviour" that included posting anti-government leaflets. Correctional time in various prisons had done nothing to blunt his determination to challenge the state authorities, despite losing his qualification so that the only work he could get was that of a production worker.

Zech had a prophetic sense of his own destiny, convinced that he was to play an important role in bringing down the state and reuniting Germany. He was a member of an underground network that had been growing in number over the past eighteen months – a group that sensed that the time was drawing near when they would be able to "storm the Bastille" without fear of recrimination. The age of Gorbachev's "glasnost" had dawned and it would only be a matter of time before the Wall came down and, as "revolutionary movers and shakers", *they* would be at the forefront of history.

Why Zech chose to approach and confide in an old school friend was something of a mystery. Roland had never given the slightest indication to anyone that he was anything other than a model citizen of the GDR. Zech was taking an enormous risk in approaching his old chum, but something about Roland suggested that he would be open to considering, at least, a subversive role within the network.

Zech's group needed a journalist – someone with the creative ability to write and disseminate anti-government literature that could be circulated discreetly to interested parties. This was the PR that the underground movement needed to gather momentum.

Had he approached Roland two weeks earlier than he did, then he might have met with a polite refusal. Roland adored Heike and Bruno and he wasn't about to risk their future happiness by writing anti-government propaganda.

The incident that was to change Roland's mind was the shooting of a young woman and a man little more than a kilometre away from the apartment. It had been a particularly cold evening, not quite dark, the inevitable finale to another dull autumn day that had not shone for anyone in East Berlin whatever their status.

Roland was nearing home having trudged from the tram stop (he took the car only when an assignment called for it). He passed, as he always did when walking, a short section of chain-link fence – a section that had never been blocked in by concrete probably because it was generally out of sight to those passing by.

The fence acted like a trap to anyone fool enough to attempt a crossing at this point. The border guards knew it as "The Spider's Web" based on a catalogue of attempts where people were either caught or killed when making an escape. It was a tempting spot, with the deep, black canal beyond. Roland, as a local, also knew it well, and whenever a shot rang out – though such incidents were getting rare – he and Heike would look knowingly at each other: The Spider's Web has claimed another victim.

Throughout his life in Berlin, he'd heard many an incident. Shots rang out from time to time accompanied by shouts and screams; it was not unusual, but such incidents were out of sight for the most part, hidden behind the ever present, ever more fortified Wall.

He didn't see the couple at first, the fence being some metres away from the pavement and screened by bushes that had run wild through deliberate neglect. There was a patchy trail of a muddy path where the grass didn't grow, evidence of some regular footfall created mostly during the summer. You could walk along the district canal at this point, and some did, though it was nothing scenic, just a shortcut.

Roland paid scant attention to the couple who, out of sight, seemed to be arguing, and so he continued to walk, thinking little of it. It was only when he heard shouting that he stopped to peer through the scrub in case the shouts were directed at him.

Before he could see clearly, he heard what sounded like the shaking and pulling at the fence as if someone was attempting to climb it; then the woman screamed with ear-splitting pitch. There followed the inevitable crack of a rifle shot then another and then a rapid burst of fire from a machine gun. Instinctively, he dived for cover as rounds hissed past him. He could hear a male shouting from what seemed to be across the canal, coupled with the hopeless screams and weeping coming from the other side of the scrub.

Horrified and unsure of how to react, Roland lay rooted to the damp tarmac as if paralysed. His blood chilled. What was best? Get up? Walk on? Walk home – get the hell out of it! No! Don't be so stupid – he was in the line of fire. If he suddenly stood up now the guards would open fire on him or at least associate him with the attempt to escape; yet there was a person moaning just a few metres from where he lay.

He had always wondered that one day he might be caught up in something, be a witness to a shooting and that when it came he would act in a truly brave manner and assist as best he could. Now, come the moment, he couldn't. The female voice cried out as if she knew someone was close by. 'Help me! Help me, would you? I need help! Don't leave me here, I beg you not to leave me here.'

Roland could see her quite clearly from his hopeless position. He was about to reply; he drew breath, opened his mouth but the words of comfort wouldn't come. A fast car, siren blaring, tyres screeching and spraying gravel like it was all some stunt out of a Hollywood movie, stopped within feet of where he lay.

A plain-clothes officer jumped athletically out of the marked car, bent down to Roland still lying prostrate and lifted him from the ground as if he were a broken doll discarded at the roadside. 'What's happened here?' he demanded.

'They were arguing… a man and a woman. I was walking home – I live on Held Strasse. Then shots rang out.'

'What were they arguing about?'

'I don't know. I didn't really hear what was being said. They were just arguing… I thought they might have been addressing me for a moment. So I stopped and looked but they were hidden from view. I wanted to help… you know.'

The officer told him most sternly that 'traitors can't be helped' and that once he'd given his details he would be free to continue but could expect someone to follow up if need be. That was all.

'The girl will be alright?'

There was no answer to that question. Questions are never answered; he should know that.

That evening, he recounted everything to Heike: 'She was a beautiful young woman… *Is* a beautiful young woman. She was wearing this tight skirt and jumper and I thought she looked like a film star when I eventually saw her. I felt like a character from a film stumbling onto a film set. That's strange, isn't it? Cue my walk-on part character!' He smiled, trying to make light of it, but he wasn't fooling anyone least of all himself.

'You see, it was such a dirty, scrubby piece of rubbish ground to… lie in and cry for help!' With that his anger broke and he hammered the tabletop with his fist before collapsing his head into his sobbing chest. This wasn't the Roland Heike knew. She gripped his arm tightly.

Lifting his head again, his vision blurred with tears, he focussed his mind on what he was trying so desperately to share: 'Just lying in the mud calling out for someone. She wasn't like a local – that's what I don't understand. It was like what she was wearing had been saved from another era and treasured, and she must have felt that if she wore this combination she would fit into the West. Does that make any sense?'

'What happened to the boy she was with?'

'He was dying at that very moment – it wasn't instant. I've never seen anyone die before. I've never even seen a dead person – and I'm a journalist – you'd think… but it was like his soul was departing right in front of me. I think a bullet ricocheted near to where I was just metres away. Ping! I was that close, you know. I think… I think he wanted to get across there and she didn't. She was trying to stop him – that's what they were arguing about and he wouldn't hear of it. Maybe she never wanted to cross in the first place.'

'Why don't they block that place up?'

'Because the canal drowns them and the government likes that. Better they drown trying to swim because if they reach the other side they get shot and that means paperwork. How many times have we heard shots ring out from there, eh?'

It was a long, sleepless night. He tried to sleep, tried to relax, but the Sandman just wouldn't come. Where was the Sandman when he was most needed?

At half past midnight, she encouraged him to sit down at his typewriter and write it all out by way of purging it from his system.

So the typewriter became the "angry machine" as he hammered out everything he could remember, everything he could still feel. Writing without constraint this time for a readership that would never be.

Come breakfast, he was exhausted.

Stupidly fatigued, he had to go to work because it was likely that the Stasi would want to talk to him and better that they find him there than come to the apartment. Heike comforted him with hugs and kisses, and coffee, holding his trembling hand across the table, but even this gesture just seemed to exasperate his condition.

Roland the gentle pacifist; his mother, Greta, shot and raped by Russian soldiers. She had kept the rape a secret from her children and from her Berlin-born husband, Niklas, who at thirteen had looked the Führer right in the eye and sworn that he would protect Germany with his life just as the dictator stroked his skinny, pale cheek with the back of a cold, "loving" finger.

Niklas would joke to Roland: 'Son, stroke my face with your finger. Go on, stroke my cheek right here – my left cheek.' And Roland would stroke his father's stubbly, gaunt, ashen-grey cheek, knowing exactly what was coming: 'There! You stroke the same cheek that Hitler stroked. What do you think of that, eh? Your old man touched by the devil himself!'

The old man was still a young man then, when Roland was small.

As a boy in 1945, he'd found Greta lying in a basement, and every year he told his children the story of how he found her close to death. They thrilled to hear it over and over again until such time as they'd grown too old and there was nothing new to add. Not one to be put off tradition, Niklas would always recount the story with immense pride, as if he'd fathered children for this very reason.

'I was sent out into the street to defend our city. Führer's orders. All hell was raining down on us. I was just a boy of fourteen handed an old rifle by a dying man – an old soldier left over from the First War, he and that gun of his. He couldn't get up, like some old mule that had collapsed and was breathing his last. He insisted I take it and then kaput, I think for him. Poor old beggar dressed for his demise in the very same uniform he'd worn as a young man for the Kaiser!

'All around there was chaos and carnage everywhere you looked. I was in a nightmare only it wasn't a nightmare and I wasn't asleep. My hearing was shot to pieces, my eyes, my mouth full of dust and dirt. I was numb and I was dumb – no more feeling, no love, no fear, nothing. The devil had stroked me and here I was in Hell and I hadn't even been outside of Berlin in my short life! Hell had come to my home – opened up like some hungry cavernous monster that was devouring the city. You children cannot believe what we saw. Hell was here – right here!'

'Tell us about Mother. What did you do? How did you help her?'

'You must understand I was lost and nowhere was safe. All the buildings in the street I knew were either destroyed or coming under attack. So, I was drawn to this sack of coal and I went to grab it thinking it could be useful because I might need it for keeping warm. I don't know, I wasn't thinking clearly. Anyway, the black, dusty sack moved and groaned. Your mother was hiding under it. I jumped and my heart went through the ceiling. I tell your mother now that my heart jumped when I first laid eyes on her, but it wasn't love then, it was shock. She knows, she understands. I fell in love later – two seconds later!'

'Two seconds? What took you so long?!'

'I put my coat around her then got her out of that basement and just in time because no sooner were we out on the street than a Russian flamethrower burned that house to the ground and we would have been in it. I made her run. I had my rifle in one hand and your mother in the other hand and we ran for our lives. Little did I know that she had a bullet in her.'

'Did you shoot a Russian with your rifle?'

'I don't know. I fired it in their direction and they fired back; but that's when I broke my vow with the Devil. I now had a reason to live! I needed to get your mother to safety, and I knew that if the Russians were to catch us we would be killed – *I* would be killed.'

'Were you a Hitler Youth?'

'No, I was a Berlin schoolboy given a hat, an armband and a lot of bullshit.'

'What did you do then?'

'We ran out of the city as fast as we could. The Russians surrounded the city on all sides. We were trying to get to the countryside where we could eat berries or even grass because we were so hungry; you wouldn't believe how hungry and thirsty we were. We could drink from a stream if we could find one. Pinch some eggs from a farmer or some apples that he might have stored. That was our greatest dream – our goal. There was nothing in the city except the spectre of death for everyone.'

'Did you reach the countryside?'

'Eventually, yes.'

'Did the Russians try to stop you?'

'We came across two uniformed men with pistols. They weren't Russians but SS, and they drew their pistols from their holsters and demanded to see our papers and to know where we were going. I said I had to get the lady to the hospital because she was dying, and I thought they might let me go because we were Germans and Berliners, but no. They would have shot us both but luck was on our side. An almighty explosion went off just metres from where we stood and we all hit the ground from its force. BOOM!

'When the dust settled and I looked up, the two SS men were gone and so we got up and started to run again. Minutes later I heard shots ring out behind me and I think now that those two men took shelter then tried to shoot us as we ran, but it was our lucky day. We were never stopped again.'

'Then what happened?'

'We ran and walked for days and days trying to head for the West, keeping the sunrise behind us and the setting sun ahead of us. We thought we could get to Austria, even though we really didn't know where Austria was.'

'How far did you walk?'

'I don't know how far. Probably a week or more we walked, keeping to the fields and woods. The Russians were everywhere. We saw soldiers and avoided them as best we could. They weren't looking for us I don't think. They had bigger fish to fry. If you want my opinion, I think it was a miracle we escaped. Then one night, deep in the countryside, we came across American soldiers.'

'Did you have your gun?'

'As soon as I saw them I threw it on the floor and put my hands up. I'd left your mother lying under a tree out of sight. She was so tired and sick, you could not imagine. I thought she would die without help. But the Americans helped her. I told them I was her brother and that we were escaping and meant no harm.'

'How did they understand you?'

'One of them spoke good German and said his name was Dekker.'

'Did they put you in prison?'

'They put me in a lorry that took me to a doctor and I was examined. They patched up all the silly little grazes I had. Do you know, that was the first time I'd ridden in any vehicle? In my life! I was so excited! That ride was like some sort of reward. I didn't even have a bicycle before the Russians came. You children have it so easy!'

'Were you a war criminal in prison?'

'I was with the POWs in a camp. I was never a soldier, but I wasn't in there long. They checked that I wasn't a Nazi and they put me with a farmer and his family, and they were nice people who looked after me and adopted me with official papers. I tried to get word back to my family, but it was a long time before I knew.'

'What did you know? What did you find out?'

'That my family were dead: mother, father, Paul my little brother. He would have been your uncle. I was the only one left so I worked on the farm and kept smiling because no one loves you when you are sad.'

'What happened to mother? Was she on the farm, too?'

'One day, I went shopping with my adoptive mother who said I needed new clothes – especially trousers. I didn't want to go at first, but she insisted and said I was very ungrateful for their love if I didn't go, and I apologised and went willingly because I didn't want to hurt her feelings. It was the best thing I ever did in my life. There, in town, working in a tailor's shop, was your mother. I recognised her straight away and she recognised me and we became inseparable again. It was wonderful!'

'Why didn't you stay on the farm? We could have been farmer's children.'

'Farming wasn't for me. I was a city boy, and your mother was a city girl. We could only return to Berlin in late 1951 – just before you were born, Roland. It was such a ruin still, but there was something that drew us back to the city of our birth, and we were home. The Austrian devil had gone forever. He'd been banished. That said, there was still the Russian devil to contend with.'

'What was it like?'

'In 1951, walls of once great buildings, shops, houses, factories stood like the jagged teeth of a man who'd had a severe beating. People were still picking belongings out of the rubble. There were some cars at least – American cars, British cars, Russian cars, some Volkswagens, but not for us, of course. People were still looking for their loved ones, their families. I looked for mine, your mother looked for hers. They were all gone. The Russians were everywhere – soldiers mostly. Stalin replaced Hitler. One madman had lost, while the other had won. But it was better than the thunder that had been in my ears when I left. When we ran from the city, the ground shook all the time, there was dust and smoke and stink everywhere. In 1951, at least it was quiet again, the smoke had cleared and the dust had settled and people tried to go about their business. But they were new people – not the people that I'd known. All the people I'd known were gone.'

'Everyone had gone?'

'There was someone I recognised. It was the day when I was walking along Behrenstrasse on my way to work – this wasn't long ago – a year or so – and there I saw the same man who tried to stop us leaving Berlin.'

'One of the Nazis?'

'The SS man was now a *Volkspolizei*. We looked at each other and we knew… He was older, I was older, but we knew. We were like two characters in a play brought back on stage again for one last performance. Do you know what I did?'

'What did you do?'

'I went up to him – square on – shoulders back and as wide as I could make them – I'd been working hard for many years by then – and I went up to him and said, "Will you kill me now?" He said, "Why?" I said, "Because you still have your gun, only you have changed sides. Once you were a fascist, now you're a communist."'

'What did he do?'

'There was nothing he could do. He turned and walked away. I never saw him again, but he's out there somewhere doing something horrible because someone tells him to do it.'

'Do you hate him?'

'I hate those who create him and others like him – the parents, the teachers, the politicians. It is important you remember this – you must remember that fascists and communists are the same. They are fanatics in need of power. Without power they wilt like flowers in the frost. They strap their guns to their waists like cowboys and they tell nice people like you and me to jump. And we say, "How high do you want us to jump?" And they tell us, and we do what we are told like good people do. And if we don't jump, they put us in prison as if we were bad, but we're not bad, are we? No. And if we still don't jump high enough, they shoot us. So we are always good people, aren't we? We jump when we're told. That man was a survivor. He became a Nazi to survive and then he became a communist to survive. People do strange things to survive.'

It was the only political thing Niklas ever said to his children, and Roland never forgot the warning. He hadn't ever spoken about politics in the family or to friends. He knew better than to do so.

Heike the Westerner frequently spoke about politics. She'd spent years and years telling Roland how great the Eastern bloc was and how corrupt the West was; and Roland would nod but say very little, certainly nothing that contradicted her opinion. She'd grown up with the freedom to complain – and complain she did.

Only now was he becoming political. Only now that death had kicked him in his face, only now was he taking an interest in another language and listening to foreign radio broadcasts; only now was he changing his mind about his place in East Berlin. He wasn't prepared to "jump" any longer. He would make his own way "out" of East Berlin. Yes, he would help in the subversion. Yes, he would do his bit – willingly. Yes, he would see the overthrow of the corrupt regime. Yes, with his help they *would* succeed.

He wasn't about to implicate Heike in this mission. She wasn't to know under any circumstances. The less people who knew the better. He had been warned by Zech: 'Tell no one', but the warning was overdramatic and unnecessary. East Germans knew from birth how to keep a secret even from their nearest and dearest family members. If Heike asked, then he was working overtime. New pressures at work, improved technology meant extra training.

The days that followed the shooting at the Wall were the days when Roland struggled most, desperate to make sense of what he'd witnessed. To him, the woman was Heike. In his nightmares it was Heike crying out for help, lying bleeding. He was the man – twitching, draining blood; his protest dying in the mud of a dirty little track that ran beside a polluted canal.

Whatever the motivation of that couple, whatever had taken them so far, they were nothing if not brave. Roland – a born journalist – badly wanted to know who they were and what their story was; it infuriated him that he knew he could never enquire and get to the root of what had brought them to such a crisis.

This was the time to be the man he believed his father had been – to get out of Berlin, to flee or at least resist. He wasn't going to jump anymore, not for any bastard communist or fascist. No devil was going to stroke his cheek and tell him he was "a good boy". What had been such an entertaining story when he was a child was now inspirational to him. The story might even repeat itself: people might try to stop him and even try to shoot at him; but he'd keep going. And if, in his flight, he had to live on grass and whatever he could find, so be it!

'Okay, you've got me. What do you want me to do?'
'Write something for the Lutherans. Write for the peace movement. Write for the Marxist intellectuals. Tell them… No, give them a message that the new Germany is emerging – the twentieth century is ending and we will not tolerate further militarisation. That we are not cannon fodder or even tin soldiers. You're the journalist; you'll think of something.'

The group met in plain sight – in an annexe of the library for that first meeting, arranged by someone within the group, but never in the same place twice and never in front of the public. Preliminary discussions were coded and brief. If confronted, their cover story was to be that they were members of a chess club. Absolutely inoffensive for sure, but chess was never likely to prevent an arrest and questioning; it was at least a cover. *What's your problem, comrade? This is a chess club – I'm a chess player. Is that a state crime now?*

At home, Roland would work into the small hours tapping away at his Voss typewriter, its keys and mechanism covered in ash, a cigarette between the fingers of his left hand and a glass of vodka or coffee or a mix of the two to keep him awake. Unseen from across the room Heike would glance at him admiringly, though quite unaware of the rebellious content of his seditious articles.

Roland could "hide" in plain sight at home. Heike had never peered over his shoulder at a single word he wrote. 'It's all about the durability of tractors,' he would say if he thought she was interested. 'It wouldn't interest you – it's sending *me* to sleep.' So she never asked, but just liked the way he looked as he sat leaning over his ash-infested desk with tobacco smoke rising, cigarette butts in the ashtray and a half finished drink. She thought he looked like a great novelist grafting at a manuscript that would one day wow the literary world, and so in her head she mentally "photographed" the scene and filed it close to her heart.

Roland reminded her of Peter, not in any physical resemblance, it was more particular expressions and demeanour. Her brother was never far from her mind. Occasionally she might see him – just the odd, once in a blue moon, distant glimpse. She didn't approach; he never saw her and he stayed away from their apartment. Roland barely knew his brother-in-law apart from those early days of sharing; at least, that had been the case, but things were about to change.

Peter Savers

Peter the enigma they called him. A newly qualified engineer by trade, he was a gifted and experienced man who could repair any machine known to man or build any structure. His debt, he believed, was owed to East Germany.

*

She rehearsed saying out loud these words: *Do you know how stupid I was with my own brother, Hanne? Can you believe that I never knew him? I never enquired after him or tried to get to know him. I just knew he could fix engines and build things – anything. When I left home he was still a boy riding his bicycle. I didn't give him a second glance. The world was all about me because I saw myself as some sort of victim, some sort of hangover from the last war – or rather a consequence of it. I was pleased when he joined us in East Berlin – that he'd got away from the West.*

"*Where is Peter now,*" *you ask? I can only say I don't know. I never did know where he was.* "*So why didn't you know?*" *you ask. I don't know – I really don't know.*

*

"The enigma" had never again imposed himself on Heike and Roland; something they truly appreciated. He was always welcome, but he never came. This wasn't unusual in the East; people kept themselves to themselves – even close relatives often preferred to keep their own counsel.

They talked about him on occasion, wondering how he was getting on, whether there was someone in his life. They talked about him just before Roland set off for his first meeting – 'a journalistic assignment' he told Heike.

That night, with the exception of Zech, everyone in attendance was a stranger to Roland. Just as well, he felt. He didn't want people recognising him and through association jeopardising his role.

All was good until some twenty minutes into the meeting; a tall, slim, bearded man with metal-frame spectacles and long thinning hair came into the library annexe apologising profusely for his lateness.

Roland recognised him straight away – the same fatigued youth handed over by Uncle on their very doorstep. He was in many ways very different in dress and style to the boy who'd been shoved unceremoniously across the threshold that night thirteen years ago; he looked so much older, darker, more haggard; but even if the outward appearance was vastly different, the gait, the sway-back stance, the exaggerated movement of the mouth when he spoke were unmistakeably Peter Savers.

Tonight there could be no welcome for the errant brother-in-law. It was clear he was not a new hand, and Roland surmised that maybe Peter was actually right at the centre of the circle as evident from the various greetings and hushed tones. He was the hub from which everything emanated.

For God's sake!

Maybe if Roland kept a low profile Peter might not see him and would disappear again. After all, what was *he* doing here? He'd left the West of his own volition and the Stasi had to be watching his every move as they did with Heike. No way would he be at the heart of a subversive movement such as this without their knowing – certainly not motivated by a desire for political reform.

He didn't move for fear that movement would draw attention.

In the end it didn't matter; Peter left after a few minutes, barely glancing at anyone else in the room and quite unaware that his brother-in-law had seen him.

Roland quickly moved on Zech: 'I can't help you with this.'

'What do you mean?'

'I've recognised someone in your group. I can't do this – sorry!'

'Who is it? Don't you trust them?'

'No, I don't trust them – nor should you!'

'Tell me who it is you suspect.'

Roland took a pencil from the desk and pulled a discarded sheet of paper out of the bin. He scribbled Peter's name and passed it to Zech.

'Who? We have no one of that name in this group.'

'The man who came in late! The man you spoke with at the commencement of this meeting. *He's* Peter.'

'Maybe you've mistaken him?'

'I haven't mistaken him – he's my brother-in-law and he defected from the West thirteen years ago. The Stasi will be watching him like hawks and without a doubt they'll be controlling him.'

'But he's at the heart of this movement. He was one of the instigators. I've heard him give talks and he talks from the heart.'

'Of course he would, Zech. He's a puppet and his masters are pulling the strings. He has no choice but to infiltrate a movement such as this.'

'So what do we do? Shut it down? And for how long?'

'I don't think you've got a choice.' Roland glanced out of the window to the street. Two storeys below, his eyes fixed on a sinister man who appeared to be watching the entrance to the building. 'See that man? The one standing there facing us in that ludicrous fur coat, hat and silly glasses? That'll be the minder. He's not even bothered about being conspicuous – he's watching in plain sight. They can pick us off anytime they like.'

Zech rounded on him: 'Don't you think I've been careful? How stupid do you think I am? Do you think I just wandered in here? He's our guy – he's watching *our* backs. No, you don't need to know his name. We'll check your brother-in-law. If he is a spy we can deal with him.'

'What do you mean, "deal with him"?'

'We would question him – at length if need be. What do you think we'd do? Shoot him? This is a Christian peace movement, Roland. Our aim is to turn swords into ploughshares across the world. We're not murderers. We know we're being watched and listened to very closely, but there's nothing anyone can do. We're not breaking the law in seeking worldwide condemnation of nuclear weapons. Both Germanys have to lead the world in this respect – the responsibility for world peace is on our shoulders.'

'But in the process we're bringing down the government, aren't we? Isn't that what we're about? Destroying Honecker and his cronies?'

'We're bringing about change, Roland. That's what this is about – change. It's not a coup. We're not looking for revenge; we're trying to create a stable, new Germany that unites us all. And a man like you can help us achieve that.'

Confrontation

In his head, he went over the scene again and again: Zech and Peter talking earnestly out of earshot. Maybe Peter was behind Zech's approach to him – Peter was the real motivator behind this particular group and had requested that his brother-in-law be included for whatever reason. After all, everyone had been approached individually – chosen as disciples and based on some estimate of trustworthiness. But a Judas would bring ruin to them all.

The risk was too great. Roland could not go back to the group with Peter there. Thank God Peter hadn't spotted him. What a stupid thing to even consider! Getting involved with a bunch of subversives, and for what? Imprisonment? The loss of his family?

So, for a time, he put the whole crazy idea behind him – no more meetings.

It was then that the woman at the fence returned to haunt his sleep in particularly vivid dreams. Each and every night without fail she would reach out to him before dying in his arms. So real were the dreams he could smell her aroma; feel the material of her bloodied clothes; even making love to her as she called out his name repeatedly before eventually accusing him of rape.

In these nocturnal visions he begins as her saviour, then her lover, then her tormentor and eventually her executioner. In each dream he knows her so well, their history shared; he calls her by a familiar name that he can never remember upon waking. And every time, her facial features morph into those of Heike.

'You should see the doctor about your nightmares,' Heike scolded him as she cradled his sweating body in her arms, his screams having shattered the night's peace.

'The whole place is a nightmare,' he replied, '… the whole stinking place.'

Some days later, by chance, he ran into Zech at a tram stop, which was odd in that for so many years their paths had not coincided, yet in recent months they seemed destined to meet as if on a collision course. Maybe Zech had been following him.

Zech wasted no time: 'I dealt with the "problem". You need to come to another meeting.'

'Why?' asked Roland incredulously.

'Because there's so much work for you. The movement needs a talented writer like you. Words free this country, not guns or tanks.'

'And just who will free *me* when the Stasi decides enough is enough?'

'The world order is changing, Roland. Things are moving swiftly. Soon there won't be a Stasi or a politburo. But we've got to give freedom a final push. *They're* already hesitating.

'If we don't do this, if we leave it to the world's politicians, then this country and Eastern Europe will never be free. We're taking inspiration from the Poles and the Czechs, and now it's our turn, Roland. Come on! Join us in the struggle.'

Roland's eyes scanned the broad, busy street for a bolthole, but there was nowhere for him to hide. He knew that in the days to come he would have to stand up to be counted, because to leave it to others was comparable to an act of cowardice. Suddenly, on the opposite pavement, he spotted the face of a stranger he knew only too well: a woman walking, her eyes downcast, her hands buried in the depths of her raincoat pockets, her long, dark hair covered by a floral-patterned scarf. His heart missed a beat; it was the woman at the fence; the woman who haunted his sleep. There could be no mistake. She was just metres away, alive, at liberty, and en route to who knew where.

It was not a moment to hesitate; he had to confront her. Much to Zech's astonishment Roland sprinted across the road, adroitly avoiding traffic and other pedestrians and causing one irate taxi driver to blow his horn and shake his fist. Roland called after her: 'Excuse me!'

She stopped and turned. 'Yes?'

His momentum hit a brick wall. What could he say or do? Passers-by glanced at them standing paused in the middle of the pavement like two stage-struck actors who couldn't recall their lines. 'Yes?' she repeated, unsure of just what he wanted from her.

He raised his hand in surrender: 'I'm sorry! I thought for a moment you were someone I knew.'

In the group, people talked earnestly in pairs rather than a discussion that involved everyone. This left Roland feeling somewhat isolated.

The "journalist" in him wanted to mix and enquire: find out who everyone was and what they were doing there; find out what they expected and just when there might be a satisfactory outcome. Did they expect to fight and die? Or be imprisoned or banished to God knows where? He wisely kept quiet, buried his head in a book on grass management and tried to conceal his nerves.

Zech beckoned him over: 'Roland? Come with me please.'

Good! At last maybe he'd be given something to get his teeth into and then get home. It had been a long day.

He followed Zech across the creaking floorboards into an anteroom cluttered with boxes of old books and library stepladders in need of repair. Three men were waiting for them – two were smiling strangers, one most certainly wasn't: it was Peter.

'What on God's green earth are you doing?!' exclaimed Roland on recognising his brother-in-law. 'Don't you realise our connection?'

'Max is fine about it, Roland,' said Zech.

'Max? Max? His name isn't Max, it's Peter – Peter Savers – and he's my wife's brother! What's more, he's a defector from the West. They watch his every move!'

Peter lit a Juwel cigarette before offering the packet around – calm and composed as could be. 'Roland is right – absolutely! They monitored my every move from dawn to dusk and every minute in between. And there was good reason for that – I'd just kicked in from the West and they didn't know who the hell I was.'

Roland couldn't believe his ears; it *was* Peter; there'd been no confusion on his part. How could any of them survive this now with such a traitor uncovered?

'Once they'd finished interrogating me,' Peter continued, 'I was put into a job in engineering, working in the steelworks at Hennigsdorf. In my spare time I studied hard at night school. I wanted to get into a university if that was possible, in engineering, and my factory enabled that.

'After I graduated I became a teacher at a polytechnic. My dreams had all come true: I was a happy man teaching metal craft and even physics on occasion. Then, last year, a group of my students approached me and asked if they could express themselves like people did in the West, and I was from the West so…

'I asked them what they meant by that and what they intended and they told me that they wanted to erect a bulletin board where all students could pin their thoughts and feelings on anything and everything, from the meaning of life to Erich Honecker's sex life. They wanted to see just how far they could test the system.

'Well, there was nothing that could be said about Honecker's sex life that we knew of; it had to be factual – no jokes, you understand. So a number of them wrote about their support of what was happening in Poland with the labour strikes, or the dangers posed by the neo-Nazis, or a soldier's love for his machine gun, that sort of thing. They even began a petition criticising Honecker's annual military parade. I encouraged all this; I saw no harm, as times were changing – *I thought*.

'The bulletin board quickly became a source of anger as other students and teachers criticised its content. But in our defence we said that that was what democracy was and that was what such a bulletin board should do if it was to work effectively – get people talking, discussing and arguing things out. But there were those who demanded retribution, as all this was heretical in their eyes. They wanted the ringleaders kicked out of the school and the education programme. The ringleaders, however, wanted to see it through – a storm in a teacup in their heads and mine.

'Within days it got serious – overly serious. The students were effectively put on trial by their fellows and teachers, while those who had originally welcomed the idea of such a bulletin board distanced themselves. A kangaroo court was set up, but not everyone was compliant. They were very brave despite being so young.

'You know, for those kids expulsion meant never getting the job they wanted, yet they were bright kids. Their future was decided from then on – street cleaners, toilet cleaners. They were humiliated in front of everyone in the school and summarily kicked out – their personal details immediately passed to the Stasi.

'As for me, of course, I was sacked with immediate effect for having encouraged this and then arrested and questioned at length. I was threatened with jail, but released. Possibly because they believed that I'd been planted by the CIA and if I'm at liberty I'll inadvertently lead them to others.'

'Well, you've succeeded, because you've led them directly to us!' stormed Roland.

'No. I changed my identity as best I could and it works, I know it works. Peter Savers is dead. He died at the Wall trying to escape eighteen months ago. You even witnessed his death, Roland. That was pure coincidence.'

A CIA man approached me shortly after my release and I told him my story. There are spies operating here in the East as I'm sure you're aware. Anyway, he planned an escape route for a man who was desperate to get to the West and arranged a false identity for him – *my* identity. In turn, I became Max Konczak – the son of a Polish war veteran. I shaved my head, my eyebrows, and the CIA man kindly broke my nose with a very adept punch. It was enough to alter my appearance somewhat. I also wear coloured contact lenses. Do you like my green eyes? Not the colour I was born with. 'So, thankfully they didn't look too closely at the man who died at the fence. The ID in his pocket did the trick. He was set up – a hapless victim. I was in the clear.'

'What about the woman?'

'She's a CIA operative. She met him, took him to the fence and then alerted the guards by arguing with him. She wasn't supposed to get shot, but that's the risk you take. God knows how you happened to be passing. But it's part of the reason why I asked Zech to bring you into this movement. We need you.'

'Are you working for the CIA?'

'No, I'm working for a new Germany. I will always be a communist, but what's going on here is crazy! Honecker is a brute and that wife of his is even worse if that's possible.

'Don't get me wrong, there is much that I love about our system, but the trial of my students turned my life around. This particular branch of the peace movement is motivated by those like me who want to bring about change for the better. Communism *can* include democracy – they are not exclusive.

'This opposition has its roots in that school. Those kids were brave enough to stand up and be counted. We have to follow their lead. You know, as we speak, people on both sides of the Wall are beginning to learn about my students. Our people are seeing it on Western news media. People are beginning to question the system. They were bright kids from good families, but they were hung out to dry just for expressing themselves. That's what young people do, no? At least, that's what they should be able to do.

'You see, it's not just about what those kids said on the bulletin board; it's about the standard of the education system here. And we're a long, long way behind our cousins on the other side of the Wall.'

Roland was indeed aware that some students had been expelled from a city polytechnic. He'd even discussed it with Heike when they listened to the breaking story on Voice of America. How odd to think that Peter had played his part, or so he claimed. There was no choice but to trust him – things had gone too far.

'Why didn't you come and talk to us?'

'What? And implicate you?'

'No! Before then. Why not share your good news about your degree and your teaching post?'

'Because we were better off apart. I wasn't going to play into the hands of the Stasi by turning up at my sister's every now and then, or writing letters. They expected us to be working as a team, and that included you! They watch Mama, you know, even though she's in the West – they watch her. She's an old lady who doesn't deserve to come under surveillance because of what I did or what my sister did. They watch all our family in the West. They have files – I've seen them. And do you think they don't watch you? Come on, Roland! They think that Heike is working directly for the CIA, that she's a sleeper. You're in danger – the three of you are in danger and you need to get out of here.'

Peter was absolutely right. We watched all of them, all of the time.

Later meetings were different. New faces were appearing.

Strangers looking equally as lost and as nervous as Roland had done. But now there was a feeling of optimism in the air, the feeling that they were making a difference. People – strangers – were talking and making plans. Things were on the rise and happening quickly. The initial talk was always of Gorbachev and perestroika and especially glasnost.

'Did you hear the BBC last night?'

'Yes, I heard that. The Americans say it's their influence that's making a difference, and Thatcher says it's her, but the BBC makes it clear – it's Gorbachev. He's moving mountains.'

'I heard that he's pulling troops out of Afghanistan.'

'He's meeting with Kohl and Honecker. At this rate we could bring the Wall down by autumn.'

'Reagan is doing his thing, too. He has an interest in a united Germany.'

'He has an interest in his American empire. Don't be fooled.'

No one believed that Honecker would bring the Wall down of his own volition or that Kohl might even pressure him to do so. There was nothing in their respective histories to suggest that either man would take one step toward demolishing the Wall and unifying Germany.

Someone suggested that Brandt would have brought the Wall down single-handedly. But the truth was that no one in the group wanted any politician to do that. Zech slammed his fist on the table: '*We* – the people – we'll bring the Wall down and no one else!

'It's imperative we bring the Wall down before Honecker fortifies it with the latest terror weapons – lasers, security cameras, computer-controlled weapons that negate the use of guards. The stinking Wall might not have been Honecker's creation, but he's done more than any other leader to make it impregnable.'

Meetings were short, comprising just enough time to make

contact, then decide the next part of the plan before everyone dispersed.

'Roland – you meet up with Kristof during the week and find some way of making progress with the Lutherans. They're planning a demonstration. Hans – check out Dieter Meier. Maybe he can help with leaflet distribution? …'

Pity the buggers outside on the street watching, taking notes, looking out for those who might be watching them. The fat man with the dark glasses and the dark woollen overcoat; he didn't even try to blend into his surroundings. Next night, it was the tall, thin man who Roland believed followed him on occasion in the cold and rain. Roland's nightmares were replaced by insomnia, something he'd never suffered from before. When he did eventually fall into a deep sleep, his dreams would expose him as being naked in public; naked at work even though everyone else was clothed; naked on the journey home, catching the train. People averted their eyes, but they all turned to look and comment on his nudity.

Heavy men would pull him off the street shouting obscenities at him and twisting his arms before forcing him into a car that was too small.

He would awake to a black depression. Looking across the bed at Heike, she might realise in a moment that he was carrying a secret. He wasn't about to let that happen. How would she react if she realised that he was working to bring down the state? That he was in cahoots with Peter, but that the brother she'd known was dead? A man called Max Konczak had taken his place.

*

Do you know, Hanne, that I was such a bloody-minded little communist that my own husband couldn't confide in me? That's the sort of cousin you have!

Some thoughts had to be blurted out loud. Not much further now.

*

It was the unexpected arrival one evening of Uncle wearing an unfashionable trilby hat, his old suit covered by an equally outdated belted raincoat, and to all intents and purposes quite alone – no lackeys this time.

Cautiously glancing out of the only street-facing window, as so few people called, she'd seen Uncle Frederick only once in the past four years. She'd always hoped that one day he would call again as of late he'd been such a stranger.

Politely standing on the step, he'd aged quite noticeably, she thought, much more frail, more bent. Perhaps that wasn't so surprising as she imagined he had to be well over eighty. He stood patiently as the bitter east wind blew the trim sides of his white hair, while holding his hat as if ready to doff it to her upon the door being opened; but his icy, grey, rigid demeanour suggested trouble of some kind.

She glanced back at the kitchen wall clock. Roland had not arrived home and he was often home by 7 pm, yet in his place here was Uncle with a mission he clearly had to complete.

Her heart missed a beat; she suspected something had gone wrong, something involving Roland. She greeted the old man cautiously, like an errant child who had failed to maintain close links with her "family". His demeanour was so entirely different, as if he were someone else entirely. Maybe it was just the cold and the onset of age being so cruel? Maybe she was just being paranoid?

'I need to come inside. They've arrested Roland. It might be an idea if you tell me what you know.'

His entrance, when it came, was actually quite abrupt, pushing past her and into the living room. He'd never behaved so brusquely before. This time he was here as a state official, an inquisitor, not a sympathetic family member or friend. He had been rehearsing this scenario for all the many years since being assigned as Heike's "mentor". The time had come, as so many of his colleagues had expected. She must have "turned" Roland, though there was no evidence to substantiate this idea.

He removed his hat but held on to it firmly. She noticed that the white hair had not totally obliterated his once blond hair. It was a strange observation while she waited for him to deliver his news.

'I have to admit,' he began, 'you had me fooled.'

'Fooled? Why would I fool you?'

'You have no interest in the GDR, Heike. Your father was an American. He was CIA. Your education was CIA. It wasn't your fault, child. You were an innocent, they manipulated you; but you've done your job well.'

'Job? What job? My father wasn't CIA! He was many things that I didn't care for, but never CIA!'

'Oh, please, don't underestimate your father or the CIA. They are clever people. They take their time – time is on their side.'

'I told you – I told *them*! All those years ago when I first came here I told them everything they needed to know. I left nothing out. You know I didn't.'

'I couldn't quite figure out your role, Heike. I knew you had been sent with a mission to accomplish, I just wasn't sure what it might be. We have evidence, you know.'

'Evidence? What evidence?'

'You have been listening in to foreign broadcasts – teaching Roland English. You have a radio, no?'

'People have radios and TVs – made here in the GDR. I

was teaching Roland English so that he could go on foreign assignments for his newspaper. That was all.'

'Is this how you treat the people who took you in?'

'Is this how the GDR treats its citizens, Uncle?'

'They could take your boy into care if you're put in prison. Do you understand?' he whispered, as if afraid that Bruno might hear.

'I am already a prisoner.'

Irritated, Uncle looked to the front door, donned his trilby and strode out into the darkness, leaving Heike to close the heavy oak door after him. She collapsed against the wall, dropping to the floor.

The "honeymoon" was over, that was clear. Her adopted tribe were not so much turning against her, but admitting that they had never accepted her in the first place. In their view, she was, and would always be, American – worse, a CIA mole and sleeper. Ironic, considering she hated America, hated the CIA.

This was worse than being locked up. She could survive imprisonment. Her beloved "uncle" thought she was a traitor and that she had let everyone down; their trust, their belief in her as a good communist. What had Roland done? What on earth had he *done*?

She would phone his editor immediately. No, of course not. What would he say? "I don't know anything – sorry!"

Why didn't Uncle arrest her? Little point in doing so maybe – she wasn't going anywhere. They had her where they wanted her – under house arrest. It was *their* apartment, *their* building; they could do what the hell they liked. How naive to think they'd welcomed her, made provision for her. How bloody stupid! They simply put her into a cage and closed the door.

Uncle had known about the radio and particularly Roland's English lessons, and no one outside the family had any inkling. The apartment was clearly bugged and Uncle had orchestrated it. He'd controlled everything.

Heike's immediate response was to pull the place apart, but what was the point? The damage was done – the state listened and watched, and pulling out wires now would only bring the Stasi to the door with an arrest warrant and an eviction notice.

If they insisted on listening for the truth, they should have the truth.

'I'm a stupid bitch!' she ranted at wherever she suspected the hidden mics to be secreted – the ceiling, the light fittings, wall sockets.

'All I ever wanted to be was a good communist and a good German. I'm not a fascist and I'm not American. He probably wasn't even my father! The CIA didn't teach us. Mrs Moran taught us; Mr Abrahms taught us; Mr Coleman, Miss Taylor, Mrs Albright. Do you want me to go on? They weren't CIA. We learned American history, we learned to speak and write English, we learned math and lots of things, but what I learned most of all was to hate the capitalist system!

'All these years you've been listening – to what? My husband and I eating? Making love? Our son crying – laughing? All you've done is waste your time and spent God knows how much money in the process.

'Are you crazy? Did you really think I was a spy or some sort of CIA agent waiting for an opportunity to bring you all crashing down? You're crazy! You know that? CRAZY!'

The very next morning, as soon as Bruno was safely in school, Heike set out in search of Roland, or what had become of Roland. First a bus and then a train to the Ministry for State Security in Berlin-Lichtenberg, Ruschestrasse 103, House No. 1. She knew it well enough.

She had lost all fear of any reprisals, as matters could not be any worse than they already were. Always in the back of her mind was a story told by a woman in Bavaria whom she'd known as a child and who had remained a good friend right up to the time Heike had left the village.

The woman, Frau Julia Groebel, had told Heike of the time her husband had been arrested by the Gestapo and taken to a prison in Frankfurt. Against the wishes of her parents, Julia boarded a train for Frankfurt with the aim of confronting the Gestapo. Without a second thought to her own safety, she walked boldly through the prison door and demanded to speak to the commandant, like a latter-day Christian confronting the lion keeper.

Once inside, she insisted that she be informed as to why they'd arrested her patriotic husband. The commandant, an unremarkable man of slight stature called Scher, who looked to her as if his true vacation was that of a café patron, duly received Julia in his office and listened intently to what she had to say. His easy demeanour caused her to relax immediately – to think that there just may be some hope. Despite her initial hysteria, she had the floor; he seemed sympathetic and appeared to be no monster. If anything, she thought he seemed somewhat embarrassed, that this tirade of hers was really not necessary as it was all a perfectly understandable mistake and this was a wonderful place.

When her long rehearsed plea for her husband's clemency was complete, Scher simply nodded. He did not reply to her questions or enter into any conversation but instead summoned the guards to bring the boyfriend to his office immediately so that she could see him. It looked hopeful.

Then came the noise: the sickening sounds of something heavy being dragged as if it were furniture; someone moaning as if struggling to carry the weight. A sickening sound accompanied by a vile smell now pervaded Scher's office.

The guards were dragging along the stone-tiled floor the

beaten body of her bloodied and heavily bruised husband. They dropped him to the floor at her feet, where they commenced to kick him in the trunk, groin and face until his groans fell silent.

Julia fled from the building not daring to look back. By the time she reached home two days later the house was empty and ransacked: her parents had been arrested and transported to a labour camp.

Heike too would demand to know what they had done with her husband, insist that someone in authority speak to her. She would even speak to Erich Mielke himself if it got Roland released.

Her blood turned to ice at the thought of what she was doing, but the idea that Roland's battered and bleeding body could be dragged before her was a thought too far. She was still certain that this was modern Berlin. Such things didn't happen anymore.

Did they?

It was audacious! The idea that this little *hausfrau* from the suburbs could storm into Stasi HQ and demand her husband's release! But of course she *was* audacious. Aged nineteen she'd walked into East Berlin from the West of her own volition. Naive and innocent she'd stared communist hardliners in the face and not flinched. Convinced of her idealistic motives in seeking "shelter" from the wicked West, the weeks she'd spent incarcerated and interrogated had convinced her that she was a true child of the state who had been welcomed and certified fit for citizenship.

Why, she was Erich Honecker's model citizen.

Of course, Julia had been an ardent National Socialist, as had her husband, yet their politics and commitment to the Party did not save them. There would not be a sanctuary for those who kissed the feet of the dictator. Such devotion was utterly pointless. Heike repressed the idea that the state would turn on her as the Nazis had often turned on their own followers.

Standing outside looking in, confused by the vast complex of modern high-rise block buildings, Heike had come too far to be put off her grand entrance: but how to get in? Berliners did not walk in of their own free will. This was not an information bureau for citizens to use and access; to the contrary, it was a city within a city that existed to control them, not inform their curiosity.

The buildings might – in the eyes of the naive – also have been a hotel or office complex. There was nothing particularly military or penal in their structure or design, and Heike suspected that it was somewhere here that she had been brought the day she approached the border guard with her plea for defection.

She remembered the inner place but not the outer as, like her friend Julia, she'd not looked over her shoulder.

'Please, my husband has been arrested. I need to talk to someone. Can you help?' she asked a bemused guard who'd been watching her.

'Give me your papers,' he grunted, proffering the palm of his hand as if awaiting a gratuity. She dutifully handed over her ID card but could offer no official letter inviting her attendance.

'I need to see something more than this, *fräulein*.'

'I'm a friend of Herr Frederick Wendt. He is a leading Party official. You can call him. He will vouch for me.'

'You'd better come with me, *fräulein*.'

Comrade Inspector Bertrand Froi eventually received her, but only after several hours of her sitting patiently, sitting on hands, rehearsing words. He was a solidly built, plain-clothes officer still young enough to be idealistic and ambitious who immediately disarmed her with his gentle approach and proffered consideration for her wait. She had not expected such a "gentlemanly" reception, but there would be no private audience, no invite to an office in the inner sanctum. As colleagues came and went through reception doors, Froi had no intention of being detained a moment longer than he had to be.

The cold, hard facts were this: 'Your husband has been arrested and is currently being interrogated because of his membership of a group that is attempting to destabilise the state. This is criminal activity of the most severe order.'

'He has *not*. That's ridiculous! He's a working journalist. He works for the state.'

'It was fortunate that we were able to infiltrate the group before any real damage could be done.'

Then it dawned on Heike: the extra-long hours; his excuses of having to stay late for training in new technology was the most likely cover for group meetings. For two months he'd been attending "training courses" and catching up on work at home. He hadn't been honest with her.

'So what do I do?' she asked. 'Can I see him?'

'There was a time when you too would have been arrested along with your husband, but we don't consider that necessary. You have friends in high places.'

'What will happen to him?'

'Your husband is facing a lengthy prison sentence. If he co-operates, he will find that the system is lenient.'

'Who will pay the rent? I have a son at school.'

'Then you'd better find some work.'

There was little more that could be said.

This time when she stood, she trembled. The bluster was gone. Froi had won an easy victory. *Well done, Roland!*

Only the exit doors remained.

No. It didn't have to be complete victory to Froi. She

turned defiantly. 'How big is this group?' He didn't answer, so she continued: 'I am saying that if this group was so big that most of the population of East Berlin – the GDR even – was a part of it, what could you do, Comrade Froi? Can you answer me that?'

Froi didn't answer.

'Good day, Frau Bermann.'

Oddly, as Froi walked away from her towards the long corridor from which he'd emerged, Heike felt a calm settle over her. Peace. Someone was touching her, holding both her shoulders, calming her. In asking that last question, she'd released something – a burden lifted. All would be fine; there was a reassuring feeling of lightness. Roland would be fine. *They* would be fine. The end was in sight, though quite what that "ending" was she didn't know.

The feeling of lightness didn't last long.

At journey's end, later that evening, she discovered to her horror that there was something of a parallel with Julia's story. Someone had been to the apartment in her absence. The front door was unlocked – she was sure she'd locked it. Inside the entrance hall the mat was at an angle. She never left it like that; even this morning of all mornings when she was angry and frustrated and nervous, she wouldn't have left the mat like this and the door unlocked. And inside the study Roland's typewriter had a fresh page of A4 paper wound into its rollers with one word typed on it: "Correction".

It had to be Bruno, yet he was nowhere to be seen. She called out his name again and again, upstairs, downstairs, outside.

No answer.

By 6.30 pm he could not be found. There was nothing to indicate he'd even come home and gone out again to play. Heike was often infuriated by her son's tardiness, but this was unusual. He had been brought up to understand that providing he did what his school and his parents required of him, he was free to play in the streets. Mealtime was sacrosanct – a definite appointment for 6.30 pm every evening. Failure to attend was not an option and he knew it. He was normally in the apartment by 4.30 pm on school days and in general was a boy of habit. Tonight, of all nights, there was no sign of him.

Panic quickly overcame her. She recalled Uncle Frederick's words: what were they? "The boy would be taken and put in care…" or something like that.

Roland was a grown man, much as she loved him, but the thought of her child being taken by the state would be too much to bear. She must find him. Shaking, she grabbed her coat, opened the door and recited a quick, uncommunistic prayer.

In answer to that prayer, there, revealed immediately on the street just metres away, was Bruno cheerfully emerging from a car.

Thank God! Maybe a teacher is dropping him home.

She greeted him sternly: 'Where have you been? Whose car was that?'

'He's a Russian man who visited the school and told my teacher that he would be picking me up as you were busy tonight. Was that alright, Mama? I'm not late, am I?'

'You're not late. They shouldn't have kept you. Was the man an official?'

'I think so. He was an inspector. He wanted to talk to me after school and I answered his questions.'

'What sort of questions, Bruno?'

'Family questions. He was interested in my welfare. He wanted to know if I was eating enough at home, if I had a bicycle to use, were we happy as a family.'

'Did he ask about me or your father?'

'Yes, he knew you and Papa – what Papa did for work. He just wanted to make sure we were happy, that's all.'

'What did you tell him?'

'Nothing. We're happy, aren't we? Is tea ready? Is Papa home or is he on assignment again?'

The following morning Heike awoke from a deep sleep to hear Bruno making his way noisily along the corridor, stomping the length of the wooden floor with leaden, heavy feet, blowing his nose, making grotesque nasal noises to clear his sinuses that only his mother would tolerate – typically Bruno. Any other day, it wouldn't have bothered her, but this morning was different. She would have shouted at him, but inside her head she heard a voice that wasn't hers – a voice that said: 'Cherish that sound.'

Optimism today.

Pessimism would have to take a back seat. Lightness had returned! Today she would find work – somewhere, anywhere.

'Mama? What have you done with the bread?' Bruno shouted across from the kitchen.

'Bread? What's wrong with the bread?'

'Nothing. It's just different. I've never seen it like this before.'

To her astonishment, there in the kitchen was Bruno examining a wrapped loaf of fresh bread of the kind they couldn't get in East Berlin. It was most definitely a West Berlin loaf. She hadn't seen a loaf wrapped in such a way since leaving the West seventeen years before.

'Is this a new thing with bread? It's even sliced! What happened to the bread I was cutting yesterday? Did you use it all up?' asked Bruno as he held it up to the light, examining it every which way.

She snatched it off him. 'Hey! Mama!' he protested.

'No, I've never seen this bread.' There had to be clues. Close examination proved useless: it didn't even have the aroma of East Berlin bread.

'Maybe Uncle Frederick left it for us. We must thank him,' said Bruno.

'Maybe he did. Yes, we'll thank him when we see him.'

Sipping coffee, Heike noticed other things that were not right. A framed picture that was askew and at least three others on the kitchen wall that looked as if they'd been deliberately knocked askew. Even the sugar bowl was full, yet she hadn't refilled it in a week. She looked at Bruno but knew in her heart of hearts that he was no prankster. His head was full of many odd, juvenile things, but never pranks.

'If someone offers you a lift this morning, Bruno, don't accept. Be polite as always but don't accept.'

'Why not?'

Heike got up and turned both taps on full blast. Bruno was aghast. This was new.

'Not from strange Russians. Sssshhh!' She put her finger to her mouth then to his lips and leant across the table where she could whisper. 'You know to keep quiet – keep your thoughts to yourself and trust no one – especially Russians. You know what happened to your grandparents! The Russians would have killed them without a second thought.'

'I'll ride my bicycle. I'll be fine!' Again, she urged him to whisper. So he did.

'Don't worry, Mama. The Russian was asking me about what sort of work I wanted to do when I leave school. He was an inspector. It was all above board. That's what he said.'

'How good was his German?'

'Very good for a Russian, but that's why he's inspecting German schools.'

'Did he give you his name?'

'No, but I think his name is Comrade Putinski? Putinskia?

Putinscov? I'm sure I heard that from a teacher.'

She turned off both taps. 'Get your coat, I'm taking you to school.'

'What do you think I am? A five-year-old?'

'No, I'm going to see if I can get a job with your school. We need the money.'

*

The stubborn rabbit was determined not to move off the road, so rather than brake at speed Heike pulled on the wheel to avoid it, assuming the car would cope with the sudden demand on its ultra-modern suspension system, but it didn't. Gravel at the side of the road on a slightly damp tarmac caused a spin that turned the car violently 180 degrees so that by the time it came to a stop she was facing back the way she had come. *My God! What next?!*

Thankfully there were no other cars. She might have careered off the highway into the ditch on one side or over the embankment on the other side.

The rabbit, unflustered, leapt off the tarmac into the verge and out of sight with not a patch of fur ruffled. Inside the car, slightly shaken, Heike reached for a tissue to blow her nose and took a moment to ponder whether this was a sign that she wasn't supposed to meet up with Hanne again.

She sniffed, threw the spent tissue to the floor and gazed upwards through the sunroof. 'What do you want me to do, Angel? Head for home? Or are you really making sure that I will go and tell all this, eh?'

Shaking, she turned the car around in an awkward five-point manoeuvre. From here, just a few more kilometres – another ten minutes behind the wheel at most. She'd come too far to turn back, and it was a personal thing with Heike, the girl who'd walked into East Berlin and made a life – never turn back.

We can keep you forever

Roland was in a poor way. Alone, in a claustrophobic cell, he tried to make sense of what had happened. It made little sense: on leaving his newspaper office for home, a car had pulled up from which three large Stasi officers leapt out and charged towards him. He was their target for the day.

Screeching tyres was just one of their hallmarks. He'd heard it before, he'd seen others pulled off the street, but in respect of his own misadventure he'd initially thought the car was braking for someone else or that it was a traffic accident.

He hadn't seen the men closing on him, so rapidly it was futile trying to run or dodge. He was their prey, the wildebeest succumbing to the hyenas. They appeared intent on killing him right there on the pavement.

Instinctively, a somewhat last-ditch attempt, he swung his briefcase at them as if it were a medieval mace, but they were bigger men and well practised in the art of surprise and capture. In fact, the swing didn't serve him at all because it simply provided his assailants with an arm to grab. They swung him around, put his arm behind his back and bent him painfully forwards, swiftly depriving him of any retaliation.

'I'll happily pull your arm out of your shoulder socket, so forget it!' growled one of them. Swiftly and adroitly handcuffed, that was the end of any further resistance. Better to keep his mouth shut and say nothing.

Pushed into the centre of the back seat with a stocky bastard either side of him, he felt their respective weights pushing down on his slim frame. This was all so typical. Every East Berliner had witnessed something like it; everyone looked away and carried on with their business. Nothing to see here, but the underlying message was always a warning to those witnessing: Don't mess with the state!

The journey seemed to take an age, the third man driving – driving that was frenetic and just plain mad, with his shoe to the floor, swinging the car around as if deliberately shifting the weight of his heavy colleagues to press against Roland's chest, crushing him to the point of near suffocation. At this rate he would be dead by the time they reached HQ.

If so, who would care? Another body? Put it in the morgue and fill out a form. Send flowers to the widow. The cemeteries had plenty of unmarked graves for dissenters like Roland. Who'd bother about another one?

After what seemed an eternity, the mad driver pushed the brake pedal hard and in the same heavy manner that he'd abused the accelerator. The car came to such a rapid stop that the men in the back were almost ejected through the windscreen: 'Damn it, Jaeger! You'll kill us all!'

A uniformed guard stomped up to the car and insisted on making a visual check of its occupants.

'We have a delivery,' explained the driver, gesturing with his thumb in Roland's direction. Satisfied, the guard ordered the barrier to be lifted. 'Pedant!' cursed the mad driver under his breath. 'Every time we come here there's a new boy on the gate just out of school and eager to show his NCO what a trustworthy little lad he is. I'd shoot 'em all!'

The last few metres beyond the barrier opened out into a puddle-saturated quadrangle. Relieved of the two men pressing down on him, Roland gasped for breath.

'Get out, scum!'

With one hand, the larger of the two men grabbed hold of Roland's jacket collar and hauled him off the back seat as if he were nothing more than a sack of potatoes picked up in the supermarket. Held tightly between them he was pushed face first through heavy steel doors into what seemed to him an endless, windowless corridor to a dimly lit reception desk manned by just one uniformed officer. His feet had barely touched the floor.

From this inner reception, draughty corridors emanated outwards in all directions – a chamber designed to keep out sunlight and freedom of expression. Roland was about to be signed into purgatory.

His body rammed hard against the high reception desk, he pleaded with his captors: 'What charge? What have I done?'

'Empty your pockets!'

He dutifully emptied every pocket: handkerchiefs, a wallet with a small amount of cash that was counted immediately before being placed into a clear plastic bag. There was nothing on his person to incriminate him. Another uniformed officer arrived and took his jacket, tie, belt and shoelaces, noted down what he'd taken and placed them, too, in a bag, which he labelled.

'Stick him in a cell.'

Locked up in what was known as a "cage", his only hope now was that the end was in sight for the GDR, but what he feared most of all was being sent deep into the Soviet Union – a fear eventually made all the more real by his jailer.

'We can keep you as long as we have a mind to. We need never let you go. We can keep you forever.'

There was plenty of time to think in the cage – plenty of time to reflect on recent events. Nothing to read – that was all part of the intimidation; nothing that might occupy his mind; just a bed, a stainless steel toilet and perpetual electric light. Once the physical shock exited his system, he could begin to think; and that was the worst part.

Peter had to be behind this! Peter? Max? Whoever he was, whoever he'd become, he was the traitor – the Judas. It was all too coincidental.

Heike must never know about the betrayal. The secret would die with him.

There were moments between sleep where on waking he swore blind he could hear Peter's voice at the far end of a corridor saying things like: 'You got him? Good! This will teach him to screw with the state.' Maybe it was an hallucination? He couldn't be sure anymore.

He *was* sure that he was the only prisoner in the building. Perhaps Zech and the others got away with it. Maybe he was the sacrificial lamb. After all, the place was as quiet as the grave, not even a damn clock ticking.

He wondered whether this was what Heike went through. Brave girl! All this confinement and deprivation, and for what?

He stared at the walls while imitating the sound of a ticking clock by tapping his foot on the floor, trying to keep a pace, seeing just how long he could keep it up. The only interaction was a plate of odious tripe passed through a hatch, with tepid water. The light was never turned off and there was no flex by which he could hang himself, no exposed element whereby he could have electrocuted himself – not that suicide was his thing; he had a wife and child to live for.

Eventually, whether a day had passed or an interminable week he had no idea, he was summoned to explain himself. Again, his inquisitor introduced himself with that very same statement: 'We can keep you… forever.' For the second time it scared the hell out of him, but this time he rebelled: 'Would you permit a book? Perhaps *Alice Through the Looking Glass*, as things here seem quite surreal.'

This was not an intimate meeting: the interrogator sat at a distance from Roland behind a desk abutting another desk positioned lengthways on. The interrogator was well out of reach and so distant as to force Roland to lean forward to hear anything he might be accused of.

The man wasn't frightening: no uniform, no whip, no manacles at the ready, no heavies. This ordinary bureaucrat with the demeanour of a regular state official who might otherwise make decisions on city planning sat alone, the sort of middle manager that Roland had so often interviewed in the line of his work when visiting factories.

Quite unremarkable.

Cameras and tape recorders had to be working somewhere just out of sight, so Roland listened for an electric motor; glanced around the austere, grey room for a camera lens; not that either would make any difference to his case or liberty. This was a suspicion on Roland's part because nothing was obvious, but then, it wouldn't be.

On the interrogator's desk were a couple of files – one of which was Roland's and had been in the making from the day he was born.

He was not prepared for imprisonment. He wanted to be brave like his father and mother, but he couldn't run as they had done. He couldn't escape through the rubble and burning buildings; he couldn't swim across the river or hide by night. He was being held to account by a regime and he'd upset them; and although they weren't about to pull out his fingernails or shoot him – only because they didn't need to – they could most certainly play with his mind.

'Your wife, Heike, insists she doesn't want to see you again…'

The interrogator paused just long enough for the shock to enter Roland's system. He then picked up a small, framed picture that had been lying on the desk. Affecting the manner of an impatient teacher having received overdue, unfinished homework, he shoved it across the lengths of both desks for Roland to examine. 'She was here this morning. She gave me this and insisted you have it and keep it as a memento of your lives together.'

The picture was Roland's favourite image of Heike with Bruno as a toddler playing in the park. He'd snapped it using the Praktika brought home from the office for unofficial, family use. He would take it to the park to practise with different lenses and filters before developing the film in the bathroom.

There was just something about the composition of the photo and the way it was so delightfully exposed. He loved the subjects and was proud of the way it had come out. Telephoto lens. Heike and Bruno in clear focus, her short, silky hair blowing across her elfin face, the background out of focus. In all, it was a good snap, through luck more than judgement on this occasion.

He was, nonetheless, a very capable photographer making the most of limited equipment. He was a good developer, too, experimenting with f-stops, exposure time, film stocks and photographic paper. Although black and white, the photo captured Heike at her most beautiful with her gaze turned adoringly toward Bruno – mischievous as ever pulling against his harness, eager for the "off".

She would not have given it to anyone for she cherished it every bit as much as he did.

'I don't believe you. My wife would never give you that picture.'

'You want proof? I have proof.' The interrogator shoved across another picture, this time a large print of the lobby – a still from a security camera. This image, too, was perfectly clear – Roland could make out the uniformed figure of a guard and what looked to be Heike clearly meeting with a plain-clothes officer. It was certainly not a fake. He knew how to fake photographs; this was not one.

Roland was now resigned to his fate. He'd brought this on; he alone had agreed to work with the group, no one had coerced him. His only hope lay in President Gorbachev. If he was the reformist that so many were beginning to believe in, then there was hope. Even if Honecker were to stand firm without material backing from the USSR, the GDR could not continue to hold out against the West.

What concerned him more was Heike. She was an ardent communist who refused to believe that her adopted state was anything other than perfect. 'A land without fascists – what could be better?' she would often say, as if in a constant state of euphoria. She meant every word. In her mind, American "fascists" had replaced Germany's fascists, with their own corrupt officials spiriting away members of the Third Reich for the benefit of the US as it sought to replace the British Empire with its own – not an original idea but one influenced by her GI father; an idea that he espoused with pride.

Heike firmly believed that the US had even assassinated President Kennedy with a view to starting World War 3 with the Russians, another belief planted in her mind by Joe and reaffirmed by Melissa who would tell her:

'Every good American gets shot! Did you ever notice that?

'JFK, RFK and Martin Luther King… and who pulls the trigger each time? The CIA; the FBI; the Mafia. Then they blame Khrushchev! It is the most dangerous country in the world and they will kill us all if we're not careful.

'The British and French are too much in their debt to raise so much as a finger in protest. Look at Vietnam! And when students protest they get beaten or shot – killed by their own policeman. And they call it peace? They actually call their country a democracy?

'What difference your hand across your heart and your hand

held high? No difference – no difference. Sweet Land of Liberty? Liberty unless you're black, red, yellow or just plain poor!

'In 1941, they didn't want to fight Hitler. They had no intention until such time as the Japanese attacked Pearl Harbor and Hitler declared war on them! They were forced into war. Hitler knew they hated the British more than they hated him. They'd have gone to war with the British Empire given the chance, but not Hitler and his National Socialists. And following the war they've interfered with virtually every state on the planet in an effort to build their own empire while closing down European empires.'

Melissa's words, Heike's sentiments.

Roland drifted back into his own body. Stuck before his inquisitor, he could not see a happy outcome for his marriage. The Stasi could do what they wanted with him – send him to a Gulag if need be, but without Heike he was lost.

She might have forgiven him a mistress or some fleeting affair, but betrayal of the state and its doctrine would be unforgivable in her eyes.

Now I have my story for Bruno, thought Roland back in his grey-painted claustrophobic cell with its single bed of wooden boards, cold steel lavatory pan and basin. *Did I tell you about the time I was incarcerated in a Stasi prison? No? Then I'll tell you…*

Heike didn't know how to make contact with Uncle Frederick. She never did have his address or phone number; he always initiated contact. That was his prerogative. He was too high in rank to be reached through conventional channels because he had the "ear" of Honecker and he played a significant role in the workings of the Presidium of the German Democratic Republic.

If it were possible, Heike would have appealed to him for Roland's freedom: for *his* sanity, for *her* sanity. But that last meeting at the apartment was to be their last; she never saw or heard from him again.

For the next month, she spent her days close to a window in the belief that at any moment his familiar figure would appear as always. If she was sitting down, she'd leap to her feet on hearing an unfamiliar noise; stop what she was doing, put down whatever she was holding, turn down the radio. Cars were of particular interest if they stopped outside.

'Mama! It's not Papa. You're wasting your time!' Bruno would call out every time she reacted to a car outside. And he was right – quite right – but she couldn't help herself.

If she wasn't looking out of windows, she was looking at clocks or the calendar. Windows, clocks, calendars; that's what living in East Berlin was doing to her.

For one month, two people were in prison in the very same city: one was incarcerated in a tiny, bare cell, which at least was warm – too warm; the other in an apartment that was too cold because she couldn't pay the heating bill.

One wanted to read and write but had no materials; the other had all the materials but no inclination to read or write anything. Both prisoners suffered appalling mental deprivation, yet neither sustained any physical scars that they would ever be able to point to. It would be as if it had never happened, because they could never prove it to anyone. But happen it most certainly did.

Roland was released following a month in detention. He was free to leave, but the proviso was that he was not to be employed as a journalist, nor could he leave Berlin without authorisation. Instead, the authorities made arrangements for him to work as a road sweeper. There were no jobless in East Germany. He would also have to obey a curfew.

'But how are we going to pay the rent on a road sweeper's wages?' asked Heike. 'We'll manage. Between us we'll manage.'

Events, however, were speeding up.

*

By the time Heike arrived in Aalenburg it was dark, and without a working satnav she was going to have to find the Roundhouse the old-fashioned way. Hanne didn't own a "handy", so there was no way of calling or texting: "I'm here! Come and meet me!" *Why can't you come into the twenty-first century, Hanne?!*

She asked the duty manager in the little supermarket.

'Ah, yes, I know it. It's a holiday rental cottage now. Not sure who owns it these days, we never see them here. They travel down from Frankfurt. There is a keyholder, but I'm not sure where they live. Shame, as it takes the heart out of the old town when strangers own properties as holiday lets. Well, why not leave the car here? It's a convoluted route if you try and drive from this point, and very narrow. It's only a short walk…'

*

The night that it happened Heike had been to a similar shop just before tea. Its stock was meagre in comparison to its equivalent in the West, but it had the essentials, from cakes to hardware. It was convenient and the shopkeeper was always affable.

That evening was unremarkable – warm and still. Dogs and children filled the pre-holiday air and some form of normality had at least returned to family life.

Roland was still at work just ahead of his curfew and

would be home soon. Tea was slightly earlier now than it used to be due to his shift rota as a street cleaner, but Heike would not eat before her husband was home. Family mealtimes were traditional and would remain undisturbed regardless of work patterns.

The intention was always to settle down to eat around 7.30 pm; mostly it was achieved, but there were very occasional exceptions and lapses, especially as the nights were drawing out; Bruno was somewhere and the fact that he was a restless teenager and growing quickly made him unpredictable.

There was some other factor that Heike could not quite pinpoint.

His personality had changed since his father's arrest and he seemed to be having difficulty coming to terms with just what had taken place. To Bruno, his father had been emasculated by the state. For a father to be robbed of his profession was unforgivable and he blamed both his father and the state government in equal measure. So the only thing for him now was to make a stand and yell like a rebel just like the Billy Idol song.

The sound of someone yelling somewhere outside just as Heike was taking plates out of the glass cabinet for warming in the oven unnerved her. She glanced at the clock; it was just after 7 pm.

Then two distinct shots rang out their snap and crack so close by that she dropped a plate. There was no mistaking the sound; it was automatic rifle fire – someone had been shot and they could only be metres away.

Maybe it was a panic reaction to Roland's recent incarceration and run-in with the Stasi, but some inner fear sparked deep within Heike. At her feet were a hundred pieces of broken china, the remnants of a much-loved plate. On any other day she would have cursed her clumsiness and swept up the debris with barely a second thought, but instead she saw the wreckage as a metaphor. Something she held so dear had just shattered, but it wasn't the loss of a stupid old plate. A feeling was surging through her system, boiling from within, forewarning that the shots were to do with either Roland or Bruno – maybe even both of them.

*

She tried to recall whether she'd ever been to Aalenburg before. There was something familiar about it. The main street was familiar for sure, as was the church tower and the river. Must have been a long, long time ago.

She tried to neutralise her thoughts. Concentrate on something else. Pretty little town – very pretty.

Stupid girl for not moving *here* back in the '70s instead of defecting to the East! There would have been a man here for her, though perhaps not a "Roland", but someone. It would have been a quiet life with a local job in a little company – maybe the brewery? They sell internationally. This is where they're based; such a tiny place for such a world-famous beer; a small museum, too, of course. She'd always fancied the idea of being a curator.

Here, she wouldn't have lost a baby. Roland wouldn't have been arrested… He wouldn't have lost his job.

Stupid mini market! Fancy calling in there for directions. For Heaven's sake, Hanne! Where are you?

*

She ran out into the street toward the Wall, calling out their names as she ran, tears streaming around her face. This was not going to turn out okay and she knew it.

Ahead of her: the dead-end – the Wall. Now she could

stop running; a small crowd of onlookers, a parked car. Perhaps he'd been run over. Perhaps they weren't shots – it was the impact she'd heard.

Her angel grasped her hand softly but firmly; she could feel its celestial grip tighten around her palm and fingers. There would be no turning back because if it was to be her man or her boy she would pick them up and take them home to tend to their wounds – the state would not have them.

With every step, certainty in her own fate grew. If they were dead at this godforsaken spot, she would die too. She would run at the Wall whereupon they would open fire and kill her for sure; and if one bullet failed to do the trick, she'd try again, but there would be no returning home without her beloved family.

Above her, the neon streetlights were beginning to flicker into life. Ahead of her in the near distance she could see the tops of the taller, finer, more modern edifices of the Western sector, tempting in their close proximity yet also taunting the misfit who had turned her back and disparaged their security all those years ago.

She recognised some of the faces that had gathered to gawp. The man on the bicycle now heading home nonchalant and unconcerned glared at her in passing as if to say, 'What did you expect?'; unsympathetic neighbours and cowards, all who dared not show solidarity for fear of association that would drag them into the whole bloody mess.

Below the crowd of gawping heads, it was, as she had feared, Bruno, lying face-up on the dirt-covered tarmac, deathly still, blood draining from his face, draining from his head into a deep, wide pool at his side.

She knelt to lift his head, oh-so-gently cradling it lovingly in her hands, his eyes desperately searching to focus. Someone at least had placed a white shirt by way of a pillow and to catch the river that oozed from the open wound. A voice in the crowd called out: 'I can take him to the hospital. I have a van. He won't last if we wait for an ambulance.'

And so four remaining bystanders carefully lifted the lifeless boy into a VW van, its dusty cargo space quickly emptied of building tools.

*

'Do you know where the Roundhouse is?' she asked a boy.
'I do! Would you like me to show you?'
'Yes please! Is it far?'
'Not far, but it's a steep climb up the hill. Mama says it's too steep, but I don't think so. Mama is old.'
'Really?'
'Yes, she'll be thirty-seven next month.'
'Oh! That is nothing! I am much older.'
'Will you be alright climbing the hill?'
'I'm sure. Lead on, young man.'

*

Bruno would be one of the very last casualties of the Wall, though not the very last. The teenager was lucky in that thanks to the skill of a remarkable surgeon well practised in bullet wound surgery, together with a dedicated nursing team, his life was saved.

In the months that followed, he made a recovery that rendered him a little lame in mind and body. He would never be quite the man he'd dreamed of becoming, but his recovery was swift and that was a godsend for which he always counted his blessings, as did his parents.

It wasn't until summer's end that the truth emerged.

Not daring to take Roland with her for support, Heike

returned to Stasi HQ once more, this time demanding answers of Comrade Inspector Froi.

On this occasion she knew the place, knew the procedure. He courteously made more time and actually invited her into the inner sanctum where he even offered her a seat in his office in order that she might take in the enormity of the seriousness of the issue. But again, and not surprisingly, there was nothing apologetic in his demeanour.

'Your son was reckless, Frau…?'

'Frau Bermann.'

'Frau Bermann. He was shot because it appeared to the guards that he was trying to cross the Wall. That was foolhardy. Our enquiries show that your son was out of control when there was no school.'

Froi removed his spectacles, stared into the middle distance and concentrated on cleaning the square lenses.

'Have you heard of Radio Glasnost?' he asked.

'No… no, I haven't.'

'It's a subversive radio station and quite illegal. Your son was running tapes for them.'

'Tapes?'

'Cassette tapes. Recordings of subversive content for use by those who seek to bring down the GDR. He was under surveillance and being followed. One of my officers tried to apprehend him. Your son ran and attempted to climb the Wall. That's when a border guard opened fire.'

'I don't believe it.'

'You should, Frau Bermann. Where were you? You're his mother! By rights, on his release from hospital we should have arrested him as well as you and your husband. He should have been taken into care – for his own well-being.'

'Then why didn't you?'

Froi didn't answer.

'Have I friends in the right places?' she asked.

Grim-faced, Froi was not about to acknowledge her question, but rather stood, donned his spectacles, straightened his shiny red tie and tugged at the hem of his grey jacket, before beckoning her to leave, with these parting words: 'You're a very fortunate woman, Frau Bermann. Very fortunate indeed.'

Their one aim now was to get out of East Berlin as quickly as possible. Like secret agents meeting on a park bench in a spy novel, they discussed over a sandwich lunch their escape.

'I have it on good authority that if we can get to Leipzig, the Lutherans will help us. We'll make a bid for Hungary. They're already protesting – openly, you know. They're confident – *we're* confident – that the Wall will be opened up by September and later demolished.'

'We can't be sure, Roland. And what about Bruno? He's not fit to travel.'

'He *is* fit to travel.'

'And if the Wall is going to come down as you predict, why risk fleeing the country? We'll be followed as soon as we leave here! There's a curfew on you, or have you forgotten?'

'Not if we're careful. There are no guarantees that Honecker will cave in, but we have to try. To stay here is to accept everything that's happened to us. It shows them that they've won – we're cowed into submission; and we mustn't let them win!'

'It's not that we're letting them win – you're trying to be the hero your father was, and you're taking me with you like he took your mother. But the difference is we have a son who may not understand what's going on. He drags his right foot now, or haven't you noticed?'

'And the corner of his mouth droops. I know, but he'll be fine. He's stronger than you think, Heike. What else do we do? Sit here in East Berlin waiting for the knock on the door? Waiting for them to come back and put him into care? They'll bide their time, but they will come back, you can be sure of it. They'll come back the day your "uncle" dies. He's the one who's spared Bruno, and possibly me, too. But "spared" isn't the right word. They haven't let us go – we're like mice before a cat and the cat has got us right where he wants us.'

'So how do we get to Leipzig without them stopping us?'

'There's a notable Lutheran doctor called Luft who has shown an interest in Bruno's recovery. He's well connected, but he's no admirer of Honecker. He's going to send a letter to our family doctor who'll make arrangements for us to travel with papers. Armed with documents, they daren't stop us.'

*

The Roundhouse was quite easy to find after all – near the top of the hill. It wasn't round nor was it detached, but it had a quaint round tower abutting its only gable end. There was a marked place to park outside so she could have driven up the cobbled street and parked, which would have been preferable as she was now breathing heavily having climbed the hill with a twelve-year-old boy egging her on and wondering why she was so slow.

She put a couple of euros into his jacket pocket, knocked on the door, but no sign of life seemed to stir from within; no lights on, no car outside, and Hanne would have been stuck without a hire car. *Perhaps this isn't the right place? I must be mistaken, but that cannot be.*

She knocked again – harder this time.

A neighbour emerged from a door across the narrow street. Heike turned. 'I'm supposed to be meeting my cousin here – an English woman?'

'English? I thought her accent rather strange. Yes, I spoke to her yesterday. Tall woman? Yes?'

'Yes.'

'I really don't know; I can't help you. Maybe she has popped out for something?'

'Maybe. I was hoping to see her before she left. Perhaps she had to go home early. Thank you!'

'She was expecting you?'

'Yes – yes, she was.'

It was not like Hanne. She would not forget their arrangement; Heike was sure of that.

*

On arrival in Leipzig, there was no one to meet them. Roland had been assured there would be a representative from the Lutheran Church, but no one showed, so they waited patiently.

*

Heike was eager to tell Hanne the story, so that she could say: *You see, this trip to Leipzig was a bad idea. We should never have left Berlin. I should have said this to Roland the moment we arrived but I didn't; I remained patient and receptive to a new direction.*

Hanne, maybe in the West you didn't understand, but we had everything we needed in Berlin. Roland had a job – nothing special, but it was work. It was only when the shooting happened and the dissenters approached him to write their bulletins – that's what swayed his mind. Our rent was minimal. Bruno's school was good; he was happy. Maybe there could have been more choice in the shops, but we knew how to get the things we wanted.

She would know where to begin when Hanne returned – *if* she returned.

*

In Leipzig, Roland had no such qualms. They had arrived at the culmination of an exciting period in which the city was leading all of East Germany in peaceful protest. All through October, ever larger numbers of people were gathering each Monday at the Nicolaikirche, openly using the traditional day of prayer – the Montagsgebet – to draw support from far and near.

'Roland! The church is wonderful! Let's go in and have a look – come on!'

'We're not tourists, Heike.'

Roland was reluctant to leave the security of the car.

'What harm can it do? It's beautiful. Come on, Bruno, you need some exercise after being cooped up in the car all this time.'

They were confident that if they left the car within sight of the church, all would be fine, but best to lock it as some of their most precious possessions were on board.

Outside, they craned their necks staring up at the tower that rose above them, unable to see the very top.

'You're very welcome to go in, the door is always open,' a woman invited them, smiling, showing them the way.

'Thank you!'

'Should I tell her I'm a communist?' whispered Heike.

'We're all communists,' said Roland; 'that's why we're here.'

Inside, the interior – vast and splendid as only a truly great cathedral can be – opened up before them.

'It's so big! Mama, look at the trees up in the roof. Can you see them?'

'They're not trees, Bruno. Those are columns and they're holding the ceiling up. They are fashioned to represent palm trees. It's a feature, maybe?'

'What's a feature?'

'Those are features,' Heike pointed to the ceiling; 'artwork like you do at school.'

'It's like an old Roman building.'

'It's classical architecture, Bruno.'

'The pews are so… so white!'

'When did you last enter a church, Heike?' asked Roland.

'Too long ago, maybe? I don't know. This is something truly special.'

Evangelical Lutheran Minister Mathius Beck loved the job of meeting and greeting visitors. Bruno spotted him first: 'Watch out, here comes a man in a black dress.' Beck, who had the kindest features of any human being they'd ever seen, was beaming from ear to ear, striding out from where they didn't know, but with a look of delight that suggested he'd been waiting for them and now they were here – the most important visitors ever. No one was like this in East Germany – this had to be a different place entirely. Had they crossed the Wall without realising it?

'Welcome, my friends! My name is Mathius Beck – I'm a minister here at Nikolaikirche. Would you like to light a candle? Say a prayer?'

Bruno nodded, though not quite knowing just what was expected of him, so Beck gave him a small, white candle. 'But I don't have a match,' said Bruno.

'This way – you can light it like so…' He showed Bruno how to light the candle from one already aflame. 'And then we place it here in the frame – that's right – and the flame of the candle keeps the prayer going.'

'I've never said a prayer before. How do I do it?' Bruno asked.

'It's easy. Just think of something you really love.'

'Anything?'

'Anything. Who do you love?'

'Mama and Papa.'

'Then your prayer is for them. Place it in the frame. The flame is your love for them.'

Bruno was more than satisfied with his candle prayer. Now he could see his love, feel its warmth against his cupped palm as the flame danced and flickered. The minister stepped back and glanced up, Bruno following his gaze.

'If you look behind you – yes, up there – you will see the biggest church organ in the world.'

'Are they silver pipes? I bet they are and I bet they're loud!' exclaimed Bruno.

'Would you like to see somewhere that other visitors never see?'

'Oh, yes please!' said Bruno, thrilled at everything he was witnessing.

They followed Beck in silence through a small oak door out of the main church into the vestry. Stone steps gave way to a steel staircase that spiralled up and up and up, past the clock mechanism, 189 steps in total, each one counted by Bruno, who would have been quicker if it hadn't been for his poor, dragging leg. He assured them it didn't hurt and that he couldn't wait for whatever was around the corner.

Finally reaching the top of the ever winding staircase, Beck pushed open a hatch above his head and climbed up and out of the tower into a stiff breeze, turning to help first Bruno, then Heike and Roland. They looked back down in astonishment at the street below where they had stood only half an hour previously craning their necks from street level.

'What do you see?' asked the pastor.

'That's where we stood. We can see everything from here.'

'See all the people below? Like ants? On Mondays they gather here at the church and march through the streets…' –

he pointed into the distance – 'those streets and those streets, too.'

'Why?' asked Bruno.

'Freedom. They march in protest for freedom.' He turned to Roland. 'That's why you're here, isn't it?'

'Yes,' said Roland.

'Then join us.'

'What about the Stasi?'

'The people are too many. There's nothing the Stasi can do. You see all those cars?'

'They're like toy cars!' exclaimed Bruno. 'And the trams! Look at the trams!'

'On Monday evenings, there are no cars down there, no trams – just people. Hundreds and hundreds of people, and their numbers are growing each week.'

'How can we help?' asked Roland.

'Just walk with us. It's a peaceful march of peaceful people.'

'But we're communists,' said Heike.

'This won't stop you from being a communist. You'll be in good company. They are *all* like you, but they are marching for a greater freedom.'

On the way back down, Heike told Pastor Beck their story: Roland's arrest and Bruno's shooting. She emphasised the danger that she felt they were in and that to remain in one place for too long could lead to their arrest and, worst of all, Bruno would be taken from them. That, she couldn't bear.

Back in the vestry, Beck linked arms with Roland and Heike and explained:

'This is what people do when they march. They march as one – one people, one voice. Come on, Bruno, link arms with us.' And he did.

'Stay and march with us on Monday. We are expecting many thousands of people. It will be an historic occasion.

Then you will make your way to Hungary and the Austrian border.

'As a minister whose church is at the centre of the protest movement, I am a man frequently in fear of arrest and so I've distanced myself from some in my congregation who seek my counsel on a near hourly basis as if checking the weather. "Is it safe to go outside, pastor?" they ask.

'For such occasions, I have prepared a little speech that I give in all sincerity and it is this: The time is right for the people to make their voices heard and this is going to happen. But you should be aware that although Gorbachev will put pressure on Honecker – in this the 40th anniversary year – there are hardliners in the Politburo who are vehemently against Gorbachev. If those forces destroy Gorbachev, the Iron Curtain will tighten so much it will strangle us all.

'And don't think there will be any encouragement from the West. Western leaders like Thatcher, Mitterrand and Bush fear a unified Germany and might do anything to keep the status quo, despite what they say in public.

'Word is the Hungarians are dismantling the border fence with Austria – now. That's your route out. It may only be the brief opening of a window, so if you have any sense you'll take it.'

*

"If you have any sense, you'll take it." Heike remembered the sentence word for word, coupled with the deadly earnest expression of Pastor Beck.

If I have any sense, I'll drive home now, thought Heike; but the urge to see Hanne was too strong. She desperately wanted to see her cousin more now than at any time in their relationship. She wanted to unburden herself as if always the good Catholic she had to make a confession. The next reunion might not be the right time for either of them. Hanne might not be able to make it – she'd attended very few over the course of a lifetime – or Heike might not be able to make it. Who could predict what the coming years would bring? No, it had to be now. She would bring the car up and wait for Hanne to return.

*

The Nikolaikirche was full every day – full to brimming. People came and went for services as always, but even Martin Luther – whose church this was – would have been astonished by the comings and goings of the proletariat.

Roland in particular couldn't contain his excitement. Here was the epicentre of the movement he'd been writing for, risking his liberty for. The memory of capture, interrogation and imprisonment was all too fresh in his mind, but his doubts were vanishing quickly. The "war" may not be over yet, but the allied camp had been found, and if the numbers of people here at the Nikolaikirche were anything to go by, then victory was just around the corner.

On Sunday evening, always the journalist, he sat down in their room in a hostel and wrote the following in longhand:

This is indeed the most exciting time for all East Germans. Leipzig is alive with the most delightful unrest this reporter has ever witnessed. It's not just the city, it's all of Saxony and maybe the entire Eastern bloc, and there is only one name on people's lips – Gorbachev (or "Gorbi" as so many people call him). The protest movement here is entirely democratic and peaceful, and has been gathering pace since its beginnings in 1983. As I write, the city is holding its breath in anticipation of tomorrow's march through its historic centre. The "Monday Marches", as they have been known since they began, are gathering in strength. Tomorrow, it is expected that the demonstrators will number in their tens of thousands, though no one is sure just how many will turn up or what the reaction of the authorities will be. The unrest felt by many East Germans, particularly those under fifty years of age, as the state celebrates forty years of containment: its people seek new horizons for themselves, their children and future generations. East Germans have become disillusioned with one-party politics. It is possible that the authorities will use force to break up the march. In the last few weeks alone, some demonstrators have been arrested, but due to the peaceful nature of the protests the police have so far held off taking action. Since September, not one shop window has been broken and the only casualty has been the traffic, which is now diverted on Monday evenings. No one knows for sure exactly what the outcome is going to be, but the people of Leipzig feel empowered for the first time.

'Tomorrow – what are we going to do, Roland?' asked Heike with heavy heart.

'We'll march, of course!'

'You sound very confident.'

'Why shouldn't I be? The people want change, Heike. This isn't just a small group of agitators meeting in a pokey little shed up an alley, this is thousands and thousands of East Germans and we need to be among them.'

'Don't you think you've done your bit?'

'There's more to do…'

'And I've done my bit. Picking my child up off the road, mopping his blood from his face, trying to get you out of jail! I've done my bit, too! Don't forget, we're also here to see the doctor. Let him examine Bruno and then let's be gone.'

'Okay, Heike, that pain is mine also. But if we drive away without having marched with our fellow citizens, then we will never feel at home in a united Germany. In years to come – maybe next year – someone will say, "Were you in Leipzig when they were marching for Germany's freedom?"

'Yes, we were in Leipzig, but no, we didn't march with our fellow citizens, because we felt we'd done our bit. So we drove on!

'Heike, everyone here, everyone who will be on the streets tomorrow night, will have done their bit also. *They* will have picked their loved ones up off the road; *they* will have family or friends incarcerated in a prison cell somewhere. *They* all have their stories – often much worse than ours! How can we be so selfish?

'Isn't this what communism is supposed to be about? People working together for a common aim? This is the *real* communism! Not spying and secret police and interrogation, shooting, blocking people in with walls and fences, mines and booby traps! That's not communism, that's totalitarianism. That's all we've ever had – totalitarianism – and we've been fooled not once, but twice!'

This had never been asked of her: *What would you do, child, if the state were to be challenged from within?* No one had thought to ask it all those years ago when she arrived, suitcase in hand – the willing defector.

Heike glanced across at Bruno, sleeping. Sitting down on the edge of his single bed, stroking his head, she glanced around the tiny room at its cell-like dimensions, harsh white walls, steel-framed windows. Already, there were hundreds of voices outside somewhere, and it wasn't even Monday.

'Are we marching, Mama?'

'I thought you were sleeping?'

'Are we?'

'We'll see the doctor tomorrow and if he's happy with your progress we'll march in the evening.'

Herr Doctor Wolfgang Luft was the son of a legendary Austrian surgeon – Professor Arnold Luft, a man noted in the annals of twentieth-century European history not only for his skills in the operating theatre but for his determination to keep the politics of National Socialism out of his hospital.

Arnold Luft's maternal heritage was Jewish, a fact that remained undiscovered by the Nazis. He had no concern for the religion of any man; a communist by politics, reluctantly tolerated by those who would otherwise have melted his body in the flaming ovens of Auschwitz.

Saved by his brilliance as a surgeon, he was responsible for repairing the shattered bodies of fighting men who would otherwise have died of their injuries. No respecter of flags or salutes, he would literally turn his back on those who openly displayed their support of Hitler and the Nazis.

It was the immediate period following war's end that was to have its most dramatic effect on Luft and his family. Having returned to his native Austria to continue his work, he was expelled in 1956 for his communist membership, his beloved clinic shut down and refitted as a hotel.

He never recovered from the irony of having been tolerated by the Nazis, only to be exiled by his own Austrian government. He settled in East Germany with his wife Annette and only son, ten-year-old Wolfgang.

Wolfgang grew up in Leipzig, and after training as a medical practitioner he continued his father's pioneering work as a surgeon, inheriting not only brilliance and carefully constructed notes but also that stubborn and determined disregard for authority of any kind.

By 1989, aged forty-five, he was an eminent surgeon and a legend in his own right with a particular fascination in gunshot wounds to the head. Bruno was yet another case study.

'Sad business,' he said, on meeting Bruno for the first time. 'You were running wild, were you?'

'Yes,' said Bruno. 'I love running wild. You ought to see the place where I live – it's a wild place.'

Heike immediately admonished him. 'Bruno! Don't be silly! We live in Berlin, Herr Doctor.'

'They tell me Berlin is a wild place, Frau Bermann, and your son has just confirmed it. Why did they shoot you, Bruno?'

'I don't know why. He was a madman – really mad. Shouting at me. I kept on running. So would you!'

'Of course I would. When is your birthday?'

'It's… it's…' Bruno sighed as the date eluded him. 'When is it, Mama? My birthday?'

'October 21st.'

'What year?' asked the doctor. Heike was about to answer, but Luft stopped her. 'Not you, Mama – Bruno. Tell me what year you were born?'

Bruno glanced at Heike – initial panic; then fixed on the doctor with steely determination to get this bit right.

'1922.'

'1922, eh? My! You are older than you look!'

Bruno grinned; he liked the idea of looking more mature than his fifteen years.

'How old are *you*, Herr Doctor?' asked Bruno with no sense of audacious audacity whatsoever.

'Younger than you,' replied Luft.

'That's alright, then!' chuckled Bruno.

Luft turned to Heike and Roland. 'I'd like to keep him here for a couple of days, for observation.'

'How long, Herr Doctor?'

'I don't know. I would just like to find out a bit more about his wound. From what I can see now, he's a lucky young man. Were you there? Was there much bleeding?'

'I arrived shortly after the shooting – maybe five or ten

minutes. He was bleeding profusely. I tried to stem the blood. I thought I'd lost him.'

'Neurological recovery can take a long time – months, years. Bruno has youth on his side and the bullet has skimmed his skull and in doing so will have taken with it some tissue. I need to work out the trajectory of the bullet, which is why I want to keep him for a day or so. And I understand there was a bullet in his shoulder, but they removed that, yes?'

'Yes.'

'Is he getting fits? Epilepsy?'

'No, only nightmares." What does he see in the nightmares?'

'He doesn't see anything. He tells me that he's in total blackness and that there's an evil presence, so he growls at whatever is scaring him, and I can hear him growling like a dog, but he says it is a place without light.'

'And this nightmare recurs often?'

'Not every night, but it makes him afraid of sleeping. He tries to keep himself awake and then he's mentally and physically tired a lot of the time. When he does sleep he sleeps half a day given the chance.'

'And do you give him the chance?'

'If it's not a school day, then it's fine.'

Luft offered his hand to Bruno by way of a handshake. 'Shake my hand, Bruno.'

'Why?'

'Just shake my hand. Cement our new friendship.'

'Okay.'

Luft took the boy's hand, shook it and then held it gently for a moment.

'What do you feel, Bruno?'

'What do you mean?'

'What does my hand feel like?'

'Warm…'

'And…?'

'I don't know…'

'Is it a tight grip?'

'No… it's a nice grip, like you're a friend. There's a boy in our school who is very strong and he grips people until they hurt. He's really bad.'

'What else does my hand feel like?'

'It's rough, like Papa's hand.'

'Good.' He released Bruno's hand, took out a pen and scribbled something on the back of a card.

'Is that okay, Herr Doctor?' asked Heike, anxious.

'Yes, nothing to worry about. His sensory ability appears quite normal, but I do need to carry out some tests with Bruno.'

'Will it hurt, Herr Doctor?' asked Bruno.

'No, Bruno, we're not going to hurt you at all. No needles. I just need you to play ball with me, so to speak.'

'I like playing ball – football, tennis, catch. Those sorts of games?'

'Yes, those sorts of games.'

There was no choice now but to do the march. They were stuck in Leipzig, and what else was there?

It concerned Roland particularly that Heike was showing signs of something bizarre – something he hadn't heard for over fifteen years. Heike would turn to look and talk to a chair or some other object as if she were addressing Bruno in person.

'No, Bruno, I'm not going out in that coat. You know I don't like that coat.'

'I didn't say anything,' Roland would reply, astonished as there had been no discussion, no aim of going out at that time or what best to wear. Why would she mistake him for Bruno?

'I wasn't talking to you, I was talking to Bruno. Bruno?! Do as Herr Doctor tells you. He has your best interests at heart, remember.'

Roland took hold of her and pulled her tightly into his body, stroking her light brown hair, tears streaming down his cheeks, burying his cheek against the top of her head. 'That bullet hit you, too, didn't it?'

'Do you want to know about *my* nightmare?' she asked.

'Yes, tell me about your nightmare.'

'It's where I climb a mountain and my legs are really tired because the path winds round and round, but it's a beautiful mountain and eventually I reach the top and I can see everything and it's all so truly beautiful.'

'Why is that a nightmare?'

'It's a nightmare because neither you nor Bruno are with me – I'm alone, completely alone.'

On Monday evening they marched without Bruno through Leipzig, placing themselves in the middle of the middle of the middle; if there was a middle, which, of course, there wasn't.

'WE ARE THE PEOPLE!'
'WE ARE THE PEOPLE!'
'WE ARE THE PEOPLE!'
'WE ARE THE PEOPLE!'

Roland shouted in an effort that Heike might hear, even though she stood right beside him: 'THIS IS GOING TO CHANGE GERMANY, BUT MOST OF ALL IT WILL CHANGE THE WORLD!'

It was impossible to hear him – impossible because 70,000 people – so closely packed together that they were stepping on one another's toes – were shouting as one. 'THANK GOODNESS BRUNO ISN'T HERE!' she yelled back to Roland, but he could only nod and smile as the collective shouts of the crowd drowned out every other noise.

'NO VIOLENCE!'
'NO VIOLENCE!'
'NO VIOLENCE!'
'GORBI! GORBI!'
'GORBI! GORBI!'
'GORBI! GORBI!'

The stillness that eventually came with dawn banished the night into the pages of history. Voices universally hoarse; hearts filled with a collective happiness no one had dared believe possible.

The normally inert East Germans had at long last marched in unison, roused like all revolutionaries by a gathering passion of naked aspiration to be free from the control of the unelected.

The Wall was beginning to crumble: cement dust falling at their feet.

'Your boy is free to go. I'm done with him – thank you!'
'Will he be alright, Herr Doctor? In the future?'
'The future is yet to be written, Frau Bermann. Bruno? Your head is fragile. Use it for creative thinking but don't think you can become a boxer or a football player. Stay away from mad axemen and those maniacs with guns.'

He pointed Bruno in the direction of a neighbouring room.

'So, you go away and amuse yourself while I give your parents a prescription. Okay?'

Bruno shook Luft firmly by the hand, stepped back, saluted him, wiped a tear from his eye, turned and marched out – the perfect soldier guard.

'He's been watching *Volkspolizei* all his life!' joked Heike.

Luft gestured for them to be seated. Taking out a notepad

from a desk drawer, he began to scribble a note.

'When you leave here this morning, make your way to the Czech border; I hear that certain opportunities are opening there; and then you can make your way to Hungary and onward to Austria. I'm writing out a route for you to take, and I'll wish you the very best of luck.'

'And Bruno?'

'If he doesn't play rough and uses that brain of his for more cerebral pursuits, he'll improve his cognitive ability, but, as you will already be aware, he's not the bright child you once knew.'

'Will he improve given time?'

'Of course, I have no doubt. With the twenty-first century just around the corner there will be advances in drugs and treatment. Time is on his side. He's lost brain tissue that he alone can't replace, but technology may well provide an answer in the years to come. Our research, as I'm sure you know, is producing results every year, but as yet we can't grow human tissue. Be patient; don't shelter him. Let him live his life to the full. There's nothing to stop him leading a normal life, but if you try to protect him you'll stifle him and that will rebound on you. Bring him back to see me two years from now. Write to me if you think anything significant is affecting him, but I'm confident in his ability.'

The map almost obscuring the car's tiny windscreen, Heike navigated them out of Leipzig while Roland coaxed the little Trabant to go yet another kilometre and another and another. Each kilometre was a miracle in the Trabant: uncomfortable, claustrophobic and frequently unreliable.

Because of its small petrol tank and no petrol gauge, they had to stop frequently to refuel. When Roland turned off the ignition at a petrol station it would often not restart with a hot engine, so they would get out and with the help of others push it away from the pumps and sit patiently while it cooled down like some exhausted donkey.

Once cooled, it would tease them. Each time the key was turned the little motor would turn over one – two – three times, giving every expectation of firing into life, but then promptly give up the ghost, leaving the starting motor spinning, whirring and engaging sweet nothing.

Each time this annoying little habit happened, they'd sit patiently and play a little game: 'Count, Bruno – come on!'

'We'll count to thirty then try again, Papa.'

'No! Wait until that other car's pulled off the forecourt – then try.'

'Give it two minutes next time,' and so on.

Always, Roland would jump out, having grabbed his plug spanner from under the seat, and unscrew each charred plug, whereupon he'd wipe any surplus liquid and carbon from the sparking end. He'd learned from his father – who'd learned from a US Army motor pool driver in 1946 – to use a pencil to apply lead to the base and contact end of each plug. The very act of doing so gave the "stubborn donkey" a breather, which helped in a small way and prevented him from going completely mad.

Once, the Trabant had been Heike's pride and joy, and it was on this very bonnet that she'd leaned back and posed for a picture that would be posted to Cornwall and her favourite cousin – Hanne.

She thought of Hanne a lot during the journey, because Hanne had often told her of the long drive to reach Bavaria from their farm in Cornwall. How it would take days and days, and that when they eventually reached Oma's she and her little brother Marco would be ill for days and days; and that Oma would be sympathetic for five minutes, before losing her patience with them if they remained in bed when there were things to be done.

Oma never liked the idea of children being spoiled, and

allowing too much by way of recovery was spoiling them rotten. What could you expect of the English? They'd never starved!

The little Morris van was like the Trabant in that it was a people's car, not a Mercedes, Jaguar or Cadillac but a true car of the proletariat. It was a gutsy little vehicle, simple in form and the way it was engineered, but able to do its job without any fuss or nonsense. Hanne had written to say how she remembered the Morris Minor van with tremendous affection despite the travails of the journey; and how sorry she'd been that Hugo had eventually got his big Mercedes – the car he'd craved for so long.

In Heike's opinion, Hanne would have made a good communist. She'd have been happy in the East; Heike was sure of that. The British were almost "communists" – the ordinary people were anyway and some of the politicians definitely were. They weren't like the Americans because they had a true, natural understanding of socialism brought about by centuries of abuse of power and their invention of the industrial process.

Britain was the home of the welfare state and nationalised industries like steel, coal and railways. British people were known the world over for their patience and egalitarian nature; they queued for everything. London was where Karl Marx was buried and people visited his grave every day, such was their affection for him and his ideas. Even Ho Chi Minh had lived and worked in London.

One day, she and Roland and Bruno would visit Britain and they would make Marx's tomb the focus of their pilgrimage. Then they would go to Cornwall via Stonehenge.

'Where is Cornwall? Where is Stonehenge?'

Not so much questions from Bruno, more a complaint about his cramped conditions in the back of the car and his mother's endless chatter.

'Cornwall is on the Atlantic coast and Stonehenge is an

ancient ring of stones built by people long before the time of recorded history.'

'Who cares, for God's sake?!'

'Bruno! I'm trying to keep your spirits up.'

'I've got no room here, Mama. All this stuff! Why did we have to bring it all? Why didn't we stay in Leipzig? I liked it there.'

No one had envisioned the journey continuing well into the East German hinterland.

'We can swap places if you like? I'll sit in the back. You can help Papa with the map reading or hold the steering wheel for him when he cleans his spectacles or blows his nose.'

'Should I put the gear lever knob back on the stick when it falls off?'

'Yes, that too.'

The tasks succeeded in keeping Bruno occupied, for this was a very different young man to the one before the shooting.

Bruno could become – at times – very moody and withdrawn; it wasn't just the journey, he'd been this way ever since returning from hospital. Nor was he the quick-witted boy of old. He had trouble remembering the most simple and mundane of subjects.

For example, he would try to put together a sentence about a person or animal and then become aggravated because he couldn't remember the species of animal or the person's name. This would make him particularly frustrated:

'You know, the animal that lives with that man and woman in the house near our street.'

'What animal, Bruno? A cat? A dog?'

'Yes, a cat. The man likes it, but the woman chases it away. But it comes back when she's not looking.'

'Does the man feed it?' But Bruno's mind immediately forgot the subject only to replace it with some other question.

'Will we have to go to the shops when we arrive at the place we're going to?'

'Yes, we'll have to eat.'

Misfiring, the Trabant's tiny two-stroke engine was in bad need of serious attention. 'We need to find a garage otherwise we're going to be walking the rest of the way,' Roland warned them.

'But we're nowhere near the border.'

'I can't help that. Our little donkey doesn't have four legs – it has two – and it's limping.'

By the time they reached the next petrol station, the isolated roadside premises was closed for the evening, and with no sign of accommodation in the neighbourhood they would have to spend the night in the car.

With nowhere to eat or get a drink it would be a long night. Heike had packed a gas stove and a camping kettle, so with a container of water they were at least able to boil some water for black coffee that they could have with some biscuits they'd picked up in Leipzig. A kind woman from the Lutheran Church hostel had pushed a bag of bread rolls at them just before they left.

'You were going to refuse them!' said Heike out of the blue. But that conversation had passed 500 kilometres back.

'Who are you talking about?' asked Roland.

'Doesn't matter. The woman at the hostel in Leipzig. These rolls made me think... I don't know!'

Ironically, this unexpected deprivation of comfort seemed to excite Bruno who now began to view it more as an adventure than a never-ending car journey. 'Maybe we could walk the rest of the way,' he said. 'I could run ahead of you and come back to pick you up with a truck.'

Again, Heike recalled Hanne telling her about the journey to Oberwinkel in 1963. 'Uncle Hugo would insist on making progress, so they rarely stopped. They had bread rolls like this and would stop overnight to sleep in the car. Then the next morning they'd be on their way again. Now I know how it was for them all those years ago.'

'The difference being they weren't trying to escape the country,' Roland reminded her.

It was still dark when Heike awoke from a safely-home-in-Berlin dream to see a man's bearded face peering at them through steamed-up windows. Built like a mountain and every bit as craggy, his appearance startled her so much she almost screamed. Having gained her attention, he tapped on the misty window with the edge of a small steel hexagon nut held deftly between large, oily, nail-bitten fingers. 'Do you want some fuel?'

His soft enquiring voice did not match his grizzled appearance.

'Yes please!' Heike replied, winding down the window to see him clearly.

Waking, Roland leaned across. 'We also have a problem with the motor.'

'That's not surprising. These tiny boxes on wheels were never made for long journeys. Come on, I'll have a look for you.'

'Thank you! We're most grateful. We've got money.'

'Why don't you freshen up in there,' said the man, gesturing to the now open door of the garage. 'Make yourself a cup of coffee and my wife will be over shortly. She'll find you something to eat.'

'That's most kind – thank you!'

The man peered at the battered registration plate. 'Berlin? You've come a long way! I'm surprised the little car has got this far.'

'We're having a touring holiday,' said Roland.

'Please! I understand. I may live and work out here in the sticks, comrade, but I'm not unaware of what's happening. All of Germany seems to be on the move. There are a lot of people on the road at the moment, some of whom are getting stuck like you because their little boxes won't make the distance.'

'The motor was misfiring, otherwise it's been fine.'

The man opened the bonnet and took the fuel cap off to dip the tank with a hinged measure that he kept in the top pocket of his overalls. Wiping the measure with a cloth and inspecting the lack of fluid, he told them: 'No wonder it's misfiring; the tank is very low and all the dirt is going into the carburettor. That's no good now, is it? What say I quickly take the tank off, wash it out and put some fresh in? Won't take a minute or two and that will give you time to have a drink and a bite to eat.'

No sooner had he made his invitation than his wife arrived with the cheery promise of putting together a little breakfast for their journey.

'Good morning!' Frau Humboldt was every bit as friendly as her husband, with a mop of greying hair that was unruly and dry as tinder. He tall and broad, she only as tall as his waist, both past retirement age – at least five years past.

On seeing Bruno she reached up, cupped her right hand around his head to caress his fine, chestnut brown hair, before gently pulling him towards her for a hug as if he were a long lost grandson. 'What a handsome young man! You must be so proud of your boy.'

'I'm Bruno.'

'I'm pleased to meet you, Bruno!'

'I was shot in Berlin. Can you see the groove in my forehead?' He bent forwards and brushed back his fringe to show Frau Humboldt the 2 cm long scar on his left temple.

'And you survived to tell the tale? Not many do.'

'He was very… *We* were very lucky!' beamed Heike.

'Then you deserve a special breakfast! I have some eggs.'

Outside they could hear the tinny engine of their Trabant being revved. 'That sounds hopeful,' said Roland.

'My man has always been good with motors and anything mechanical. There was a time when he worked for Mercedes Benz, you know, and Porsche.'

After a few minutes the sound of revving stopped and all was quiet again. 'Perhaps I ought to go out and see what the situation is.' Roland was anxious.

'Finish your breakfast. My man will tell you soon enough.'

Frau Humboldt had made them a simple breakfast of fried eggs on toast, 'a little speciality and a ritual,' she said, something the couple enjoyed every working morning.

Ducking under the doorframe of the workshop, Herr Humboldt reappeared, this time looking rather more serious. His news was not good. 'I'm afraid, comrade, your little car is not capable of reaching the border. The head gasket is blown and I can fix that, but there are numerous other little problems that will conspire to let you down. If it fails in Czechoslovakia, I assume there will be a language problem and they may just be awkward for any number of reasons.'

'We set our hearts on Hungary. A recommendation from someone we met,' Heike appealed to him.

'If your man – and your boy – would care to assist me, I can replace the head gasket and it won't cost you a fortune – I can assure you of that. But I strongly advise that if you wish to continue your motoring holiday you turn around and head southwest for Gera. From there, head south again for Rudolphstein. There is a crossing there for all traffic. You might have to wait there a day or two, but from what I hear things are looking – how shall I say? – promising.'

It took little more than an hour to replace the head gasket, an hour in which Heike paced around the premises trying to get her head around what they should do next.

It was good to have a walk again if only around the small garage after so long cramped in the car. She thought about the future and how they could never try this again as they'd be too old and then the border would be more of a barrier than ever. In her heart of hearts, she really wanted to turn around and go home right this minute. She'd had enough; but Roland was absolutely correct in his summing up of their particular situation: they were prisoners in their own home and they would never be sure of their liberty. A day might come when they would both be arrested and imprisoned, and Bruno would be carted off to some correctional facility. She couldn't bear the thought of losing another child.

'If you take my advice, you'll head south for Rudolphstein. But whatever you do on your motoring holiday, take care and, particularly, don't push that little motor too hard. For the south, turn left out of here.'

Beaming smiles of gratitude as they drove away, Heike couldn't help but like the couple immensely. 'What nice people!' she said, but Roland didn't reply. There was a caution in both of them that had been forged over many years of living in East Germany. Trust no one.

*

Heike switched on the ignition for the car clock. She would give her cousin five more minutes to return. If not, then head back home and forget it; it wasn't meant to be.

*

'He's right, of course,' sighed Roland, 'this little car's not up to going the distance. We'll be lucky to get to Rudolphstein.'

'I can't find Rudolphstein on the map,' said Heike, infuriated. 'Do you think he was telling us the truth?'

Roland didn't answer, fearing that they just might have been set up and that it was all a trap. Perhaps this was always going to be a country they could never leave.

With every passing kilometre, the Trabant seemed to be getting progressively more fragile: more rattles, more squeaks, as every bump in the road seemed destined to break its suspension or chassis in two. It would have been a joke in other less serious circumstances. In the event it should die, their unofficial plan was to abandon the car to its fate and find a bus or train station, taking with them only what they could carry.

Later that morning, the brave little "donkey" died with a last gasp on a lonely road in the middle of a vast forest that had probably begun in Poland and undoubtedly stretched deep into Czechoslovakia and culminated in the Alps. So much for a train station or bus stop, there wasn't even another car to be seen.

It was silly to think of shoes in the enormity of it all, but Heike could only think of how impractical her shoes were for walking anywhere. Perhaps it was because she hadn't planned beyond the possibility of them travelling beyond Leipzig.

'Have you got nothing else?' Roland asked, incredulity getting the better of him.

'No, nothing – I'm sorry.' She had, of course, packed for Roland and packed for Bruno, but given scant thought to her own needs.

'I thought we'd be staying longer in Leipzig. I could have got something there. How was I to know that we'd be traipsing across Germany in a stupid little car that was barely capable of leaving Berlin?!'

The Trabant was kaput in every sense of the word. In

tribute, Bruno picked some leaves from the verge, placing the flora reverently on its bonnet in recognition of what he described as the machine's efforts which were nothing less than: "brave" and "valiant" and "… not the fault of the car."

No amount of fiddling under the bonnet or cajoling or swearing would make any difference. There was no longer a spark of life from any of its two meagre cylinders; the "donkey" would have to be abandoned.

Preparing for a third consecutive night in the lifeless Trabant, joking that only East Germans could take the cold and the confinement, sleeping in the seated position, thirsty and hungry. Their assumption was that far from being in a dense forest they were actually very close now to Rudolphstein – probably close enough to walk the estimated 10 or 20K, depending on the route. Without the car it would be better to walk through the woods because the authorities were sure to pick them up ambling with cases in hand along the road.

Before leaving the car, Bruno insisted on peeling off the cartoon stickers that Heike had put on the dashboard many years ago when it had first been acquired. Bruno was small then and she'd stuck them on in an effort to make it look more of a family car and so much less austere.

'I never did like these silly stickers!' he said, before peeling them off with his thumbnail and placing them carefully into his jacket pocket.

'Then why are you keeping them?' asked his mother.

'So as not to litter the forest.'

'If you hang on to them, one day someone in the West might pay a lot of money for them,' said Roland.

'That's what I'm banking on!' replied Bruno, grinning.

Heike had not walked through a wood since she was a girl. As a child she would spend long hours in the countryside picking flowers and letting her imagination run wild. And when Hanne visited that summer of '63 she'd shown her English cousin all the secret little places she'd loved.

As a child, she'd return home with squelching cloth bumper boots soaked by the long, wet meadow grass. The squelching made her laugh, the water having warmed up inside each boot. She would take them off and wring them out like dishcloths.

She recalled her "bumper-boot" expeditions now with Bruno to keep his mind off the distance, exclaiming that 'bumper boots were the most comfortable boots ever, ever made by man; and there was nothing nicer for the feet than a new pair.' If only she had them now.

'Were they American?' asked Bruno. Heike didn't answer.

The wood, like all dense woods, offered no horizon – no hope. There were occasional signs warning not to leave the footpaths because of unexploded ordnance. Every incline, every clearing, seemed to offer new hope, but their hopes were dashed each time as they reached what they believed would be the end only to see ahead of them more and more trees.

Bruno's gammy leg and awkward gait slowed them to a snail's pace, though he convinced himself that he was by far the fittest and fastest of the family who was taking it slow in order to wait for his infirm parents.

Any excuse to stop and rest was a good excuse. It was at these times that Roland recounted the epic trip that his parents had taken as kids at the end of the war and how they'd run and walked for days and weeks until eventually finding the Allies in the form of US soldiers. 'So we mustn't give up,' he urged; 'my parents would consider this a walk in the park.' This remark did not endear him to either Heike or Bruno.

By late afternoon, the thick, dull November light was falling rapidly towards total darkness. Still there was no end to the interminable forest, until, that is, they came across a clearing that looked hopeful in offering a way out.

The vista that met them, however, offered false hope. Below in the steeply banked valley was the broad expanse of the heavily mined border fence.

This fence was like nothing Heike had ever seen as a girl. This part of the border was not just a wire-link fence but a veritable obstacle course of wire fences, coiled barbed wire, steel vehicle traps and mines in the sand.

They discussed their limited options: 'The inner wire is probably electric or booby-trapped. There's no way we could cross it.'

Heike burst into tears. 'All this way, and for what? Four hours we've been walking! Four bloody hours! And all because you wanted to bring down the state!'

For the first time, she hated Roland; and Roland knew it.

'I'm going back to the car.'

'We'll never find the car in darkness. We'll have to find shelter here and continue as soon as it's light. This path we're on is parallel with the border. We can't turn around now.'

Without a further word, without warning, Heike spun around so quickly, so passionately, swinging her right arm with a momentum that could have brought down a prize fighter; the back of her clenched fist impacted Roland's cheek with such ferocity that it knocked him off his feet.

Stunned, he remained on the ground. It wasn't the blow, but the intention that had felled him. His beloved wife of sixteen years had snapped because she blamed him for everything that had befallen them in the past twelve months.

'Are you still going to find the car?' he asked, rubbing his jaw.

'No. I'm going to stay here and get this family out of this bloody mess!'

They walked on for a further half hour until there was not a glimmer of light to see their way. As the dim early evening light of the forest gave way to darkness, the strobing light of a watchtower some distance away startled them. Unsettling as it was to begin with, it did provide a flash of illumination to see their way forward.

There, ahead of them and barely visible amongst the decaying stalks of bracken, was the irregular shape of a moss-covered bunker, probably dating from the last war. It wasn't perfect, but at least it offered a concrete floor on which to lie, with some overhead shelter. For the first time, they would be able to sleep stretched out, if they could sleep at all. Not that there was any comfort to be had.

Bruno had seen TV programmes about the wilderness of the forests and the noises of the countryside. How thrilling was this to be actually a part of it! The sounds were real and the whole sky was truly, truly black. He'd never seen such a black sky before; he'd never heard the calls of anything bigger than a pigeon in a park. Now he was surrounded by blackness and the calls of the wild. Sandwiched between his parents, it was the greatest night ever.

There was only one big downside: he was soon shivering with cold. The noises of the forest were "brilliant" in his words, but creepy, too. Who could rest amongst owls, foxes and goodness knows what else? 'Are there any wolves here?' he asked.

'I don't think so,' Heike reassured him.

'Bears?'

'Perhaps in Poland, not here.'

'Would the bears know that they're not in Poland?'

'Why? … I don't know. They probably prefer Poland.'

'Boars. There must be boars here… Do you think we'll see one?'

'Not if we go to sleep we won't. Goodnight, Bruno!'
'You want me to be quiet?'
'Yes.'

Roland desperately wanted to reach out to clasp Heike's hand, to wrap his long arm around both her and Bruno. The very night they needed their warmth there would be no embrace. He could have lifted their spirits with yet another story about the time his parents fled Berlin, and how they too must have spent similar nights in the open; but instead of good-humoured put-downs he might otherwise have anticipated, he feared a serious rebuttal from Heike. Best to keep his silence and his distance.

When light eventually returned to relieve them of what had been undoubtedly the longest, hardest, coldest, most uncomfortable night of their lives, the world that revealed itself was one that was offering hope. 'Did you sleep, Mama?' asked Bruno.

'Did I sleep? I don't think I slept for one second!'
'What about you, Papa? Did you sleep?'
'No, I didn't sleep, Bruno. What about you?'
'Yes, I slept. A bit uncomfortable, and a bit cold, but I slept. Oh, it's raining!'

Stiffly stepping out into a theatrical array of sunbeams piercing the dripping canopy of mature pines, Roland reached for his spectacles. In the distance he could see smoke wafting through the morning mist; in fact, he could even smell smoke. Somewhere a fire was burning and they desperately needed to warm themselves.

They set off now with renewed vigour, but Bruno's gammy leg was stiffer than ever. He could barely walk, and so with an arm around the shoulders of each parent they set off in silence toward the beckoning smoke that was coming from the chimney of a house on the edge of the forest – two houses in fact.

Resident Ute Kempelmann spotted the hapless trio from her garden just before 9 am and, fearing there'd been an accident, ran out to meet them.

'Oh, you poor things! What happened?'

'Our car broke down. We got lost.'

'Welcome! Come in! Come in! I'll get you something to eat.'

'Where are we?' asked Roland.

'This is Burgstein. We are just a couple of houses. There used to be a village here a hundred years ago, but the inhabitants all emigrated to Canada and America. This is all that remains.'

'And Rudolphstein?'

'Rudolphstein?' exclaimed Frau Kempelmann, unsure as to why that was their destination. 'It's not far – 15K – but you have to go around the river. I'll do you some breakfast and then my neighbour Hubert will take you. My husband is at work, you see.'

'That's very kind – thank you!'

'You see,' whispered Roland to Heike, 'I knew this would be a happy ending.' Still grimacing, Heike didn't answer.

'You'll never believe it, but I dreamt this would happen!' Frau Kempelmann was as excited as a child at Christmas. 'You see, I have premonitions – I have always had them. For weeks now I have been waking up and telling my man about this recurring dream where a family comes out of the forest and I'm here to help them. Isn't it extraordinary!'

There was no exaggeration in the tale except that Herr Forrester Martin Kempelmann had made it quite clear to his wife some months ago that he didn't want to hear another mention of a recurring dream or any talk of silly premonitions. That very morning, however, whilst on his rounds, he discovered the abandoned Trabant and made a full report by radio.

'My man finds all sorts of unexploded bombs in those woods,' said Frau Kempelmann. 'It's his job to clear the area for forestry. During the war the Nazis stored ammunition here that wouldn't be seen by Allied aircraft. You were lucky not to have been blown up.'

'Wow! Bombs!' exclaimed Bruno. 'Have you got any here? We could blow up the border fence and walk across!'

'My son has an active imagination.' Heike squeezed Bruno's hand in an attempt to instil a little discretion.

'My imagination is active because I was shot – trying to cross the Wall. I can show you—'

'That's enough, Bruno! Our son has the most vivid… You know what they're like at this age. Have you got any children may I ask, Frau…?'

'Frau Kempelmann. Forgive me, I should have introduced myself earlier.' She shook hands with them before pointing to photographs on the mantel and on sideboards of children of various ages. 'None of them mine, I'm afraid – nieces, nephews and two children from my man's first marriage. They live with their mother in Gera. We see them every other weekend. They love it here.

'Please – sit down and relax while I bring you some breakfast.'

It took Frau Kempelmann just ten minutes to warm some croissants and make a pot of coffee. She chatted to them all the while about the home and the family she'd married into and how lucky she felt. Initially, she could hear acknowledgements from the living room, but they grew less with every passing minute. By the time she returned with a large, stacked tray, all three of her guests were snoring soundly.

Heike came to with a start.

'Forgive me! Roland! Bruno! Wake up. I'm sorry, but perhaps when we've eaten we should be on our way.'

'My friends, I completely understand. Eat your breakfasts. I'll call my neighbour, Hubert.'

'We'll come with you. We mustn't sit down too long or we'll never get up,' said Heike.

After breakfast they followed Frau Kempelmann out into the front garden where she called across to her neighbour's house: 'Hubert! Hubert!'

A man appeared at a small upper window on the gable end of the house. His fleshy upper torso covered by a white cotton Aertex vest, he looked as if he had only just risen from bed and was still going about his ablutions when interrupted by Frau Kempelmann's shouts. He pushed open the window. 'What is it, Ute?'

'This family are lost and need your help to get to Rudolphstein. Can you take them?'

'Rudolphstein? Yeah, yeah! A minute – just a minute.'

'Hubert is a wonderful man. He is retired, but works part-time. If anyone can help you, he will.'

'We are very grateful – thank you!'

Reluctant to return indoors, Heike and Roland were keen to see the garden while they waited for the neighbour to appear. The house and garden reminded Heike of her childhood home. The very same aroma of pine and autumn decay, covered stacks of chopped timber; the stillness in the air and the call of rooks and blackbirds; even a robin chattering away on the frosty grass near their feet, appealing for anything they might wish to discard for his breakfast. This was as close to her rural roots as she had been in seventeen years of living in East Berlin. It was all so familiar and reminded her of just how isolated she'd been in the city with its wall, divorced so entirely from the country. Maybe this was where the future lay for them. Not in some city but in the country.

Many years ago, Hanne had brought from England a copy of Thomas Hardy's *Far from the Madding Crowd* especially for Heike. Hanne jokingly referred to the title as "Far from the Maddening Crowd", the humour of which Heike had not initially understood. She understood now: this place was truly far from "the maddening crowd".

For the second time since leaving their home in Berlin, she felt a sense of calm and well-being. It was clear to her that folk in the isolated, rural areas were so much more open and friendly. She'd always known this in her heart of hearts.

The slam of the neighbouring door jolted her out of a blissful reminisce. She turned to see a very different neighbour from the man who'd leaned out of the window just minutes before. Stern-faced and on a mission, here was a stocky, balding man dressed in the all too familiar uniform of a *Volkspolizei* officer.

'You are lucky Hubert was at home today. If anyone can help you he will. Thank you, Hubert!'

There was little more that could be said. Always polite, Heike and Roland thanked Frau Kempelmann for her kindness in making them so welcome and giving them such a lovely breakfast.

Now it was time to accept their fate.

The game was up.

Roland would be sent to prison somewhere in the East for sure, with little chance of reprieve. Heike's fate was uncertain. They could only hope that Bruno would be treated sympathetically, because he would be removed from their care without doubt. It had been a good try and they'd at least made a spirited go of it, but the eventual outcome was unlikely to be kind. Fortune had turned away again. At least this wasn't going to end with a shooting, and that was at least a mercy. With heavy hearts they clambered into the small, unmarked car that was also the officer's family transport.

'You are lucky!' he told them. 'I wasn't on duty this morning but I had a call from my neighbour, Comrade Kempelmann, whose *frau* you just met, telling me of an abandoned car – a Berlin-registered Trabant – and then you turned up next door. I assume you are the owners of the car?'

'Yes,' was all Roland would say, nodding.

'Where are you taking us?' asked Heike.

'You are from Berlin?'

'Yes.'

'You are a long way from Berlin.'

'We were on our vacation.'

'Are you visitors from the West?'

Roland hesitated. 'No.'

'Did you happen to see from the wood down into the valley and the border fence?'

Neither Roland nor Heike were prepared to answer for fear of incriminating themselves. Bruno, however, had no such reticence. 'Yes, we saw it. Didn't we?'

Hubert reached across Roland to the glove compartment; their initial fear was that he might be reaching for a pistol; instead, he pulled out a packet of opened cigarettes, deftly extricating one with his free hand before pushing in the car's cigar lighter.

'That is where a man was shot in '82 on that very steep bank you were looking at. He was only in his early thirties – young, fit – but our patrol had no choice – he gave them no choice.'

'I was—' Bruno was about to tell the officer about his own shooting, but Heike quickly stopped him by squeezing his knee and putting her forefinger to his mouth. 'You still have some croissant on your lips, Bruno.'

She could see the cold, grey eyes of the officer glance at them in the rear-view mirror. Like all policemen he was suspicious and cared not one jot whether they were on holiday or not. He clearly knew the political situation and would be on high alert. She daren't imagine what he might do with them.

For some inexplicable reason, the officer was driving deeper and deeper into the countryside where, in this intensely wooded area, it was difficult to get a bearing. If he were going to hand them over, then surely he'd head for the nearest town?

Perhaps he was under orders from someone in Berlin. It was possible that someone, somewhere was giving an order direct to him. The Stasi must have lost patience: *Take them to the woods; make out they tried to run. Don't worry, there'll be no comeback. She is a CIA sleeper with known terrorist connections; he is a political agitator. Shame about the boy.*

In the front seat, Roland was clearly worried. For a long time, the officer said nothing else – didn't so much as sniff or clear his throat – then he asked matter-of-factly, 'You have friends or relatives in Rudolphstein?'

'Yes,' said Roland, 'friends and relatives.'

'You don't look of pensionable age,' queried the officer.

'What do you mean?' asked Heike nervously.

'Pensioners with a permit can cross. Didn't you know that?'

'No,' said Roland.

'You have the necessary permits and passports – yes?'

Roland simply shook his head.

'You don't know anything about Rudolphstein, do you?'

Neither Roland nor Heike answered for fear of incriminating themselves.

'I thought not,' said the officer. 'Do you know that last year or even last week, you would not have got within 5 kilometres of here?'

Suddenly, he pulled into a lane that became narrower with

every passing twist and turn. Roland turned to look back at Heike in an effort to somehow communicate his concern: *Is he going to take the law into his own hands and shoot us here?*

They could possibly overpower him. He was not a young man – not particularly big. If Heike grabbed him around the neck from the back seat and held tight, Roland could grab the officer's pistol, at which point he'd have to surrender. That's if they didn't crash in the process. Worse, Bruno might panic and interfere. Of course, the alternative could be that he was taking them to meet other *Polizei* who just might be crooked and looking for a bribe.

The uneven tarmac surface of the lane became concrete, then broken concrete, then just a stony, uneven track. The car slowed to a snail's pace as the surface disintegrated beneath its tyres. If they were going to jump him, now would be as good a time as any. Heike, anticipating her husband's intentions, braced herself for action.

If ever there was a time for telepathy then this was it.

Rounding a sharp bend, slowly revealing itself, there ahead was a situation that beggared belief. To the side of the track, a row of cars parked up as if a festival or sporting event were about to take place with this as the gathering point. Some cars seemed abandoned, their boots and doors wide open; others had only just been parked, with their occupants milling around and preparing for something – Roland and Heike could not imagine what.

'This is as far as I will take you,' said the *Polizei*. 'Good luck!'

Cautiously, they climbed out of the car, closing the doors, whereupon the officer immediately put it into reverse and accelerated backwards without so much as a second glance at them.

Bewildered, they stood for a moment watching the others – families and couples just like them putting on boots and making sure they had what they needed before climbing through a hedge. Before them was an open grass field, which in one direction seemed to stretch for as far as the eye could see. Ahead of them, at the top of a slight incline, was a small wire fence some 800 metres away.

People were walking and running across the field to the fence where there was an opening.

'Come on, this is our chance!' urged Roland. 'That's the Czech border. They're opening up the border.'

'I don't believe it!' said Heike. 'The border is bigger than that silly little fence!'

'Then ask these people,' said Roland, gesturing to those who were already making their way across.

'What's happening?' she asked of a woman who was tying the shoes of her young daughter.

'Haven't you heard? The Czechs have opened the border. We can cross to Hungary and then Austria. Grenz has ordered it.'

'But that's not the border.'

'No, but beyond that fence the gates are open. There's a crossing point.'

Heike turned to Roland and Bruno, smiling with relief: 'We'd better go, then.' Climbing through the gap in the hedge, they found themselves walking alongside some fifty other East Germans advancing in line toward the fence as if they were an army; and as they tramped through the wet grass their pace quickened somewhat, as if they feared the border might suddenly close. Halfway across their pace quickened again to a trot, as if an unofficial race were underway; even Bruno was keeping pace. Two-thirds now and the trot moved up a gear into a run. Still Bruno kept pace, and what's more he was loving every step.

The end in sight at last, just metres to go, excited voices could be contained no longer. Faster and faster, ordinary folk running like demented athletes for the Gold medal position, cases and bags gripped, tiny tots grasped, sprinting like fury now because in their caged minds there was a man somewhere out of sight with a machine gun who might open fire at any second and fell the lot of them like ninepins.

What a hideous prank that would have been; but even as they reached their goal, climbing under or over the little wire fence, everyone suspected it. The unseen guard had to be ready; he must have them in his sights. This was the cruellest joke; this could not be true.

Easing back their frantic hurry, passing through the gates, Heike stared in disbelief at each and every border guard because they were looking as bewildered as she did. They seemed subdued, hopeless, as if all of a sudden the Cold War had been declared null and void, but at any second the joke would be called in.

She looked at one guard in particular. She thought she recognised him; that it was the guard she had met as a child with her cousins; the friendly guard who'd offered them chocolate and spoken to them so nicely. He even had a dog with him. But no! How could it be him? That was so long ago.

*

Someone tapped on the window; it was Hanne.

'I'm so sorry! So sorry! I just had to pop out to get some wine and something to nibble on. I thought I could do it before you got here. The man in the shop said a woman was looking for me. I hurried straight back.'

'Never mind, Hanne – you're here now. What a wonderful place you have rented!'

That evening, Heike told her story in full. It was done, a weight lifted from her shoulders. The schnapps helped them to laugh and listen and exchange notes, but there was something Hanne had to ask of her cousin.

'What of Roland? Are you both…?'

'We are still married, but we've lived apart for many years now. That incident in the woods changed us both and I never felt quite the same way about him again.'

'And Bruno?'

'Bruno has his own place near me with Judith – his wife, you know. But our hearts are still in East Berlin. That city behind the Wall was our lives, our home, and for the most part we had no complaints. I would have stayed, as would Roland and Bruno. We'd be a family still – maybe.

'Roland has gone back and lives not far from where we lived. I go to see him, we are friends and neither of us has taken up with anyone else. The memories draw me back and I'm still a communist you know, in my heart and mind, but I'm a true communist not a Leninist or Stalinist or Trotskyite.

'Bruno's generation will be the last of the East Germans. We were an entity unto ourselves and when our day is done we'll take our experiences with us, just like Uncle Hugo's generation were different. I hope there will never be anything quite like it again, but the world is always an unstable place.'

'And what of Peter?'

'Peter – where would I begin? Roland told me everything later. Peter was an enigma to everyone. Some have told me recently that he was in the employ of the Stasi, whilst others tell me that he was working for the Americans and the British just as he had claimed. I don't know the truth and to this day I don't know where he is. Maybe… maybe one day he'll let me know, but for now I have lost him as a brother. Perhaps he no longer trusts anyone. Who can blame him? It was a society that didn't trust itself.

'You know, Roland and Bruno were in the crowds that smashed open the Stasi HQ in Berlin. That's when Roland got his beloved camera back. It nearly killed someone when it fell out of its case and down the stairwell! Never mind! It didn't hurt anybody, but it was close, you know. Anyway, once in there, Roland used his journalistic ability to root through papers, finding references to him, Bruno and Peter – and me, of course.

'It took a while, but he found what he was looking for, as did many others who wanted to find – not the truth, I should say, but the "truth" according to the government and the Stasi.

'Yes, everyone discovered "the truth" that day when they broke into the HQ. You see, Hanne, it turns out that Peter and I were willing stooges of the state. We walked right in and said, "Okay, here we are! Do with us as you please," and that's just what they did.'

'Would Peter have betrayed his own family?'

'I don't know, Hanne, I really don't. They had something on him, of course they did. He was an agitator in their eyes.

'It's occurred to me in recent years, as more information has come out, that maybe from the moment he followed me into East Berlin they used my name to trick him into being a spy and informer. That's how so much of it worked, you know. We'll look after your sister providing you're a good boy and do some work for us. Or maybe he just fancied himself as a spy.

'He was a pawn to begin with and who knows what pressure they put on him working in the steelworks? But he became a hero with regard to the school, and history just might remember him for that. Perhaps I wouldn't be talking to you now without those schoolchildren that he inspired.'

'I find it so hard to—'

'Believe? I know, me too.'

'Sounds like something out of a John le Carré novel.'

'If we'd had a proper father, this might never have happened. We didn't though – we had a drill sergeant for a father. And everything Peter and I did was to pay him back for the way he treated us and the way he treated Mama. But whatever the cause, we have to take responsibility and not blame those who were themselves "victims" of a sort.

'You and I, Hanne – we're the children of Hitler and Stalin and Mussolini, and their shadows stretch a long way. I look at Bruno's little daughter and I say to her, "Not you, little one. For you it will be different." And I believe it will be – I have to believe that.'

The cousins talked well into the small hours. The schnapps flowed, as did the wine – red wine. Music played in the background, music from some obscure station specialising in hits of yesteryear. Heike did most of the talking. She has since assured me that she recounted everything and left nothing out, and I believe her.

Me? Well, you must understand, I was no longer eavesdropping. I'd long since retired. I was out in the open and taking notes in the most ethical manner. I have been unemployed for many years now, but the compilation of notes is all that I know, so my "journalism skills" are all that I have.

I was Hugo's "ghostwriter", you know. His biography, though little more than a local memoir of a highly successful flower grower, I think, was one of my finer literary achievements. Of course, he got all the credit, quite rightly.

As for Heike, well, she is very bright and I suspect that deep down she realises that it was me – the ears of the state apparatus as it once was listening for endless hour after interminable day. It is a subject we've never broached and probably never will. To Heike, I am simply the feature writer who approached her with a story idea for a magazine – an exposé of how it used to be on the other side of the great divide. I thought hers was a particularly interesting story. Well, I would, wouldn't I?

The reunion?

There are plans afoot for another family gathering, and if Hanne, Heike and Heidemarie have anything to do with it then it will continue for many years to come.

*

'You won't tell Heidemarie what I have told you, will you, Hanne?'

'Not if you don't want me to, but maybe one day you ought to tell her.'

'She would not understand.'

'You never know until you try. Maybe you're… underestimating her?'

'Maybe. *Auf wiedersehen*, Hanne!'

'*Auf wiedersehen*, Heike!'

Chapter 6

Lookout

Before leaving for Frankfurt and home, Hanne had one last mission to accomplish – to walk one more time among the hills overlooking Oberwinkel and to the lookout tower she'd loved as a child.

She'd always hated leaving Bavaria to return home to dull routine and who knew what. Today was no exception. She wanted the holiday to continue. The accommodation was such a fine little house with its round tower, the weather was very amenable – neither too warm nor too cool – and even the hire car was much better than her own.

Germany always pulled her then held on to her when she was within its grasp. If it weren't for the family at home, she'd happily stay for as long as she wanted. Silly, really, considering that the boys were grown men and that Sandy would be happy here, too, even though he didn't speak German. Maybe they were her excuse for not staying longer.

Holidays did this to everyone – lulled you into a false sense of security. The belief that there would be no problems there, that it would be a long, long vacation for the rest of time.

It could never be. She dropped the key back into the caretaker and drove to a place on the high outskirts of Oberwinkel where she could leave the car and amble off on her walk to the deer lookout. Hopefully, it would still be there.

The track was as it had ever been, and as a bonus she could see in the distance a horse-drawn vehicle approaching her. *How lovely!* she thought. *And what timing! That's what I like to see.*

As it drew closer, she stood aside to admire the bay cob pulling its heavy oak wagon of occupants and their belongings. At first, she assumed they were gypsy travellers, but the driver – a rather severe looking man – was dressed in Bavarian traditional costume, together with his wife and two children, with what appeared to be all their worldly goods. She smiled at them, but their reaction was one of disdain as the driver cracked the whip above the horse's flanks, causing Hanne to jump and the cob to quicken its pace.

Maybe they are on their way to a traditional fair. Those things can be stressful for those taking part.

Not many minutes later, also approaching along the same track, were two boys pushing a handcart loaded with a large sack of grain. Again, she stood aside for them to pass and again they did not acknowledge her. They weren't particularly old – probably both under ten years – and were dressed in the manner of children of the '30s.

She was now sure that a traditional folk fair *must* be gathering or be underway somewhere in the district and that the boys were probably members of the same family that had passed with the horse and wagon. She called out, 'Grüss Gott!' but neither boy responded nor looked back at her.

It didn't matter that there was no response. People have their reasons, and it was such a beautiful morning for a walk. She was convinced this was the right thing to do before heading for home. Well worth getting up early and putting the house in order first thing. If only Sandy could be here with her.

As the temperature began to soar she stopped to catch her breath. Above her, two buzzards squealed as they gained altitude on the warm thermals of a cloudless sky.

Ahead, yet another element of what was becoming a rather bizarre and fragmented carnival came into view and this time kicking up dust. Three German soldiers kitted out in combat uniform and carrying rifles. This unnerved her for a moment as she assumed that they were soldiers on exercise for some reason.

For a third time, she stood aside to let them pass, and it was then that it was clear to her that the men were wearing WW2 uniforms; they weren't in modern uniform at all. Again, they didn't acknowledge her gesture; it was as if she wasn't there.

Re-enactment? Surely such things were frowned upon here.

It occurred to her that these rather surreal travellers were "ghosts" of a kind and perhaps ghosts of her making. If so, then what was around the corner? She didn't have long to wait. Now feeling a bit more apprehensive as to what she was experiencing, she could feel something drawing her forward, that she must continue her walk. This was most unlike her, but the pull to carry on was overwhelming.

She hadn't gone many more paces when again she saw ahead of her an even larger column of spectres the like of which she struggled to believe, yet there they were solid in form and proceeding directly toward her.

If these are apparitions of an age past to which I am the ghost, then why not stand in their path?

Coming directly at her a US military jeep towing a large field gun, and behind that a Sherman tank followed by assorted infantrymen all in step. She stood her ground until such time as the apparition appeared so real in sight and sound that it would run her down, and so like a rabbit she leapt at the very last second to avoid being run over. Not one face turned to look at her and not one voice was raised in annoyance.

The dust kicked up covers her from head to foot and chokes her; but rather than curse, she is amused and even thrilled by the experience.

If I'm being shown something, then this really is a show and a half!

Looking back along the track from whence she'd come, to see if she can see the progress of the troops, or the boys or the wagon, but there's no sign of anything or anyone.

Too liberal with the schnapps last night. Oh, if only Heike could have been with me for this!

In any other circumstance, she would run fleeing from the scene, fearing for her sanity; but this morning, the sheer pleasure of witnessing so many phantoms thrills her like a fairground ride.

What next?

As if on cue, two men approach in the distance, walking a large dog. It is only as they get closer that she sees them clearly in uniform. Yet again, she stands aside. This is the best of all those who have passed her: it is the friendly guard dressed as she remembered so well from that summer's day in 1963, his sleeves casually rolled up, his field cap tilted in jaunty style, and prancing at his side, head held high, the chocolate-loving Alsatian. Yes, her memory was spot on! He was indeed a ringer for Clint Walker.

He could have been a movie star who might have achieved great things had the world he'd known been different. Neither man sees her; the dog doesn't see her. They walk on into the far distance watched by an incredulous English woman in late middle age.

Ten minutes on, breathless, she reaches her goal.

The deer lookout is still in place; the ladder and platform are just as they were all those years ago, though she suspects that the timber has been replaced as least twice since that summer of '63. She puts her foot on the first rung and worries that now it is too steep and that she doesn't want to find herself stuck and unable to get down like some woosy pussy up a tree.

I'm not so old that I can't do this.

She convinces her rational fears that it really isn't difficult, and before she knows it she reaches the platform and makes herself comfortable.

As then, she must be quiet. The deer must still be around somewhere. She settles her breathing as best she can.

Below, a child's enquiring voice startles her. 'Hello! What are you doing?' she asks.

'I'm looking for deer,' Hanne replies.

'There are not as many as there used to be,' says the girl. 'Can I come up and join you?'

Hanne shuffles across the platform and beckons the girl to join her. Together they sit side by side looking out towards the far horizon.

'If we're very quiet, we might see a doe and her fawn,' the girl tells her.

'Yes, if we're very quiet.'

***

For exclusive discounts on Matador titles,
sign up to our occasional newsletter at
troubador.co.uk/bookshop